THIN YELLOW LINE

M. J. URREA

Dedicated to my husband, Javier, for his vision, patience, kindness and support.

Many thanks to my husband Javier Urrea, my son Alejandro Urrea, my sister Hope Hubbard and my friends who read the manuscript so many times they can quote it: Thu, Ana, James and Lisa. Also thanks to my nameless contacts with the FBI and to Gary for his tireless professionalism.

CHAPTER 1
CHERRYWOOD

"Click, click, click" was the clean, steady sound of the clock on the wall of Dr. Ted Snyder's office. His patient, Dr. Jeanine Hunter, felt like she was living in some sad cliché. Everything she had ever imagined about a psychiatrist's office surrounded her: the black, leather couch, the amber light emitted behind deeply crème colored lampshades, the smell of expensive leather, richly stained hardwood floors, and fine pieces of art. The style of the office expressly communicated that Dr. Snyder was well to do. Though he would profusely deny it, everything from his manicured fingernails, expensive pipe tobacco, and eclectic décor demonstrated he was clearly a popinjay in every sense of the word.

Dr. Snyder was one of the few tenured physicians associated with the University of Texas Medical Branch at Galveston's medical school that still maintained such an elaborate and sophistically kept office. Most of his colleagues occupied spaces that were slightly more than glorified corporate cubicles. But Dr. Snyder, an old dinosaur, had earned enough tenure to procure such a delicious office of this size and scale in the Old Red building, the architectural icon of the University.

Jeanine sat quietly on the couch. The steady 'click' of the wall clock was her only tether to reality. Dr. Snyder, content for the time being with her silence, did not press her to speak. As the four o'clock hour approached he glanced at his Rolex, removed it, set the time and moved it back and forth forcing it to keep time as is customary for such a timepiece. He replaced his watch with a sharp snap of the metal band, leaned forward placing his elbows on his desk and engaged her one last time before their session ended.

He let out a low frustrated sigh, removed his metal-rimmed glasses and delicately set them down. "Dr. Hunter, the phrase silence is golden is true in most cases. And while I can intuit a great deal from your silence, I believe it would be a better use of our time

1

if you would actually talk to me. After all, I am trying to help you. Your patient is dead, your colleague is missing, and the FBI would like some answers."

CHAPTER 2
ACTIVELY DYING

Twenty-four hours prior to her consultation with Dr. Snyder, Jeanine was in the ICU watching her patient, David Scott, fight for his life. David was very special to her. Yet, this was not his first near death experience. David had end-stage AIDS. Having been close to death on half a dozen occasions, Jeanine had perfected the preparation-for-the-worst speech she had given to his family so many times in the past. David had refused treatment for his condition and to the surprise of many; he had done quite well for about 2 years. Then, everything changed. His CD4 count, the branch of the blood cell family that defends the body against infections, started dropping and he developed every imaginable infection from esophageal Candida to tuberculosis.

Jeanine reflected on the their relationship. The first time she met David was at the beginning of her first year in residency a year ago. The Infectious Disease specialists did not think he would survive. He had no medical insurance and was at the mercy of the hospital's Family Medicine residency program that took care of indigent patients. After being in the hospital for a month, with pulmonary histoplasmosis, he was finally being discharged from the hospital. Given his financial situation, the specialists suggested a Family Medicine resident take David as their own patient; someone who would provide continuity of care on an outpatient and inpatient basis.

Jeanine volunteered. In truth, she felt he was too complicated for her to handle, but she was inspired by a milieu of conflicting emotions: the hope for his recovery, the opportunity to make a difference in his life, and the fight for a lost cause. However, there were other things to consider. Something about him endeared her and made her want to be a better physician, his physician. Yet, on the darker side of her reality, it was likely he would be dead in six months. Somehow, his established expiration date made it easier to engage in his life. However, she learned he was just as stubborn as she was and he did not subscribe to the notion of a six-month time limit. He was determined not to succumb to death and as long as he fought, so would she.

Over the last year, David had been admitted so many times he often joked he should have a wing of the hospital named in his honor. Two months ago, he went on a month long trip with his father to Italy. He came back with high spirits and in the best medical condition he'd had in years. Jeanine was hopeful that he had turned a corner in his treatment. She had become quite close to his family, especially his father Frank Scott, who trusted her so much that he also became her patient.

But AIDS is an unforgiving tricky bastard. Almost a year to the day Jeanine had met him in the hospital, David started coughing incessantly.

When Jeanine saw him, she barely recognized him. He was gaunt, barely weighing one hundred pounds, his color was sallow, he was covered with diffuse skin sores, and his liver was inflamed. Gastric fluids and blood from his stomach were being suctioned into a canister at his bedside via a nasogastric tube in his nose; lines were running into every vein and he was kept in a double isolation room with negative airflow to protect the other patients until it was determined whether or not he had active tuberculosis.

His eyes loomed as large globes inside a hollow body. He had developed acute respiratory failure from another infection; acute hepatitis and a gastrointestinal hemorrhage.

Over the next several weeks, he improved slightly but it was obvious that this infection would overcome him. David's sense of humor was still intact and he would crack silly jokes as Jeanine tried to convey the severity of his condition. He was in denial, but slowly, he realized his time had come.

The nasogastric tube and IV lines were removed, and although fragile, he was deemed well enough to go home with hospice. He decided this would be his last hospitalization. He would die with dignity at home under hospice care. David was weary of the repeated hospital admissions, his mother's tears at his bedside, the wondering about tomorrow, and the fight to keep living.

It was a hard decision for Jeanine to accept. He was only 32, a few years older than her, and he had become dear to her. She saw all of the potential of his life and felt sad that the world would never see it.

"Hey you," she said entering his room. He could finally see her face now that he was out of the isolation room and she wasn't required to wear an isolation suit.

"Hey yourself," he shot back energetically. It was his last day in the hospital and he was looking forward to going home.

"I'm going to miss you," she said.

"Liar! I know your hours. You get here at 4 AM and leave after 8 PM every night, if at all. You are happy to see my sick ass get out of here!" he chided.

She feigned hurt. "I beg your pardon! I work this hard on all of my patients, not just the pains in the neck like you!" she shot back.

"Well, you are still going to be my doctor, right? Even if I am on hospice?" he asked concerned.

She impulsively stole a quick glance at the floor. She did not want to reveal her sadness or reluctance to watch him die. He did not need that burden. She had promised to continue the management of his care, including hospice.

"Of course," she said trying to muster up as much enthusiasm as possible.

"Come on, doc. Don't be like that," he admonished again "I know you."

"All right," she answered pushing through her sadness. "I will hate to see your sorry ass go! No one else makes me laugh like you! All these sick people around and no one is laughing! What's wrong with them?"

"That's my girl!" he said with as much urban attitude as a suburban, privately educated, WASP want-to-be could have. "Besides," he continued, "I need you to write my morphine prescriptions. I don't do pain!"

She huffed at him and took a soft jab at his arm. He made harassing her an art form. She was easy to harass and that made her easy to love.

Jeanine left him to do paperwork. It took her half an hour to complete his discharge forms; and even as she signed her name on the last line of his papers, David was being murdered.

CHAPTER 3
BRICK HEAVY

Similar to the destruction left in the wake of a hurricane was the confusion, despair and emotional tumult on Galveston Island following David Scott's demise. However, these emotional affects could not be objectively measured as easily as something like property damage. The Islanders knew something horrible had occurred but the particular events were nebulous and, in the absence of knowledge, panic gave birth to speculation and paranoia.

It was in this climate of fear and desperation that the FBI thrust special agent Luke Donovan with the explicit directive to succeed at all costs and with the greatest efficiency of time and finance possible. Failure was not an option. The Bureau would not accept a poor outcome or a damaged reputation. Based on the magnitude of this case, success would be Donovan's magnum opus; and failure his Titanic.

The investigative team for this operation was comprised of five agents including Donovan. Unfortunately, Donovan was not allowed to choose the agents he wanted. His superior, Agent Crookshank, had chosen each member for this investigation. Each of them had different backgrounds: Lorna Woo was on loan from the National Center for the Analysis of Violent Crime (NCAVC) and would serve as his psychological profiler; Mellicent Swenson and Ben O'Donnell had worked as undercover field agents and had more experience than their other counterparts; and finally, Jake Glenn was a rookie on his third assignment.

Although Swenson and O'Donnell had more experience than Woo and Glenn, Donovan still considered them unqualified. This squad lacked cohesion and their usefulness to him was yet to be determined. Donovan called a briefing to assess their skills.

"Okay, roll it out for me," Donovan ordered with a nonchalant arrogance. O'Donnell started the presentation. He placed a photo of David Scott's lifeless corpse on the overhead projector.

"The stiff is David Scott. 32 years old, former manager of a chain imports store. He had three priors, all of them for narcotics possession."

"Intent?" Swenson asked.

"Negative. No intent to sell. No obvious connections to narcotics or organized crime. He was just a user. Anyway, he died yesterday in the ICU of John Sealy Hospital from complications of AIDS. When his family came to collect the body, they noticed a scar down the front of his chest. When they had the hospital check into it, they discovered he had the mummy treatment."

"What?" Woo asked as she, with great frustration and anxiety, searched for the term 'mummy treatment' in the papers in front of her.

"He had his heart, lungs and kidneys removed without the family's consent," O'Donnell informed.

"Whoa," Glenn interjected.

"Few words but a correct conclusion, yes, big whoa my monosyllabic friend," O'Donnell agreed with a sarcastic jab at his young colleague. "The hospital is not even clear if the guy actually died of his illness or if he was killed for his organs. We have our own forensics team doing an autopsy."

"That's a big leap. If he was already dying from AIDS, why would someone kill him for infected organs?" Swenson asked.

"Was his condition stable before he died?" Donovan interjected as he stroked his goatee.

"Well, he was being discharged to hospice. Hospice only takes terminally ill patients. However, they usually give the patient 6 months or so depending on the illness." O'Donnell answered.

"What does the doctor say that was treating him?" Donovan probed.

"According to the team of doctors taking care of this guy, you get several reports. Some say he should have been dead years ago and others were surprised this guy tanked so soon. Despite releasing him to hospice to die at home, they did not expect him to die immediately."

"So he wasn't a healthy specimen but healthy enough to leave the hospital on his feet versus a body bag. Ok, so the next question is was this just a mix up. You hear about mistakes in hospitals all the time. What makes this different? How did we get from died of natural causes to murdered for organs? What if they just got the wrong body and thought he was a donor but wasn't?" Swenson inquired.

"Well that's where it gets twisted," O'Donnell continued. "Nobody knows where the organs went. Plus, no one knows who did the surgery, who authorized it, or which hospital personnel were involved. According to my research, in terms of organ transplantation, everything in John Sealy Hospital is done by the book; they set the standard for the entire country. No one does anything, anytime, anywhere unless it's in triplicate and enough red tape to surround the United States... twice." He said holding up two fingers to emphasize the point. O'Donnell paused to change the transparency on the overhead projector.

"And even if, and that's a big if, this process could have been circumvented it would be nearly impossible to have had a surgery performed on a patient and have no record of it being done. It's like a space shuttle blasting off without anyone's notice."

Swenson pushed further, "Even the best systems break down. This could still be a case of mistaken identity. I'm not convinced."

Donovan noted Swenson's skepticism. He had studied her case histories and discovered she was relentlessly ambitious. She had her eyes on Donovan's position. He would have to keep a close eye on her. At this point, Donovan took over the presentation.

"Agent Swenson, I have the information you are looking for. About two weeks ago our narco-terrorism units lit up with information. The surveillance of the South American drug lord Carlos Colorado erupted in activity. The intel was cryptic, at best, but they kept referring to *Los Organos*. We assumed it was a location until this event occurred. Now it seems it is not a place but Spanish for 'the organs'. It's actual body parts that Colorado wants. Further research has revealed his one and only son has kidney failure. We've been tracking Colorado for years but he's cunning and manages to evade us. We have no photos of him and any agents that get inside his organization have been neutralized.

Although we can't touch him, he definitely has a presence here. Last year the DEA, in conjunction with the Forestry Service, discovered Colorado had marijuana plantations in the National Parks. Colorado actually created one inside a public wildlife reserve here in Galveston. But despite his low profile, he's come out of hiding and is personally involved in this case."

"Someone must have seen something," Swenson said with growing interest, "who are our suspects?"

"The staff has been interviewed several times. The last two people to see the patient alive are Doctors Monica Rubio, who signed the death certificate, and Jeanine Hunter. We have Rubio sequestered in the Houston safe house. She came forward with some very interesting information implicating Dr. Hunter's involvement," O'Donnell informed.

"Have you interviewed Hunter yet?" Donovan asked.

"We have a statement from her. Pretty basic," Glenn answered.

"What info have we collected from her surveillance?" Donovan asked.

O'Donnell chimed in, "We don't have authorization for wire taps yet; but we did get the search warrant."

Donovan was frustrated by their lack of assertiveness. "I'm not going to let this case go to hell on a technicality. She's our top suspect. All searches have to be authorized so the Justice Department doesn't throw it out. Woo, you've had access to her apartment and her files, what's her profile?"

Agent Woo was unaccustomed to giving her opinion verbally. She preferred writing her opinions than speaking to people. But to advance her career, she had to have more field experience and asked her father, a higher-level agent, to pull some strings to have her assigned to this case. Tentatively, she gave her impression of Dr. Hunter.

"Sir, I think the best way to describe her is through her own words. I was able to get a copy of her journal and I think this entry best summarizes her:

I hate my life. I'm working 120 hours a week. I'm over $100,000 in debt. I'm almost thirty and

10

even though I do not subscribe to the notion that I'll
expire if I'm not wed by 30, I don't think I'll ever
find the love of my life. Residency is a rich boy's
club. I have to work harder to prove I belong here.
This will never end and every day gets worse. Each
moment hammers into my psyche, like nails in a
coffin that I don't belong here. I grow more and more
unsure of this career. I don't know if being a doctor
is worth the sacrifices I'm making. Sometimes I want
it all to end and I don't care how. I'm always tired
and dirty. I'm just a glorified janitor for the human
condition. I don't know if I can do this anymore…

There was a protracted silence.

"Agent Woo, I don't like repeating myself. It is an inefficient
use of time. What is her profile?" Donovan asked frustrated. He had
worked with agents from the FBI's NCAVC before. They were well-
trained agents with experience in homicide, kidnapping etc. many of
whom he'd had the opportunity to train. His expectation was that
Agent Woo would bring this expertise with her; however, this was
not the case.

"She is characterized as a weak personality; she is self doubting
and needs external reassurance to succeed." Woo proclaimed
anecdotally, as if reading ingredients from a recipe.

"Agent Woo, I'm not asking for a dating profile. I don't care
about her weekend chores. Would she be likely to participate in a
scheme to murder, steal organs, and transfer them to a drug dealer?"
he asked point blank.

Woo swallowed hard.

"It is highly possible, sir. In her fragile state she could be easily
coerced. I don't think she is morally intact or capable of repelling a
financially lucrative offer."

"Morally intact?"

"I think her moral compass is easily misguided, sir. She is
irresolute."

Donovan did not try to conceal the roll of his eyes.

"How is the Island?" Donovan asked O'Donnell, deciding it better to move on than continue with Woo.

"Fear, sir. Fear is mounting all over the Island. Everything on the Island is connected to the medical school. The administration is asking if their medical students, staff and patients are in danger," O'Donnell answered.

"Good, fear is useful. We can use that to our advantage," Donovan mused.

"What info do we release to the press?" O'Donnell asked grabbing a pen in anticipation of the brief he'd need to communicate.

"Nothing," Donovan replied to their surprise, "for now I want everyone kept in the dark. The less they know the more control I have. Now, listen up. First thing in the morning I want a meeting with the hospital president. Next I want the authority for wiretaps on my desk yesterday! The fact I have to ask for them reflects poorly on all of you. You know how to do your jobs, so do them. Finally, I believe Jeanine Hunter knows more than what she's communicating. So until further notice, she is our number one suspect. That means I want that tree shaken until she's begging to tell us more information. Investigate her family, if she has a cat interrogate its fleas, find out what she ate for breakfast two years ago last Tuesday; make her uncomfortable but don't touch her. Leave that to me."

In the meantime, Donovan had research to do.

CHAPTER 4
SETTING THE STAGE

The morning of Jeanine's session with Dr. Snyder, Jeanine was called to a meeting with the University president. She was not told the purpose of the meeting but she guessed it was regarding David. Upon entering the office, she immediately used the observational skills she'd learned in medicine to assess the meeting's attendants. She met with Dr. Robert Sardo the president, her residency program director Dr. William Baker, and two other men she referred to as the "suits".

They reminded her of pharmaceutical drug representatives, only stiff and less glamorously appareled. They all seemed ill at ease except for the suits. One of them was standing in the shadows and she could not see his face. The other was a man in his mid-thirties, stocky and well built who, at first glance, appeared stodgy and slow. But after studying him for a moment, she reassessed him as much more agile, someone who could definitely handle himself in a street fight.

Jeanine sat in front of the president's large oak desk. The office was located near the top floor of Old Red, as it was affectionately named, for being built out of red brick. This 100-year-old icon of the University represented its' strength and endurance. It was one of the few buildings that survived the great hurricane of 1900 that decimated the Island and killed thousands of people. President Sardo's oval shaped office was one level below the historic cadaver lab, and its windows afforded a 360-degree panoramic view.

Sardo sat behind his oversized desk and Jeanine admired the palm trees that swayed behind him through the large paned windows. She wished she could be outside under the sway of the palm trees, sapphire blue sky, and sun instead of being sequestered at what felt like the Spanish inquisition.

President Sardo was a short, burly, man who was used to pushing people to get what he wanted. He was not accustomed to being told what to do. As with all presidents of hospitals, politics were a suit he wore well. Despite this fact, he looked nervous. Huge drops of sweat fell from his face like large beads of clear glass. These were not attributes common to the president and seeing them made Jeanine more nervous, as something or someone had rattled his cage.

"Jeanine", president Sardo started somberly, "I know you must be curious as to why we've called you here."

"Yes sir," she replied with quiet apprehension.

"These men are with the FBI," he said acknowledging their presence with a nod in their direction. "You may have spoken to some of their colleagues earlier and we appreciate the assistance you have already provided, however, we need more from you. The FBI has reason to believe that Dr. Rubio was abducted in relationship to Mr. Scott's case."

"What? Monica is missing?" she gasped.

One of the FBI agents, Agent O'Donnell, interjected. "Dr. Hunter we have reason to believe that you are at risk of also being abducted. That is why we have called you here today. We are assigning an agent to you for security. We will be monitoring your daily activities to make sure that you are protected. Furthermore, we believe that by keeping you under surveillance we may be able to solve both of these cases. Ergo discover who abducted Dr. Rubio and who stole the organs of Mr. Scott."

"Surveillance? Assigning an Agent? What does that mean?" Jeanine could see now why they were so pale. She felt flushed, shaken, overwhelmed. Her mouth went dry, her hands were wet with perspiration, and her stomach developed an acute case of gastritis with severe burning in the pit of her stomach.

The other agent stepped forward. He had a sleek, lean, muscular frame that lent itself to blending into the shadows. All this time, he had been inconspicuously monitoring everyone's responses, especially Jeanine's. He had an elegant, authoritative appearance. It was clear he was the one in charge of this meeting. He stepped toward Jeanine, out of the shadows, and into the light.

"Dr. Hunter, I am Special Agent Luke Donovan. I know this is overwhelming for you. I want you to know that we are here to protect you. We will do the best we can to keep you safe with as much normalcy as possible."

He used his voice to elicit a calming effect. Jeanine had used the same technique with her patients and although she knew what it was she could not help but fall prey to its effectiveness. Obviously, there was more they were not telling her. Something did not feel right and, until she knew what it was, she did not trust any of them but decided she would cooperate.

"Anything I can do to help Monica or find out who did this to David I will do," she answered simply.

"Thank you, Jeanine. These men will escort you to their headquarters. They have some issues to discuss with you. I will meet with you again tomorrow," Dr. Sardo announced.

Jeanine was discretely escorted from president Sardo's office to the headquarters the FBI had established on the Island. They had disguised their location in one of the warehouses near Galveston Bay's waterfront. It was another way to diffuse the Islander's suspicions.

In total, there were ten thousand square feet of space. On the ground floor, there were 3 workstations comprised of metal L-shaped desks from the 1960's. The floor was covered with miles and miles of black computer cords, power cables and the like all neatly bundled with ties to prevent tripping. Jeanine sat down in the middle of the room and felt like a kindergartener waiting for someone to give her permission to speak. She waited anxiously for the FBI liaison she was supposed to meet.

Time crawled by. She'd been waiting for over half an hour in the vast coldness of the large room whose air conditioning had been ridiculously set to 65 degrees Fahrenheit. As with anyone who is forced to wait in silence, she started to think about the circumstances surrounding her and she was flooded by waves of emotion. She was still mourning David's death and now that pain was coupled with the fear that someone may be waiting to kidnap or kill her. Monica might already be dead. She felt isolated and fought to stave off the fear and desperation that were howling at the edge of her consciousness. She had to stay in control.

On the second floor of the warehouse was a loft area accessible by a catwalk whose offices overlooked the first floor. From this area, concealed by one-way mirrors, the agents studied Jeanine.

"What are we waiting for?" Jake Glenn asked. His pale cheeks blushed red as he clasped his hands together as though waiting for fine a meal. His youthful exuberance betrayed his age and inexperience.

Donovan's ramrod straight posture was unaffected by his pupil's question. He simply kept his eyes focused on Jeanine as he took a sip of coffee too strong and too bitter to be considered palatable. Without turning his attention away from Jeanine, "Agent Woo, would you answer Agent Glenn's question please?" Donovan asked.

"Standard procedure is to isolate the subject for at least thirty minutes in a cold room forcing them to feel vulnerable. In so doing the subject is more amenable to manipulation and more easily scrutinized. Said subject is also more likely to trust a parental figure that can extract even more information," she answered with a monotone, dictionary-like cadence.

Agent Lorna Woo irritated Jake immensely. Woo was a useless bookworm who studied people but had absolutely no people skills. He sighed under his breath. Donovan maintained his statuesque posture for another half hour stroking his goatee. For whatever reason, at that same moment, Jeanine looked up at the mirrored glass and peered directly at Donovan. For a second, he thought she could see him through the glass and in that moment he felt a brief, almost tangible, connection with her. Loosing himself from this thought he engaged Agent Woo.

"Alright, it's time. Lorna, interrogate her," he instructed.

"Me?!" she said with surprise and trepidation in her voice.

"Sir, I'm just here to provide analysis. I...I...I don't actually interact with the subject," she replied, saying the word 'subject' as though it were a disease.

"Agent Woo, I am the team lead on this case. I will assign personnel as I see fit to accomplish the task. I am not asking you for your opinion. I am giving it to you." His resolve was as fixed as his posture.

Swallowing hard, Lorna gathered a handful of papers, books, notes, and journals and clung them to her chest as she prepared to go downstairs. Pencils and papers slipped out of her vice-like grasp to the floor. As she bent to pick up a hapless sheet of paper from the floor, she would inadvertently drop more paper, pencils and pens. It was comical to watch her gather this cornucopia of office supplies. She slipped, nearly falling, on numerous occasions but miraculously she maintained her balance.

Donovan sighed silently as he heard the spectacle of Lorna behind him. Although he did not face her, he could hear the calamity and see the reflection of it in the window in front of him. He shook his head wondering about the next generation of agents finally acquiescing the realization that it was his task to train his sophomoric counterparts.

With a single glance over his shoulder Donovan communicated to simply drop everything, go downstairs, and talk to Jeanine. Some things did not require words. Lorna obeyed and commenced her interview with Jeanine.

Woo sat uncomfortably behind the thirty-year-old metal desk. She slid its accompanying metal chair across the concrete floor such that it let out an ear-piercing screech. This lasted at least 30 seconds as she moved the chair to and fro, right and left, until she found just the right spot for the chair. She shifted in her seat, shuffled her papers, and dropped pens and paper continuously. Anxiety induced hives formed on her neck and face. Jeanine watched her with concern and then humor as she fought against asking if medical attention was necessary. Jeanine's faith in Agent Lorna Woo's ability to provide any sort of protection for her was ebbing...quickly.

Lorna swallowed hard, "Well," she said with her voice cracking "my name is Agent Woo and I'm just going to go over some information with you." Her voice ran through three different octaves in one sentence, sounding very much like a pubescent boy. She cleared her throat and announced, "An agent will be with you twenty four hours a day to…"

"What? Are you serious?" Jeanine asked incredulously. "Twenty four hours a day? How is this going to work? What about my patients? Which Agent?" The last question escaped before she could stop herself. She eyed Lorna closely hoping that she was not going to be her protection.

Lorna fumbled again through her sentences trying to think of what to say. From the surveillance room, Agents Swenson and O'Donnell joined Donovan. Swenson commented on Donovan's procedure. "Hmmm, interesting tactic" Swenson mused cynically. "Using Lorna, a complete social idiot, to garner a relationship with the one person who has any possibility of getting us out of this swamp."

"Swenson, your opinion is ill informed and, as such, unsolicited," Donovan replied verbally swatting her like an annoying fly. Swenson smoldered but held her tongue.

O'Donnell interrupted their discussion. "I hate to interrupt but I believe Lorna needs assistance," he declared.

Donovan's intent for Lorna was dual. His purpose was to introduce Lorna to an actual living creature while also creating an environment in which Jeanine would need to trust him. However, as he peered downstairs, he could see Jeanine was highly incensed.

At that moment he heard Lorna ask, "I don't mean to irritate you, I just need to know how many sexual partners you have had. It's in your best interest to be honest with us…"

"Look, I don't know who you are but this has nothing to do with David or with Monica. Why are you asking me these questions? Furthermore, I don't appreciate being called a liar, it's insulting!"

"If there have been too many to count you can just say that…." Lorna chattered on not bothering to listen.

Jeanine jumped straight out of her chair. Just then, Donovan approached.

"Dr. Hunter, please," he asked as he glided across the floor with an elegant unhurried stroll. Jeanine's heart was racing and she was shaking with anger. She did not care who was after her at this moment; all she wanted to do was to leave. Donovan's presence was welcoming after her discussion with Agent Woo. She hoped he was here to rescue her from this simpleton. Luke walked around the desk and sat next to Jeanine.

"Dr. Hunter, I am sorry if Agent Woo was insensitive. Sometimes we lose sight of our mission. Our purpose is not to

18

intrude into your life but to protect you from whoever abducted Dr. Rubio and find out what happened to your patient. Our goal is to work with you and not against you.

In fact, there are a total of five agents working on this case. These include: myself, Agent Woo, and the three agents upstairs who are watching us through a one-way-mirror. Jake, please open the window," Donovan called upstairs. Compliantly, the mirrored glass opened and Jeanine could see the three additional agents peering at her from upstairs.

"Honesty from the FBI? I don't know what to say" she replied.

"Give us a chance Dr. Hunter. We are here to help you."

"You are helping me by asking about my personal life?" she asked angrily.

"Our tactics are intrusive, I admit, but we have good intentions," he replied soothingly.

"Intrusive? That's an understatement. I want to cooperate, but have you considered how I'm supposed to see patients with a horde of FBI agents following me? It doesn't exactly build patient-physician rapport."

"You will not be followed by a horde, Dr. Hunter. I will be the only agent following you."

Jeanine was taken aback. Surprise permeated the room not only for Jeanine but also his agents, as well. "What?" she asked.

"I will be the only agent assigned to you."

"Where are you, I mean, um, how are you…" she stammered.

"I will pose as a foreign exchange medical student. You will be my hostess. We are correct in determining that you live alone?"

"That's not possible."

"Living alone?"

"No. I mean, yes. I do live alone but you cannot stay with me."

He blinked at her in surprise, an emotion he rarely felt.

"I'm not sure I understand your objection," he finally said calmly.

""Because!" she screeched. "It would be imprudent. Can't you assign a female agent to me?" she said in a more reserved tone.

'Imprudent,' he thought to himself. Who says such things much less believes in it Donovan wondered. "We could, but none of them have my experience. I believe this is the best option," he continued feeling solid in his point.

"In that case, I quit. I can't do my job with you inside my head, inside my apartment and inside my life. If I can't do my job I am a danger to my patients," she declared.

Luke cleared his throat. He had prepared for every possibility. "Dr. Hunter, we must request that you maintain your typical daily duties. Anyone who is involved in Mr. Scott's case is probably watching you and to alter that schedule is not an option."

"You may feel comfortable with this risk but I won't bargain with my life or with the lives of my patients," she answered defiantly. Luke rose to his full height consciously using it to intimidate her.

"Will you bargain with Dr. Rubio's life? You may be the only link Dr. Rubio has to make it back home. What about Mr. Scott? If you cared for him or have concerns for your other patients you must realize their lives are in jeopardy. You may hold the key to protect them. If that does not appeal to you, perhaps you will consider this. I have every assurance from president Sardo that every day you refuse to cooperate will be counted against any vacation days you may have. I think it would be best if you worked with us." He would not be dissuaded.

She shifted uneasily in her chair. If looks could kill, her glare would have killed Donovan stone dead. She didn't like being manipulated. She was backed into a corner. "Well, you can't stay with me. My father would not approve," she answered simply clenching her jaw angrily.

She had nothing else to say. The reasons for her objection seemed obvious to her and she couldn't understand his refusal. Her father's authority was the first thing that came out of her mouth but in hindsight she wished she used a more clever response in her defense. Regardless, her stubbornness, a trait Donovan would love and hate, was as firmly entrenched as a cat unwilling to enter a cage.

"Your father wouldn't approve of you living with a male medical student? It's 1990. What is the problem? Besides, your father does not have to know," he insisted still attempting to appeal to her less conservative side.

"*I* do not approve," she answered emphatically. At this further provocation, she was offended. Her hot eyes shot up to meet Donovan's. As angry as she had been with Lorna, her current state of frustration had grown exponentially in response to Donovan. Though his frame dwarfed hers, it was her presence that filled the room.

On this point she would not yield. She shook her head at him sadly, almost pitiably, for his lack of understanding. She wondered how it could be so difficult for him to understand that she, a single female, would not want to live with a man she hardly knew. "It takes a lifetime to build a reputation. It only takes minutes to destroy it," she finally explained.

Poignant.

He finally understood. For him, this was just another case. For her, this was a life. And after all the dust had settled, she would be left with the remains of it long after his façade had gone.

'Damn,' he thought to himself 'trumped by morality.' He did not understand this girl. But to crack this case he knew he needed to understand her and it was obvious Agent Woo was incapable of facilitating this.

"Alright," he finally answered, "we'll see what we can do." He would make arrangements to observe her in a neutral setting. As he turned to leave, he faced Agent Woo and whispered, "I think her moral compass is intact, agent."

Jeanine did not hear him but saw Agent Woo turn bright red.

+++++

In the loft above them, another conversation was taking place. "What do you think of Donovan?" O'Donnell asked Swenson.

"I think he's losing his touch. I've never heard of the agent in charge of ops taking point on surveillance. He can't remain objective unless he's an emotionless bastard," Swenson replied, as though delighted by the notion she'd proposed.

"Yeah," Ben O'Donnell mused "or he's a genius. I've studied his cases. He may be a merciless bastard but he's effective. He is known for thinking everything through and covering all of the angles."

"You respect him," Swenson noted mildly amused. O'Donnell merely raised an eyebrow in response. The gesture spoke volumes.

"I think I can do the job better than he can," Swenson finally said.

"So do I," O'Donnell stated.

"You think I can do better or do you think you can?" Swenson asked to clarify his position.

"You want his job?" O'Donnell asked avoiding her question.

"Crookshank is the SAC in Houston; he's Donovan's superior now. He's going to be promoted to deputy director. I look forward to working under him."

"You mean," he asked slyly, "you've never worked under the Special Agent in Charge before?" referring to the rumors of their sexual relationship.

Swenson eyed him sharply, allowing her icy glare to provide her answer.

"How do you know Crookshank?" O'Donnell continued undaunted.

"I've worked with him when I lived in England," Swenson answered curtly.

"So that's where you're from. The mystery is solved! I wondered about your English accent," Glenn interjected excitedly finally feeling approval to join the conversation.

"No, knit wit. I'm an American. My father was the U.S. Ambassador to England," Swenson corrected sharply.

"Oh," Glenn replied deflated as he lost his newly found confidence.

"What's that got to do with Donovan? He's got a 92% success rate. Do you think Crookshank is going to ignore that for…well…you?" O'Donnell challenged.

Swenson's response was icy and too detailed for a mere theoretical exercise. It was clear she had a formative plan to dethrone Donovan. "You might consider his ratio impressive but the Bureau does not. It might be a 92% success rate in general. But do you know who comprises the 8%? Carlos Colorado. So, in that sense, he has a 100% Colorado failure rate. If this case looks like it's going south, pardon the expression given our geographical location, Donovan's position is tenuous and his ass will belong to me."

"This isn't just a hypothetical for you. You really want this case, don't you?" O'Donnell observed. She eyed Glenn and O'Donnell hungrily.

Swenson replied, "Why do you think you are here? Donovan didn't choose us. Crookshank ordered Donovan to take us on this case because he knows Donovan is going to fail and when he does I'll be waiting to take over." Both men were silent for a moment.

"What do you think, O'Donnell? Is she behind all of this?" Jake Glenn asked, his courage replenished after his last question to Swenson. O'Donnell looked at Jeanine for a long while thinking about Jake's question.

"She is not a typical mark," O'Donnell observed. "Donovan has put her at the center of this for one of two reasons. Either she's involved with a bigger group that's behind this and she's the one that got caught with her pants down or she's bait," he finally answered.

"Which do you think it is?" Jake Glenn asked carefully.

"Whoever is behind this is too slick to let out a scapegoat. They would probably just kill her if she got caught. Donovan's putting too much energy into her just on a hunch. Either she's bait and he doesn't care or he's just going to get enough circumstantial shit on her to make her look like she's involved. You put enough blood in the water, the sharks will come and they'll bite on anything that's in the way. Too bad though. She seems like a nice girl," O'Donnell mused contemplatively.

"Too bad? Nice girl?' Are you getting soft O'Donnell? That's not your reputation" Mellicent huffed.

"Hey, you've worked enough ops to know what's going to happen here," O'Donnell defended, referring to Donovan. "He takes no prisoners and he uses everything he can to get his mark. He'll use her and when he's done there'll be nothing left except a nice neat little package for the Justice Department and a closed case."

"It's just part of the job. Somebody has to go to jail," Mellicent stated flippantly, "and if he doesn't put her there, I will."

"I just hope it's the right somebody. And," O'Donnell added "Swenson, I'd watch your ass with Donovan, if I were you. I've researched him. After college, he joined the FBI but asked for a deferment to serve time in the Israeli Defense Force. I can't ascertain how long he was there or what he did after leaving the IDF. There's an entire chapter of Donovan's life missing from the files. Apparently, this guy has enough clout to make his own records disappear."

"I know you enjoy looking at my ass O'Donnell. But don't worry, I know how to protect it," she announced as she sauntered out of the room provocatively. Ben and Jake instinctively admired Swenson's derriere for a moment before higher brain functions returned their attentions to the true issue at hand. Both agents observed Jeanine in silence. Each man was within his own thoughts.

Outside clouds were gathering. A storm was coming.

CHAPTER 5
JEANINE, DONOVAN AND SNYDER

"Your patient is dead, your colleague is missing and the FBI would like some answers." The words reverberated in Jeanine's mind. Her heart sank into her chest even as she sank deeper into the leather chaise. Her mouth went dry.

Jeanine had been requested, commanded really, to meet with Dr. Snyder to see if he could release any information hidden in her subconscious, in an effort to assist the FBI.

"Tell me what you remember about that night," he repeated. She recalled the events to Dr. Snyder. A million things happened all at once but Jeanine saw everything in slow motion. She had just laid down her pen after signing David's discharge order form, lifted her head from the nurses' station kiosk and walked back down the hall towards his room to say goodnight.

As she walked towards his room, the code blue-alert blared overhead and an avalanche of white coats and scrubs from the coding team emerged and sprang into action. Jeanine felt like she was in a nightmare; she developed tunnel vision when looking at his room. She kept trying to run but her legs were unresponsive.

By the time she arrived, Dr. Rubio, Jeanine's friend and fellow classmate, was running David's code. She was giving orders, initiating advanced cardiac life support, and nurses administered medications and did chest compressions. David was unconscious, convulsing and vomiting. Jeanine was shouting at them but no one could hear her. Finally someone asked, "Who knows this patient?"

"I do" she yelled back, "Stop the code! He's a DNR!"

The room fell silent. Everything stopped. David was a DNR, a 'Do Not Resuscitate'. He did not want to be brought back if he was dying. Dr. Rubio ordered all resuscitation procedures to stop and asked someone to call his family, as his time was short.

"Jeanine, go home." Monica advised, "I know how close you are to him. You don't want to see this."

Jeanine was dazed. She walked zombie-like to her on-campus apartment. She called David's family. They had hoped to have him pass away quietly at home. Dying in the hospital is not what they had expected. They rushed to the hospital hoping to be there in time before he died. They did not succeed. At midnight, Jeanine's phone rang. It was Monica calling to let her know David had died.

It was the same story every time she told it. Nothing new came to her mind. Dr. Snyder considered what she said. He had read her statements provided by the FBI, of course, but he wanted to evaluate Jeanine as she recounted the details. Dr. Snyder had three decades of experience as a psychiatrist and had spent his entire career at the University.

He had narrowed his patient census significantly recently and his only patients were physicians or medical students. He enjoyed working with residents deemed at risk for not completing their programs. He was a particular favorite of the medical students and residents because he was an intercessor on their behalf defending them against an administration that would just as easily fire a struggling student than root out the reasons regarding their failed performance.

Dr. Snyder's other unique quality was that he sincerely believed in the brotherhood of physicians. While his colleagues deemed residents and students as pawns, he regarded them as fellow brethren and would only call them by their proper title rather than their first name or some denigrating nickname (he considered all nicknames trite).

His shortcoming, however, was his arrogance. He considered non-physicians as lesser creatures that deserved no higher station in life than to be tolerated, if that. He was narcissistic; he had a sharp temper and was incapable of mercy or forgiveness.

He had been working with Jeanine on a weekly basis for a few months, prior to David's death, because the administration felt she was struggling through her residency program. They had not made significant progress. Today's session was additionally challenging, in his mind, because they had the added distraction of Agent

Donovan's presence, which stirred up a deep-seated resentment in Jeanine that, even she, found surprising.

"Pardon the observation, but you seem more irritated to be here than usual. Might I assume the presence of your FBI shadow has something to do with that irritation?" Snyder asked.

"I don't agree with his presence here," she replied resentfully. Dr. Snyder leaned back into his comfortable chair and stroked the immaculately trimmed beard on his narrow chin.

"It is obvious why he is here, Dr. Hunter. The FBI has told you they are here for your protection and to elicit information from you regarding Dr. Rubio's disappearance and the situation with Mr. Scott. Whether that information is conscious or subconscious is irrelevant. It is clear to me that they are also here to catch a glimpse of your psyche. Why they think they will be any more successful at seeing into your mind than I have been is beyond me. But that is beside the point.

I might assume that you are also somewhat of a suspect in this case. But, heavens, that could not be possible because the FBI would be violating your rights. Yet, I am intrigued. I think you should have the opportunity to know thy enemy, as they say. Why don't we try something different for this therapy session? Agent Donovan is it? Agent, why don't you tell us about yourself?" Dr. Snyder finished with a smug grin feeling pleased with himself.

"What?" Donovan asked, as he was lulled back to a state of consciousness. He had been propped up against a wall in the far corner of the office leaning into the shadows of the room trying to be unobtrusive. He silently questioned whether his attendance at these sessions would prove profitable in any way. The last thing on his radar of possibility was that he would be evaluated.

"Yes, Mr. Donovan, I am most certainly speaking to you. I reluctantly allowed you to attend our sessions. If you have the gall to attend then you should also have the wherewithal to participate. If you are going to listen to Dr. Hunter's innermost thoughts I think it fair you reciprocate." His perfectly enunciated words hung in the air like the pungently sweet scent of the tobacco smoke from his pipe.

Before Donovan answered, he took a moment to consider Dr. Snyder. He was an extraordinarily thin gentleman in his late sixties with strawberry blonde hair that had lost its stronghold to an abundance of grey. He was a very well groomed man with impeccable taste who wore tailored three-piece suits. He spoke with a brisk eloquence that could cause one to mistake him for an Englishman. In Donovan's previous conversations with the psychiatrist, Donovan noticed he possessed the terrific tendency of evasion. He was adept at asking penetrating questions but he, himself, was elusive. Snyder reminded him of a lesser version of himself.

A deep, rumbling, negativity was growing in the pit of Luke Donovan's soul. Now that he was in the proverbial spotlight, he could see why Jeanine despised this process so much. No one enjoyed being dissected. As the eternal and awkward silence raged on, Donovan considered this as an opportunity he could use to get closer to Jeanine.

"All right," he started slowly, "what would you like to know, Dr. Snyder?" he asked in a perfectly unaffected tone. Dr. Snyder's smiled widely and Donovan imagined him as a spider salivating at a juicy fly caught in his web.

"I think it best that Dr. Hunter ask the first question," he announced.

At this point both Jeanine and Luke shared a simultaneous emotion: total surprise. Up until this moment, Luke Donovan had not been a person, he was an entity to be despised, a representative of evil and now thanks to Dr. Snyder he had regained the rank of human being. She studied Donovan thoroughly.

"Where are you from?" she asked.

"Maryland"

"No, where are you from, originally?" she asked almost frustrated he did not understand her question.

"I grew up there," he answered again.

"You have an accent and it's not from Maryland," she sighed dismissing his reluctance.

Both men were intrigued chiefly because Donovan's accent was so subtle. Dr. Snyder had not even detected its presence and he thought himself to be quite the observer. For Donovan, it was a probing question, in that he had tried for so long to hide his accent from others and he'd become quite good at it. In his line of work it was necessary to be inconspicuous; an accent could be lethal.

Jeanine could see from his mannerisms that this observation was affecting him. A thousand thoughts flashed across his face. Before he spoke, she could tell he was holding something back.

"I was born in the United States but my father is from Ireland. I lived there for a while," Donovan answered expectantly awaiting her reply.

She shook her head negatively as she looked at him. "No, there is something else. I can hear the Irish but…there is something else…something…Middle Eastern?" She asked distantly as she tilted her head in contemplation as though trying to see through him.

"Impressive," Donovan replied honestly.

"Indeed!" Dr. Snyder agreed with a father-like-pride as though he was responsible for her detective abilities.

"My mother is from Israel. I spent several summers there. We moved to the U.S. permanently when I was ten. I've been trying to lose both accents ever since. Most people don't even notice. How did you?" He asked.

"Do you speak another language?" Dr. Snyder added.

"It's trivial. Just something useful at parties I guess," she fumbled awkwardly.

Donovan observed lying was not her strong suit. Most of his agents would give their left arm for half of the talent she had. But she was genuinely humble, almost embarrassed, to admit such a talent. Donovan was impressed.

Dr. Snyder interrupted, although not wholly satisfied with her answer, turning back to Agent Donovan.

"You are a walking contradiction; a Jewish, Irish Catholic? You must have had an interesting childhood."

Donovan had learned to appreciate his differences and even use them to his advantage. Even now his uniqueness proved profitable.

"Actually, my father was Protestant, not Catholic, and my mother was Israeli by birth but she practiced Christianity. It is believed that my mother's family descended from some of the first Hebrew Christians, after Jesus and a few of his closest friends, of course!"

He chuckled a little. He had not told that little anecdote about his family in years. His eyes met with Jeanine's and for a second they exchanged pleasant glances. Something about her eyes was appealing.

Dr. Snyder observed something between them but it disappeared just as quickly as it formed. "Your experiences must have affected your personality," Snyder continued.

"I know who I am," Donovan shot back sharply unappreciative of Snyder's probing.

"And who are you exactly?" Jeanine asked directly.

"The one sent here to help you, Dr. Hunter," Donovan replied sharply.

She swallowed hard and lowered her eyes to the floor. She said nothing else. Precisely at the end of the hour she looked up at the clock. It was time to go. Donovan knew she was hiding something. He needed answers and these therapy sessions were not getting him there. He had to push her for more.

CHAPTER 6
THE MENTOR

"Are you sure you want to do this?" she asked. "Once you start down this path, there is no going back." Luke Donovan paused for a moment.

"I wouldn't be here if I wasn't sure. I just need some help, Renee." He was not convincing. Renee skeptically raised her left eyebrow and cocked her head to the side.

"All right," he admitted, shifting his defensive posture to one of respect for his older venerable mentor "you have me. You always did have a way of sorting through the bullshit."

"You know me, Luke. I'm as constant as the sea. That's what you need in your life; a woman who'll be your bullshit detector. But that's not why you're here," she observed wisely.

Renee had been an active FBI agent for over 30 years but she benched herself five years ago after being shot in the hip by a suspect. Luke respected Renee because she was the heart and soul of an ideal agent. She did not play political games. She became an agent for the sole purpose of upholding justice for all those who had been wronged. Ironically, Renee felt her injury was a blessing in disguise. It gave her the opportunity to appreciate all of the things she never took the time to enjoy; and she even managed to save a disintegrating marriage.

She stopped working cases and only did research which in itself was still a daunting task but one she could accomplish easily. She was equally successful, if not more, at solving the mysteries no one else could piece together. This was probably due to her uncanny ability to read people. A skill, she believed, was lacking in the younger generation of agents.

Other FBI agents, intimidated by her gruffness, called her the 'old battle-ax'. Her inner strength was admirable and for those who could get close enough to her, that strength was conferred to them. She either liked you or she didn't and the opposite was also true. In

31

honesty, she was a hard person to get along with. She had a mouth like a sailor and an attitude like a president. She would be heard and she would be heard distinctly. Most of the politically oriented, upwardly mobile agents could not abide her, nonetheless, they respected her as she was one of few who could accomplish what others could not or would not. Hence, she was, in essence, the tool they needed to succeed. To excel in the FBI you had to be successful at solving cases especially when it came to large cases with media attention.

At this juncture, Luke needed Renee's opinion about Jeanine. "Renee, I've reviewed the case with Agent Woo, my profiler, but I do not agree with her assessment of Dr. Hunter. Woo is intelligent, although, not in any particularly useful way. I think her conclusions are saccharin at best."

"I've already reviewed this case," she said with her ruff tobacco stained voice. "Your analyst has her head up her ass," she replied.

Her statement caught Luke by so much surprise that he could not suppress a laugh and his coffee shot out of his nose. "So much for tact!" he replied laughing and wincing simultaneously as he wiped coffee from his face.

Undaunted and pleasantly entertained at his response, Renee continued as they sat in her 1970's style ranch house with wood paneled walls. They were sitting in a room crowded with thousands of FBI files some of which Renee was currently using as a makeshift desk. The room was so congested Donovan had to navigate through a distinctly-carved, premeditated path just to make it to a 12-inch wide seat which had seen better days in its previous life as an old milk crate. This was the uncomfortable seat upon which Luke found himself perched. He had to keep shifting his weight from one buttock to the other to avoid that enduring pain one always experiences when sitting on a hard surface.

He wasn't surprised that there were so many files in her house or that he had to snake through it just to find a place to meet with her. But he was impressed by how well she could bring order to chaos. She knew the place and location of every dust-free well-manicured file.

Renee continued. "Woo is so inundated with textbooks and convenient labels that it's disgusting. I don't know why they keep popping out these nitwits, must be nepotism. I hate that shit! No experience, no knowledge of people...." She stopped herself, shaking her head at the situation. Renee sighed and looked at Luke squarely in the face.

"This case is going to cost you something Cochise. This Dr. Hunter is like no other mark you've worked before. And for you, sport, that's saying something. The way to get to this woman is through trust. And it has to be genuine. She's sincere and to reach her that's what you will have to be. She has instincts, good ones and she listens to them.

Your analyst thinks Hunter is suffering from an "ugly duckling" phenomenon and that as soon as the right prince comes along she'll swoon and drop her pants. That's a load of shit. She's not waiting for somebody to justify her existence. She's up to her neck in the disgusting shit of human beings. Yes, she's tired, she's frustrated and she could probably use a shot of Jim Beam and a good fuck but you're not going to get close enough to offer either to this girl if you approach her like she's just another case.

Her "moral compass" is wound tight. She's not conservative, she's not liberal, she's right and you can't politic your way into that kind of heart. Woo mistook her kindness as weakness, her thoughtfulness as passivity, and her gentleness as lack of an aggressive nature. Let me assure you; she is not weak, slow, or stupid. She will not let someone into her inner circle simply because they smile and smell good. To reach her, you are going to have to let down your own barriers. She will see through anything else.

You had better make sure you are prepared to do that. From personal experience, I can tell you a case like this can pull you in so that you can't distinguish the truth from the illusion you are presenting. Can you do that hot shot?"

Luke had been absorbing all that Renee had said. She had dissected this case to the bare bones. He wondered how she could know so much about this woman with so little observation. Still, some of her observations had already been confirmed. Donovan recalled the events of Dr. Snyder's last session with Jeanine and how she cornered him on his accent. He wasn't sure he could honestly answer Renee's question.

"I won't make you answer, sport. I don't want to force you to lie to me. I know you are not ready but you'll do it anyway because that's your job. But I can tell you now you are headed for failure if you don't wrap your head around this."

Luke only smiled in response, as anything else was too painful to attempt. Renee was like an older sister who never pulled any punches. And like all older sisters you can only take so much truth at one time before the pain becomes too much to bear.

Renee leaned back in the wooden office chair she was sitting in and its un-greased spring hinges creaked tentatively as she leaned back to relax for a moment. She took in a deep breath and let it out slowly; kicking herself that she had given up her habit of smoking as she could really use a cigarette right now. She'd start again next week.

The light in the room was shifting, as the morning had grown old. The source of illumination was provided by three sets of narrow windows. Each window was six inches wide and five feet tall and separated by about six inches from the next window. Each set of three windows was separated by five feet of wood paneled wall.

From where they were sitting, Renee's husband could be seen outside in the yard unwinding the water hose and getting ready to water the yard. He was wearing a yellow polo shirt, a khaki colored baseball hat and plaid polyester golf shorts that no grown man ever had the right to be seen in public wearing, as they were far, far too ugly. He was getting tangled in the hose that was encircling him like a hyperactive snake wrapping around his waist and going over his head until he almost tripped...several times.

"Luke, look at my husband. He's out there in the middle of an August day, watering the yard and tangled up in a garden hose. He's not the brightest crayon in the box. But for some reason, unknown to me, he loves me. Do you see those ugly golf shorts he's wearing? I gave those to him twenty years ago. I think they are made of some ancient, cursed, polyester that just can't be killed. They chafe like hell but he wears them for only one reason. Do you know what that reason is?"

Luke only looked at the kyphotic, sixty-something, year old man studded with age spots, wondering why anyone would wear something that hideous.

Renee continued. "He wears them because I gave them to him. And that's the only reason that matters to him. What matters to me is that I didn't even pick them out. I was at a conference and forgot it was his birthday. I had an assistant, obviously one who hated me or had poor fashion sense even for the 70's, to go buy them for me so I could give them as a present. He wears them because he loves me and wants me to know he appreciates me. But when I look at him wearing those shorts I am hurt. Not only by how fucking ugly they are. But I hurt because of all that I missed all those years that everything else was more important than him and that fact is even uglier than the shorts."

She paused for a moment before she continued. "Do you know why I'm telling you this? No, of course not. Let me put it this way. Have you ever driven down a two-lane highway? It's the craziest thing in the world. To think that the only thing separating you from utter fucking disaster is the power of paint someone splashed on the road simply staggers the imagination; a thin yellow line is your only barrier of defense. The suggestion that two, thin, solid lines of paint are all that separate your car heading north at seventy miles per hour from a fully loaded 18-wheeler headed south (also going seventy miles an hour, you guess) in the middle of the night should fucking paralyze you.

Just consider these two possibilities: only a few inches separate you from life versus being the ultimate road kill in the human remains specimen jar in some crime lab. That's a thought that will keep you awake at night. But people drive those roads every day.

Luke, I'm telling you this because no one else has the balls to do it and I do. At some point in your career you will have to make a decision about what is important to you. In this business, they try to sell you the goods that everything is black and white. By now, you should have realized, well, that maybe it's not black and white and the differences between right and wrong, good and bad, sane and insane are not as wide as we would like to make them.

You need to ask yourself why the brass chose you for this case. You know, as well as I, that no one is made lead on an investigation of this magnitude without a reason. Have you been chosen because of your reputation to find the right body for the crime or because you have a reputation to find anybody for the crime. Are you are the kind of agent that thinks that thin yellow line down the road is just paint or do you think it protects you by some law of the highway universe? If the former you're all right. If the latter you're gonna end up as road kill and the FBI is gonna be drivin' the fuckin' truck!"

She paused. "I guess there is a middle ground, you could just end up with a wife that buys you ugly fucking shorts!" She smiled at herself as she made 'a funny' as she called it. But Luke was not laughing.

He felt an inescapable wave of tension flood over his muscles. It was hard to hear this. He did not come here for his own analysis but he respected her too much to stop her. It hit home. Renee could tell she'd reached that part of him he rarely let others see. She had to take advantage of the moment for one more crack of unsolicited advice. It might be a while before he returned.

"You need to let go of the past Donny boy, including your ex-wife, if you expect to move forward. What she did to you was shitty; to be frank, but what's done is done. And, by the way," she said, "I know you did not ask but I am going to tell you anyway. Hunter is not the criminal in this case. She's not the one. It's just not in her. Have fun driving home, stud."

CHAPTER 7
BURNED

Dr. Savage had been Jeanine's mentor from the first day she entered medical school. Each student was matched with a faculty member and, while their paring was random, it was nonetheless perfect. His temperament and maturity steadied her serving as a lighthouse to her psyche during the tumultuous and stormy sea of her medical career.

In order to preserve Jeanine's reputation and honor the request for discretion, Donovan arranged for a small but controlled electrical fire in her apartment. This caused extensive damage to her unit substantial enough to render it unlivable. Donovan also secured assurances from President Sardo that Dr. Savage would be amenable to having them reside with him and his wife.

The Savages lived on the Island in a large colonial home with a detached carriage house. It was not unusual for Dr. Savage, as a faculty member, to host visiting medical students and residents. Since it was a University practice to pair students on rotations, regardless of sex, Jeanine's honor would be protected and Donovan could still have direct access to her.

This scheme also validated, in some respects, Donovan's claim that Jeanine's life was in danger. While she was despondent over losing her apartment, she was pleased that her belongings were intact and that she would get to stay with Dr. Savage, someone whom she trusted implicitly. Unknown to Agent Donovan, Jeanine suspected Donovan's involvement with the fire. It was all together too convenient, especially since the damage was specifically isolated to her unit. Nonetheless, she was glad to be with the Savages.

Their carriage house had two bedrooms, a small kitchen and a sitting area. The main house, a two-story parakeet yellow colonial, was built in the late 1800's. It had been damaged half a dozen times by tropical storms and hurricanes over the years but, fortunately, never to any great extent. Dr. Savage, its fourth owner, had successfully preserved as much of the natural charm as possible. It was, for lack of a better word, quaint with its original hardwood flooring, lovely crown molding and period specific architectural elements from the crystal door handles to the chandeliers.

Despite the circumstances, Jeanine felt very peaceful here. There was an innate and palpable stillness in Dr. Savage's home that was spiritual and tranquil. Lush tropical plants and flowers like banana trees and oleanders surrounded the property. One corner was left open with a view Galveston Bay. The light danced on the water like happy flecks of gold. She enjoyed standing under the shade of one of the large palm trees, listening to the rustling of the palm fronds in the wind and watching the water.

Donovan observed her from the kitchen of the main house. After a while, she came inside and joined them for a breakfast Dr. Savage had prepared. His wife, Mrs. Savage-Roundbottom, was a night nurse and had just completed her shift.

"Home so soon, dear?" Dr. Savage asked flatly from the kitchen table. To hear them speak to each other, you would never guess they cared for each other. It was like watching two strangers have a conversation. But for them, it was an intimate dance.

"Yep, I'll be in the bed now," she announced flatly with her rich Minnesotan accent, and walked past them as though they were not there. She was a very matter of fact woman.

"Hello, Jeanine, nice to see you back. Glad you brought a friend," she stated dryly.

And to her husband, "please have them to sit down hon'. It's rude, don't you know? Goin' to bed now," and she walked through the kitchen and up the stairs with a large disinterested yawn.

"Luke, you'll have a chance to get to know Mrs. Savage-Roundbottom better once she wakes up. Even though she's been out of Minnesota for 20 years she still has that damn accent," Dr. Savage said. "Besides, I still love to hear her explain to new people why the name Savage-Roundbottom makes sense. I still don't understand it but that's the woman I married."

"So, how are you kiddo?" Dr. Savage asked turning his attention to Jeanine. That simple question hit her with the sudden pain of reality. She grimaced but tried to recover her countenance. To anyone else but Dr. Savage, this momentary grimace would have left them unaffected. But being a keen observer and caring for Jeanine as one of his own children gave him a father's insight that was not easily fooled. He did not address her distress. He would wait for that. She gave him a generic answer.

"Oh, same old same old," she said trying to create as much spirit as possible. She wanted to talk to him but not in front of Donovan.

"Well, Luke, President Sardo tells me you are an exchange student from Ireland?" Dr. Savage asked.

"Yes, sir" Donovan answered.

"Well, what differences have you seen between American medicine and that of Ireland?"

"Honestly, I haven't seen enough to form an opinion yet."

"I see. From the experiences you've had in Ireland, what do you think your medical specialty will be?" Savage continued.

"At this point, I think it's still too soon to say. I'd like to have more experience before I make a decision."

"Hmmm. That's a good strategy. What influenced you to come to the United States?"

"The U.S. is an interesting country. And I have some relatives that live here."

"Oh yes? Where do they live?"

"Baltimore," Donovan answered.

"Well, I would have hoped you could have gotten an assignment a little closer to Baltimore than Galveston!" Dr. Savage observed.

"It was a random assignment. I'm happy to be here."

"You are fortunate to have been assigned to Jeanine. She's a fair yet fastidious teacher. You will learn quite well with her and still preserve your humanity. That is something I admire about her. She has not forgotten why she wanted be a doctor. I cannot say the same of all of our colleagues."

"I look forward to it sir." Just then, Donovan looked at his watch. "Please excuse me. I have a meeting at the University." He thanked Dr. Savage for the breakfast and left. Savage could visibly see relief in Jeanine's posture.

"Ok kiddo. What's wrong?" Savage asked. Jeanine rubbed her forehead with her hand. Her head felt like it weighed a million pounds. She could not hide the truth from him but she could not disclose all of the facts. "There's so much, Dr. Savage."

He could hear the strain in her voice. "I don't even know where to start," the air felt heavy in her lungs. "All I can say is that, everything feels so heavy. I feel," she paused feeling the acid churn in her stomach. She could barely finish her thought. "I don't know that I can do this."

"Jeanine, as your mentor and as your friend I wish I could help you." He said genuinely.

"So do I," she said forlorn. She leaned back in her chair with a deep sigh.

"Have you spoken to your father? I know you haven't spoken much recently. Maybe now is the time to reach out to him?"

"I don't know how, Dr. Savage," she answered.

"What do you think your father would say about what you are going through?"

"He would tell me to focus on God. To think about the purpose He has given me in life."

"And what purpose is that?"

"I have always dreamed of being a doctor; of helping people. But now it seems that dream is…"

"What has changed?" he asked concerned.

"Everything has changed," she sighed.

He was quiet for a moment. Then, leaning forward he rested his elbows on his knees.

"When you were my student last year, one of the things I admired about you was your tenacity. You believed, most ardently, that God had given your life a purpose. Do you still believe that?"

"Yes, of course" she said without hesitation.

"So you believe the God of the universe loves you enough to care about your eternal soul?"

"Yes."

"And you are absolutely certain about that?"

"Yes!"

"So, if He cares so much about your soul, don't you think He cares about your life?"

"Sometimes I wonder," she pondered, "compared to more important things in the universe my life seems unimportant."

"Well, let's say you help someone who was hit by a car. They've been in a coma for three weeks and they finally wake up. They recover beautifully and right before they are discharged they tell you they are missing their wallet. You search the entire hospital to find it. Why? Because when you save someone's life they are valuable to you. What's important to them becomes important to you. If this is the case with mere mortals, it's certainly true with God."

"Thank you Dr. Savage," she smiled feeling reassured and hugging him.

"All right, all right. Enough private displays of affection," he groaned affectionately. "By the way, what's with your student?" he queried.

"What do you mean?"

"I'd say he works hard at saying nothing at all. I've had more meaningful conversations with wet paint. I know less about him now than before I met him."

"He's from Ireland. That's all I know."

"Hmmm," he mused unconvinced. And for reasons he wasn't completely sure of he was also deeply concerned.

+++++

"What did you get? Hear anything useful?" Donovan asked upon his return to FBI headquarters. He had placed recording devices in Dr. Savage's house.

"I think so, boss. Listen to this," Agent Glenn chirped happily.

Donovan listened to the conversation between Jeanine and Dr. Savage.

"There's definitely something between her and her father. Dr. Savage indicated their relationship has been strained recently." Glenn informed. "I've gotten all the records from her bank account. She's been sending money to her father every month for the last two years."

Agent Woo was also present, "We can also use the religion angle" she chimed in from behind a stack of papers on her desk. She was speaking loudly because she was still wearing the surveillance headphones.

Glenn motioned for her to remove the headphones. Donovan was silent for a moment.

"Well, sir, what do you think? The religion angle?" Woo repeated.

Internally, Donovan was torn. Normally, he would have used any means necessary to pursue a suspect. But he did not feel comfortable crossing this line, at least not now.

'Lines,' he mused to himself, 'damn that Renee.'

"Keep looking," he instructed.

CHAPTER 8
ALL THE NON-SPECIFIC HOO-HA

The day was winding to a close on a hot August day on Galveston Island. It was near dusk and the late sun was yielding amber light that cast long shadows on the downtown buildings of Galveston's Strand and Fisherman's Wharf. The city quietly resigned itself to the notion that the day was ending. Shop owners were turning over the wooden door plaques from 'open' to 'closed' while others swept the days' accumulation of sand and refuse away from their doorsteps. While this normal world was winding down, Agent Donovan's work was just beginning.

"Please, tell me Dr. Sardo, what can I expect tomorrow?" Donovan asked.

They were at FBI headquarters in Galveston's warehouse district on the bayside of the Island. Donovan had asked Dr. Sardo to meet him and Jeanine there in order to elucidate what kinds of things to expect on his first day of rounds, his first day in her world. Dr. Sardo answered ad nauseam with all the specific yet irrelevant details typical of an administrator.

"You must first understand the process of postgraduate medical education, Agent Donovan. Residents go through "rotations" (Donovan noted Sardo actually made the quotation sign with his fingers) which is a simple way to say that each month, the duration of a "rotation" (quotes with fingers again), the residents "rotate" onto a new specialty or discipline in order to complete the requirements of the residency program. The American Board of Family Practice sets these tenets forward.

Given that this is a family practice residency program, the residents "rotate" through general internal medicine, pediatrics, surgery, and obstetrics etc., all of the core specialties of medicine. In a three-year period, they will rotate several times through each discipline in order to saturate their knowledge base.

As one group of residents "rotates" onto a discipline, or service, as it is often called, another group rotates off of that service. In this way, the community, especially the underprivileged, has access to health care while the residents complete their education. Once they graduate, they are completely capable of performing in all areas of medicine as a family doctor.

For the sake of efficiency, each service is made up of 4 to 5 residents (typically a third year, second year and two first year residents also known as interns). A faculty physician who is directly responsible for the care of the patients leads the team. The teams are organized in a hierarchical fashion with the faculty physician as the most senior lead and the third year resident being the next highest and so on and so forth. The duty of each member of the team is first and foremost education and then direct patient care. The residents bear the brunt of the work, particularly the interns as it has been proven that immersion in the practice of medicine is the best way to learn it.

The faculty member is always available. The upper level residents, the second and third years, are responsible for teaching the interns and any medical students, should there be any. It is the most efficient means of educating residents and we are quite proud of it."

He concluded with his chest quite puffed up with pride. They were standing in the center of Donovan's office. President Sardo was standing directly in front of Donovan in the center of the room. Jeanine was standing behind the president to the right of his shoulder. Donovan could see her slowly moving away from Sardo as he spoke. With each word from his mouth she was slowly leaning further and further away from him. It was an obvious physical manifestation of her internal dislike for him.

She would not stand next to him, look at Sardo or meet Donovan's gaze. It was like watching one of those nature shows on television that use high-speed cameras to video tape the phototropic movement of plants toward the sun. But in this case, Donovan noted she was leaning away from the light.

"Thank you president Sardo your description is quite useful. I will consider this information as I construct my surveillance team. I will speak to you again tomorrow."

Donovan replied as Agents Swenson and O'Donnell entered the room. "But we haven't discussed your role on the team, yet," President Sardo interrupted sensing that he was being excused.

"Agent Donovan, the administration considered your decision to follow Dr. Hunter on rounds. We have significant concerns regarding how this will affect patient care. While we understand the need to protect Dr. Hunter, we feel your presence will compromise her ability to interact with her patients and develop a rapport with them. They may feel intimidated by your presence."

"What conclusion have you reached?" Donovan could see they had already come to a decision and that based on Jeanine's half grin it would be unpleasant for him. "Dr. Hunter," President Sardo called instructing her to reply. Trying, but not very hard, to wipe the half-grin from her face, she answered the question.

"You will be my medical student," she answered with satisfaction. "That will explain why you would be essentially useless on a medical service while following my every move. It is the quintessential role of the medical student: To be actively and intently doing nothing," she concluded enjoying the brief moment of power she could exercise over Agent Donovan.

"Useless?" he mused whimsically. "Well, that's not so bad," he replied. "At least I get to wear the white coat."

"Well, not exactly. You get to wear a short coat," she replied with a sardonic grin.

"A short coat?" he asked incredulously with a raised eyebrow.

"Only doctors wear the long white coats you are accustomed to seeing. Medical students wear the short coats. It's a rite of passage. Of course, along with that title of medical student you have the responsibility of being the gofer, pun of all jokes, rookie, etc." She finished.

"I see this is amusing you, Dr. Hunter," he replied with tongue in cheek. His own agents were also rather amused. In actuality, he did not mind the role. Before he was an FBI agent, he'd definitely had more demeaning undercover roles. During his brief stint in the Secret Service, he'd had the opportunity to become well acquainted with a dumpster sitting outside a hotel the vice-president would be using. For 48 hours he was given the charge of watching and wading through the refuse receptacle for any suspicious activity. This, by far, would be much less disgusting.

"No, Agent Donovan, I am sure you will be able to handle this quite well," she replied lightheartedly.

"Since this is an internal medicine rotation, we will have a complex patient load. We wake at 3 AM and we leave when all the work is done," she stated returning to her former state of seriousness.

"3 AM?" he asked skeptically.

"3 AM," she answered with quiet resolution. There was no wavering in it.

President Sardo went to leave the room but before he did, he turned and said, "Agent Donovan, the administration is trusting the safety of our doctor to your supervision. Please keep her safe and find out who is killing our patients."

Sardo gave a nod to Jeanine. He was now satisfied that everyone's role was well defined: everything had a point of order, a place, and a position. Jeanine did not acknowledge him; he irritated her to the point of nausea, as all administrators did. She did not trust them. Quite frankly President Sardo expected her to respond, but was not affected by the fact she did not. He would have her cooperation and that is what mattered most.

Upon Sardo's departure, the air in the room freshened, at least to Jeanine. It was a similar sensation one feels when their least favorite uncle exits. There is quiet respect for the uncle's position in the family with an underlying resentment of his presence. And when that presence is gone, there is an overwhelming sigh of relief.

"Dr. Hunter, what can I really expect tomorrow?" Donovan asked. Jeanine thought for a moment before answering. Donovan could see the gears in her mind turning over the question.

"President Sardo had all of the definitions right; all the non-specific hoo ha, if you will. If you needed a dictionary definition he'd be the best human being to physically represent one. But the tangible activity of being a resident is a lot different than what you read on paper."

"Hmmm," Agent Swenson chimed in "like the difference between a field agent that actually does the work vs. others that just give orders?" It was a question with an obvious slant at Agent

Donovan. The simile was not lost on Donovan or on Jeanine. Donovan's response was simply a quiet acknowledgement with a palpably expressed, *"Back off!"*

Jeanine continued.

"He's an administrator. His last significant human interaction was probably in the womb."

"That's a little bitter, doctor" Donovan said with emphasis on the word "doctor". "Not a phrase that is becoming of a caring, sensitive physician" he probed.

She shook her head negatively and walked to the bay windows on the other side of Donovan's desk. "Are you investigating me Agent Donovan?" she asked with her back to him. She had to ask him in this way. Looking directly at him made her nervous, as his presence was intimidating to her. She hated this fact but denying it was nonsensical.

"What do you think?" he answered.

"I think you are a liar. I think you will politicize your answer and tell me nothing."

He considered his position. Each action was a well-calculated chess move. He considered what Renee had told him. Despite his better judgment, he decided to try her advice, but he would not do this in front of his agents. This was too delicate to handle in front of an audience. "I'll answer your question but answer mine first. What can I expect tomorrow?" He studied her face in the window's reflection.

She turned back to face him and, pausing slightly, she wet her lips before answering. What came to mind was her attending physician for tomorrow's rotation, Dr. Rucker.

"Brown," she replied facing him squarely.

"What?" he asked incredulously, wondering if he had heard her correctly.

"Yes, you heard me correctly. Tomorrow, the attending physician is Dr. Rucker and he is the color brown personified: safe, passive, noncommittal, and weak. It is the color of boring, squeaky shoes," she answered succinctly.

"People who speak in similes are unintelligent pawns," Swenson announced with biting sarcasm.

"Actually, those were metaphors. A simile uses terms such as 'like' or 'as'. For example, you are as annoying as nails on a chalk board," Jeanine retorted hotly as the blood rushed to her face.

"So what does that have to do with me?" Donovan asked. This question brought them back to the subject, as Donovan shot a hot glance at Swenson that commanded her to keep quiet.

"He is a peculiar man whose existence is governed by paranoia and speculation. He is the fulfillment of the saying 'those that can do and those that cannot teach' as he has no survival skills whatsoever outside of an academic institution. His low sense of self worth is exemplified by his constant need to prove his intelligence. To do this, he chooses one resident from the team to torture with incessant questions and meaningless tasks. We call it 'pimping'. Rucker will try to make himself look better by belittling one of his pupils much as possible."

"What else can you tell me about him?" Donovan inquired.

"His inferiority complex is only heightened by his last name. He always assumes people are calling him 'fucker'."

"Are they?"

"Of course, usually in response to his pimping, but the faculty call him that too. Also, he is married with no children and when you see him…" her voice trailed off as she gathered her thoughts, "let's just say he adamantly denies any homosexual tendencies but no one is actually convinced." Jeanine added.

"So, Rucker is pathologically paranoid. I sense that makes your job more difficult?" Donovan probed.

"It makes my job impossible. Our profession demands commitment but he does not have the slightest inclination of how to do it. As Rucker is the team leader, he makes the final decisions regarding patient care. Regardless of what is best for the patient or what the patient wants, he will waiver on every issue and second guess everything making it impossible to accomplish anything."

"Accomplish? Isn't the accomplishment to take care of patients?" Agent Swenson asked pointedly.

"Despite Dr. Sardo's canned speech, let me assure you he has made it very clear to us that medicine is a business." Jeanine answered, acknowledging agent Swenson's question. "The longer patients stay in the hospital the more money the hospital loses. The hospital gets paid based on the number of admissions of paying patients. However, insurance will only pay a certain amount and once that amount is gone the hospital is not making money.

From a medical standpoint, the rate of a patient's complications during a hospital stay increases exponentially the longer they are admitted. So, there is a magic window of opportunity where a hospital can make money and keep people healthy and after that window is gone the cost of keeping the patient in the hospital rises not only due to the lack of money available from their insurance company but also from the aspect of complications from nosocomial infections, hospital errors, etc.

Therefore, it is in the best interest of everyone to deliver efficient patient care. As much as President Sardo would have you believe it's all about education, residents are charged with the responsibility to get patients admitted and discharged as quickly as possible.

With Dr. Rucker as the attending, we will admit patients who don't need to be admitted because he is afraid not to admit them. We will keep patients in the hospital because he will be afraid to discharge them. And all the while the administration will give us the ambivalent charge of taking care of patients with excellence but getting them out as quickly as possible."

"Sounds a lot like the FBI to me," Swenson said out of the corner of her mouth as she took another obvious shot at Donovan, which was met with a quick glare this time but still no verbal response. Donovan concluded Swenson was testing him; seeing how far she could push him, like a child testing their limits.

"It sounds like you don't want to work, to me," Swenson added as she slighted Jeanine again. It was obvious Mellicent had bought the party line that Jeanine was guilty until proven guiltier. She considered Jeanine spoiled, lazy and ungrateful.

"I would think your focus would be to keep patients alive rather than worry about hospital policies. Isn't that what a good doctor would do?" Jeanine could hear the malevolence in Agent Swenson's voice.

"You say 'good doctor' like it's an oxymoron like 'government intelligence'" Jeanine shot back.

Swenson glared at her; she was not accustomed to being trumped.

"Agent Swenson, the real world of residency doesn't run as smoothly as things do in the FBI where I am sure everything goes according to plan. Despite your opinion, I am trying to keep my patients alive."

Agent Donovan intervened, "I think that is enough information for now, Dr. Hunter. I think we have a clear picture of what to expect."

Jeanine looked hard at Agent Swenson, who, turned on her heel and coolly left the room. As a child, one of Jeanine's babysitter's was named Mellicent that had a similar characterization to Mellicent Swenson: cold, calculating and pale. Mellicent Swenson also fit this characterization perfectly and Jeanine did not like her. Her icy blue eyes were set closely together in her face; they were accentuated by her platinum blonde hair that was pulled so tightly into a bun Jeanine was sure her eyes would have popped out of their sockets like champagne corks. The agents exited Donovan's office via the catwalk going downstairs to their respective desks. Jeanine and Agent Donovan were alone.

Jeanine appeared beside herself. She rubbed the tension building in the back of her neck and paced in front of Donovan's large harbor facing windows.

"What's on your mind, doctor?" he asked.

She admired the view of the boats docked in the harbor and the glint of moonlight as it reflected off the water. He approached her taking note of her posture.

"Doctor Hunter, may I ask what you are thinking?"

"No," she answered.

"I am trying to help you," he countered.

"Are you?" she snapped over her shoulder.

"I'm wondering when you were going to tell me that David was murdered and that I was a suspect?"

He was taken aback but recovered quickly. "Who said anything about murder?" he questioned evasively.

"President Sardo did. He specifically told you to find out who was killing our patients. No one said anything about David being murdered. Until now, you indicated the only crime was that his organs were illegally harvested. Now it appears he was actually killed. Plus, Agent Swenson's not difficult to read. She thinks I killed him."

"Let's say your assumption is correct and Mr. Scott was killed, you were one of the last people to see him alive."

"That's hardly a justification for suspecting me! I'm a doctor," she said exasperated. "I'm the last person to see a *lot* of people alive. If that is your only basis for suspecting me then over half of the staff should be under arrest! Am I a suspect in every patient's death?"

"No, you are not."

"So why is this different?"

He edged closer to her. "That's what I'm trying to determine."

"No, that's what you have already determined. You determined he was killed and you think I did it."

"Isn't it possible that Dr. Sardo just miss-spoke when he said 'killed'?"

"Unlikely. For him to use the word 'killed' is more than a simple slip of the tongue."

"We'll have to agree to disagree."

"Is that something they teach you in FBI school?" she asked frustrated.

"What?"

"How to tell someone to 'fuck off' politely?" she flushed at the use of the curse word.

"Yes, it's actually called conflict management. Is it working?" he said with a half grin amused at himself and intrigued with this verbal interplay.

"Not really. Despite what you say or don't say, I think Sardo meant what he said."

"Of course you do. But it got you to change the subject."

"There's still Agent Swenson," Jeanine pressed.

"Yes, she still exists. What is your point?"

"Existentialism aside, she obviously thinks I'm guilty of what you are refusing to accuse me of. She regards me with disdain."

"Is that something they teach you in medical school?"

"What?"

"To use words no one else in the 20th century uses? Disdain?" he teased.

"No, I learned the big words in college," she bantered back hotly. She was not enjoying this as much as Donovan was. "Please answer me."

"She disdains everyone," he answered truthfully.

"But especially those accused of murder?" she continued. She was persistent, tenacious in fact. He would not allow her to defeat him in a battle of words or high-browed metaphors. He let out a sigh, leaned against his desk and touched his shoulder to hers as he joined her in the view of the harbor.

"Dr. Hunter, I've been an FBI agent for over fifteen years. You are not going to get me to say anything I don't want to say."

"That may be true. But as a doctor, I've learned to hear the things that people don't say."

"I'm not *saying* anything."

"Indeed, and very loudly too," she observed.

He acquiesced. Perhaps this was the time to exercise Renee's judgment. "Dr. Hunter, I cannot comment on the specifics of this case. No one has said anything about murder. As for the rest, yes, you are a suspect."

Jeanine felt her stomach sink to the floor and she was not too far behind it. Her knees went weak and she almost collapsed. Donovan braced her by the arm and lowered her to sit on his desk.

"I'm sorry. I did not mean to upset you."

"Why? Why would you think I could.... that I would do something so.... like this?" she stammered.

She was obviously affected by this, more than he had expected. The reaction seemed genuine by Donovan's determination. Perhaps it was one thing to ponder she was being considered as a suspect, but to hear the cold truth was overwhelming. He paused for a while.

"Why don't you tell me the truth?" He asked looking down at her as she rested on his arm.

"What truth?" she asked pushing away from his embrace as though finally becoming aware of it. "What do you want to know?"

"Tell me who you are."

'What?' He thought to himself. 'That's not what I want to ask!' He recovered from his thoughts.

"Is an understanding of who I am going to change your perception?" she pressed.

"Forgive me but I've noticed you have a strong resentment of authority. You are considered an outsider by the administration and most of your colleagues. That singles you out among possible candidates who could do this. The typical profile of this type of criminal is someone who operates outside the norm: someone who may display anti-social tendencies or someone who might be tempted to join the criminal world. So, doctor, you are a suspect. Show me why you shouldn't be." He finished quietly.

The look she gave him was shock and dismay. She did not understand the creature standing before her. And for a split second he saw himself through her eyes; he did not like what he saw. Anger and frustration flowed over her in waves. Tears welled up in her eyes and she blinked them back. Her words were strained through bitter and angry tears.

"I don't know what my…socializing with faculty members over potato salad has to do with my performance as a doctor or my behavior in society," she said bitterly, "and I don't know what kind of…weird, screwed up personality analysis you people are doing on me. But analyze this fact: I loved David! He fought for his life every day and it was my honor to help him. Now you accuse me of killing the man I have been trying to save for the last two years! Do you have any idea of how insulting that is? And you expect me to open my life to you? To trust you? So you can use my own testimony against me?"

Her words were breathy and tight in her chest. Her hands were clutched in tight fists at her sides. Though tears were silently streaming down her face, there was a strength that beamed through her with a force and spirit that Donovan had rarely seen and dared not affront.

She steadied herself and with calmness said, "I don't know what you want from me, Agent. If you are going to accuse me, then accuse me, otherwise leave me alone!"

She turned away from him and walked toward the door wiping tears from her face. Donovan contemplated their conversation as he stroked his goatee. He leaned against his desk continuing to admire the view of the harbor.

As she turned the handle, he called to her, "Don't go far, doctor, I'll be right with you."

She paused for a moment before walking through it. She did not bother to close it behind her. It was a silent yet poignant rejection of him and all he stood for.

He   had   lost   her.

CHAPTER 9
KNOW ME

After leaving FBI headquarters that evening, Donovan accompanied Jeanine to the hospital. She was starting her inpatient medicine rotation and her custom was to acclimate herself to the patients she would inherit on her new service. It was her way of making sure she was ready for the first day, which was always difficult. They entered the elevator of John Sealy Hospital and headed up to the ICU. She faced the elevator doors as it ascended. Donovan stood behind her.

"Are you really going to follow me everywhere?" she asked over her shoulder.

"Yes, doctor. I thought we had already discussed this."

"Yes we did. I didn't know how literally to take you."

"If I say it, you should believe it," he said undaunted.

"Do you really speak that way?" she asked irritated.

"Affirmative," Donovan stated authoritatively.

"What is it you want from me?" she asked.

"I need to make out your character."

"Why are you trying to define me?" she asked almost pleadingly.

He didn't like talking to her back. He needed to see her face. Talking to her back made him feel cold. Her words sliced into his heart. He shifted his position in the elevator to see her face. "Yes, I am trying to define you."

She raised her eyebrow and slightly rolled her eyes. "Is that a difficult thing to do? To define you?" he asked. "Others more skilled than you have tried and failed," she cut her eyes at him as she recalled her encounters with Dr. Snyder. He admired her spirit. He had a weakness for feisty women.

"You don't like being defined?" he pressed.

"I don't like being caged," she shot back quickly.

"I'm not trying to cage you. I'm trying to save your life." Her eyes softened slightly as if to say, "*Touché*"

The elevator doors opened and a doctor entered. Donovan watched the interaction between them curiously. It was obvious that they knew each other. The doctor stood very close to her. She tensed with his approach.

"Hey Jeaniney, where have you been? I've been looking for you," the man said.

"Jourdan, don't call me Jeaniney," she snapped back.

"Why not? You let those other guys call you Licious."

"That's a nickname. I allow it out of professional courtesy."

He ignored her response. "Look Jeaniney, I wanted to talk about the other night. I forgive you."

She shot him a look of hurt and anger but maintained her composure. "You forgive me?" she asked incredulously. Her eyes were bright with frustration. "I think we should talk about this later," she advised, as she was quite consciously aware of Donovan's presence.

Jourdan looked around the elevator and saw that Donovan was wearing a short white coat, signaling that he was a student. "There's no one here that matters," he replied pompously.

She wrinkled her forehead at the insensitivity and condescension of what he just said. She also realized that nothing she could say or do would convince him to alter the path he was on. "Look, I want us to be friends, Jeaniney. Why can't we do that?"

"Because you don't know what it means to be a friend."

"Of course I do! I know you better than anyone! I know you are still mad at me because I wouldn't go dancing with you. But see how well I know you? I bet you went out anyway huh?"

"Yes, I did. What is your point Jourdan?"

"The point is we are great friends. We each need somebody like that in our lives right now. I need you Jeanine. I miss how we talk about everything. I need someone I can trust. You are always there for me," he urged.

"Jourdan, for a long time I confused familiarity with intimacy. It's like people who confuse sex with love. Just because you know my habits doesn't mean you know me or have the right to demand my time. In your world, you are the center of your universe. Everything revolves around you. I have needs too."

"Really?" he replied hotly "How would you know anything about sex? From what I can tell, you don't have any needs below the waist!"

She recoiled as if burned by his words. She felt hurt and embarrassed and even more so with Agent Donovan listening to all of this. "I've never been burned either but I know enough about it to know I never want to be," she replied quietly.

Jourdan cursed himself for letting his anger get the best of him. He hung his head like a dog found guilty of stealing his master's food.

"Look, Jeanine, I'm sorry. What do you want? I'm really trying to be decent here. Everybody knows your reputation for not..." his voice trailed off as he tried to communicate to her delicately. But grace was not one of his attributes. "Everybody knows you are tight. For my own reputation, I could say we're doin' it but I don't because I like you. I like being friends with you. But you are making it impossible."

Jeanine closed her eyes. She pushed away the tears that wanted to come. She would cry later. Donovan noticed a strange calm come over her face. The tension in her frame eased. She turned to face Jourdan with a surge of confidence and decisiveness. Her words were not biting or angry, as they could have and should have been. Instead, she was gracious and disarming.

"Jourdan, I would like to thank you. You have reassured me that my decision to end our friendship was the right one. I have high standards and the basis of my relationships is decency; it is not the summation of it. If the best you can offer me is decency, then I am glad to have it. But I have to have more. I hope you can understand."

Jourdan was summarily confused, annoyed, and worst of all, rejected. He thought to say something and, as the nasty concoction was about to erupt from his mouth, he caught Donovan's eye. The look he was receiving strongly suggested he hold his tongue. The doors to the elevator opened and Jourdan left without saying a word or even looking at Jeanine.

After he left, she felt a wave of sadness flood over her again. She did not have many friends. She felt isolated and alone and the only one in the world with her, witnessing her lowest moment, was a man who could possibly arrest her.

As the elevator resumed its previous course it jerked upwards causing her to lose her balance. She stumbled and caught herself on the rail of the elevator. Donovan instinctively reached for her arm to help stabilize her. She met his stare with tear-glazed eyes.

"Is that enough definition for you, Agent Donovan?" she asked quietly. For once in his professional career, he felt ashamed of his work.

"I'm sorry," he replied.

As the elevator doors opened, she pulled away from him and went to the racks of charts. She plunged into her work, reading pages and pages of chart notes to prepare for the next day, trying to forget her troubles and grief. Donovan was struck by her. She was a complex character full of contrasts: grace and uncertainty, composure and anxiety, weakness and strength. One thing was for sure. Renee was right. This case was going to be different than all others.

+++++

Back at the carriage house, Jeanine sat at the antique vanity by her bed. She was aimlessly regarding a dusty corner in the room. It was moments like this when she wished she knew more about drinking alcohol. That not being the case, she just ate more of her Tums tablets to calm her burning stomach.

She heard Donovan enter the carriage house and shortly after he tapped her door. She turned to acknowledge him. Her room was dark except for the flicker of a candle on her vanity. He pushed away from the door jamb he'd been leaning against, out of the shadows and walked slowly toward her, into the flickering candlelight. He had a panther-like prowess about him and under any other circumstance Jeanine would have considered him rather attractive.

"Dr. Snyder thought it was fair for you to know me; for you to evaluate me just as I am evaluating you. You asked me who I was and I told you that I was the one sent here to protect you. But that didn't really tell you anything about me." He paused for a moment and knelt before her before beginning again. This speech did not appear to Jeanine to be rehearsed.

"I believe in God, I believe in right and wrong, I believe a person is defined by what they do more than what they say. I believe in honor and dignity and that if your word has no meaning your existence is worthless. Dr. Hunter, I know you don't like me much right now. Not me the person, maybe, but me as a representative of the FBI. You resent the fact the only solution we have presented is to invade your life."

His face was full of thoughts. But of all the thoughts that ran across his face Jeanine could see no signs of deception.

"Recently, someone told me to be honest with myself about my job and who I am. I don't know that I have the self-awareness to do that. But I can tell you that my life and my job are both intertwined. Above all things, I want to see that justice is done. I want to make sure that the innocent get protected and that those who break the law get what they deserve. I've seen a lot of innocent people suffer and I work to the best of my ability to try to protect them. I will find out who did this and when I do, I will make them pay for it. In a word, I am relentless."

"And by the way," he said lightening the mood as he rose to his full height, "I believe walking in the rain is therapeutic for the soul, that besides U2, the best band…. ever…Prince is a musical genius, that mint and chocolate were never meant to coexist, that horoscopes are ridiculous, that people who put bumper stickers on their cars about their children are in denial, adults should never wear clothes sporting cartoon characters, and that Christmas presents were meant to be opened on Christmas Day not on Christmas Eve."

Jeanine smiled slightly but did not answer. Donovan left and walked back to his room to prepare for the next day.

CHAPTER 10
DEATH IS THE COLOR BROWN

Jeanine woke with a start, gasping for air. She'd overslept and she was late for work. Not today of all days! She was on call today. She couldn't start off already behind. Call days were the worst days of all to show up late. The room was pitch black save the amber hue creeping in through the sheer curtains from the street light outside her window. She instinctively shot up from bed and looked at the alarm clock at her bedside. The glowing green numbers showed 02:30.

Damn! She thought to herself as she fell back onto her pillow in disgust. She'd woken up thirty minutes too soon and cheated herself out of blissful sleep. She flopped back onto her bed in the darkness, desperately trying to go back to sleep and reclaim that last half hour. It was no use. It was like waking up from a pleasant dream and trying to find it again. Once it's gone it's gone. Her mind was already running over with thoughts of things she had to do. She hated it when she woke up before her alarm. It almost always happened on her call days and was just another insult to injury.

She lie awake thinking but trying to sleep. She knew that if she did go to sleep it would only be for five minutes and then the alarm would sound. Then she would have to hit the snooze button which would eventually lead to her being late…. again. She hated being late. She had never been so late so many times in her life, but since she started residency she had lost any appetite for life or for the little polite things that went along with it. Why get up early to suffer more? At least when you're late you can have some control over your life even if it is only a lie to yourself.

The clock radio blared its annoying BEEP BEEP BEEP. She lay in bed now somewhere between dreams and consciousness; that wonderful place where everything moves in the gleam of silver twilight and you are suspended in animation and nothing can hurt you. But it is only a fleeting thing.

She sighed deeply and groaned as she sat up. She walked zombie-like into the bathroom stumping her toe on the vanity she'd only been sitting at hours earlier. "Oh!" she called out in the darkness. She was sure she had woken everyone on the property. She did not have her bearings down in Dr. Savage's quaint little carriage house.

She emerged from the bathroom soon after and was dressed in her hospital scrubs, typical ponytail and her white coat. She spent a second shaking her head negatively at her reflection wondering about her appearance and resolving that something must be done. Afterwards, she quickly grabbed her keys, a piece of toast, and was about to get her bag and dash out of the door when she stopped dead in her tracks. She remembered Agent Donovan. He was sleeping in the second bedroom down the hall.

Damn, she thought to herself. He was not up. He was going to make her late. Damn she thought again. That's three 'damns' before 3 AM; this was definitely not a good sign. She politely knocked on Donovan's door. There was no answer.

"Agent Donovan?" she asked tentatively, "Are you awake? I have to go to work now."

There was still no answer. She wasn't sure what to do. What if she opened the door and he was one of these trigger-happy posttraumatic stress disorder FBI guys who shot first and asked questions later? She could imagine him sleeping in the room wearing his holster with his hand resting on his gun ready to whip it out and shoot who ever intruded. She would have to chance it. She had to start rounds at the hospital. As she slowly pushed the door open she was halted by another thought.

What if he slept naked? That thought was even more frightening than the first. Her heart skipped a beat and she removed her hand from the door as if it were hot. She quickly cleared her mind of the vision. Pushing these thoughts out of her mind, she determined that she had to enter regardless of the consequences; between bullets or nudity though she was not sure which one was worse.

She turned on the light in the den hoping that it might alert him that she was about to enter and dissuade him from shooting her. She knocked once again and was greeted by silence. Finally, she gently pushed open the door and entered.

He looked like one of those television models that sleep perfectly without a wrinkle in the sheets. Though his 6 foot 1 inch frame was too long for the full sized bed, he nonetheless, lie perfectly and peacefully in the middle of the bed. The covers were neatly folded across his bare chest.

On his desk, he had neatly organized his jewelry: a watch, a bracelet, and two rings, in straight lines exactly ¼ inch from each other. Jeanine turned on the small lamp on the nightstand next to his bed.

"Excuse me. Agent Donovan, you have to wake up now. Agent Donovan, wake up, please," she urged quietly.

Donovan's eyes slowly opened to the sound of a sweet voice calling him to wake. His eyes slowly opened from small slits to their full size. Jeanine watched his face, as the innocence of sleep gave way to the knowledge of wakefulness.

"Agent Donovan, we have to go to work. You have to get up now," she urged.

Donovan sat up quickly and looked at the small clock on the nightstand. It read 3:10 AM. He looked back at her in disbelief as he was still trying to get his bearings.

"I know it seems early but we have to leave now if we're going to make it in time."

She could see understanding spread over his face. Donovan nodded his head in agreement and Jeanine left the room to let him get dressed. He soon emerged and they were off to the races.... literally. She transitioned almost instantly from the sweet voice that lulled him awake to doctor mode. She walked at a brisk pace, even for Donovan, to her car, a 1979 Oldsmobile Cutlass Supreme that used to belong to her maternal grandfather. She could see from Donovan's face that he had reservations.

"It has character," she defended, answering his unspoken question. She had obviously defended this beast before. The morning was unseasonably cool as the dew point made the ambient air feel colder than normal. He ponderously admired the car.

"It's been years since I've seen one of these," he reminisced as he opened the door for her. She revered him incredulously. She never had a man, other than a relative, open a car door for her.

"These doors must weigh at least 50 pounds!" he laughed to himself.

"I'm sorry it's so far below your expectations," she replied feeling insulted.

"I did not mean to insult you," he said realizing he was offending her, "I'm actually impressed. I used to have one. It's like seeing an old friend."

"It's never let me down," she answered, still a little sensitive about her car.

She turned the key in the ignition and the car choked and sputtered. She pumped the gas and kept turning the key but the car would not start. She sighed and rolled her eyes.

"Judas!" she said to the car as she flashed Donovan a sheepish grin. She whipped a Uni-ball pen from her from the pocket of her scrubs, popped the hood latch and got out of the car. Donovan soon joined her and watched as she unscrewed the butterfly nut off of the cover to the air filter, propped opened the choke on the carburetor with the pen and got back into the car. She turned the key and success! Once it started, Donovan took the pen out and replaced the cover to the air filter and got back in.

"I'm impressed," she said eyeing him with interest "most people have no idea of what I'm doing."

"Nowadays, most people drive fuel injected cars. But this…this is a great car," he said nostalgically as he patted the door. "But, I think you're due for a new one!"

She nodded with a quizzical brow as she considered Donovan's character. He was not what she expected.

Finally underway, Jeanine drove down Seawall Boulevard to the hospital. There was a strange stillness about this time of the morning. The streets were calm and silent with the darkness of night. It had rained overnight and all that could be heard was the sound of the car driving on the wet pavement and the gentle swoosh of the waves lapping onto the beach. The day had not yet awoken and there was a sublime peacefulness mixed with anticipation. The quiet sounds of the morning had not become polluted by the hum of busy lives and even the sea seemed to sleep. She parked in the doctor's parking garage, ironically, next to a brand new Mercedes Benz.

At a pace, which to Donovan seemed a jog, she reached the hospital from the parking garage and flew up eight flights of stairs to John Sealy Hospital's top floor (the elevator was too slow to use). She only spoke to him once during this time and Donovan did the best he could just to keep up.

"It's 04:00 and we have ten patients to see this morning before I meet with the rest of my team. This will go quickly."

With dizzying speed, Luke Oren Donovan watched as she used the computer to scroll through the list of her patient's medications and vital signs. Then she proceeded to the chart racks at the nurses' station. She had three patients on this floor, four patients on the fifth floor and three in the ICU. She dashed and darted into and out of the patient's rooms barely saying a word.

At this time of the morning, her main concern was to make sure the patients were still alive and that none of them had had any complications over night that she needed to address. The purpose of early morning rounds was really for show. The patients were still deep in sleep and could not really answer any questions about their previous night. But for insurance purposes there had to be a note in the chart that the patient was seen several times during the day regardless of whether that first visit was actually informative.

Invariably, some patient would want to talk to her about their bowel movements and she would, resignedly, engage them. As much as she hated the idle questions, she had the hardest time pulling away from her patients. Which is why she had to get up so early to round on them that and her interminably meticulous nature. At times, she had to use that 'okay I know you are talking but I have to leave now' tone of voice. It was a rude way to excuse oneself but it had to be done to meet the schedule.

Her countenance was serious. She was focused on what she had to do and was ever hoping she could get through rounds before her on-call beeper went off. Morning rounds were a delicate dance of speed, medical decision-making, calculations, and note writing. One had to be efficient and accurate. But this was difficult for Jeanine, a talent she had not mastered. Finally, she'd seen her last patient. It was almost 6:00 AM.

"We have to go to the conference room now, meet the other team members, and discuss our patients. Then we'll go to the main conference room and have morning report where we'll talk about our patients as well as those admitted by the other hospital teams."

Initially, Donovan decided not to intrude, but observe her almost surgically precise movements. Finally, he felt this lull in activity would give him a chance to engage her.

"What, no breakfast?" he asked semi-jokingly. He was a creature of habit and breakfast was always on his to do list after jogging 5 miles. "Was that supposed to be funny?" she asked sharply.

"No, not really funny," Donovan replied feeling small under her harsh gaze. Clearly, he noted to himself, Jeanine was not a morning person.

"I'm sorry, if you want breakfast you'll have to wake up earlier or wait until morning report. There are chicken salad sandwiches in the doctor's lounge. I wouldn't eat them though, if I were you. The cafeteria makes them from left over chicken and you can never tell how old they are. We call them salmonella sandwiches because they'll usually give you diarrhea." She said it so matter-of-factly he thought she was joking. She wasn't.

"Well, if I do get sick, at least I'm in the right place for someone to take care of me," he remarked smartly.

Jeanine stopped silently, turned to Donovan and merely gave him a look. Although she did not say a word, the look on her face unmistakably said, *'Are you serious?'* It was obvious she was in no way amused. She was completely oblivious to the humor he was trying to display and with that same look she was able to make him feel as small and inappropriate as a schoolboy. Besides his mother, sister and Renee, she was the only woman who had ever done that to him.

She turned and headed down the stairwell to the conference room on the first floor. Donovan watched her descent before launching after her down the stairs. He was intrigued.

She flew down five flights of stairs with just enough time to make it precisely at 06:30. The other members of her team soon joined her. They too had that same look of Monday morning blues mixed with a deep sense of dread. One of the residents appeared completely haggard. Donovan reasoned this must have been the resident that was on call last night.

He perked up when he saw Jeanine and gave her a nod indicating the torch had been passed. It was the same process every morning in the hospital; some going in, some coming out just like the waves on the beach.

They commiserated for a moment and shared data on a few key patients. It was not simply a change of call from one resident to the next; this was also a change of rotation. Five residents were leaving the service and Jeanine's team was taking over.

They greeted each other with cold civility; they were a gloomy bunch. Donovan was surprised at the lack of camaraderie; perhaps that was something that did not exist among doctors. The team was composed of five residents: two-third year residents, one-second year resident (Jeanine), and two interns. Before they all sat down he could hear them all murmuring a name in unison like a collective moan, "*Rucker*".

The aforementioned Dr. Rucker soon joined them at the round table in the conference room. He was a 5'11", 170-pound Caucasian myopic individual with an unusually feminine gait and mannerisms. Donovan had to do a double take. It was difficult to stifle the laugh welling up within him. Despite his best intentions, all he could see was brown, just as Jeanine had described him. Rucker was wearing brown, lace up, leather shoes with brown socks and brown slacks and a white short-sleeved button down shirt with brown stripes and a brown tie.

Dr. Rucker greeted the team in his characteristic mousy, southern accent.

"Good morning everyone," he chirped with more enthusiasm than was necessary. Based on Rucker's build, Donovan expected to hear a strong, deep voice. But out of this broad chest came a sad little Truman Capote imitation that was deeply disappointing yet thoroughly amusing. Rucker over-enunciated his words (out of fear that someone would misunderstand him) and spoke very intentionally and very slowly. What would normally take someone ten minutes to say took Rucker at least half an hour. Donovan could see the silent groan emanate from each of the doctors on the team as the words eeked out of Rucker's mouth.

Donovan could empathize. It occurred to him how ridiculous it was to have a group of otherwise highly intelligent people led by an incompetent fool, not by merit, but by lack of a better choice. It felt all too reminiscent of the FBI. Donovan mused that all human systems were the same regardless of their background.

"I see we have a guest amongst us," Rucker observed referring to Donovan.

"This is Luke Donovan. He is an exchange student from Ireland," Jeanine informed.

"Oh really?" Rucker pouted placing his hands on his hips.

"No one told me they were adding a medical student to our team. No one ever tells me anything! I just suppose someone in the administration was behind this. They are always throwing things my way without my consent. It is ridiculous! I get no respect whatsoever. I should be treated as a tenured professional not as some half-wit!"

He kept on at this for several moments, speaking mainly to himself about the horrors of the administration with several frantic moments of paranoia mixed in.

"Well," he started again after collecting himself and realizing the team was ignoring his little rant (for once he was happy they were ignoring him). "I think this would be a good opportunity to educate the world about the sophistication of our medicine. Hmmm, now to whom should I assign the medical student?"

He looked at all the residents as he pondered who should receive the charge of the responsibility of the student. Jeanine knew he would choose her. She was the only woman on the team, the only second year resident, and the only one who was making eye contact with him right now. And the obvious choice of the resident he would choose to harass.

"Dr. Hunter I am holding you personally responsible for the education of this student. And," he continued much to their dismay in a sappy Irish accent, "I hope you'll do us proud lassie!" Jeanine's jaw literally dropped open in the shock and embarrassment that Rucker could be this uncouth. She and Donovan exchanged glances.

Just then, Kent Carlton, one of the third year residents chimed in. "Dr. Rucker, as a senior resident on the service I feel it is my duty to render my opinion on this subject. I believe the responsibility of this task should be given to a more seasoned resident, someone who could truly educate the medical student and provide a much better glimpse into our medical system. Perhaps, one of the interns would be a better choice?"

Jeanine sighed to herself. What an insulting little snipe! She rarely used the word hate, but when it came to Kent Carlton it seemed appropriate. From the very first day he met her he treated her with cold indifference at best and at worst with insult. Today, he obviously chose the latter. He did not really care who trained the medical student. But to suggest an intern with less than 2 months of experience was a better choice than an experienced second year was an insult he knew Jeanine would appreciate.

Donovan could see the internal struggle in Rucker between these decisions. He could see Rucker debate the options and change his mind. As he began to speak, Donovan interjected.

"Sir, with all due respect, while my primary objective is to learn the differences between American and Irish medicine, part of the focus of my elective here in the States is to observe the role of women and minorities in medicine. While I am sure everyone here is a capable educator, I believe my objective would best be achieved by studying Dr. Hunter. I don't see that any of the other 15 residents in your program would be able to provide that perspective."

His request was respectful yet formidable and could not be denied. Rucker merely nodded in agreement. Kent Carlton, however, would have the last word.

"It is unfortunate Dr. Rubio is not here." It was another cut at Jeanine. She glared sharply at Carlton. He disregarded it without a thought.

Donovan watched this interplay with interest. He wondered why she did not verbally respond to him. Did she feel guilty because she was involved in Dr. Rubio's disappearance? Did she respect the hierarchy of medicine so much that she would not respond to a superior with disrespect? Or was she intimidated by this obvious asshole?

Donovan also scrutinized Rucker carefully. He surmised there was no way this imbecile was part of any conspiracy to pirate organs. Intimidating, he was not. After studying Rucker, he moved on to the other members of the team. He had a dossier on all of the residents of the program giving him a background on who Jeanine was working with (of course it was prepared by Agent Woo so he had to bear that perspective in mind).

The two third-year residents were Kent Carlton and Douglass Bryan. From the profiles he had read, they were highly anal creatures with over developed god-complexes. Both were married but Bryan had a weakness for extra-marital pleasures. They shared the drive for making money and did extensive moonlighting. Bryan had a reputation for spending money as fast as he could earn it.

Carlton's weakness was his love of being right; he was a gifted physician in that he learned quickly and had an almost photographic memory. The academic aspect of medicine was easy for him; he did not have many of the struggles with concepts or retention his fellow colleagues endured. In most normal cases, he was adequately pleasant but as intelligent as he was, he was equally arrogant, cruel and heartless.

The two interns on the team were Adam Black and John Ivory, fresh out of medical school. There was not much information on them as they had just started this program a few weeks ago and were obviously not involved in the crime.

"Well," Rucker started again, "why don't we discuss our patients." Rucker pulled out the list the twenty patients who were under their charge.

"Dr. Hunter, why don't you explain to the medical student what we are doing?" Rucker asked. She nodded and began to explain how morning rounds worked.

"This service is comprised of five residents. The interns and I are given the responsibility of direct patient care while the third year residents are responsible for managing the service. Each morning, the interns and I will see our respective patients and present the patients in the morning to the team to discuss the events that occurred overnight and our management plan. Then, the resident who was on call the night before will present the new patients that were admitted to our service overnight.

After we discuss these patients, we meet the other two hospital teams in the main conference room to discuss the new patients admitted overnight in what is called morning report. Here we discuss any interesting patients or patients that present specific challenges or learning points. After morning report, we go see the patients on our own service, a process we call rounding, which gives the team a chance to see every patient on the service. After rounding, we meet to discuss the patients again. At that point, we break to do our individual work, and admit new patients to the service if there are any. Once the work is done, we see the patients again and meet again as a group to discuss any changes."

Donovan could not believe how long this rounding process took. With all the incessant rounding it was unclear to him how any work actually got done. Rounds literally meant making the rounds around the hospital. Every moment of their day was devoted to movement. Unfortunately, the movement was not progressive but only circular.

"Dr. Hunter, you did not define the differences between a pediatric, adult, and geriatric patient. You did not mention obstetrics, gynecology, or the ICU. I think we will have to have a discussion about your own understanding of the range of this service," Rucker informed.

And so it had begun; the incessant picking for which Rucker was well known. Jeanine knew it was best to choose her battles and this was not one worth fighting.

"Yes sir," she replied. The rest of the team silently moaned at his nitpicking.

Jeanine could feel her blood pressure rising but she said nothing. She tried to remember that the purpose of all this was to help Agent Donovan find out where Dr. Rubio was and who had absconded with her patient's organs. She held her peace but prayed that her pager would ring so that she would have to go rescue some patient from some evil fate and save herself from the boredom of Rucker!

As though God was listening, Jeanine's pager sounded, BLING-BLING, BLING-BLING! She reached down for it and recognized the number as being from the emergency room.

"It's the ER," she replied getting up to return the call. Rucker leaned forward, as if to consider whether or not he should allow her to answer the call. While Rucker was battling his internal misgivings, Kent Carlton did his job to focus on the task at hand.

"Dr. Rucker, we should discuss our patients," Carlton advised.

Rucker replied, "I suppose so, but I would like to wait to see what Dr. Hunter is talking about with the ER."

Donovan could hear Douglass Bryan mumble under his breath, "damn, it's already been forty five minutes and we haven't talked about any of the patients yet."

At that time, Jeanine hung up the phone and returned to the conference table. "Dr. Rucker, I need to go to the ER. We have two patients there who need to be evaluated. One of them is having a heart attack and the other is an elderly woman with difficulty breathing."

Rucker was torn between decisions. Any normal attending physician would have dismissed her to the ER (which was across the hall from the conference room), gone with his team to morning report and then start rounds on the most critical patients of the service. This would have been the best way to manage their limited time. But Rucker, being so afraid of things going wrong, decided to do everything at once.

"I think the entire team should go to the ER and when that's done, we round and go to morning report."

Luckily, Jeanine was thinking ahead. "Dr. Rucker, morning report is in 10 minutes and I know you hate missing it so...." He cut her off before she could finish. It looked bad if the attending physicians did not attend morning report, at least in his mind. "All right then," he finally acquiesced, "you go to the ER and we'll go to morning report. But as soon as you are done or we are done we need to rendezvous to discuss all you have done."

Then Rucker scurried down the hall with his rubber soled brown leather shoes squeaking after him like some kind of geek homing device. His gait was so unusual that his rear end twisted furiously in the polyester pants he was wearing. Donovan could imagine sparks flying off his behind.

Rucker's grip around Jeanine's throat was not imaginary, and Donovan did not like it. He understood why death was the color brown;   and   Rucker   was   brown   personified.

CHAPTER 11
RAIN IN THE ER

It was 07:45 and Jeanine ran to the ER with Donovan right on her heels. She quickly saw the two patients she had been summoned to see in the ER. The first patient she admitted to the service had a heart attack. He was a 52-year-old smoker with hypertension and hyperlipidemia. The second patient she saw was a 75-year-old woman with emphysema. She was stable and Jeanine collaborated with the emergency room physician and decided to send her home.

She met with Kent Carlton to present her patients. As Jeanine was a second year resident, and had proven herself to be adequate, she did not need direct supervision. However, as a formality, she still had to present her patients to her upper level residents for review.

"Hey Kent," she started methodically as she took a quick glance at her PDA to review her notes, "these two patients were pretty straight forward."

"What's going on?" Kent asked with interest. Donovan noticed they could still maintain a professional rapport even though they personally disliked each other.

"The first patient was a 52-year-old Caucasian male smoker with uncontrolled hypertension who presented with one hour of acute anterior chest pain during sexual intercourse. He had EKG and cardiac enzyme changes consistent with an anterior MI. I've started oxygen, morphine, aspirin, a beta-blocker and nitroglycerin; admitted him to the ICU and consulted cardiology. Dr. Liberty is the cardiology fellow on call. I've called him and he will do a cardiac cath today as soon as possible." She finished with military precision.

Donovan was impressed with her professionalism and clarity. He was getting used to the melodic way doctors discussed their patients' medical conditions. Jeanine, in particular, had a rhythmic quality to her presentation that was characteristic of the more experienced physicians.

"Sounds good," Carlton nodded in agreement, "go on to the next patient."

"The next one is a 75-year-old Black female with a twenty year history of emphysema. She ran out of her medications a week ago and has had shortness of breath for two days. She was given IV Solu-Medrol, oxygen, and nebulized bronchodilator treatments with albuterol and Atrovent over the last four hours by the ER staff. Her O2 sats are back to normal and she says she's back to her baseline. In talking with the ER physician, we agreed to let her go home today with her typical medications and be seen in our outpatient clinic tomorrow and again the day after to make sure she's still stable."

"I agree. Sounds like a good plan but, did you run that by Rucker?" Carlton asked flatly. She sighed, already reading Carlton's mind, "No. I did not consult him," she answered. Carlton rolled his eyes and grimaced. "You know what he's going to do?" he chastised.

"I know, I know," she sighed "But you know this was the right thing to do. She was a little old lady who was without her medications for a week. To put her in the hospital would have been the worst thing for her. To expose her to pneumonia is the last thing she needs. My way, she'll get to see four doctors in three days while staying in the comfort of her own home without excessive exposures to other ill people for much less expense. She'll get better healthcare as an outpatient and she'll get better! Besides, technically she was still the ER doc's patient and not Rucker's yet."

She stopped while closing her eyes and taking in a deep breath before she continued, "But you are right. I know what he'll do. He will freak out that he did not get the entire history of her life from birth while she was here in the hospital. He'll make me call her at home and ask her to drive back to the emergency room so that he can see her. Then after three hours of pain staking interrogation, he'll decide to admit her to the hospital where she'll stay for three days until she gets pneumonia from the patient next to her. Then she'll have to go to the ICU on a ventilator and then she'll finally get to go home after three weeks of hell."

She was rubbing her neck and she could feel flicks of acid building in her stomach.

"Yep," Carlton agreed, "well, whatever happens, leave me out of it." He replied with that selfish I'm-glad-it's-you-and-not-me attitude. "I wash my hands of it. By the way, your student looks bored" he said referring to Donovan who had been quietly watching all of this while standing next to Jeanine.

Carlton turned and walked away happily going to see his patients in his clinic and glad to be away from Rucker.

"Gee, thanks!" she answered sarcastically to his already turned back.

Douglass Bryan, the other third year resident emerged not long after Kent left and gave her a synopsis of the patient census. "I have to go to my clinic now so it will just be you and the interns in the hospital today. Rucker, of course, will be expecting you soon. Good luck!" he said with a half-baked grin as turned and headed out the door.

The smell of wet, humid, electrified air filled the ER. It was raining heavily outside. Even though there were no windows in the ER, the unmistakable smell of rain was pervasive; especially when the wind picked up and brought in the smell of salty seaweed. It was only present for a moment, when the glass sliding ER doors opened. Somehow, it comforted Jeanine that it was raining outside when she was working. It made her feel like she was not missing anything like a real life.

As she admired the rain, she remembered Donovan said he, 'believed walking in the rain was therapeutic for the soul.' She wondered about that for a moment just as his eyes met hers. "Would you rather be out there? In the rain?" she asked him.

He gave her a half grin, glad to know she was thinking about him. "Of course, but it's always better to go with someone than alone," he replied.

Jeanine looked at her watch. It was almost 10AM. She glanced at the doors of the ER that led up to the patient wing and glanced back at her watch. She was mentally calculating something but Donovan could not tell what. Was she waiting for someone? A contact or a lead he could use, perhaps? Donovan mused.

She sat down behind the large ER work desk and whipped out the notes Carlton and Bryan had given her as well as some other scrap pieces of paper and note cards she had been carrying in her pockets. With lightning speed, she started entering the patient's information into her pocket computer.

Sensing that Donovan was curious she said, "I'm entering the patient's information into my PDA. Scraps of paper and note cards are too unreliable. They disappear or someone spills coffee on them; computers intimidate Rucker so it comes in handy. If he ever asks me a question that he's not sure of the answer to, I whip this out this puppy he usually stops arguing with me and just agrees so that he won't look wrong. Also, it's nice to have a database that doesn't change in size even if your census does. If I have three patients or three hundred on the service, this little guy," she said as she gestured with it, "it doesn't get any heavier. Besides, it's good for bounce backs too."

"Bounce backs?" Donovan asked.

"It's a term we use to describe patients who are discharged from our service but are readmitted after a short absence," she said using her fingers to denote bounce back in quotations.

"I didn't know anyone still did that."

"Bounce back? Of course, we aren't dealing with the world's healthiest population here. Galveston has been designated as the hospital for the indigent and uninsured of Texas. So people will drive hundreds of miles to get here for free care. Sometimes all we do is patch them up just enough to go home and come back in again."

"No, not that. I meant use quotation marks with their fingers. Besides Dr. Sardo, of course," he said teasingly with a boyish grin.

Humor was not something she expected from Donovan. He seemed too stiff for it. Jeanine raised her eyebrows seductively. Donovan had not noticed her eyes before. But as he looked at her, he realized she was one of those women who could melt a man's heart with just one look. It was just, until now, they had been covered with so much sadness and pain he could not see it.

"Funny!" she huffed.

He laughed back, starting to feel a little uncomfortable, but he could not figure why.

They were standing in the emergency room at one of workstations. It had a tall counter that could be used as a writing surface but was best used as a place to lean against. Jeanine was resting her arm on the counter while tapping her pen on one of the clipboards. Suddenly, the monitors in the telemetry beds of the ER became fuzzy. It lasted for about 2 minutes and then it was gone.

"The telemetry units are acting up again. I thought they fixed that," she observed.

"What happens now?" Donovan asked as he shifted his stance.

"In a perfect world, we'd get to take a break, eat something, review our patients in a sane manner and then go take care of their needs and maybe have five minutes to use the bathroom. Usually, at least 2 members of the team are called to work in the outpatient clinic during the day, either the morning or the afternoon. The senior residents, Bryan and Carlton, both somehow got scheduled to have their clinics Monday morning. That's unusual. What should have happened is that one-third year is always available while the other is working the clinic.

Anyway, since I am not in a sane world, Dr. Rucker will rush through the emergency room doors to your right as though his hair is on fire, he'll review my work with a fine toothed comb, tell me everything that I did was wrong and call back one of the patients I just discharged because he's afraid she will go home and die and he will be responsible for it.

Then we'll go up to each individual floor and discuss each patient ad nauseam for the next three hours, we'll break for an hour to do the work we talked about doing for three hours only to be called by Dr. Rucker to round again on the same patients we just discussed for three hours. He'll be upset that we haven't finished the work he told us to do this morning and he won't accept the excuse that we were in the process of doing that work when he called us back to round again because he's unrealistic and insane.

Then, in addition to the work we have to do from morning rounds he'll add more work to the evening rounds and change his orders from the morning rounds causing everyone to be completely confused. Of course, since I'm on call, I'll be running between the ER and upstairs all day playing catch up on pretty much everything."

Donovan just looked at her in disbelief sorry he had even asked. 'It can't be that bad' he thought to himself. She turned to look at him now, and reading his mind said, "Yes, it is that bad." He was taken aback for a second as he was wondering how she could know what he was thinking when to most people he was a mystery.

"I hope you know what you are doing by volunteering to be my shadow. I don't think you are going to sleep much or do anything else for that matter," she said sadly.

"From what I have seen, you are a mature and dedicated physician who genuinely cares about people. Regardless of how little sleep I get as I protect you, I feel better knowing that I am doing this for someone who is worth it" he replied sincerely. He could see her cheeks blush underneath her cinnamon complexion.

"Are you just saying that to get into my head or do you really see that?" she asked.

"See what? That you care about your patients? Everyone sees that Jeanine. Even the ones who pretend not to," he replied.

She had felt that no one understood her or how hard she worked for her patients. Luke Donovan was the last person she ever expected to understand her. She did not answer him but her eyes told him everything he needed to know. She was quiet for a moment listening to the steady fall of rain outside the ER doors. Finally she leaned close to him, making sure no one else around could hear her, quietly asked, "have you heard anything…about Monica?"

He caught the subtle scent of her perfume as she stood close to him causing him to feel unusually unsettled. "No, not yet. But the…um…we are working on it. Don't worry, we'll find her," he stammered trying to reassure her.

True to form, Rucker burst through the ER doors at precisely 11:30. Sweat had penetrated the armpits of his short-sleeved button down shirt and had left large wet stains. From the moment he went to morning report all he could think about was Jeanine in the ER and all the things that could be going wrong.

"What!" he exclaimed with a shriek.

"What sir?" Jeanine answered back nervously as she felt the deep need to run away from this avalanche of brown anguish rushing towards her in the person of Dr. Rucker.

"Don't 'what' me! I want to know everything that happened here in the emergency room with our patients." He asked nervously, as his brown loafers squeaked over the recently waxed snow-white emergency room floors.

If Luke Donovan had any lingering thoughts that Dr. Rucker was involved in murder, Rucker's current behavior abolished the idea entirely. He was a delicate flower of a man and did not have the thrust for dirty deeds.

Jeanine spoke slowly and deliberately so that Rucker could hear every word. Her presentation of Mr. Morrow was so crisp it sparkled.

"Mr. Davis Morrow is a 52-year-old Caucasian male who I admitted with an acute MI." She whipped out copies of Mr. Morrow's EKG and lab work and presented them in a way that Dr. Rucker and the interns who finally caught up with him could easily follow. Donovan was amazed at how physicians could succinctly summarize all of a person's life in a matter of minutes, a few pieces of paper, and lab tests.

"As you can see," Jeanine continue, "he has ST segment elevation in the anterior leads of his EKG. Furthermore, he has remarkably elevated troponin levels, which are also consistent with an MI. I suspect the left main artery is involved given his history of hypertension and ventricular hypertrophy also evidenced on the EKG. His chest X-ray does have a small amount of cardiomegaly but I pulled his records from his last admission a year ago and the heart size is unchanged thus I do not believe he is in heart failure.

I started him on the standard protocol of a beta-blocker, aspirin, oxygen, nitroglycerin, and morphine and arranged a room for him in the cardiac intensive care unit. I also consulted the cardiology service. Dr. Liberty is the cardiology fellow on call today and he agrees with my assessment. He will do Mr. Morrow's heart catheterization as soon as possible."

Up until now, Rucker had been quite impressed with her presentation. Everything she had done was perfect and while he had been looking and listening for something to criticize there was nothing. Yet, he could not let her think her work was perfect.

"What!" he exclaimed again with a note that took all of them aback. The interns took slow steps back so as not to be hit by any of his verbal fire.

"You consulted a specialist without my consent!" He fired at her angrily. "I talk to the specialist first! That is too much of an assumption on your part! You may be a second year resident but I am still in charge, Dr. Hunter!" he scolded.

"And where are your notes? Where is the history and physical report?" He asked as he paced back and forth before the ER desk. Before he could finish the question, Jeanine whipped out two copies of the history and physical report.

"Here are two copies sir. I know you like to have one to keep with you and one to take home. The original is in the patient's chart. For your convenience I have also ordered his old records from the archives for comparison. If you like, I can cancel his heart cath and leave him here in the ER but delaying his care may send him into heart failure. I assumed you would not find that acceptable, sir."

She had played this game with Rucker before. For now, the battle was going in her favor as she quieted him with her precision. Being obsessive compulsive about details is not a prerequisite for being a physician but it is a honed skill that is gained upon graduation.

"That will do," Rucker replied begrudgingly. "Go on to the next patient."

Jeanine took in a deep breath. She knew this would be the moment Rucker's head would explode. There was no point delaying or trying to side step what she did. There was only the truth.

"The next patient was Mrs. Ruth Thibodeaux, a 75 year old Black female with longstanding COPD who ran out of her medications and came to the ER with shortness of breath. I analyzed the patient and her data," she said as she put her records, oxygen saturations and lab work in front of Dr. Rucker.

"I gave her oxygen, intravascular Solu-Medrol, nebulized albuterol and Atrovent and after watching her saturations improve I sent her home with instructions to see one of our colleagues in his clinic this afternoon and see me tomorrow in my clinic."

Rucker's eyes widened and his face reddened so that he looked like a cherry flavored lollipop.

"You did what!" He exclaimed as his voice went up three octaves.

"I sent her home sir," she responded unabashed. For once Rucker did not know what to say. No resident had ever done this to him before. He'd always heard of other attending physician's allowing it but he never once considered it in the realm of possibility for a resident to do it to him.

"I believed it was the best thing for the patient," she continued undeterred. "Her chest X-ray was negative for infection, her oxygen saturation was at 96%, she has the tools to give herself nebulizer treatments at home, should the need arise, and I gave her samples of her medicines from the ER. In my opinion, it was best to release her so that she would not be exposed to a life threatening pneumonia."

She could see the interns wincing behind Rucker in anticipation of what he would do to her. She stood still and confident and would not cower despite Rucker's ranting. She was not perfect but right was right and she would stand behind it. Rucker collected himself and stood up straight; he was eerily quiet.

"What you believe is not important!" he spat at her indignantly. "What is best for the patient is not important! What is important is that you respect me Dr. Hunter and that is something I will accomplish before you leave this service!" he squealed.

Donovan's chin hit the floor. Rucker was ridiculous. Talking to her in this way was probably the only way he could get a decent erection.

"John," Rucker called "I want you to call Mrs. Thibodeaux and tell her to come back to the hospital. Now don't you worry, I'll stand right next to you and tell you just what to say," he instructed with that syrupy, nauseating, southern patronizing accent.

As he was instructed, the intern dialed the number and Dr. Rucker silently mouthed every word he spoke.

CHAPTER 12
GRAHAM

"Are you alright?" Ivory whispered to Jeanine in the stairwell, as Rucker's team ascended the steps to continue morning rounds. He was wondering if Dr. Rucker had affected her. She did not seem any worse for wear.

"I'm fine. You grow thick skin around here," she replied casually.

"Why did you do it? Wouldn't it have been easier just to admit the patient instead of send her home?" Ivory asked under his breath. Donovan listened attentively to her answer wondering the same thing.

"Doing what's right for the patient is the reason we are here. Sometimes it's harder to do what's right but you will sleep better at night knowing that you did the honorable thing instead of just the easy thing. Always remember that," she advised. Ivory stared at her curiously before catching up with Rucker who was walking ahead of them. Her words toiled in his mind.

Reaching into the inside pocket of her lab coat, Jeanine produced two packages of individually wrapped graham crackers and handed one to Donovan. He had never been so happy to see food. His hunger had grown from an irritating trickle to a steady roar over the last several hours.

"That obvious?" he asked, referring to his hunger, which he had hoped he was hiding better than he was.

She smiled in response, "I am a doctor you know."

"What else do you have in there?" he asked trying to peek inside her jacket, "Don't hold out on the food!"

She laughed heartily and playfully exclaimed, "You will never know!"

A strange look came to her face as she said those words. For a moment, she had forgotten he was an FBI agent. As the reality of his existence returned to her mind, she considered he might know abundantly more about her than she ever realized. The moment was not lost on Donovan. He graciously took the crackers without another word and they silently continued on rounds.

They ascended to the top of the stairs arriving at the eighth floor. They had four patients to see on this floor. Rucker began to inundate the residents with his perspective on patient care.

"There was a study that showed that patients perceived you spent 18.9% more time with them if you sat down when speaking to them versus standing up when speaking. Of course, I will be the only one who will be able to sit because there is only one chair in the room. So, try to look sympathetic so that the patient will think you are sincere. This is a tip that will prevent us from getting sued. Jeanine, make sure you are writing these tips down for the medical student so that he can take them back with him to Ireland." Rucker instructed.

They thoughtlessly plodded on following Rucker like a herd of sheep listening to his not-so-clever anecdotes. After needlessly spending an hour on two stable patients that had been waiting anxiously to be discharged home, they headed down to the seventh floor that was the geriatric floor. They still had not discharged the patients they had just seen but discussed their dismissals at length.

This rounding process was incredibly boring and inefficient to Donovan. They talked about the same information over and over again without really coming to any conclusions or doing any work. Unless, of course, work was defined as Dr. Rucker creating that sucking sink-hole sensation of depression within Donovan's chest due to his mundane micromanagement. When were they admitted, how old were they, how many bowel movements had they had, what medicines they were on, how much urine they had produced between 2 and 3 AM, what they ate for breakfast on Tuesday a week ago, blah blah blah. Donovan wondered how this was productive.

Rucker, on the other hand, validated his existence by hearing this same mundane information even though he'd read it in the chart only hours before.

"Junior Dr. Donovan, (he always called medical students, junior doctors) we are going to see Mr. Graham. He has pancreatitis. What do you know about pancreatitis?" Dr. Rucker asked.

Since Donovan and Jeanine were bringing up the rear of the team, she could tell Donovan what to say without alerting Rucker.

"It's an inflammation of the pancreas that is either idiopathic, caused by heavy alcohol use, obstruction of the biliary tree, or in rare cases due to scorpion stings. It is usually a medical emergency requiring IV fluids, nothing taken by mouth, and a work up to determine the cause, if any. In severe cases, patients may require TPN to maintain their nutrition if the inflammation cannot be controlled in a timely fashion to prevent starvation. Their amylase and lipase levels are checked regularly along with their electrolytes."

"Very good!" Rucker exclaimed with more glee than was necessary. "You can tell that junior doctor Donovan really studied that topic. The rest of you would do well to be so clear and concise, especially you Dr. Hunter. You could learn a thing or two from your student here." Rucker proclaimed as they reached the top of the stairs.

Jeanine just smiled. If those same words had come out of her mouth he would have criticized her. Donovan quickly realized Rucker was a fool. Still, it perplexed him why everyone seemed to give Jeanine such a hard time. Was it because she was a woman, was it because she was Black, or was there a history he was unaware of?

As the day wore on, there was one moment that broke the monotony of the process. Rucker gingerly knocked on Mr. Graham's door to announce his arrival with words dripping with honey sweet intentions and a warning to the patient to shield their eyes because of the bright overhead light he was about to turn on.

Donovan swore if he heard the words, *"Bright light, bright light"* in that sad little southern twang again one more time he'd ring Rucker's neck. As Rucker sauntered across the room with all the grandeur of Florence Nightingale, it occurred to Donovan that Rucker was the way he was because he was afraid. He was afraid of being sued, afraid of patients, afraid of looking like a fool, and afraid of being wrong. Donovan surmised a life lived in fear was a terrible thing. It depreciated his existence.

As Rucker went to sit by Mr. Graham's bedside, he discovered there were no chairs whatsoever. So, to satisfy his internal need to sit, he knelt next to the bed on his knee. This was awkward for several reasons. The top of hospital bed was four feet above the ground. In order to see Rucker, Mr. Graham had to lean over the bed rail and almost fell over the edge of the bed. Everyone did the best they could to suppress their laughter.

"How are you today!" Rucker yelled at the elderly gentleman as though he could not hear him. His overly sweet southern accent was in full force. Donovan noticed that all the patients were watching either one of two shows on their hospital TV's. Either it was the *Price is Right!* or *Little House on the Prairie.*

"Which one do you like?" Jeanine whispered to him clandestinely.

"I'm partial to *Little House*," he replied in similar fashion.

"Me too," she smiled back. "You can follow the plot in every other room to keep your mind occupied. But it's like playing chicken, you want to look like you are listening to the attending without getting caught watching TV."

The entire time she was speaking, it appeared she was completely focused on Dr. Rucker and making notes of what he said.

"Don't you worry you will miss something important?" he asked.

"With Rucker?" she asked incredulously.

"No. Right now, he's rounding on old information from 4 AM. All of their vital signs and lab work from that time were incomplete. The lab doesn't even draw their blood until after 07:30. The real meat happens between 10:00 and 15:00 hours when most of the labs have returned and you have to make decisions on what you've seen."

"So, why *Little House?*" he asked.

Having Donovan around was actually a little fun, Jeanine thought. The interns were always too nervous to talk or joke with her on rounds especially if the upper level, Carlton and Bryan were there. With them there was no room for levity.

"It reminds me of home. I used to watch it every day when I was a kid," she replied.

"What about you?" she asked.

"I like the clothes. I think the fashions will make a comeback." They laughed quietly.

"You're good at this. The Bureau should have recruited you," Donovan stated.

She broke her gaze from Rucker's face and peered at Donovan. In all seriousness she replied, "What makes you think they didn't?" And just as quickly, she flashed the most furtive smile. Just when he was going to address her again she turned away and checked Mr. Graham's IV line. Donovan was left wanting for more. Something he had not felt in a long time. Finally, Rucker was done interrogating the patient.

"When you gonna let me go home, doc?" Mr. Graham asked anxiously.

"Well, when you are completely pain free and your labs are within acceptable limits." Rucker answered.

"Well, hell doc. My belly is always hurtin'. I gotta truck to drive and a livin' to make. I gotta get outta here day after tomorrow," Mr. Graham replied gruffly.

It was clear he was trying to be honest and not disrespectful. But Dr. Rucker took offense to any curse word. "Now, now, Mr. Graham," he started patronizingly, "I think we need to watch our speech and let us do all the thinking for you. And aren't you a little old to be driving a truck?"

The air was taught with anticipation, as the volcanic explosion from Mr. Graham was imminent.

"What did you say you college educated, polyester pant wearing prissy, son-of-a-bitch?" Mr. Graham roared as he sat up in his bed and balled up his fists.

"I'm sorry all of us don't have a shit load of money in our back pockets like you, doc! But I gotta family to support and I can't be in here linin' your pockets!" He was glowing red with anger.

"Well, I guess I better go now. Nice to see you!" Rucker yelled as he hastily stood up to make his escape. He knew he had crossed the line. Thankfully, he could send Jeanine in later to do damage control. She was good at that sort of thing.

Then, suddenly, Dr. Rucker shrieked like a young schoolgirl, "Ewwwhhh! Oh my, what is on my pants?" Mr. Graham began to chuckle. His entire body shook like a bowl of red Jell-O as he was an obese gentleman with plump red cheeks. If it was December he could have taken a job as a mall Santa.

"Ya damned fool, my urinal is right there. I musta missed it a couple a times. Why the hell would ya kneel down there anyway?" Mr. Graham asked. Rucker ran out of the room amidst a hail of laughter.

Rucker returned about a half an hour later, around 14:00, wearing a pair of scrubs he borrowed from the surgical floor. During his absence, and knowing he'd be in a foul mood upon his return, Jeanine had taken the opportunity to get some work done. She sent the interns to discharge the two patients they had been seen earlier while she finished some paperwork and ran some lab values on the computer. Donovan was curious.

"Why did you send the interns to discharge those patients? Aren't you risking Rucker's wrath again?" he asked.

"Rucker has already approved their discharge. If I can get them out before 15:00 they will not be charged for another day in the hospital but if we wait to finish rounds with Rucker, they won't get out until after 18:00. As you have seen, Rucker is going to be angry with me whether regardless of what I do. In which case, I'm going to do what is right despite his anger."

They regrouped and finally finished rounding. They had missed any chance for lunch. Dr. Rucker left quietly, still reeling in his embarrassment, which was a good thing for the team as he left without assigning them additional work to do. So, they quickly scavenged food left over from a pharmaceutical company sponsored conference.

Afterwards, Jeanine efficiently managed the remaining work by assigning patients to each intern while she handled the complicated patients in the ICU and admitted more patients from the ER. This late in the afternoon, she knew Carlton and Bryan would not be back to help them, as they did not enjoy dealing with Rucker. By 17:00 most of the work was done, which in Donovan's mind, was a huge credit to Jeanine's efficiency.

"Adam, you are on call tomorrow. You better go home and get some rest. Try to forget this place for a couple of hours. Tomorrow will be better. The first day on the service is always the hardest.

You did good work today. I know it doesn't feel like it but you are doing well," she said kindly.

Adam Black looked at Jeanine and seemed to see her for the first time. He had heard all these negative things about her from Carlton and Bryan: she was lazy, unintelligent, and nasty to work with. But none of these things were true. He could see how hard she was working. And, in the several weeks he had been an intern, no one had ever acknowledged his work or even lent consideration to him. He appreciated it. He simply said, "Thanks 'Licious" and turned and went home.

Donovan watched the exchange. He could see everything Adam Black had thought. But he had to ask about the term "Licious". Jeanine grimaced slightly.

"Just a nickname, don't ask!" she warned.

"It's part of my job, ma'am" he replied with a tip of an imaginary cowboy hat.

"The FBI really wants to know why my chief resident last year decided all interns needed nicknames?"

"You never know what small, insignificant details may uncover," he replied slyly.

"Oh, I see," she relied smiling, "well, mine started as a play on my last name. Hunta, then Huntalicious, and that evolved into Licious."

"What!" he exclaimed through a laugh. She shook her head smiling.

"Despite what you have seen, some of us actually do like each other. Last year we had a fantastic senior class. They were good doctors who really taught us a lot and showed us how to survive. Somehow, I don't know how, the name Licious just stuck. The entire hospital knows about it. Even some of the faculty members call me Licious. Either that or Hunter because no one goes by first names here. Maybe it's because Monica and I were the only women in our class and they didn't know what to do with us."

"Gee, you have survived the first 14 hours. So what do you think of your first day?" Jeanine asked Donovan as they rode up the elevator to the doctor's lounge.

"Well," he started quite seriously, "It is not exactly what I expected. You guys use the word 'round' as though it was a verb to connote action. I was summarily disappointed to discover it is really a noun synonymous with the word death." They both laughed.

"I did not think it would be this bad. How do you get anything done?" he asked.

She sighed, "It's not always like this. For as bad as it can be, there are also times when it's like...a machine...when it just flows and everything is right."

Donovan mused silently.

"I have to ask, Agent Donovan," she started, "how do you do this?"

"This?"

"I mean your life. You go undercover; I guess that's the right word. You assume a different life. What do you do with your family? Your friends? And, what happens if someone recognizes you? How do you handle that?"

"I doubt anyone will recognize me here."

"Why?"

"First, I rarely go undercover so I'm not worried a previous perp would recognize me. Second, I don't have any family to report to."

"So, all you have is your work?" she asked regarding him pitiably.

"You seem surprised. Am I any different than you, for example?"

"No, pardon me, I assumed. You just seem like someone who would be married."

He eyed her for a moment carefully thinking of what to say. He remembered his advice from Renee, 'be genuine' she advised.

"I was married," he said simply, "we divorced five years ago."

"I'm sorry," she responded sincerely.

Just then, Jeanine's pager went off, it was Dr. Rucker paging her to come to Mr. Graham's room. Donovan and Jeanine met Dr. Rucker at the elevator. He wanted Jeanine to "smooth things out" with Mr. Graham after their heated conversation. Additionally, he wanted her to insert a Foley catheter.

"We really need to make sure this patient is comfortable with our care. I know you have a good rapport with Mr. Graham so I want you to make sure he is not going to sue me…err…sue us for keeping him here in the hospital."

"I'll do the best I can sir," she replied respectfully. Jeanine may not have been considered as the academic all-star like Carlton but she was known for having great bedside manner. She had saved many of her attending physicians a great deal of embarrassment just by being a good listener and really talking to the patients. Rucker was a fool, but he knew he needed her for this.

"What's a Foley catheter?" Donovan whispered in her ear while they were in the elevator.

"For some patients, we have to know precisely how much urine output they make. It tells us how well hydrated they are. Also, since we are giving them fluids, we expect a certain amount to be produced. If that amount is less than expected they could be retaining fluid and that can be catastrophic especially if they have congestive heart failure, for example.

So we insert a Foley catheter into the urethra. It's about the size of a drinking straw in width and about two feet long. The catheter directly captures the urine from the bladder and feeds it into a bag that hangs by the patient's bedside. Once it is inserted into the bladder a small balloon is blown up to keep it from slipping out accidentally. The balloon has to be deflated before it is removed to prevent injuring the urethra."

Jeanine watched Donovan's face change colors for a second when she described passing the catheter into the patient's penis.

"Are you alright?" she asked noticing his obvious discomfort.

"Affirmative," he answered unconvincingly as the color slowly returned to his face.

As they ascended, *Dust in the Wind* Muzak was playing on the elevator speakers. Donovan and Jeanine started singing it quietly under their breath.

"You two seem to be in tune. Who sings this I wonder, *Boston?*" Rucker asked.

"*Kansas*," they replied simultaneously.

"I'd think that band was a little old for your time, Dr. Hunter" Rucker said.

"It's not Prince or U2, but I like the classics. Besides, it helps me relate to older generations," she replied slyly taking a jab at their age.

She flashed a look at Donovan recalling his appreciation of the aforementioned artists from the previous night. Both Rucker and Donovan felt her age comment and protested.

"I'm not that old!" Rucker said protested as he pursed his lips, bobbled his head like an old woman, and placed his hands squarely on his hips. Even Rucker could be human at times.

In equal protest to Jeanine's age comment, Donovan mouthed, 'I have a gun' to her. Jeanine happily scooted out of the elevator as the doors opened feeling contented that she could tease both Rucker and Donovan and get away with it.

As they reached Mr. Graham's room, Rucker posed a question. "Should I tell you what to say?" he asked as his paranoia was rising steadily.

"No, sir, just let me talk to him. If I need help I'll ask."

"Hey there old man!" Jeanine exclaimed with a familiarity of old friends.

"Hey, there sweetness how are you?" he replied equally.

Rucker's face went ashen. How many rules had she broken he thought to himself.

"I just wanted to check on my favorite patient today," she said sweetly.

"Aww honey, you just sayin' that cause I'm cute!" he bantered back.

"Well, if it wasn't for your wife here I think I'd have to take you off the market," she continued flirtatiously.

"Honey, you can have him!" Mrs. Graham injected smartly.

Donovan watched the interplay. They were all laughing and carrying on as if they had known each other for years.

"How long has she known him?" Donovan quietly asked Dr. Rucker.

"2 days," he answered.

"You'd think it was 2 years," Donovan observed.

Jeanine went to sit on the foot of Mr. Graham's bed but hesitated. "Is it safe to sit here? There aren't any bodily fluids here I should be aware of?" she joked.

Mr. Graham glanced over at Dr. Rucker who was standing in the shadows by the door hoping not to be seen. "Hey man, I hope you don't have any hard feelings about that? That was just an accident. You know, one a those, what do you call it, occupational hazards?" He joked.

"I think Dr. Rucker is alright. He really wanted to check on you. That's why we're here. I know you want to go home, but you aren't ready yet. Remember we talked about this?" Jeanine reminded. He reluctantly nodded yes.

"You've had this pain for a long time," Jeanine continued. His wife responded for him, "Stubborn jack ass. I told him to come in here last week but he wouldn't listen to me!"

"Ah woman! Let the doctor finish talkin'!"

"Oh so you'll listen to her? Well she's not the one goin' home with you" Mrs. Graham mumbled under her breath.

Jeanine continued trying to soothe the point. "Well, what's important is that we all work together to get you healthy, Mr. Graham. We won't have any answers overnight. This process took years to get started and it will take a while to figure it out, so you'll have to be patient with us. But look on the bright side; you'll get to see me everyday! What can be better than that?"

Mr. Graham roared with laughter so loudly the windows shook. "Alright, alright doc. But they told me about this thing with the, what is it, momma?" he asked his wife.

"A cathter," she replied.

"Yeah, a cathter. Those nurses told me about this thing." Mr. Graham peered over at doctor Rucker who slunk more into the corner. Donovan also eyed him harshly as he considered the procedure Rucker was forcing Mr. Graham to endure.

"If I just gotta have it, I don't want some junior flip doin' it. You all only get one shot at this. I want you to do it so it's done once and done right!"

"Alright, old man, I'll do it and I'll do the best I can but I make no promises unless you can produce some of that barbecue sauce I hear you are famous for."

"Girl, you got it!" he shot back "All the sauce you'll ever need!"

After Jeanine inserted the catheter, she went to the wash station in the hallway to clean up. "You made it look easy," Donovan observed. "Really? I was nervous the entire time! It's easier to insert them in surgery when they are unconscious but awake is something different."

"No, not the catheter! I didn't watch that. I meant talking to him. You seem natural at it."

"Do catheters make you nervous, Agent Donovan?" she probed with a sinister grin.

"Let's just say it's not on my top ten list of things I'd like to have done to me" he replied.

"I just treat them like they are my own family. I think the legal system and even our own medical ethics makes us too cautious. We put up barriers to protect ourselves and in the end, they just end up being.... barriers."

"Medical ethics?" he asked.

She sighed as she put on her lab coat; she'd removed it to insert the Foley. "All doctors are required to take medical ethics courses. One of the recommendations in our course is to keep a certain level of distance between the patient and ourselves. It's not a hard and fast rule. As a recommendation, it's actually a little vague. The idea is that you don't allow yourself to develop a personal relationship with your patient that would negatively affect your judgment. But it's hard to be a machine. You know, not care about your patient. There's no line in the sand."

"Have you ever gone too far? Crossed the line? Cared too much?" he probed. She eyed him sharply; keenly discerning the FBI agent in him.

"Have   you?"   she   replied.

CHAPTER 13
A PLACE WITHOUT DIGNITY OR HONOR

"It must be hard for you." Mrs. Thibodeaux stated. The 95-pound Black woman sat squarely in the middle of her hospital bed. She was so small that the twin-sized bed swallowed her. Though small in frame, her personality was gregariously warm and friendly. Mrs. Thibodeaux was the 75-year old patient Jeanine had discharged almost 14 hours ago.

Dr. Rucker felt uncomfortable with Jeanine's decision to treat Mrs. Thibodeaux with outpatient therapy. Therefore, he insisted she return to be admitted for her acute exacerbation of chronic obstructive pulmonary disorder.

As standard hospital procedure, Dr. Rucker demanded that Mrs. Thibodeaux have an intravenous line even though she did not really need one. However, Mrs. Thibodeaux suffered from small veins that rolled thus no one was able to place the line. The gentle woman had endured fourteen attempts by various nurses but they had all failed. Even though she was one of the kindest people Jeanine had ever met, Mrs. Thibodeaux was running out of patience. When Dr. Rucker called one of the pulmonary specialists to put a central line directly into her chest wall for intravenous access, Jeanine could no longer contain herself.

Jeanine had not sat down for the last 6 hours finishing busy work for Dr. Rucker. Yet despite her fatigue, Jeanine armed herself with previously undiscovered fountains of energy. She asked Dr. Rucker to wait on his central line and allow her to try to place the IV.

"But what if you don't get it?" Rucker asked, chasing after her as she walked down the hall toward Mrs. Thibodeaux's room with the IV supplies.

"Then you can ask the pulmonary docs if they think she needs a central line," she answered angrily as she continued to walk down the hall.

'Hold it together Jeanine' she thought to herself, 'he's still the boss.'

Jeanine was infuriated with Rucker for many reasons. She was still here in the hospital doing unnecessary grunt work. This was the first call night she ever had in her entire residency career in which the ER was eerily quiet. They had not called her for so much as a 'hello' in about 6 hours. All this time, she could be reading on topics she needed for her patients or maybe even get some sleep.

To make matters worse, poor Mrs. Thibodeaux, who did not even need to be in the hospital, was now about to get an IV stuck into her neck that carried the risk of deflating one of her lungs. Jeanine's ability to respect his position was quickly ebbing. This is the state that Mrs. Thibodeaux was addressing with her prior question.

"It must be hard for you" she said kindly.

"Yes, ma'am" Jeanine replied, "If I don't see a good vein I won't attempt it. But if I see one that's reasonable, I will not miss."

But Mrs. Thibodeaux was not referencing the IV line. "No baby," she said in her sweet elderly voice, "it must be hard working with such a group of assholes."

Donovan and Jeanine could not help but laugh out loud. Jeanine looked at her patient with jaw dropping awe. She was stunned that such a delightful gentlewoman would use the word 'asshole' with such clear accuracy and precision and that she could see so much of what was happening even though Jeanine had not said a word about it.

"No ma'am," she answered obviously lying "they are all very nice people." Jeanine had learned long ago to 'always support the team' regardless of how she really felt. But Mrs. Thibodeaux's smart eyes discerned the issues.

"Honey," she started as she watched Jeanine clean her left arm's antecubital fossa.

"I'm an old woman. I've seen many things and I've been many things. And one thing I know for sure is how to read the sweethearts from the assholes. And there ain't a sweetheart among 'em just a whole lot o' assholes, honey. Except maybe this one with you; he's got the looks of sweetheart in an assholes body," she said referring to Donovan who was standing on the other side of her bed.

"Do I hear Louisiana in your voice?" Jeanine asked trying to change the subject.

Donovan shifted his weight feeling fairly sure he had just been insulted. Mrs. Thibodeaux just smiled. Jeanine successfully placed the intravenous line and started a saline drip to keep it open. Donovan watched and listened with affected interest.

"Yes, I grew up in Crowley, Louisiana. Then my husband and I moved here to Galveston over thirty years ago."

"It must be a small world. I have friends in Crowley," Jeanine smiled back. Mrs. Thibodeaux beamed with pride.

"Well, hey, look at that. You did it! Now, honey, tell me why I needed this thing?" she asked.

Jeanine sighed and smiled thinking about how to answer. "Don't think about it honey, just tell me straight," Mrs. Thibodeaux advised, as she read through Jeanine's discretion.

Jeanine, in turn, read the old lady's face and realized she could not lie to her. "Well, ma'am" she started slowly "the complete truth is that it's all about fear. You see the hospital wants to be prepared in case you need IV access to give you fluids. If you have no IV access and we need to give you emergency medicines it would be a hindrance to give you the best medical care. Besides, it would be hard to justify your being here in the hospital if there was not an IV. Your insurance might not pay for your hospital stay because they would say your admission was unnecessary."

"Yes, I understand that. But you and I both know that I don't need to be in this hospital in the first place."

Jeanine's forehead wrinkled in confusion. "Why did I come back you want to know?" Mrs. Thibodeaux asked.

"Yes," Jeanine asked bewildered.

"Because of you," she answered quietly. "I have never had a doctor take such good care of me. When you were with me in that emergency room, you thought of everything. No one has ever done that for me in this hospital and I've been here enough times to know how they act! And when that little worried doctor called my house and told me to come back, well, I thought to myself, I did not have anything else to do and he said I would get to see you again, if I wanted to, so I just came right on back."

"But, Mrs. Thibodeaux, I could still see you in the outpatient clinic," Jeanine answered still perplexed.

"Honey, I just have to say, and I hope you don't mind me calling you 'honey', honey. I don't mean any disrespect, baby. But what I mean to say is I am very proud of you. All of my life, I have hoped to see a Black doctor. And my prayers have been answered. But not only are you a good doctor, baby you are a good person. I saw how hard you were working and I just wanted to see you again."

Jeanine, overcome with emotion, struggled against the tears that were coming to her eyes. She managed to compose herself. Yet, admittedly, she had felt her tiny existence was just that, tiny, and had no impact on anyone.

"Thank you Mrs. Thibodeaux. I'm glad I could help you." She laid her thin, delicate hands on Jeanine's and talked to her about her family.

Through the thick veil of her exhaustion Jeanine could feel warmth deep down to her soul. There are a few moments in a doctor's life where they feel fulfilled by the purpose for which they were born. This was one of those moments.

After a little time had passed, Jeanine left Mrs. Thibodeaux's room. Donovan silently walked with her down the hall toward the nurses' station. Before they reached the station, Donovan caught Jeanine by the elbow, pulled her to him, and gently wiped the remaining tears from her cheeks with his handkerchief.

"Thought you might need this," he said warmly. He peered down at her as one of the most interesting creatures he had ever known. He didn't know what to think of her but he knew she was special. Jeanine appreciated the gesture, dabbed the tears from her face and handed back his handkerchief.

Just then, Dr. Rucker flew by in, for lack of a better word, a tizzy. "Are they here yet?" he asked frantically. His hands were shaking; he was fidgeting, and pacing back and forth at the nurses' station. "Where are they? Didn't I ask for that tray to arrive stat?" he continued unglued.

"What is the purpose of using a word if it has no meaning? I did not say 'promptly'. I said 'stat'!" Rucker complained.

"Aggh! I'll just start it myself. The tray is already here. Where is the pulmonary fellow, dang blast?"

Jeanine looked on in quiet confusion. Watching Rucker fly around was always amusing. Half the time he asked questions of the nursing staff so quickly that before they could answer him he had already asked another two questions. And while they were trying to answer his questions, if he bothered to listen, he would have had the answers he wanted.

The experienced nurses knew him well enough to just let him run around until he was so exhausted that he just would leave. The less experienced nurses, infected with his anxiousness, would run around after him as he paced back and forth trying to keep up with his ridiculous pace and answer his questions. It was like watching a beheaded chicken floundering around and throwing up hundreds feathers and debris while followed by a swarm of nervous flies.

"Mrs. Thibodeaux could be dying! Doesn't anyone care!!" he shouted.

"What?" Jeanine exclaimed as she realized he was still planning on the central line.

"Dr. Rucker, Mrs. Thibodeaux does not need a central line. I started an IV," she informed him.

Rucker never skipped a beat. He just kept nervously fluttering around the nurses' station like an anxious, beheaded chicken.

"Yes, yes, IV, IV. But she still needs a central line. That IV could fail and then where would we be? No, this will never do. She must have a central line," he proclaimed.

"With all due respect sir this is ridiculous. She barely needs an IV and now you want to put in a central line? That procedure could collapse her lung and give her a pneumothorax. Why is this necessary?" She demanded to know.

Rucker was annoyed by her interference. "Let me remind you, Dr. Hunter that I am the attending on this case and I believe I know what is right for this patient. And furthermore, if she had any confidence in you, she would have remained home and not returned to the hospital for more treatment!" he snapped.

Jeanine just looked at him incredulously. She knew it was useless to argue. Donovan could not believe this guy. He wondered what friends he could talk to with the State Board. Maybe he could call in some favors and have this guy's license pulled.

Tired of waiting, Dr. Rucker impatiently grabbed the kit to place a central line himself. "Now, are you going to assist me?" he snapped. "No, I will not" she replied hotly. She would not justify an unwarranted procedure.

"No? I'll do it myself!" he exclaimed as he marched down the corridor in his tight brown polyester pants.

Donovan could hear the nurses talking about Rucker after he left.

"Those pants are puttin' out sparks from his behind! Look how he's walkin' down the hall Francine! No straight man walks like that!"

"You better be quiet Marjorie. The only reason he has this job is because his wife is on the hospital's board of directors."

"Sparks, girl! Sparks!" the nurse cackled as she admired his derriere.

Moments later, Jeanine could hear Mrs. Thibodeaux wail in pain. Jeanine clenched her teeth in anger and frustration. She placed her elbows on the nurses' station desk and propped her head on her hands. She felt powerless. Donovan was red with frustration himself.

As soon as Rucker was finished, Mrs. Thibodeaux developed shortness of breath. The monitors in her room starting beeping alerting the staff of an ominous sign. Her oxygen saturation dropped steadily from 98% to 95%, 92%, 89%, and she became disoriented and confused. Jeanine quickly ordered a portable chest X-ray to determine if Rucker punctured her lung.

She and Donovan ran down to the radiology department to read the film with the radiologist. "Hey, Jeanine. How ya' doin'?" asked Bobby Schneider, the radiology resident on call.

"Not good Bobby. And I think I'm about to get worse," she panted. He looked her up and down and shook his head sadly. "Fucker huh? I know your pain," Schneider replied sympathetically.

"Yeah, I think Rucker gave her a pneumo."

"A pneumo?" Donovan asked over her shoulder.

"A pneumothorax," Jeanine replied as she studied the X-rays on the view box. "It is a punctured lung. The lung deflates like a balloon inside the chest wall and the patient develops shortness of breath. It can push over the midline structures like the heart and for some it can be fatal especially in patients with compromised lung function like Mrs. Thibodeaux."

Bobby put the x-ray on the view box. Sure enough, Jeanine could see the fine line delineating a collapsed lung on the left side. The lung markings clearly did not extend to the edges of the lung as they were supposed to.

"Damn!" Jeanine exclaimed as she cursed Dr. Rucker. "Thanks Bobby" she called over her shoulder as she up the 5 flights of stairs from Radiology to Mrs. Thibodeaux's room.

Once Jeanine arrived, she flew into Mrs. Thibodeaux's room but it was too late to prevent the inevitable. She was in respiratory failure and Jeanine called the code and started CPR. Jeanine called out orders in dizzying speed and intubated the patient, placing a tube down her throat and into her trachea so that she could be mechanically ventilated. Donovan watched from the hallway trying to stay out of the way.

The pulmonary team arrived as Jeanine worked feverishly to insert a chest tube into the left side of Mrs. Thibodeaux's chest. It was difficult for Donovan to watch not only from a personal perspective, but also from a physical one.

Here it was just moments ago this profound, wise little woman was vivid and dynamic. Now, she lay comatose and barely clinging to life while Jeanine used a scalpel to open her chest and violently insert a tube into her chest. It was arcane and primitive but it was the only way to save her life.

Jeanine finally got the tube into place. The X-ray technician wheeled in his large portable machine and took another chest X-ray. This revealed Mrs. Thibodeaux's lung had re-inflated due to the placement of the chest tube. But, she was still critically ill and on a ventilator. They moved her to the ICU.

"God damn family doctors!" Dr. Baxter roared. He was the pulmonary fellow on call.

"Starting fucking lines when they don't know what the hell they are doing. They just give us more work to do."

The two pulmonary doctors glared at Jeanine, who was wearing scrubs stained with Mrs. Thibodeaux's blood. Rucker, who had slunk quietly into a corner hoping not to be noticed, had no intentions of defending Jeanine for his actions.

Dr. Baxter laid into Jeanine with both guns. Although he knew Jeanine was not the one who placed the line, he followed the rule of shit rolling down hill. He was a fellow and was superior in rank to her, but not to Rucker. He would yell at her but would say nothing to the attending whose fault it really was.

"What the hell were you thinking? What the hell convinced you that she needed a line in the first place? And in the second, if you thought she needed one what the hell made you think you were qualified to touch one much less insert one?"

Jeanine was speechless. In her mind a thousand things were running through her head. *Rucker is standing right behind me. He'll clear up this mess. He'll tell them it was his idea. He'll defend me. Wait! Am I crazy? Rucker isn't going to defend me he can't even defend himself! Why is this guy yelling at me? This is not my fault! Geez say something! Defend yourself! Don't let this guy walk all over you! Move! Breathe! Speak!*

The words would not come. All she could do was blink back in silence as her cheeks turned red from frustration, anger, and the embarrassment of having the entire floor watch her be humiliated. She felt ridiculously insignificant. Dr. Baxter glared at her for what seemed to be an eternity. The small gathering of nurses, doctors, and even patients stood paralyzed and watched as Dr. Baxter and Jeanine stood locked in what seemed to be a staring contest that Jeanine would painfully and slowly lose as her eyes inevitably met the floor with a palpable thud.

Jeanine slowly realized her mouth was dry and it just dawned on her that her mouth had been open this entire time. She closed her mouth and remained silent.

Suddenly, over the loud speaker, she heard "Dr. Hunter, please report to the ER stat. Dr. Hunter to the ER stat."

Dr. Baxter rolled his eyes. "Well F.P. go fuck up some one else's life. You seem to be good at that." His words were as sharp as glass.

As Jeanine turned to go to the ER, the air hitting her skin felt like glass particles cutting into her. She desperately wanted to scream, cry, vomit, do something to let out the rage inside of her but she could do nothing. She could feel the heat of eyes watching her leave. There were many different expressions. Some sympathized, some seemed happy that she was getting ripped apart, some were surprised, but the one that hurt the most were those eyes of disappointment. Those were the ones she could not handle. It was ripping her apart inside. Those glass sharp words Baxter had used were tearing into her stomach and giving her a powerfully fierce gastritis. She walked down the hallway chewing on antacids.

Donovan watched the entire scene bewildered as much as everyone else. The entire thing was a debacle. He had wanted to say something; come to her defense at least, but nothing. And in the end, the one that was suffering the most was Mrs. Thibodeaux. There she lay in her ICU bed clinging to life because Rucker insisted she be admitted, and insisted on a procedure she never needed. As much as he hated to think of it, he also blamed Jeanine because she had not done enough to defend her. He could not purge the thought from his head that she should have tried harder to stop Rucker. Although, admittedly, there was not much else she could have done. He pulled himself from his reverie and followed Jeanine to the ER with more questions than answers.

Jeanine and Donovan had been awake for almost twenty-four hours now. Jeanine had been walking for some time now and did not even know how she had made it to the ER; it must have been autopilot. She did not even consider Donovan or realize he had been with her this entire time. Her mind would not allow her to think outside of this moment. That was probably a good thing because if she had thought about agent Donovan, or more specifically the reason why he was with her, it would have sent her over the edge. As it was, she was not very far from the brink.

"Hunter! Where have you been? We've been paging you for half an hour?" the ER doctor called as she walked through the doors. He did a double take when he looked at her, "You been drinkin' kid? You look like shit. Did you have your pager off or what?"

Dr. Russell was the ER doctor on call. He was in his mid to late 40's, not too much older than Donovan. All the residents called him Davey Jones because he had a strong resemblance to the actor. They even shared some features: a bright smile, dimples and that ever so lustrous and buoyant hair. Of course, Dr. Russell's hair was more salt and pepper and after working fourteen hours in the ER he was not so fresh but he still looked better than most of the other physicians and was disarmingly charming. He referred to the residents with endearments like "kid" or "sport".

Jeanine answered him, surprised that her voice that had just abandoned her, only moments before, was now finding its courage again. She swallowed hard to get her voice to participate, as her throat was still very dry.

"I was on the telemetry floor and the ICU. They've been having interference up there with monitors and pagers and...."

"Oh, those damn telemetry floors. We keep telling admin to fix that problem. You can't receive pages when you're too close to those machines. Anyway, we got a doozy for ya' kid. I got a guy in bed 14 who's here because he couldn't find his penis. I tried to turf him to Urology but he has no insurance so they want Family Medicine to admit him and they'll do the consult. The thing is he can't find his penis because he's over 700 pounds."

Jeanine suddenly developed tunnel vision. All but the door to room 14 grew dark. She was sure she had probably passed out for a second but the sound of Dr. Russell's voice pulled her back to reality.

"What? What did you say?" she asked trying to convince herself that she heard him incorrectly.

"Yeah, I kinda glazed over that little...err...big detail. Yeah, he's about 700 pounds and he has been sitting in his own urine for over a week. He usually just aims at a bucket on the floor but for the last 7 days he has only been able to dribble so..."

Jeanine looked at her watch. "Russell it's two o'clock in the morning. You mean to tell me that after a week of not being able to pee he suddenly realized at two o'clock in the morning that this is finally important enough for him to come to the hospital?" she asked incredulously. Righteous indignation was increasing exponentially.

"Yeah kid," he said as he patted her on the back, "he's all yours." He said as sympathetically as possible. Then, in a flash, he was gone to see the next patient. The patient was now officially her problem.

"I don't believe this," she moaned. She did not know whether she would laugh or cry. Donovan stood back, noting the look in her eye, and wondering what it meant. It was difficult to describe. Wild, bewildered, savage, insanity was the closest description he could use to qualify what he observed. In just a few seconds, each emotion passed through her face.

From one second to the next he was not sure if she was going to go screaming out the door (which in his mind she had every right to do at this point), or find a blunt object and start bludgeoning the next passer-by, or if she was going to start crying uncontrollably. Was this the spirit of the woman who was behind David Scott's death? Was this the side of her personality he had been waiting to see? The action that followed was not one that he expected, in the least.

She walked to a small office that was labeled "doctor's office" in the corner of the ER. It was the size of a closet with dim lighting and the smell of stale food and old socks. In a style reminiscent of a Tai Chi-style calm, she closed her eyes, took in a slow, deep, cleansing breath, and rubbed the muscles in the back of her neck. In that same instant he could see her mouth moving silently. 'Was she praying?' he wondered.

Slowly her eyes opened, and there it was. It was peace that he saw in her eyes. The gray mist over a vast still ocean, an internal quiet that led to external action.

She didn't say a word to Donovan. She walked passed him, picked up the patient's chart and headed into his room.

"Good morning, sir. I'm Dr. Hunter and this is my medical student, Luke Donovan," she announced crisply. "Let's find out what's going on with you."

Donovan did not understand this world. She had been awake for over twenty-four hours and had been working for twenty of those hours with only a few moments of rest and food. This was pure insanity and there was no dignity or honor to it.

CHAPTER 14
MATTERS OF THE HEART

It was 06:00 on the 3rd of August. Jeanine and Donovan had just finished rounding on her assigned patients. As her call night came to a close, Jeanine stood by one of the hospital windows watching the sunrise. Donovan felt awful; like the worst hangover he'd ever had but without the pleasure of ever being intoxicated. They'd been awake now for thirty hours with only 30-minute catnaps here and there over the last few hours. That sleep was interrupted by constant calls from the ICU regarding Mrs. Thibodeaux or their other patients.

Much of last night Donovan wanted to forget. He peered over at Jeanine as the soft morning light bathed her skin in beams of sunshine. The sun's powerful photosynthetic effect seemed to revive her spirits purging away some of the filth that accompanies the custodianship of other human beings. As morning broke, the realization of a new day came and, more importantly, a new opportunity to forget the horrors of yesterday and embrace the potential of what lie ahead. Silently, she and Donovan joined Dr. Rucker and the rest of her colleagues to begin today's discussions.

"So, what's on the agenda for today, troops?" Rucker asked energetically. Donovan noted that Rucker was completely unaware of the suffering he'd caused. He approached the day with none of the scars Jeanine had endured.

"Jeanine, we are going to allow you the honor of being treated as an upper level resident," Carlton announced.

"As a second year, I am already an upper level resident so what's the change?" she asked.

"You kept everyone alive, more or less, and now you will be given the privilege of supervising the interns on call just as Bryan and I do."

Jeanine's mind was processing this information. She was never good with things on the fly. For a moment, Jeanine was elated.

Does this mean no more call for me? She thought to herself. Since the third year residents did not take primary call they only supervised the interns and usually they did that from home.

"So, what does that mean?" She asked cautiously trying to avoid premature celebration.

"Let's not quibble about the details now during rounds," he advised, "I just thought you'd like to know how much we respect you," he proclaimed. For a moment, Jeanine remarked how Carlton almost looked attractive with his dark green eyes set against his jet-black hair. But, as she caught the corner of his eye, something sinister was brewing within him that dismissed all compliment and sent a shiver down her spine.

The team rounded in its usual fashion, slowly, very slowly. They started with Mr. Richard. Overnight, Jeanine had consulted the urology service to assist the patient. They had taken Mr. Richard to the operating room to surgically place a Foley catheter in his penis so that he could urinate. That was the simplest aspect of his hospital admission.

Because Mr. Richard was so large, it took an unusually large amount of anesthesia to sedate him. Consequently, it was quite difficult to arouse him afterward. Even though the surgery only took 15 minutes, his lungs were still paralyzed due to the anesthesia and, therefore, he had to remain on the ventilator in the ICU.

The other complicating issue for Mr. Richard was the reason he could not find his penis in the first place. His scrotum had swollen to the size of a basketball due to an infection called cellulitis. This engulfed the penis to the point he could not see it much less urinate. So, to assist his recovery, he was treated with multiple intravenous antibiotics for the infection.

"Jeanine, I was very impressed with the way you handled Mr. Richard," Rucker informed unexpectedly. She kept waiting for the other shoe to drop. She just knew there had to be an unpleasant admonishment in there somewhere. If not from Rucker, then Carlton surely had one. But the moment came and went and the team moved on to the next patient in the ICU, Mrs. Thibodeaux.

Donovan revered the frail little woman. She seemed older now; she was less like a person and more like an entity, a science experiment. There were tubes and wires coming and going out of every orifice of her body. She was purposefully sedated to the point unconsciousness because without it no one could tolerate artificial life support. The physician's surrounded her bed and discussed ventilator settings, acid base status, urine output, arterial blood gases and the like.

Jeanine took the lead on this case, as she knew the patient better than anyone else. She remained at Ms. Thibodeaux's bedside for a few moments after the team had left. Donovan observed her regard for Mrs. Thibodeaux. It was a mixture of sadness and regret. But there was something else. He could not pinpoint it but the room itself affected her.

"Hunter," Dr. Rucker asked nervously, "what is the state of her family?" He really wanted to know if any of them were angry that Mrs. Thibodeaux was in this state and if they were considering suing him. He had to tread carefully around Jeanine on this issue. He did not want to give her cause to expose or exploit him.

"I have spoken to her family. They are anxious about life support. They insist that this is not what she would want. They do not understand why she is in this state, given the fact she was not that ill before she came to the hospital," Jeanine informed flatly.

Jeanine would offer nothing else to calm his guilty conscience. Her reports to him were matter-of-fact. He had lost any rights to her civility. And whatever the consequence, she would not be the facilitator as she was with Mr. Graham.

"Are they angry? Do they understand she was a sick woman before she came here? Should I have the ethics committee speak to them? Does she have a living will?" He asked in rapid-fire succession as he anxiously tapped his fingers on the nurses' station desk.

Donovan noticed how scared he was; it was not hard to miss. What was missing was any sense of remorse. He had put her in this condition but his only fear was for himself.

"Of course she doesn't have a living will," Bryan scoffed in a whisper to Carlton, "those kind of people don't have living wills."

"Which 'those people' are you referring to, Douglass?" Jeanine asked irritated cutting her eyes at him. Bryan's prejudices were well known amongst the residents. Jeanine had a low threshold for his racial intolerance.

"Don't get defensive Hunter. It wasn't personal it was just an observation. How many people like her have we treated? If you're honest with yourself, you'll agree that most of those people don't have living wills or medical powers of attorney," he replied flippantly.

Jeanine clenched her teeth and continued. She was exhausted and was not up to the task of confrontation at this point. "She's one of those people, as you call her, who does have a living will in fact. Her grandson is an attorney and he gave me a copy of it yesterday. It is on her chart as is required by law" she finished sharply.

Bryan shrugged it off. "Law of averages," he replied dryly.

"Let's stay in touch with the family. I don't want any surprises," Rucker advised nervously, as he conveniently ignored the other pressing issues.

Rounds went on like this for several hours until they finally reached Mr. Graham, their last patient of the morning. Unfortunately, his pancreatitis was advancing and inhibiting the pancreas' normal function of regulating blood glucose and digestion. He had developed acute diabetes and his calcium levels were dangerously low. Both were ominous signs. He had to be placed in the ICU to begin intravenous feeding through a system called TPN.

"What's TPN?" Donovan asked Jeanine.

"It stands for Total Parenteral Nutrition, it's liquefied nutrition through an IV," she answered quietly as they stood at the back of the room while the team consulted with the gastrointestinal specialist who would take over this portion of Mr. Graham's care.

"It's very complicated and you have to monitor it very closely. The electrolytes in the solution have to be calculated precisely or the patient can die. We are trying to intravenously supplement the nourishment he should be getting from food. Humans were not meant to be sustained in this way."

"You're worried about him," Donovan noticed studying her expression. As she answered, she never took her gaze from Mr. Graham's face.

"I've seen sicker patients with the same condition rebound and improve. But he's not going to make it. He's giving up," she answered quietly. As Donovan studied the old man, he noted the change in his character. The normally burly, boisterous, red haired firecracker of a man had become solemn and quiet. Yesterday, he was bigger than life flirted shamelessly with Jeanine. Today, he did not even bother to make eye contact.

His wife, a thin Caucasian woman in her forties who looked like she could have easily been sixty, was despondent. She had lived too hard, tanned too often, and smoked too much. She was tired of living in the hospital and watching her husband worsen. Mr. Graham's prognosis was grim.

Finally, at the completion of rounds, Rucker departed and left the team to divvy up the remaining work. Sadly, the healthiest of their patients was Mr. Morrow, the gentleman Jeanine had admitted with the heart attack. Except for Mr. Morrow, the patient census looked rather bleak. Rucker would return in an hour, of course, to harass the on call doctor.

Meanwhile, Jeanine was looking forward to going home; it would be nice to feel human again. Simple things like feeling the warmth of the sun, breathing the free air, and taking a shower had become treasured commodities for her soul.

"What time are you done today?" Donovan asked almost reading her mind. He, too, was exhausted. It was now 40 hours since he'd slept or showered and he needed to check in with his agents. She looked at him curiously. He could not decipher the meaning of her glance.

"At 16:00, I hope. I have some paperwork to do for the time being. There's a resident conference room beyond this nurses' desk. You can wait there for a few minutes while I access the central computer for labs. "

Donovan complied and, from this vantage point, he observed the nurses were talking about Jeanine under their breaths.

"I think she just needs to get laid," Corinne stated blatantly.

"That's your answer for everything" Sadie smirked "but I be damned if it's not true!" They both cackled loudly as they huddled next to each other feigning useful work as they hovered over some loose charts.

Donovan noted the residents and hospital staff had come to accept his presence with as much courtesy and attention as a gnat. Because of the hierarchy of medicine, as a medical student (especially a foreign medical student), he was deemed insignificant. Only a few of the staff would actually acknowledge his presence, much less speak to him.

Donovan gained relevant information just by standing in the nurses' stations: which nurses were having affairs with which doctors, which doctors were getting divorced and did not know it yet, who was having sex in the call rooms etc. Most of it was idle gossip but, interestingly, quite accurate as he would later learn. The cackling of the two gossiping hens still annoyed him.

"Why do you think she is so uptight?" Sadie asked oblivious to Donovan's eavesdropping. Just then, Jourdan, Carlton and Bryan approached the nurses' station.

"What are you two hotties talking about?" Jourdan asked flirtatiously. This was obviously for flattery. The hotties he referred to were not in the least attractive. They were both in their mid-fifties, un-kept, hair-chinned and horribly obese. And Donovan was sure they hadn't showered in days.

Donovan recalled Jourdan was the insensitive jerk Jeanine had spoken to in the elevator the first night he was with her in the hospital.

"Oh, just talking about uptighty-pants over there," Corinne answered smugly.

"Oh," Jourdan replied with a sex-starved grin as he admired her from the doorway massaging his chest. "Oooh yeah. Luscious Licious!"

"Forget it man," Bryan said nonchalantly. "You have as much of a chance with her as you do with my wife," he scoffed with a glance in Jeanine's direction.

Jourdan fell mysteriously silent, too silent in fact. Bryan cast him a long, suspicious glance. Fucker, Bryan thought to himself as he postulated the relationship between Jourdan and his wife.

Jourdan guessed Bryan's thoughts and simply ignored them, adding fuel to the fire.

"She was all into you last year, Dr. Jourdan," Corinne asked in her deep East Texas drawl that added a few extra syllables to Jourdan's name stretching it out like a melody.

"That was up until he kicked her uptight ass to the curb!" Sadie finished laughing more loudly than she should. This caught Jeanine's eye. She guessed the subject and decided to ignore them. It wasn't the first time this had happened. Donovan noticed that she caught Jourdan's eye before she went back to work. Her expression reflected her disappointment and disgust. She felt betrayed.

"Whatever happened between y'all?" Sadie asked slyly.

"She had her nose wide open for you. Hell, she would have eaten the peanuts out of your…"

"Ok, ok, we get it. She was hot for him. What happened?" Corinne interrupted impatiently.

"What makes you think we didn't" Jourdan asked furtively.

"Nah, I can always tell." Corinne informed as she carefully scrutinized Jeanine for signs that she'd been deflowered.

Bryan was quiet; he was still thinking about his wife and Jourdan and could not continue this exercise about Jeanine. His mind was in other places. Donovan took this opportunity to get more information on Jeanine from her colleagues' point of view.

"What kind of doctor is Dr. Hunter?" he asked Kent Carlton who was standing nearby and pretending not to be listening to the nurses' conversation. Carlton raised an eyebrow but did not give Donovan the courtesy of making eye contact.

"She'll graduate," he replied simply as he flipped through a patient's chart with disinterest.

Donovan probed more deeply.

"I ask because my course requirements require an evaluation of my mentor. I would hate to give her an inappropriate assessment." Donovan's announcement was irresistible. It immediately caught Carlton's attention; and forced him to engage Donovan. With smug arrogance, Carlton pronounced his opinion that only a few women should be allowed to practice medicine. In his judgment, they were too emotional to be intellectual or competent.

"So you believe her emotions make her a liability?" Donovan inquired.

"Don't you?" Carlton replied haughtily as he closed the chart he'd been using.

"She's not trustworthy," Carlton continued matter-of-factly "dependable or accurate. I wouldn't trust her to treat my dog."

"What, may I ask, has occurred for you to form this opinion? Did she hurt someone?" Donovan pressed.

"No, not yet," Carlton replied flatly.

"Do the other women in this program exhibit the same traits?"

"Yes, most of them, Hunter is the worst though."

"So, let me understand. You basically despise her because she's a woman?"

"Don't make me out to hate women. I like women. I'm married to one. I have a daughter. But this is medicine. You have to be able to think past your PMS, your culture, and your sex. I don't think she's capable of doing any of that." Carlton turned away to finish his work.

The world was a small place. Donovan had heard this speech before from colleagues in the Bureau. He looked over at Jeanine with fresh eyes and pitied her for all she had to endure. It was obvious, the reason she didn't spend time with her colleagues outside of work; she was an outsider in every sense.

He looked up to see Jeanine staring at ICU bed 11. This was Mrs. Thibodeaux's room but she wasn't in it. She'd been taken to radiology for some imaging. Still, Jeanine's fixation on the room was obvious.

Black addressed his curiosity, "That room has bad juju."

"What?" Donovan asked eying the 5 foot 2 inch miniature physician strangely. "That's the room her patient died in last month," he answered.

"What happened to him?"

"He had AIDS," Black answered.

Donovan considered Jeanine again. That was the look he could not discern earlier when they were with Mrs. Thibodeaux. He wondered what fueled her. It must be difficult, in this place, with so many demands to remain whole. What gave her the capacity to keep going forward? Was there ever a point when she succumbed to the well-traveled roads and seductive powers of money and greed?

CHAPTER 15
HEART LAB

Jeanine completed her work and went to use the restroom. On the way back to the nurses' station, she had the strange sensation that someone was watching her. Every step she took on the cold, white, ultra-polished floors was echoed by similar footfalls. And while she had not worked with Donovan long, she knew it was not his presence of which she was now keenly aware.

She nervously looked over her shoulder but she saw nothing suspicious. Suddenly, her pager sounded, startling her. She did not recognize the number. As all of the phones near her were occupied, she had to use a phone in a remote and isolated area. She dialed the number, introduced herself after the line answered and awaited a response.

The other end of the line was disturbingly quiet. The only thing more disturbing was the repeated sensation that she was being watched. The hairs on the back of her neck stood up and she anxiously looked around waiting, for what, she did not know.

"Jeanine?" a voice behind her called.

She jumped out of her skin as she heard her name called. It was Donovan.

"Where did you go?" he asked in an agitated tone; then seeing her expression he asked, "What's wrong?"

Her hand was laid across her chest as she panted softly. She was unsettled.

"I got a page and I was returning it. I couldn't find a phone on the other unit so I came to this one. When I returned the call, the phone answered but no one spoke. I could hear them but they didn't say anything. And I know it's strange but," she paused "I could feel that someone was watching me."

Donovan took the receiver from her and listened. Someone on the other line hung up the phone. Donovan paused for a moment trying to decide if she was lying to him. "Is it common for all the phones on a unit to be occupied simultaneously?" he asked suspiciously still wondering why she was on a unit by herself.

"I don't know. I've never noticed. I'm just trying to answer my page" she replied.

"Who was on the other end of the line?" he asked.

"I don't know, they never said anything," she answered again. He decided not to press the issue but filed it away for further thought. They returned to the intensive care unit.

Upon entering Mr. Morrow's room she was surprised to see he was gone. Donovan could see the wheels turning in her mind; she thought he had died. Her shoulders were tense and her eyes were wide with anticipation. She checked the floor to ceiling dry erase patient status board for Mr. Morrow's location.

"Cath lab!" she exclaimed with a eureka-like enthusiasm as she darted out of the room and down the hall with Donovan fast on her heels.

They entered the cardiac catheterization lab through a series of three security doors. Each door had a specific code required in order to enter. Jeanine pressed the keys 9911 on the keypad and the vacuumed door seals crisply released permitting their entry. The code to every door was the same. So much for security Donovan thought to himself. As they walked into the cath lab-monitoring suite, they ascended a case of metal stairs into what looked like a television control booth but only more narrow.

John Sealy Hospital was an older building and post-construction additions were often unique. Jeanine informed Donovan the suite had been a semi-trailer with doors on both ends. It had been converted into an architectural nightmare; it was oblong and filled with numerous television monitors that flashed images and data in various colors and shapes that were all foreign to Donovan. It was so jammed with equipment that the walkway only permitted the passage of one person at a time. It was dimly lit for the purpose of viewing the monitors more clearly.

The control room looked out on the three heart catheterization suites via large glass windows. Typically, one cardiologist, usually with his fellow, and a team of nurses performed the heart catheterization while another cardiologist in the control booth monitored and reported to the operating cardiologist, the procedurist, what if any coronary artery blockage was present. The monitoring cardiologist was also there to help in case the patient went into full cardiac arrest on the operating table, which was known to happen during this procedure.

This is where Donovan and Jeanine found Dr. Anthony Liberty, the cardiology fellow on call. As they entered the control room, Donovan noticed how the pitch of their footfalls changed. The floor beneath them was a data floor, under which there were probably miles of cords and data lines. Before they entered, Jeanine addressed Donovan, "Tony is a fellow in cardiology. This means he has finished his residency in internal medicine, and now he training to be a cardiologist. In the overall scheme of things, he ranks higher than a resident but less than an attending."

They quietly entered the cath room and almost immediately the monitors flashed. Jeanine glanced thoughtfully at Donovan for a second. Donovan took notice.

"Hey Tony," Jeanine greeted jovially. "Well hey there yourself!" Dr. Liberty answered brightly with a smile larger than Texas and an accent to match. He was from Kaufman, Texas a small town near Dallas. Of all the doctors Donovan had experienced thus far, Anthony Liberty was the happiest and purest soul he had seen. When he smiled, the entire room lit up like the sun. Donovan could see why she was fond of him as a person and a colleague. He actually enjoyed what he did for a living and had a down to earth sincerity that made an instant friend of anyone he met.

"Tony, this is Luke Donovan," she said as she introduced Luke "he is an exchange student from Ireland."

"Nice to meet you! Welcome aboard! You have a good teacher in Jeanine," he answered as he firmly shook Donovan's hand. Donovan had to look long and hard at Dr. Liberty. At a glance, he looked all of about twenty. He had a young face with bright blue eyes and strawberry blonde hair cut in a youthful style.

Becoming more serious, "Alright, alright, I read your note on this guy. Good write up by the way. He's next up for a cath. He got bumped yesterday for the wife of a congressman with mild chest pain.... you know the drill."

As Liberty spoke, he noticed Donovan was still standing. He motioned for Donovan to come closer and pulled up a chair for him to sit and join their discussion. "Here, have a seat Luke. Let's look at this EKG together." Donovan was impressed that he had given him a second thought.

"So Jeanine, what do you think?" Dr. Liberty asked.

"I think the ST segment elevation in the anterior leads definitely points to a blockage in his left main. I bet he has single vessel disease and a stent would have him on his way to recovery and out the door in 2 days."

Dr. Liberty nodded in agreement. He then proceeded to carefully explain all of this to Donovan.

"This is a good teaching case Luke. Let's think it through. We have a male over age fifty that has risk factors for heart disease: he's a smoker, he has hypertension, high cholesterol, and he's overweight. He had exercise induced chest pain and, even though Licious did not say it, I'm sure he has a family history with heart disease probably in the men of his family and all before age fifty.

Licious did everything right. She got the patient assessed quickly, put him on medications to control his blood pressure and decrease the workload on the heart with oxygen, nitrates, a beta-blocker, morphine and stopped any further blockage with aspirin.

At this point, we could try him on antithrombolytics like heparin or we could cath him and see where his coronary artery obstruction is. All that is to say, we could give him medicine to prevent him from closing off any more of the arteries that supply his heart with blood or we could go take a look at those arteries with our catheter and even hope to open up some of those blockages at the same time."

Liberty had a slow and careful way of explaining things on a very basic level that Donovan could understand. He possessed an air of humility and appeal that made the listener instantly want to engage in the conversation.

"Good job Jeanine. I think he will have a blockage in his left main." He leaned over to Donovan, "the left main is usually the big artery that goes down the center of the heart anteriorly" he explained. "But there are other subtle changes too." Jeanine carefully examined the EKG's rhythms. "Look at his rhythm, he has a hemi-block too," Liberty stated.

Jeanine sighed remorsefully feeling disappointed in herself, "God, I didn't even see it. I just rattled off this guy's life like it was a scene out of a script. I'd already read the last chapter and had him at home in his lazy boy ready for his next heart attack. It's the benefit of my get 'em in get 'em out philosophy." She felt that deep sinking sensation in the pit of her stomach that recurred whenever she made a mistake.

"Hey, don't beat yourself up kiddo," Liberty responded putting his hand on her shoulder to comfort her.

"Donovan, could you give us a moment?" Liberty asked. Donovan walked out of sight but not out of earshot.

"Why am I doing this?" she asked rhetorically as she rubbed her forehead with her fingertips. "I'm an insignificant family medicine resident! I'm practicing cardiology, gynecology, obstetrics, orthopedics, internal medicine, and pediatrics among other things! I know just enough to be dangerous!"

She was shaking with anger and frustration and was holding her head in her hands.

"Listen, Jeanine, let's stop before you have a coronary!" Liberty said consolingly.

"The bottom line is that you saved this guy's life. He came to this hospital for help and he has received the highest quality of care he could ever hope for. What I showed you on his EKG, though important to me as his cardiologist, does not in any way affect his care. Everything in your management has been exactly right.

Licious, I am trained to find the subtle things on his EKG; I'm a cardiologist. I know family medicine is frustrating sometimes because you are pulled in so many different directions. I could not do family medicine. That's your gift just like this is mine. Remember medicine is a team effort. We work together because one person can't know everything. Some things you will see, some things I will see, and some things we will figure out together."

Donovan listened to all of this with interest. There were so many dimensions to her persona. She was sharp and courageous yet intimidated and tentative. She was a true gem: beautiful and flawed.

Just then, Mr. Morrow was wheeled into the cardiac cath-operating suite. Dr. Wolf was the attending cardiologist who would be doing the catheterization. He was in his mid-fifties and looked like he himself should have been on the catheterization table. He was pale from too much indoor work, over weight, over worked, and only had two volumes: very loud or very quiet.

Whether loud or quiet he was like a knife and was always cutting. He walked into the control booth wearing a buttoned lab coat that was desperately struggling to stay closed over his belly that had grown much larger since the time he had first bought it. Dr. Wolf was known for being exceedingly harsh with his fellows yet equally flirtatious with the female residents.

"Liberty!" he roared venomously from around the corner.

"What the hell is going on?" he asked less loudly, after spotting Jeanine.

Liberty did not miss a beat. He downshifted from advice giving friend to competent-robotic-worker mode. Despite the toxic lava that Dr. Wolf spewed, Liberty was undaunted. He was numb to the sharp sword of Dr. Wolf's tongue who tried, unsuccessfully, to push every button to make Liberty lose his cool.

To Donovan, it was a well-orchestrated dance. Wolf would yell, rant and rave. Ask for a tool, a supply, a form, hell even a paper clip and Liberty would graciously provide everything he asked for magically as though pulling them from the air. For the life of him, Donovan could not see why anybody would want to give Tony Liberty a hard time. It would be like being harsh to kitten. Liberty had an answer even before Wolf had questions. And that was the sum of it. Maybe that was the essence of a physician's training: to learn the all the possibilities so that they would be ready for any challenge.

"Liberty, why is this guy still sitting in the lab! Why hasn't he had his cath yet?"

"He just arrived from the floor, sir," Liberty replied quietly as he adjusted gauges and instruments.

"Why didn't you page me earlier to do his cath?" Wolf continued to argue.

"He just arrived from floor, sir." Liberty answered again.

"What are you a broken record? I heard you the first time. If he was taking too long to get here why didn't you go down to the floor yourself and get him!" Wolf scorned.

"I was monitoring our patients in the Critical Care Unit and I could not leave them unattended. Besides, your congressman's wife was being cath'd as well" Liberty responded.

"Look," Wolf said poisonously as he lowered his voice to a little above a whisper. He stepped toward Liberty, invading his personal space and brought himself right above Liberty's head to emphasize his point, "you may already have a job lined up in that backwards ass town you call home. But for the next 6 months your ass still belongs to me so don't push me!" he scorned.

Wolf straightened himself and with kindness equal to the malevolence he'd given Liberty he turned to Jeanine who had been quietly watching. She respected Dr. Wolf as a physician and a teacher but she hated the way he treated the fellows under his direction. To Donovan, it was a constant mystery how these people who called themselves doctors could treat each other so maliciously in one instance and in the next instance help the most pitiful dregs of society with caring and compassion.

"Hey Luscious! What are you doing here?" he proclaimed loudly, his words dripping with desire. When she was not looking, he eyed every inch of her cleavage. If the already low V-neck on her scrubs was any lower Wolf would have gotten lost in her breasts. Wolf was very slick, or at least, he thought he was. He was the kind of guy who preyed on young women because they did not know enough to realize that he was full of shit. To a younger woman, he was profound, experienced, and clairvoyant. But to the sage eye he was full of himself and not much else.

Wolf knew just where to stand to get the best view down Jeanine's blouse and when to look away so that he wouldn't be caught. Donovan despised him. He loathed any abuse of power especially in someone in a position to protect and teach.

"I'm the one that consulted your service about Mr. Morrow. Liberty was showing me some interesting things on his EKG I had not considered."

121

"That's unlikely," Wolf replied as he watched Liberty prep the patient in the OR.

"You should really be kinder to your fellows." Jeanine encouraged. She knew she could say things to him that no one else could, partly because she was a woman and she knew his reputation, and partly because for whatever reason Wolf had given her that license. Even women he'd slept with (and still liked afterwards) wouldn't have tried this with him.

"Yes, milady, whatever you ask!" Wolf replied taking a deep 16th century courtier's bow. Jeanine rolled her eyes and sighed at him.

"You are incorrigible!" she answered half-teasingly.

"That's why you love me, my dear." He bantered back.

"You wish!" she answered. She was no fool to his advances.

"All in good time my dear!" he answered more assuredly of himself than he should be, as he squeezed her hand. He turned to scrub for the catheterization. But he allowed his hand to linger for a while on her hand before leaving; too long in fact. Donovan watched as she slowly and subtly pulled her hand from underneath his. Wolf caught her eye with a sly glance. She swiveled her chair around and turned toward Donovan.

"Dr. Wolf, I did not introduce you to my new medical student, this is Luke Donovan," she said taking advantage of the introduction as a distraction. Jeanine knew that introducing Donovan would give her the break she needed. Wolf's advance was making her uncomfortable. His hand would find its way down to her thigh if she would let him. Wolf turned toward Donovan for all of 2 seconds, looked him up and down, and left never saying a word to him.

"He lays it on a little thick," Jeanine said after swiveling around in her chair to face the cath suite. She felt embarrassed and disgusted by Dr. Wolf.

"It's a fine line you have to walk here," Donovan said as he sat next to her.

She turned and looked directly into his eyes. "There are a lot of fine lines around me, it seems," she replied. Her eyes were dark pools of clear water revealing an old soul. These eyes had seen pain. In a moment that seemed like an eternity, he could see she had been fighting all of her life. As a woman in an academic society she still had to fight silent battles for her dignity. She was not immune to the world of large, well-developed egos in the bodies of small men.

Soon, Dr. Liberty emerged from the OR and sat next to them in the control booth.

The procedure was starting. Donovan watched as Dr. Wolf, who was now in full OR sterile regalia, threaded a wire that looked like a thin version of a coat hanger through an artery in Mr. Morrow's right thigh. The wire had several receptors that could measure the heart's ability to contract and with what amount of force.

Finally, they had reached the heart itself. It was amazing. On the screen in front of them and in the OR for Dr. Wolf, they could see a fluoroscopic image of Mr. Morrow's heart and arteries on the screen as Dr. Wolf shot dye through them.

"Look, his anterior wall and inferior wall are barely contracting. His ejection fraction has to be less than 30 percent," Liberty said as he and Jeanine analyzed the images.

"He's got hypokinesis in two walls," Jeanine observed thoughtfully.

"Either he's had a massive heart attack or...."she stopped short.

"Or what Mr. Donovan?" Dr. Liberty asked Luke, pimping him over his shoulder.

"Or," Luke hesitated trying to think of what to say. It came to him, "or this wasn't his first heart attack," he concluded.

"Very good, Dr. Donovan," Liberty continued without breaking his rhythm of working the controls on the monitor in front of him. His job was to precisely record the flow velocities coming out of the heart so that the rest of the data could be analyzed after the cath was completed. Donovan and Jeanine shared a glance, which said 'Whew! He got the right answer.

Dr. Wolf could be heard through an intercom in the control booth. "Liberty, this guy has 3 vessel disease: 90 percent obstruction of the left anterior descending, 85% in the RCA, and 70% in the left circ. I'm going to stent what I can but call Dr. Adak and tell him we got one for him," he instructed. "Oh, and by the way, when we get done, I'll need you to pick up my laundry and mow my yard," he barked.

Donovan looked at Jeanine for an explanation. "He has blockage in three of the main coronary arteries that supply blood to his heart. All of them cannot be stented. A stent is like a hose that opens the blockage so that blood can flow again through the vessels and give blood to the damaged heart muscle. But Mr. Morrow's obstructions are too severe. Dr. Adak is a cardiovascular surgeon who will take vessels from Mr. Morrow's legs put them into the heart bypassing the blood around the obstructed arteries."

"Sounds serious," Donovan answered.

"It's open heart surgery. It is very serious," she said soberly.

Dr. Wolf finished the cath and emerged from the OR.

"Ok nitwit Libbie," he said insultingly to Liberty, "finish up the paper work. We have rounds to do. Meet me in the Unit in twenty minutes. Run!" Wolf commanded.

At that time, a very attractive nurse walked by and her eyes met Dr. Wolf's for a second or two. It was long enough. "Make that an hour." Wolf corrected.

Obviously, Dr. Wolf had some plans with the nurse in his office or, more than likely, the stairwell. It was not the first time, nor would it be the last.

Liberty quietly finished his work. "He never seems to bother you, Tony," Jeanine stated as she watched Liberty busily finish paperwork. It was really more of a question.

"When you have gone through all that I have, you realize his ranting is insignificant. He's here to teach me and I'm here to learn."

Liberty could not help but note the weight that was on her shoulders. "Have you been talking to your dad?" he asked concerned.

She sighed. "Have you been talking to Savage too?"

"No, why?" he asked with growing concern.

"He asked me the same question," she confessed.

"I know you are going through a lot right now with your patient dying. And you hate life because of residency and being 'Rucked' around with. But things will get better, trust me."

"I hear what you are saying Liberty, but you don't know what's happening"

"Do you?" he asked with piercing directness. His question caught her off guard. She felt the heat of a soul-searching scrutiny and, even though it was for her own good, it still hurt.

"God does not do anything without a purpose, Jeanine. When my wife had our twins at 27 weeks gestation and they had tubes coming out of every orifice I thought I was going crazy. I was their father, a doctor, and I couldn't even help them. I was on call every other night and when I was not on call I was in the NICU with the twins or trying to support my wife. I hardly ate, or slept. It was not my faith in medicine that carried me through that experience. It was my faith in God. And let me tell you that faith was tested to the brink. There were nights I asked God why he would do this to us."

"Then, I realized that dark days come to us all, the believers and sinners alike, so I decided to walk with God instead of against Him. So, after all of that, whatever Dr. Wolf does to me is trite."

Jeanine was tearing up.

"Why did you and your dad stop talking?"

She squirmed in her seat for a bit with the thought of confessing this in front of Donovan but she chose to ignore his presence in lieu of the benefits of talking to a friend.

"We had a fight. He said I had become cynical and skeptical. I told him it was a product of maturity. He told me that sage and wit are not polluted by cynicism and skepticism."

"Wow, you and your dad speak to each other that way?" Liberty asked with a raised eyebrow.

"That's one of our less intense discussions, actually" she said thoughtfully.

"Remember that you have a purpose and suffering is only temporary," he advised somberly.

"Only temporary?" she asked with a battered grin.

"Only temporary," he encouraged.

Suddenly, the pager on Jeanine's waist started to blare. Both Liberty and Jeanine simultaneously said, "Rucker."

CHAPTER 16
REVELATIONS

August 3rd 1500

Donovan and Jeanine flew up the stairs to the eighth floor in response to Rucker's page. By the time she had arrived, Rucker had already gone.

"Well, that's it for us. We're off to golf. Later Hunter. Take care of the service but don't call us." Carlton announced as he was leaving. This was unexpected. The intern, Ivory, was on call and Bryan's job was to back him up.

"Are you leaving? Aren't you going to back up Ivory?" she asked.

"Oh, weren't you paying attention?" Carlton replied haughtily.

"You're an upper level resident. Which means you cover the interns with us," he informed.

"Managing the interns is not the role of the second year resident. And what about my own call? Am I supposed to cover the interns as well as my own primary call? I'd be on call almost every night," she asked incredulously. She could not believe this was happening.

"This conversation is laborious. We're going to miss our tee time," Carlton replied disinterestedly.

"So let me see if I understand this," she replied angrily,

"I get to do your work and also carry my own load while you go play golf? How is that fair?" Her voice was cracking with anger.

"You see Luke, this is what I was telling you about females. They become hysterical and confuse the facts with emotions," Carlton instructed as he ignored Jeanine and addressed Donovan directly.

"Hunter," he said turning his attention back to her, "you have your orders. Unless you think you cannot handle them. This could be really damaging for you, especially since Dr. Baxter has filed a complaint regarding Mrs. Thibodeaux's central line fiasco. I would hate to have to report your poor performance to the resident evaluation committee since you're already under review," Carlton said scornfully.

Carlton was on the resident evaluation committee. He, along with a few other handpicked residents and faculty, evaluated his peers on a routine basis. Jeanine had been deemed as an at-risk resident and Carlton knew it. He had just aired her dirty laundry to the rest of the team. Donovan was perturbed and made a mental note to call his friends in the IRS to have Carlton's tax returns audited. Donovan could not abide their insufferable arrogance. While Jeanine was powerless to affect them, Donovan was not.

"What do you plan to tell Dr. Rucker regarding your absence on afternoon rounds today?" she asked, hoping to trump his authority with Rucker's, such that it was.

"We convinced him that this was his idea. Besides, did you know he used to play college golf? I guess you never learned to play? Too bad," Bryan sneered.

Jeanine should have known better. Their announcement this morning was too good to be true. She was too angry for words and too overwhelmed to think of a clever response. Sadly, the hope of leaving early now stung like poisonous venom at the base of her brain, teasing her with the hope of a resemblance of life only to be dashed again by powers beyond her control. Slowly anger was accompanied by embarrassment as she realized Donovan had been watching her demise.

Jeanine had finally collected her thoughts and pushed forward as best she could. It was up to her to manage the service since her upper levels had deemed it so. She sent Ivory to check on Mr. Morrow; helped Black calculate a rehydration formula for a hyponatremic patient, and proceeded to discharge one of their other patients. In an hour, she and the interns finished the work of the day. A feat few of her colleagues could claim.

Suddenly, she was paged overhead. She returned the call and was informed by Dr. Snyder's secretary that he wanted to see her at 1600. Just as Carlton and Bryan were about to leave she addressed them.

"Excuse me. Dr. Snyder has requested I meet with him immediately. Therefore, one of you will have to actually work this afternoon," she was smug and she knew it. It was worth it to see one of Carlton's plots blow up in his face. He always won.

"Well," Carlton sighed obviously annoyed "You had better get your therapy. We would not want you to go crazy. Don't tarry in his office. We'll call to see when your session is done and make sure you aren't wasting time."

"No, Carlton, you wouldn't want me to lose control. You never know who my first target might be," she said suggestively with a smile that made his cheeks blush and sweat in places he would rather not mention.

Even though she hated the idea of meeting with Dr. Snyder, it was nice to see Carlton reeling from something, anything.

Donovan and Jeanine had been inside the air-conditioned sterility of the hospital for over 30 hours. Once outside, they were forced to immediately acclimate to the weather. The 105 degree Fahrenheit, 100% humidity literally took the breath from their lungs. Jeanine had hoped to see some sunshine today but the weather, as though reflecting the tumult in her life, had produced a storm.

A thunderstorm that had formed over the warm waters of the Gulf was about to unleash its fury upon the Island. The grey sky was full of dark clouds pregnant with rain. The air and the trees were profoundly still with the anticipation of the storm. The deep, low rumble of thunder vibrated the ground beneath them and wispy fingers of lightening spread across the sky. Then, slowly and methodically, heavy, round raindrops pelted the sidewalk with enough force to etch the paint off of cars. The harsh missile like thuds quickly evolved into a pouring, driving rain that reduced visibility to almost nil.

Though the walk from the hospital to the Old Red building was only the distance of a city block; Jeanine and Donovan were completely soaked by the time they arrived.

"So, Dr. Hunter, it's nice to see you again," Dr. Snyder remarked. "I hope our discussion today will be productive. I have heard a good report about the way you handled yourself on call last night."

"It was call," she answered simply. Her defensive stance was slowly and steadily increasing. She could not help it. She hated being probed. Dr. Snyder was annoyed by her response but tried to conceal it.

"I heard Dr. Rucker has been more antagonistic than usual, despite that, you successfully admitted 14 patients during the night; you kept everyone in the ICU alive. I believe Kent Carlton was the last resident to accomplish something like that. But as I recall two of his patients died. How did that make you feel?"

"How did what make me feel?" she asked.

"Being successful," he said.

"What makes you think I was successful?" she inquired.

"Well, wouldn't you call a night like that successful?" he continued.

"I guess *you* would," she answered defiantly.

Snyder observed closely the body language between Donovan and Jeanine. He could see they were much more comfortable with each other than they were at their first meeting. He mused about this point for a while before speaking again.

"Why don't we try some exercises, then? Tell me what you would prefer," he instructed.

"Summer or winter?"

"Summer," she replied.

"Hot or cold?"

"Hot."

"Night or day?"

"Night"

"Dusk or dawn?"

"Dusk," she finished flatly.

"Dr. Hunter, are you really listening to my questions or just telling me the first thing I tell you?"

"I am listening," she answered shortly.

"Alright," he replied with doubt, "Why night instead of day?"

She was tired of these games. Kent Carlton was playing games with her and now she had to play games with Dr. Snyder. In her mind she thought, 'What the hell? He asked, so here's his answer. Fuck him!'

"Why night? Why night you ask? Because it's mine! All day long I play by someone else's rules. I go where they want me to go.

I do what they want me to do and when they want me to do it. I live my life by someone else's agenda, calendar, politics, etc. Someone else's foot fungus or constipation is more important than me! But after work, after everybody else's timecard is punched, it's my time. If I want to watch the sunset, if I want to read a book, or if I want to just piss it way watching ridiculous infomercials on television until 4 AM that's my business because it's nighttime and it belongs to me," she answered hotly.

Donovan was impressed.

"Is that why you are late to morning rounds?" Snyder asked; unable to resist the urge to irritate her. She huffed and shook her head.

"It's funny to me how you can do a hundred things right and the only thing that people will remember is the one thing you did wrong," she stated with clarity.

"That is the way of the world, Dr. Hunter. If you want to deserve the title of physician, you have to realize that other people's perception of us is almost as important as reality."

"Is that some code of honor you have developed for our profession? I hear that from you every time we meet. We talk about the code, the expectations others have of us, and the legacy we have inherited, and hope to pass these things on to others. But I see nothing of this in the real world. I begrudge every morning that I wake up because of this system and I hate it. We don't practice medicine. We practice asset allocation and damage control. From the moment the patient hits the door we are already scheming to get them out with the least amount of financial inconvenience to ourselves.

I do the best I can and it is never good enough. And in the event I ask for assistance from my attending physician, I am met with ridiculous questions about insignificant details that have absolutely nothing to do with the question or the patient. But they are meant to dissuade me from calling them again and to cover their lack of knowledge regarding the patient in question. So you will excuse me if I don't rush to get back to this place every day," she finished passionately.

The words flew out of her with brisk celerity.

"Color me surprised, Dr. Hunter. I've never seen such emotion pour out of you. Perhaps sleep-deprived inhibition is the key. I should schedule all of our sessions after you have been on call. However, I find your reasoning illogical."

Donovan could not help but roll his eyes. He was actually getting to the core of who Jeanine was and what she believed and now this idiot was interfering with psychojunk. What did logic have to do with it? It's not about logic; it's about being in control, you idiot! Donovan thought to himself.

"Night always leads to day. So even though you see it as your time it really isn't. It's never your time if we use your logic. So why hot instead of cold?" Snyder asked, returning to his former questioning.

She sighed, "Can you be that obtuse?" she asked angrily. "It's about control. When a room is freezing cold that is someone else doing it to me. They are in control. At least when it's hot, no one has control except me. I can take it or leave it. I can take off clothing, drink cool water, sweat etc.,"

Dr. Snyder interrupted. "But it's short sighted control. Don't you have control when you are cold to shiver? Or put on clothes or drink something hot?" He probed angrily losing his ability to conceal it.

Jeanine had had enough. "This is your game, doc. You asked the questions, I gave you answers and frankly I'm tired of playing," she was soaked all the way through with rain and her patience was at an end. She glanced at the clock it read 1700. "And looking at the clock I don't have to play any more. So, if you will excuse me, I'll be leaving now so I can finally go home. I've been here for 48 hours and I'm done," she stood up to leave.

"I appreciate your candor, but you are not excused until I excuse you!" He spat emphatically. Wounded, she sat back down withdrawing into herself. Snyder turned toward Agent Donovan. "Agent, why don't you enlighten me, you've been studying the good doctor. Maybe you can give me insight into her personality that she is unwilling to provide."

"I beg your pardon?" Donovan asked dumbfounded.

"Yes, why don't you tell me who Jeanine E. Hunter is? What secret is she hiding?"

This was dangerous Donovan thought. He did not like being in this position. Both Snyder and Jeanine watched him with expectant eyes. His mind raced thinking of ways he could use this to his advantage.

"Well," he started unclenching his teeth as he tried to look everywhere else in the room except at Jeanine. Ultimately, he locked eyes with her and plunged forward. "She works very hard. She cares deeply for her patients. She gives herself completely to what she does."

Snyder watched the interaction between them and contemplated while he sat with his fingers pressed together.

"Hmm, that's interesting" Snyder replied. "Then tell me why she is considered 'at risk' by her peers and faculty?" he asked almost rhetorically.

Donovan shot a look at quick look at Snyder who, obviously, had his panties in a wad over something. She had insulted him and he was not about to let that go.

"I can tell you why," Donovan started which caught Snyder's immediate attention. Snyder had not expected Donovan to answer.

"You think she has poor time management because she is late to rounds; you think she is detached because she does not fraternize with faculty, and you think she does not care about her work because she is not cheerful when you ask her about being on call. She's not the one with the problem. You are.

You cannot understand her because she cares too much. She gets to the hospital hours before the other residents because she actually spends time talking to her patients instead of talking at them. And because she cares about them, she lets them talk to her. She gives every bit of humanity to this place so that she hardly has anything left for herself.

She is tardy because she is meticulous. She's late because she values people more than schedules. She doesn't hate her job, as she perceives; she hates the politics and bureaucracy. Of the lot of you, I would rather have her as my doctor than any of you. Present company included," Donovan finished defiantly.

Snyder sat quietly listening to all Donovan said. He was as still as stone holding his gold Cross-pen between his fingers. Jeanine was impressed and surprised that Donovan knew her so well. He had been looking deeply into her eyes the entire time he was talking.

Snyder finally responded with a question neither Jeanine nor Donovan expected.

"So, Agent Donovan, why is Dr. Hunter alone?" The room was so quiet she could have heard a pin drop.

No one said anything for a long while. No one moved and hardly anyone breathed except for Dr. Snyder who seemed more at ease since they were so obviously uncomfortable. Only the sound of the driving rain was audible. "Well, I see you have less insight into this area of her life. Perhaps Dr. Hunter can fill us in. Doctor?" he asked.

Jeanine wanted to run, far, far, away. "What does that tell you about me, Dr. Snyder? Kent Carlton is married with children and he is a repugnant snob," she replied defensively.

"We are not talking about Kent Carlton we are talking about you, Dr. Hunter. Since you have decided not to talk to me I have been forced to piece you together from other non-conventional means. I read your medical school admission essay. In it, you said you wanted to be a doctor so that you could leave the world in a better way than you found it. You wanted your life to have meaning and you wanted to have a family. But where is your life now? The family you long for? The differences you hope to make?"

Snyder was like a black widow spider sitting back calmly and calculatingly as an unsuspecting fly was being caught in a sticky web. He sat deeply within his red velvet wing-backed chair waiting for an opportunity to pounce. Then, suddenly, he sat forward at Jeanine with a rush.

"Tell me Dr. Hunter! Be honest. Isn't it your need to fill your loneliness that caused you to develop a closer relationship with David Scott than would be considered as normal? Is it that relationship that got him killed and led to the extraction of his vital organs? Is it this need to quench your loneliness that makes you a dangerous physician? Isn't that why you spend so much time with your patients? It isn't your love for humanity! Isn't that what Dr.

Rubio thought? Isn't that why Agent Donovan and the FBI have been keeping her in a safe house all this time so that they can use her to testify against you? Don't think! Just answer! Tell me now!" He commanded vehemently.

He was shaking with emphasis.

"What!" She gasped. His words were flying at her like a hundred daggers. "What are you talking about?" she asked. She was taken completely aback. "Monica is with you?" she asked addressing Donovan directly. Even under his relatively olive toned skin, she could see he was starting to turn a faint red. He was caught with his pants down.

Donovan wondered how Snyder knew this information and why was he telling this to Jeanine? God, what must Jeanine be thinking? He did not want her to find out his secret about Dr. Rubio this way. Snyder liked the fact that he had unraveled whatever relationship Jeanine and Donovan had created. He wanted and needed that relationship to fail. Dr. Snyder kept at Jeanine, ignoring the malevolent glare he was getting from Luke Donovan.

"I find it is interesting you could hear the variances in Agent Donovan's voice that indicated his nationalities. That is a skill usually gained by someone who can speak other languages. In the last 6 months of therapy you have never discussed this in our sessions. Isn't that a part of who you are? And who you are is why you are here.

I see a plethora of doctors in my office and it is my duty to determine who is worthy to wear that white coat and who isn't. I have not reached a conclusion as to your worthiness so if you want to maintain your status in this honorable brotherhood we call medicine I suggest you do more than waste my time and tell me what I want to know. Forgive my, obtuseness. I need to understand who you are," Snyder seethed as he leaned back into his chair more calmly.

"And by the way, so does the FBI, that is also why you are here, remember?"   he   said   quietly.

CHAPTER 17
THE ELEVATOR

Jeanine rushed out of Snyder's office as quickly as possible, bursting through his office doors. She was overcome with emotion as hot tears streamed from her face. She ran to the stairwell but it was closed by maintenance.

She was coming out of her skin. She was determined to get out of that building. She could not deal with Luke Donovan; she would not. Out of the corner of her eye, she could see him emerge from Dr. Snyder's office. He had not immediately followed her out of the office but lingered there for a while talking to Snyder. She was hoping to use that lag in time to her advantage and get away.

For over a hundred years, the iconic Old Red building represented the jewel in the crown of this old and noble medical school. The building had been transformed into the anatomy lab; transplant coordination center, and administration building for the medical school. It stood as a reminder of the timelessness of medicine. Its message was simple, to remind each physician that graduated from its doors that regardless of technological advancements of medicine, there are some things about medicine that never change; it is resolute, patient and noble.

Despite all efforts, the faint but distinct fragrance of embalming fluid from the anatomy lab hung in the air. The odor clung to everything, which served as another reminder of the purpose of this building. Its main hall was lined with life sized, marble statues of the heroes of medical science from Imhotep to Archimedes. It was here where Donovan found Jeanine. They were standing on opposite ends of the hallway, fifty feet apart. Her only escape was the sole elevator; added to the landmark Old Red building fifty years ago. It was an older model with thick, silver, slow moving doors.

Jeanine had hoped to avoid the elevator, as it was interminably slow; yet it would be to her advantage if she got in first; he would be stranded and unable to catch her. They stood paralyzed, looking at each other for a while. Their standoff was like watching two Wild West gunfighters about to have a showdown. One could imagine tumbleweed blowing across the path between them pushed by a hot and lonely wind. The incandescently lit hallway was thick with anticipation. As it was after 17:00, there was no one was in the building except for them. Donovan could see what was in her mind. He could not let her get away.

As if beckoned by the same call, they simultaneously sprinted towards each other. Jeanine reached the elevator first, whipped inside, and desperately pressed the 'door close' button as hard as she could hoping that the harder she pressed it, the faster it would close.

"*Success!*" she thought as the doors narrowly closed. But then, at the last moment, Donovan's arm slid through the opening.

"Get out!" she yelled trying to push him out of the elevator unsuccessfully.

He pushed himself inside and the doors closed after him.

"Where do you think you are you going?" he asked.

"Don't you know? You know everything else! I'm just a pawn in some twisted sick game to you!" she yelled. She tried desperately to get the doors to open again.

"Jeanine, please," he pleaded trying to convince her.

"Go to hell!" she yelled angrily as hot tears streaked her face. The elevator came to a sudden grinding halt. It was stuck.

"No!" Jeanine exclaimed recognizing the significance of the elevator's movement. Donovan opened the red door to the elevator's emergency phone box but all he heard was static. He thought for a moment but whatever thought had distracted him he soon resolved against it.

Jeanine started pacing anxiously. The temperature in the elevator was hardly cool. Her rain soaked clothes were still clinging to her body, as they had not dried much since their arrival at Dr. Snyder's office. She felt hot and sticky and thin wisps of hair clung to her face.

"You might as well calm down," he instructed patiently, "I think we are going to be here for a while."

"You calm down!" she spat back at him, pacing more quickly.

"I've got to get out of here, I have to get out of here," she kept repeating. She was rubbing her neck with her hands and was starting to pant. She was not usually claustrophobic, but with the weight of the world crashing down around her she felt like she was in a coffin and started to panic.

Donovan had to catch her by the shoulders to get her to settle down. She resisted him violently.

"Let go of me!" she demanded furiously pulling away from him.

"Jeanine, listen to me," he commanded holding her fiercely by the arms.

"No! I'm tired of listening to you! How could I have been so stupid to believe you in the first place? What was I thinking? You work for the government! How could I have trusted you?" she said more to herself than to him.

"I had nothing to do with that! You have to believe me, Jeanine," his voice was soft and sincere.

"Why? Why should I believe you? Why should I believe you when every thing you have ever told me has been a lie? You said a person is what they do and not what they say. Your actions and your words are not the same. You are a liar! And what else is a lie? All that business about God, walking in the rain, mints, chocolate and music? How did you know I believed those things? Did you read it in some FBI file about me or just pop open my journal?" She was trembling with anger.

"All of that was true," he replied, "I believe all of those things."

"When lying is your business, how do you even know what you believe?" she cut at him. The remark found its mark. She had hurt him.

"Damn it Jeanine! I couldn't tell you about Monica," he explained.

"Couldn't or wouldn't?" She asked pointedly.

"What was I supposed to say Jeanine? 'Hey, your best friend has ratted you out because she thinks you spend more time with patients than she thinks is appropriate? She thinks you are involved in a heinous act and wants to help us prove it.' When was I supposed to spring that on you? Was there ever a right moment to tell you the person you believed in has betrayed you?" he asked sincerely.

"That seems a little hypocritical to me," she said with hard eyes, "since you have just done the same thing."

She could have punched him in the stomach and that would have hurt less than the look she gave him.

"I can't believe this. I can't believe Monica would do this to me. Why would she do this?" Jeanine asked angrily.

She realized that Donovan was still holding her. "Let me go, Mr. Donovan," she seethed. The rush of all of her emotions was catching up with her and she felt like she was going to pass out. The temperature in the elevator was already uncomfortably warm but with all of the excitement it was becoming unbearable.

"No," he said, "I won't let you go." He had to convince her of the truth.

"Why? Why won't you just leave me alone?" she asked wounded.

"Because," he started. But he halted because he did not know how to finish the sentence. His heart was racing, "because I want you to trust me," he finished quietly.

At that point, Jeanine stopped panting. She was looking at him sharply, almost cunningly. On a dime, there was a distinct evolution in her countenance from forlorn to seductive. Her eyes softened and Donovan could feel himself being lured into something he did not expect and could not control. He was feeling a more intense burning than Galveston's sultry, humid heat was emitting. With that look, she could have asked anything of him and he would have willingly given it to her.

"Do you trust me?" she asked softly. Her face was close to his. "I'd like to," he answered as his voice cracked from his chest. She was still inches from his face. She reached up tentatively and took his face in both of her hands; then slowly caressed his right cheek until she ran her fingers behind his ear to discover what her eyes had already seen. He was wearing a police wire.

He grabbed her hand instinctively to prevent her from finding his earpiece but it was too late. She rotated the clear piece of transparent plastic between her fingers as she pushed away from him.

"It was you wasn't it? It was your surveillance equipment in the hospital room that interfered with the telemetry units. That's why my pager stopped working. You use the word trust when it profits you most. Tell me, Agent Donovan, is there a class specifically directed toward manipulation? Or do you come by it naturally?"

Her voice was sweet and soft but her words were coming at him as fast and hard as jabs that come from a professional boxer. He was reeling from the attack; he felt surprise and hurt, something he had not felt from a woman in a very long time. He went back in his mind to determine when she could have discovered his wire. It came to him. All the interference with her pager and the glitches on the screens in the cath lab; all the strange looks she had given him when these events occurred.

Again, Renee's words reverberated in his head, 'Be genuine. She will see through anything else.'

He had to decide whether he would come clean or lie. In his mind, he heard O'Donnell and Swenson back at their headquarters screaming, "No you idiot! Disavow everything! Admit nothing! Cover your ass and lie! Tell her nothing."

But he decided to take Renee's advice, as she had never steered him wrong before. In a bold move, he threw caution to the wind and crossed a line he never thought he would cross. He trusted his heart. He needed her. He took off the shirt he was wearing, exposing his bare muscular chest, and the small wire that was taped to his sternum. She watched him curiously and her brows were knitted together in confusion.

He laid his neatly folded shirt on the floor and sat down cross-legged with a perfectly straight posture. He invited her to sit and reluctantly she complied.

He spoke to his Agents via his wire, "If any of you repeat what I am about to say to anyone, I will track you down and kill you." He was serious. They knew it and so did Jeanine. She swallowed hard nervous about what he was going to say.

"It is very important that you trust me. I cannot effectively protect you if you can't put your life in my hands. Obviously, I have failed. But I swear to you that I'll do everything in my power to keep your trust sacred. I will not apologize for wearing a wire. It was my decision to wear it and my decision not to tell you about it.

If you knew I was wearing one you would be self-conscious and would not behave like you normally would. I needed to see you, as you are, without any pretense. I felt it was the best way to do my job and take care of you. I did not mean to deceive you. I realize that I cannot convince you of my sincerity by words alone. If I were in your position, I would feel the same way. Your friend has betrayed you, your mentor is torturing you, someone that you probably know killed your patient, and I have lied to you. Yes, I did say killed. You were right earlier when you asked me that question. We do think someone killed Mr. Scott.

So, I am going to share something with you I have never told anyone else. As an Agent, believing a suspect is generally the best way to lose your job or get killed. Regardless, I am going to do what I have been asking you to do. I am going to trust you. Everyone back at HQ will hear what I have to say through this wire." She studied him carefully.

"Tell me honestly, Mr. Donovan, why did you take this case?" she asked with those piercing eyes of sincerity he had come to admire and respect.

"Honestly, I was given this case because of my reputation. I am what is called a closer."

"Like in baseball?" she asked.

"Yes. I'm the one they bring in when they cannot solve a case. I find evidence to…"

She interrupted him, "to convict?"

He wanted to look away, to disguise his guilt but something would not let him.

"Affirmative. I was sent here to close the case and find evidence to convict you. I've been following a major drug lord throughout much of my career. We think he is linked to this case. The Bureau wants this guy and you are a means to that end."

She studied him and could see he was telling the truth. She looked horrified.

"It's not something I'm proud to admit. This is the kind of case I am good at. I have never created evidence. But I can say I have stretched circumstantial evidence when the pieces seemed to fit. That is a scar I will have for the rest of my life. There is a chance that there are innocent people in prison because of me.

After my divorce five years ago, I was bitter. I became a machine that did not think about why or what. As long as I was moving, doing, or fixing, I wasn't feeling anything. But you can only do that for so long until you reach a point when you have to look in the mirror. Either you keep doing what you are doing and you don't care anymore or you make the decision to change. I think that is what my mentor was trying to tell me before I took your case. You are the line in the middle of the road."

"Line in the middle of the road?" she repeated confused.

"It's a long story. It's been over 36 hours since we've slept. I'm tired and rambling, but the point of the matter," he paused for a moment trying to collect his thoughts and pull them together into some cohesive argument. He was tired and the words were floating away from him.

"I must stress to you the urgency in which we must move forward. I believe the man behind this will strike again. I need to know what you know and…" his voice trailed off as he thought for a moment.

"What?" she asked.

"So does someone else. Dr. Snyder. He urgently wants to know what you know," he mused.

He peered at her, "you may have to tell him what he wants to know."

"And what, exactly, is that?" she asked skeptically. She knew the answer.

"He wants you, Jeanine, all of you. I don't know why. But he may be the key we are looking for. Someone leaked intel to him about Monica. But despite that, he is poignantly interested in you."

She thought quietly for a moment. She was sitting across from him leaning her back against the elevator wall.

"That must have been some divorce," she said going back to the former subject.

He moved over to sit next to her.

"We were married for 8 years."

"How did you know it was over?"

He peered at her softly and cracked a half smile. "Well, there were no telltale signs. Unless you consider, the fact she was having an affair with my boss," he chuckled a little unable to hide the grimace that followed.

"What?" she asked in disbelief, "how do you get over something like that?" she asked.

He looked her squarely in the eyes, "You don't."

His frankness surprised her. Actually, it surprised him too. His typical answer would have been something along the lines of, 'With time, family, friends and faith in God, everything works out or you just keep going and take one day at a time.'

But all that would come out of his was the honest truth. He did not care who was listening; all he cared about was earning her trust.

"So what did you do?" she asked despite herself. Curiosity had captured her and anger, as much as she craved its power, was ebbing.

"Well, at the end of things, you have to go back to the beginning. We both had an equal share in the failure. The simple answer is that I was not what she wanted. What used to be full of promise and hope turned into bitterness. We ended up hating all the reasons we fell in love in the first place."

Jeanine looked confused. He was speaking metaphorically again. There were also four confused FBI agents listening in at the warehouse. And all of them were anxiously awaiting some clarity. Donovan became more thoughtful. He forgot about the wire attached to his chest and the audience that came with it. He just focused on her eyes.

"I never believed in divorce. I still don't. It was something other people did because they did not try hard enough or because they did not really love each other. The truth of it is that divorce is always a possibility for any marriage. I felt like damaged goods when it happened to me." She listened intently.

"I will never forget the day we met. We were in D.C. at one of those drive-through dry cleaners."

"Drive-through dry cleaners?"

"Yes, they don't have those here. I miss them. I'm a slave to a good crease. Anyway, she was in the car behind me and I could see

142

that she was having an animated conversation with her passenger. She was a gorgeous blonde with silky hair and blue eyes. Everything about her sparkled like diamonds. She was perfect. She even looked like she would smell good. She was really into her conversation and had not even noticed me. I convinced the dry cleaning attendant at the window to give her a note for me and I pulled over to the side and waited for her to answer."

"What did the note say?" Jeanine asked curiously.

"It said, *'I'd like to see your left hand. It can only be as beautiful as your right hand but I hope the ring finger is undecorated. If that is the case, please call me at 555-1212'*"

"And that worked?" Jeanine asked with her eyebrows raised incredulously.

"Yeah," he sighed nostalgically, "I knew it was a long shot but that's the best I could come up with at the time. I did not have much experience, so I was just as surprised as you are that she accepted. As it turned out, she was always kind of a rebel when it came to certain things. Always doing things just to see what kind of reaction she could get out of people. To her, I was a novelty. The kind of guy people in her circle would really hate. I mean really, how many Irish-Israeli, Christian Protestant FBI guys do you know? She was born into a wealthy, well-established family. When the novelty wore off, all that was left was me, and I was not enough."

"I'll never forget one of our last real conversations. I asked her if she loved me. Her reply was *"If you have to ask, does my answer really make a difference?"* I was shocked. She continued to say, *"Why the surprise Donovan? I told you who I was before we got married. I made it plain to you I have no need for romance. If you wanted that kind of woman you've wasted your life."*

"What did you say?"

I asked her how she could be so cold. She replied, *"Cold? Call it what you will, I call it real. If I were a man you'd call me bold and aggressive. You knew what I expected from this relationship. You entered this marriage with your eyes wide open. If you do not understand it is because you chose not to see."*

Jeanine was horrified that his wife could have been that disturbingly frigid.

Donovan explained, "Sherry had certain expectations of me during our marriage. Her father was a senator who commanded a lot of respect. He had achieved a certain status and she expected me to achieve the same. Everything was on track for me to eventually leave the Bureau and work for him and possibly even run for office some day. But in my heart, I knew I was not a politician. When the time came for me to leave the Bureau, I could not do it."

"She never forgave me. When those hopes were not realized, everything else just became one disappointment after another for her. We ended up in the land of 'this is mine and that is yours' the first step in the slippery slide toward divorce. After a while, even simple things like talking to me burdened her. All I really wanted was to be with her, to hold her, to talk to her, but this became work for her too. I could see the death of our marriage in her eyes. She looked at me with emptiness and disgust. We limped along for a while, twisted, broken and in desperate need of repair.

When her father became ill and moved in with us it seemed to breathe new life into her. But that was short lived. After the first couple of weeks, she could not handle it. She could not handle seeing her dad weak, incapacitated, and incontinent. It would be hard for anyone to see their parent in that way but it was especially hard for Sherry. So, I took charge. I took a leave of absence from the FBI to take care of him. I bathed him, I fed him, I changed his diapers, everything."

He paused. It was obvious the pain of this was still there. He noted how intently Jeanine was listening. The pale glow of the lights was still enough to enhance her cinnamon colored skin. Her eyes were soft and sweet. It comforted him and he summoned the strength to continue.

"I finally had to put him in a nursing home because the demands were too great. I hated it, but it was the only way to care for him. I went back to work but my head wasn't in it. I was working on a case against Carlos Colorado. It was an ugly case. We had good evidence, a solid witness, and it looked like we were going to nail this guy but somehow he slipped out of our grasp. In the process, he killed two agents that had been my friends.

I was reassigned because my director felt my personal issues with Sherry had distracted me. My new boss had this snide, superior, attitude that was just over the top. But for some reason he took a special joy in making my life miserable. Then, one night when we were at a staff meeting, he just came out and told me he was sleeping with my wife. I just stared at him like he was speaking another language. I wanted to kill him. I'd had training in special ops, hand-to-hand combat, and served in the Israeli army. I could have killed him a hundred different ways. But, all I wanted to do was see Sherry. She admitted it flippantly. She did not care if I knew and was determined to continue seeing him. He had a promising career in the Bureau and could give her the lifestyle she wanted."

"I could handle being in a loveless marriage. I was committed to making it work, but to have an ongoing affair with my boss made me realize people were just toys to her. And that was more than I could take."

He paused for a moment.

"Jeanine, I am sharing this with you because when Sherry left me, I felt emotionally bankrupt. Divorce was not a process that happened to my marriage. It was a life-sentence that happened to me," he said as he grasped his chest.

"I felt deserted by everyone even God. And it wasn't until I met you and saw what you do for your patients that I could consider that everyone is not a suspect and that there are people in this world worth caring for."

She thought quietly for a while studying him. His confession had affected her.

"And this case, is it a chance for redemption?" she finally asked.

"Yes, in some ways. I believe, against all I have been told to believe, that you are innocent of this crime. I cannot say why except when I look into your eyes I do not see a killer. And, I must redeem myself against all I have done wrong in the last five years. During that time, when Carlos Colorado eluded me, it started a chain of negative events in my life; some were my own poor choices. I cannot blame him for those. But he is heinous. He's back in the States now and I want him so badly I can taste it. That's why I am so tenacious about your surveillance. He will kill everyone in his way. He's done it before. Colorado must go to jail or die. He must pay for his crimes. I won't let him kill you."

Donovan did not see Jeanine's expression. But the name 'Colorado' sent cold chills down her spine.

+++++

"Obtuse? She called ME obtuse? We shall see who is obtuse…" A dark figure sat alone in an unlit room in leather, winged back, office chair brooding with malevolence. He dialed the switchboard and asked to be connected to *delta delta bravo charlie*, which took him to an untraceable outside phone, line.

"Does she know anything that can affect us?"

"Possibly."

"Why is the FBI following her?"

"It is unclear."

"Can we use her to find out what they know?"

"She will cooperate."

"Will we need to persuade her?"

"She *will* cooperate."

"Initiate the persuasion immediately. Use all available resources."

He hung up the phone and thin reams of fragrant of pipe smoke rose above his head into the darkness.

CHAPTER 18
SPIRIT OF DISTRUST

As soon as Donovan and Jeanine escaped the elevator, they ran back, across the campus, to the hospital. The downpour had ended and in its wake 2-foot tall ghost like wisps of vapor evaporated from the hot concrete dancing like ships floating out to sea. The wall of humidity before the storm was a mere inconvenience compared to the sultry suffocating blanket of wet air that wrapped itself around them now.

Jeanine entered the ICU with Donovan not far behind her. She paged Carlton and Bryan but after half an hour she received no response. This made her uneasy.

"What's wrong?" he asked. "I don't know. They aren't answering my pages. It doesn't feel right." She did not want to call Rucker. It might alarm him and make the intern's call night mercilessly painful.

She checked on her patients in the ICU. All of them were fine except Mr. Graham who was having a scan performed in radiology. Finally, she decided to go home. She had done all she could do to contact her team and her specific patients were stable.

On the drive back to her apartment, Jeanine had accidentally run a stop sign, a red light, and made an illegal left turn. None of them on purpose, of course, but without sleep even simple driving decisions were difficult to make. The rest of the evening was uneventful. She and Donovan went to their separate rooms in Dr. Savage's cottage to sleep and perchance to dream. Donovan could hardly believe that he'd been awake for almost forty hours.

Morning came much too soon. At 0300 the alarm sounded and roused Donovan back to consciousness. He felt sick and hung over all at once. The small amount of sleep he had was not enough. His back and feet ached and his eyes hurt but he managed to pull himself out of bed and into the bathroom. A shower that would have normally taken him minutes was suddenly complicated and prolonged by his inability to concentrate and complete simple tasks. He was trying to load his razor but could not focus his eyes well enough to put the blade on correctly. After trying three times, and nearly slitting his index finger twice, he decided facial hair was a better option than digital amputation.

Once he finally managed to get his fingers to work well enough to take off his clothing and get in the shower, he struggled to remain conscious. He discovered, that once the warm water hit his body and his already tired muscles began to relax that staying awake was even more difficult. To make matters worse, his mind was so fatigued that he could not remember if he had lathered up or not. He actually soaped up three times and half way through the third he finally remembered that he had already scrubbed.

As for Jeanine, she was consumed by thoughts. Donovan's conversation was toiling through her mind. She found herself thinking of the world as a much larger place than her small corner of it. A small yet growing idea was gathering in her mind. Similar to the way a hurricane begins as a small wind off of the western coast of Africa, ideas were brewing in her mind that eventually became a great storm.

Two thoughts were of particular interest. The first was that she needed her father's advice. This problem required wisdom beyond her abilities. But her relationship with her father, the rock of her life, was strained and she did not know how to repair it. The second was what to do with Agent Donovan. Her heart was inclined to believe him but she would not trust her heart without prudent guidance that, of course, was directly related to her first torment. She considered her last conversation with her father. It was 2 days before David had died. At the time, she was post-call and had only slept an hour.

She recalled the conversation.

"Dad, I'm just tired."

"Jeannie-bug I'm just trying to help. I just want to understand what you are going through."

"Dad, I really don't want to talk about it. I just need to go to sleep, ok?"

"Sometimes it helps to talk about things, honey."

"Dad, I'm just going through a lot right now that you cannot understand."

"What, because I'm not college educated?" He asked sarcastically.

"What is that supposed to mean? What.... What does this have to do with you?"

"I don't know. We used to talk before you got to medical school. Now that you are a doctor, seems like you don't have time for the old man. I'm just trying to give you an out."

"Dad, look, I'm not looking for an out. Everything is not about you. I've got a lot of stuff on my plate and that has nothing to do with you!"

"I'm just trying to talk to you baby."

"Well, dad, even when I do talk you don't bother to listen! I tell you that I'm tired but you keep at me like talking about how tired I am is going to make me feel better. I've been awake for the last 50 hours and I'm really spent. I'm working in this hellhole of a place that is supposed to be about healing people but it's all about being in the military and following orders and doing what looks good rather than doing what is good. I have a patient that is dying and no one cares!"

"I'm just trying to help, Jeannie. Maybe there is some board you can talk to help your patient. You are a doctor and you have a voice. And, as a doctor, you have to protect your patient, you have a moral obligation to...."

"Moral obligation?! My moral obligation??" she kept repeating.

Jeanine felt captured by all the things she could not say. She did not like speaking this way to her father. But they were caught in a conundrum. She had no way to express all the things she had endured. She had no way of helping him to comprehend her world or what she was going through. He kept pushing her until, finally, the damn broke.

"I don't know how to tell you that my life sucks and that I am exhausted and that I hate my life and my job and I just want to die! I think I made a terrible mistake in being a doctor but I don't think you will understand that. I love that we have a relationship where

we can talk about everything and anything but right now my life does not even make sense to me! I wish you could just hear me and listen to me and not judge or criticize me."

She saw herself from outside herself like one of those weird out of body experiences. Her dad was reaching out with sincerity and to her it was like salt being poured into a wound.

"Jeannie-bug, I just want to be a part of your life. I feel like we are strangers and I need you. Don't you see God has given you a gift? How can you question His purpose?" he asked poignantly.

She interrupted. If she had to hear how much she had been blessed one more time she was going to scream. "Do you have to call me that?" she snapped at him. "I'm not a child, daddy!" she exclaimed. She let the 'daddy' slip before she could even help herself and she kicked herself internally for doing it. She wanted him to take her seriously; not like a petulant child.

"I'm sorry honey but you will always be my baby." The sigh she let out in response was all she needed to say. Without any words she said, 'No, I am not your baby!' She could feel his hurt through the phone. He tried to defray the moment with humor. "What? Are you there with someone? Is that why you can't talk to the old man? Is it that Jourdan again? I never did like him."

She was so frustrated she could hardly speak. "What!" She exclaimed. "What are you trying to say? That of all the reasons I have given you for why I really don't want to talk about my day you dismiss all of that and ask me if I am sleeping around?" she asked angrily.

"I was just joking baby. I did not mean to insult you, honey. I'm just trying to help..." he started but she interrupted him.

"You're just trying to help me. Yes, I know," she replied angrily, "I think you've helped me enough."

The other end of the line went dead silent. It took an eternity for him to respond. Then, distantly he replied, "Well, I better let you go, Jeanine."

The line went dead. That was the last time she had spoken to her father.

She went to bed and woke with these thoughts. When Donovan emerged from the bathroom Jeanine was sitting on the chaise waiting for him. It appeared she had been there for some time. She looked him over as she grabbed her duffle bag.

"You look terrible," she observed.

"I feel terrible."

"That's about right. The first day after being on call is the worst. You've had just enough sleep to feel toxic."

"When will I feel better?"

"In about two days."

"That's good. When are we on call again?"

"Today"

"Then, I'll feel this badly for four days?"

"Welcome to my world" she replied, as she gave him an encouraging pat on the shoulder.

By the time they'd made it to the hospital, Jeanine noticed the interns had already seen most of her patients. She looked at her watch. It was only 0500. This was odd. They should be seeing their own patients. When she got to the ICU, her team had already gathered. Carlton and Rucker looked at her with disdain. Ivory looked sadly pitiful. He had been on call the previous night.

"What are you doing here?" Carlton asked angrily.

"Where were you last night, Dr. Hunter?" Dr. Rucker asked in a whiney pathetic voice with both hands on his hips and his lips pursed like an old woman.

"We were stuck in an elevator in the Old Red building," she replied apologetically. Besides their lack of any sympathy she could see that something was amiss.

"What's happened?" she asked. Ivory looked at her with eyes full of sorrow.

"Mr. Graham coded, Hunter. He went into cardiac arrest last night at 1730. We coded him and he's alive if you want to call it that," Ivory said sadly. He knew how much she liked this patient. Unfortunately the nicest patients seemed destined to be afflicted with the worst medical conditions.

Ivory was shot a hot-as-molten-glass look from Carlton for even addressing Jeanine. But he was too tired to care what Carlton thought of him.

151

"I'm really sorry Licious. I spoke to his wife she's agreed to allow him to be an organ donor just in case he goes into arrest again."

As she looked at Ivory, she could see the beginning of the process she had gone through a year ago when she was an intern. The heartache of losing a patient you really care about, the inner turmoil of having to put your own grief aside to do your work and then the mixed feelings of guilt you have when you have one less patient to see. A switch just goes from on to off and you don't allow yourself to feel because you'll go crazy.

Carlton addressed her again, "Dr. Hunter, I don't know what circumstances (he emphasized 'circumstances') delayed your arrival." He eyed Donovan suspiciously, "but since you were unable, or unwilling, to fulfill your duties Dr. Rucker and I have decided that you will not be off this weekend, as originally scheduled. Your work is not up to par and the patient's should not suffer for it. I have reassigned your patients to the interns and I have supported a complaint with Dr. Baxter to the resident evaluation committee."

She was appalled. There was no reason or logic to this vehemence. "What! I was stuck in an elevator. I could not return your pages and even if could, Mr. Graham would still have coded. And why would Dr. Baxter file a complaint against me? It was not my decision to give Mrs. Thibodeaux a pneumothorax!"

"Don't bother to lie, Jeanine. You were not stuck in any elevator," Carlton replied flatly ignoring everything except what he wanted to hear. "We called Dr. Snyder's office after you refused to answer your first several pages. Dr. Snyder informed us that you had left his office at 17:30." Carlton pressed.

"Yes, I believe I said that," she replied angrily, "but I also told you I was stuck in an elevator after we left Dr. Snyder's office. He couldn't have known that. Didn't you hear me?" she snapped at him.

He sighed and looked at her as though she was less than nothing. "Dr. Hunter, you have created a spirit of distrust on this service. Anything you say requires scrutiny." He was condescending and his voice was dripping with the odd flavor of loathing and self-righteousness.

"Spirit of distrust?" she repeated. Jeanine could not believe she was hearing this. She was overwhelmed by the mere words themselves. 'Who talks like that? What the hell does that mean' she thought to herself. She scrambled to think of something to say. She hated that she wasn't one of those people who always had the quick, witty response. She managed to push through her mental block.

"Carlton, have I done something to make you hate me? I'd just like to clear the air and find out what it is about my being that disturbs you so much?"

Even as she asked the question, the fact occurred to her that Carlton might be aware of what was going on with her. Was it this business with Monica and her patient David Scott that had colored his view of her? If Snyder knew information about the FBI's activities then it was possible that others could also. He and Snyder sat on several boards together. Was that what was fueling his malevolent distaste for her? It also occurred to her that he had always been an ass towards her even before all of this started. This was giving her a massive stomachache. She shifted her weight and rubbed her abdomen.

Rucker had been listening but feigned ignorance. He did not like being in this position. He stood up to intervene several times but thought better of it and sat back down after meeting Carlton's hot stare. Suddenly, Carlton whipped his head around with the viciousness and celerity of a snake and looked at her. He attacked with the same serpentine viciousness and celerity as an angry rattlesnake.

"While I am sure you spend countless hours wondering what I think of you, be sure that I don't think of you at all. In fact, I don't like you, Jeanine. I don't like you the air you breathe, the clothes you wear or your very existence. I'm not one of these people who believe that everyone deserves to be liked or respected. I believe you get what you deserve and that God gives good things to those who deserve them.

Everything about you is loathsome to me. You represent everything that is wrong in this world. You think everyone should get a fair chance, be treated equally, and that bad things happen to everybody regardless of whether they deserve them or not. Well I believe bad things happen to bad people and if you get caught in the crossfire then too bad. Ever since you have been here, the administration has coddled you. The fact you were allowed to enter this honorable program is abhorrent to me.

Admittedly, your medical school essays and letters of recommendation initially impressed me. As one of the residents on the admissions committee of our program, I voted in favor of your acceptance. But ever since you have been here you have been nothing but a disappointment to me and serve as a blemish on my record for choosing good residents for this institution.

Good residents don't get burned out or tired or complain about the long hours. They don't spend all hours of the night holding hands with patients when they should be reading for their Boards. They don't waste time with this touchy-feely, putrescence that you embrace. Good residents suck it up and take their blows like every doctor has before them. Good residents consider it an honor to work long hours and sacrifice time from their families.

For the rest of your tenure here, however long that is, I suggest you stay out of my way. All I ask is you do your work; a charge I feel confident you will neglect. And I will do everything in my power to make sure the leaven you bring with you does not affect the quality of the other residents as it has obviously already affected your medical student. I can only assume what the two of you were doing yesterday." He scorned.

His words felt like acid as they burned through her skin and into her bones. They were coming at her so hard and so fast she barely had the frame of mind to breathe. She hated that she had ever asked the question in the first place. Her jaw dropped open and all she could do was blink back a response.

Never in her life had she felt the sting of personal hatred in this way. She had no clever retort. There were so many levels to what he had said to her that she did not know what to say. In one single soliloquy he had questioned her integrity, debased her existence and called her a whore. She had been clenching her fists during this interlude so tightly that her hands were shaking from the tension and her fingernails had dug into her white palms. Carlton's six foot four inch frame had been towering over her. She was powerless to move, like a mouse caught in the stare of a cobra.

She was aroused from her stance by her pager going off. She had to go to clinic that morning and this was her reminder page. She quietly turned and walked away. The air in the room had been tight. Despite the busy goings on of other doctors, patients and nurses, everyone had heard.

Carlton had a sense of satisfaction. He had enjoyed unloading all of this, after several months of saying it behind her back; he'd finally said it to her face. As he turned to address the interns, his eyes locked with Donovan's. This time, Donovan would not be silent.

Donovan strolled over to address Carlton in no particular hurry. He moved toward him with a regal authority that commanded respect. This was something Carlton was not used to. It was like watching a puma hunt an antelope. There was even a low, puma-like, steady, growl emitting from Donovan's chest. As both of their heights were comparable, Carlton had nowhere else to look but directly into Donovan's face.

Donovan stood just an inch or two into Carlton's personal space. Just close enough and just long enough for Carlton to feel uncomfortable.

There Donovan would wait.

"Can I help you with something?" Carlton asked trying but failing to sound authoritative. 'Gotcha!' Donovan thought. Carlton was the first to speak and in this battle the first to speak was the first to lose. He had opened his kimono.

"Yes," Donovan started slowly, "you can help me. You can help me by never speaking to Dr. Hunter in that tone again."

Carlton raised his eyebrows and was about to say something pridefully indignant but before he could, Donovan interrupted him and stepped even closer with a commanding presence. "And before you continue, you should know that I am not impressed or intimidated by your condescending arrogance. You are weak. You have chosen to threaten the one true being that exudes any sense of honor, kindness or grace in this establishment. You are a disappointment. You can't respect a colleague much less a patient because you cannot see them as an equal. Your self-righteousness is a repugnant fume in the nostrils of the God you think you serve. You will have to answer Him for that.

But while you are still here on earth, know this, if you ever question her honor or her integrity again you will answer to me. She will not be on call this weekend, you will not bring her before any committee, and if there is any disciplinary action to be taken against anyone for Mrs. Thibodeaux, it will be against Dr. Rucker. Is that clear?"

His words were slow and sharp, as he wanted Carlton to hear and feel every word of what he was saying.

The words hung in the air for what seemed an eternity. Donovan remained planted in front of Carlton, who now found himself in the unusual position of being speechless. It was not that he did not know what to say but he was afraid to say anything.

Again, in their delicate dance, Carlton was the first to act. He nodded affirmatively and silently turned away departing with bright red cheeks and his tail firmly tucked between his legs. Donovan watched him walk away and, not long after, Rucker stood up desperately hoping not to be noticed. Of course, Donovan was waiting for him to stand. Their eyes met. Rucker felt the sting of conviction in his eyes. "Right Dr. Rucker?" Rucker nervously acquiesced.

Jeanine did not have the privilege of hearing the conversation between Donovan and Carlton. Her wounds were deep and she was emotionally   hemorrhaging.

CHAPTER 19
CRASHING WAVES

The University Clinic was located in the poorest section of town to provide care for indigent patients. It was about 10 minutes west of the hospital in the center of the Island. Jeanine, still reeling from the blows she received from Carlton, barely recalled arriving at her clinic much less seeing her patients. Today, the patients came and went with complaints of all kinds: dermatoses, pharyngitis, hypertension, pityriasis rosea and Stiff-Man syndrome. She saw them all with the same robotic mentality.

Her last patient was Miguel Sanchez; a very attractive Mexican American man in his early thirties. He was a member of a local gang. He usually saw Jeanine several times a month for various gang related injuries. Jeanine was his favorite doctor and despite the clinic having over 100 doctors he would only see Jeanine. He would wait hours to see her even if someone else was available. In the last year, his number of visits had dramatically increased.

Today, he had a laceration on his hand reportedly the result of a kitchen accident. The angle of the injury, the location, and the depth of the cut were consistent with a knife fight etiology in Jeanine's determination. She cleaned and approximated the wound without saying a word. Miguel observed she was disturbingly solemn and not her usual bright and spirited self.

"What's up doc?" he asked trying to stimulate conversation.

"Nothing Miguel," she rendered. Obviously she was not in a mood to talk.

"Doc?" he said in a tone of voice that caught her attention. Try as she might, his charm was persuasive. She could no longer repress a small smile. To this end, he felt victorious. "What's wrong doc?"

"Just the usual Miguel," she answered dryly.

"You're not still seeing that asshole doctor are you?" he asked referring to Jourdan.

"I was never seeing him," she replied putting away the sutures and scissors on her procedure tray, "we're just friends."

"Hmm" he smirked, "he's not right for you"

"In your opinion, is anyone right for me?"

"No one but me," he joked with enough truth in it to make her uncomfortable.

She glanced at the corner of the room where O'Donnell was watching her with interest. He had replaced Donovan as her shadow today. She turned back to Miguel.

"Look Miguel, you are smart, too smart to be doing this. Promise me you will get a regular job."

His eyes were smart and sad all at once. "Doc," he said warningly. It was all he had to say. He was staying where he was.

"Okay," she sighed, "I'll see you next time, I hope." She would let it go for now. She did not have the wherewithal to instruct or guide him.

O'Donnell admired her for this. He thought about the path his life could have taken if no one had intervened. It was not long ago that he had experienced someone like her in his life. After seeing her patients, she had some time to herself before the rendezvous with her colleagues at the hospital.

Donovan sent O'Donnell to cover Jeanine; knowing they were on service call that night increased the likelihood they would be up all night again. While he appreciated the sacrifices doctors made, he knew he could not survive another night without sleep. O'Donnell, Donovan decided, was experienced at field ops and could be trusted to cover Jeanine while he went back to headquarters, briefed his other agents, and slept for a few hours. Before sleeping, he asked Glenn to update him on the information about Jeanine's father.

"Did you find anything useful on her father?" Donovan queried.

"His parents are deceased, no siblings, he's married with 3 kids. He's worked a dozen jobs in a dozen places. They were real nomads and then five years ago he fell of the grid."

Donovan mused for a moment. It all sounded familiar, too familiar. Nice clean family, nothing to raise suspicion. Nothing was extravagant or particularly noticeable. His life was conspicuously inconspicuous.

"Does that seem normal to you?" Donovan probed Glenn. In the most interesting conversation they had ever had, Glenn answered in a way Donovan had never expected. It was as though someone had removed Glenn's training wheels.

"Everyone's a criminal. They just haven't been caught yet."

"That's a particularly cynical view of the world, don't you think?"

Glenn didn't answer. The prepubescent, rosy cheeked, fair-skinned greenhorn had lost his virginal status. Evil had crept into the garden. Donovan was concerned but would have to investigate this matter later.

"What happened five years ago? Why is he off the grid?" Donovan continued.

"I don't have clearance to access his records. They're sealed."

"Sealed? By whom?"

Glenn handed him the limited information in Thomas Hunter's file. "By you, sir," Glenn replied curtly.

Donovan eyed Glenn curiously. He took the files from him cautiously, went into his office, closed the door and pulled the shades. Heavy thoughts weighed on Donovan's mind.

Woo had been observing them. "Why would Donovan have sealed someone's records?" Woo asked.

Glenn followed Donovan with his eyes until the office doors were firmly shut. "There's only one thing I can think of. Hunter's father was in the witness protection program," he answered. "And Donovan put him there."

+++++

In Donovan's absence, Jeanine had some downtime. She needed to be alone, to think, to vent her frustration, to just be. Naturally, she went to one of her favorite spots on the Island-the Seawall. O'Donnell accompanied her but, sensing her deep-seated resentment, he kept his distance.

She sat on a concrete bench on the Galveston Seawall and watched the waves crash against the shore. She felt like the spray of the water, as it slammed itself mercilessly against the rocks of the pier. The waves rolled, tumbled, punched and kicked relentlessly against the huge boulders of the pier. Those that managed to escape the heavy stone laden pier rolled up and fizzled out on the shore. What started off as tumultuous titans diminished and de-evolved as sighs of frothy foam on the quiet sand.

The ocean breeze whipped violently against her face. The salt, the sand, the water, and the wind swirled around her. She felt everything and nothing at the same time. She wanted to purge her soul into the sea but there was no solace, no comfort, nothing but the waves and the wind. She wanted to scream, to die, to shout, to yell, to move, but nothing would come. She felt like a shell of a person both empty and full at the same time. Mostly, she was tired of being afraid.

Passersby were filled with melancholy as they looked at her face. Her expression was a unique combination of sadness, pity, and fuck-off all at the same time. She truly wore her emotions on her face and in her eyes.

Sometimes she could come to the Seawall and throw all of her grief into the ocean and feel revived and refreshed, but not today. There was too much. Instead of feeling revived by the waves, she felt like the issues in her life were drowning her.

"Kind of dangerous don't you think? Being alone?" She heard a voice from behind her say. She knew it was Donovan.

Jeanine kept her gaze fixed on the waves as she spoke to him. "They built this wall because of the Great Storm in 1900. It's over 10 miles long and 17 feet tall. It's the only thing standing between the Island and the Sea," she said blankly.

"Over there," she pointed, "is a memorial to the nuns of a four story orphanage that was destroyed by that hurricane. There were a hundred children in that orphanage. As the storm rolled in, the water kept rushing in, one floor at a time until they were forced to the fourth floor. In a last ditch effort to save the children; each of the 10 sisters tied themselves to ten orphans with rope. After the storm, workers were looking for survivors on the beach. One of them discovered a deceased nun partially buried in the sand with a rope tied around her waist. As he followed the rope it led him to a sad and morbid discovery. All of them died except for two or three of the children who had managed to break free.

I have no idea what those nuns must have felt. I look at these waves and I feel like they are crashing into me. I have thrown myself; flung myself entirely into this life and I don't even know what it means."

The wind was mercilessly blowing her hair, whipping it around her face. She was literally and figuratively on the edge. Donovan dismissed O'Donnell and sat next to her.

"Jeanine?" he started.

She quickly interrupted. "Is there any way possible I could have a moment alone?" she asked vacantly.

"It's possible," he retorted.

"But not probable," she replied quickly.

Silence.

If it was possible to look at someone and see nothing at all that is what Donovan saw when he looked at Jeanine. She was transparent with apathy.

"Jeanine, what happened back there at the hospital…" he started trying to encourage her.

"What?" She snapped with biting bitterness. Then, softening a bit, "I'm just asking for…a moment alone, please. Can't you understand that?" She turned to look at him and the pleading in her eyes reached him.

"Alright, what do you need?" he asked against his better judgment.

"I need to be alone." That was all she would say. He searched her eyes as he gently laid his hand on top of hers.

"I'll find you," he said as he rose and walked away. He had O'Donnell tail her but gave specific instructions to remain inconspicuous. Meanwhile, Donovan had homework to do.

Jeanine returned to Dr. Savage's carriage house and decided to call her father. It had been too long since they had spoken and she earnestly needed him. Unbeknownst to Jeanine, the phones in the carriage house had been bugged. As soon as she initiated the call to her father, the line started recording.

"Sir, you should hear this," Woo informed Donovan and they listened intently to the conversation.

"Daddy" she said between sobs, *"Daddy"*.

"What is it baby? What's wrong?" he asked with concern.

"Daddy," she sobbed again in great distress, barely able to breathe between sobs, "I don't know what to do."

"What's happened?"

There was silence for a long time as he just listened to the unintelligible cry of his daughter, his child. Then, slowly, he began to do the only thing he could do-pray, "Father, give us grace and peace only as you can provide. Lead us so to fear nothing because you are our ally! Lift us up on the wings of eagles that we may soar over our enemies. Give us the clarity of your vision and the strength of your wisdom. In Jesus' name, Amen."

"What's going on baby girl?" he asked solemnly after a few moments. His voice was deep and filled with the stillness of a father's strength but tempered by his respect for his daughter's adulthood.

"I wish I could tell you everything. There is so much to say and so little time."

"Did he get to you?" he shot back quickly to defend his position.

"Who?" she asked impatiently.

"The asshole who insulted you; did he get to you. You don't have to answer that because I know he did. I can hear it in your voice."

"What do you expect me to do, dad? I'm really trying to tell you something."

"Taking an action to defend yourself is not always external," he continued, "It starts with a decision. That is where you fall short. You see, when you know who you are no one can deprive you of your internal peace. If the one who insulted you said things that were true then fix it. But if he said things that were false then let them go. A time is coming when you will have to live by faith and not by fear. Faith in the knowledge that all you have been taught is right and just; faith to go forward. Honey, you learned the fear part very well. So well that I never realized you had not learned to live by faith. Do you know when I realized it? When you were interested in that Jourdan guy. Do you recall, I never asked you if you were having sex?"

162

"Dad!" she exclaimed

"Well did I?"

"No, and I hope you are not about to!"

"No, I'm not going to ask. I don't need to ask. Because I know you well enough to know that you would be too afraid to even get close enough for that. You are so afraid to fail in your career that you have isolated yourself to relationships you know are doomed to fail. But this behavior does not isolate itself to one area of your life. It binds you. It paralyzes you. You are now afraid of success and even afraid of yourself. It's time to let go," he instructed.

She sighed calmly feeling strangely empowered. "I hear you, dad. But right now I need you to hear me. I should have told you this earlier but I didn't see it until now."

"What's wrong, honey? You're making me nervous and I don't get nervous?" he asked uncomfortably.

"Dad, I'm in trouble. I can't give you all of the details but I know what my heart wants to do I'm just not sure if it's the right thing to do." She could hear him pondering on the other end of the line.

"Honey, I trust you. Trust yourself."

"Likewise," her father added, "there's something I need to tell you."

"What, dad?"

"I haven't been totally honest with you, with the family. I really need to talk to you in person."

Back at headquarters, Donovan removed his headset. He could see the relationship between them was special. Silently stroking his goatee, he considered what it was Jeanine's heart was leading her to do. Donovan hoped her inclination was to believe him. He gave Woo a reassuring pat on the shoulder for bringing the conversation to his attention.

However, Donovan needed more information about her father. He knew something was there. He had to determine what it was. He made some calls to the DOJ and to Renee to investigate Thomas Hunter. He was certain their paths had crossed. He needed to know why. A chill ran down his spine as he considered the possibilities.

The only case that came to mind from that time frame was Carlos Colorado's. Could Jeanine be connected to Colorado? Could her father? Donovan wondered.

Donovan returned to the hospital and found Jeanine talking to Carlton addressing her at the nurses' station. "You won't be on call Labor Day Weekend," Carlton informed her. "I'd also like to apologize. My address to you this morning was unprofessional."

"Thank you," she said graciously as she noticed an odd exchange of glances between Carlton and Donovan. Carlton said nothing else and departed. Donovan had changed and looked refreshed. He was wearing cologne that Jeanine found pleasant and alluring.

"You look rested," she observed.

"I needed to get cleaned up. I didn't do a very good job this morning."

"I see your five o'clock shadow is gone" she added "you clean up well."

'Did she just compliment me?' He thought to himself. He stored the memory for later. "About this morning," he started tentatively.

"Mr. Donovan," she interrupted, "I need to thank you for giving me some time to be alone. It really helped me to clear my head and process some things." He nodded silently.

"But you already knew that, didn't you?" she asked provocatively as she pointed to her ear referring to his surveillance causing him to feel a twinge of guilt for invading her privacy. She was confident and evocative. Gone was the odor of despair and loneliness; in its place was the sweet intoxicating fragrance of assurance and boldness. Previously, he had come to admire her spirit but now she hooked him entirely.

"It's not personal, Jeanine. It's just a part of the investigation," he countered

"That's too bad," she commented pensively.

"What is too bad?"

"That it's not personal. If anything is anything it should at least be…personal," she answered.

164

"So, we're on call again tonight?" he asked changing the subject, as he shifted his weight.

"That's called avoidance you know," she chided with a raised brow.

"Isn't it medical malpractice to use your skills on someone who isn't your patient?" he asked furtively.

"Occupational hazard," she replied with a crooked grin and a raised eyebrow.

"Jeanine," he said seriously, "I don't mean to press you but…"

"But you need me to meet with Dr. Snyder again," she finished.

"Affirmative," he agreed. She nodded silently. "We have an appointment with him this afternoon," she informed. "Remember, we need to get more information from him," he advised, "try to make him reveal more information."

+++++

Dr. Snyder received them promptly at 16:00. Before they entered the office, Donovan took her by the arm to address her.

"Don't be afraid to open up to him. Besides, it's not like you have any deep dark secrets right?" he chuckled.

But even as he said it, Donovan wondered about the possible relevance of something in her past or her father's. The moment passed but not for Jeanine. She froze and the color drained from her face. Donovan tried to escort her into the room but she halted like a cat being forced into a cage.

"Jeanine?" he pressed trying to understand her hesitation, "What's wrong?" She stiffened.

"Everything," she whispered thoughtfully. Slowly, she came back to reality as if waking from a post-ictal state.

"Are you alright?" he asked noting her frame was still rigid. "Yeah," she replied unconvincingly and walked zombie-like into the office.

Dr. Snyder addressed them. "Please come in, I have another appointment after yours so we need to expedite this session. Jeanine, I have been quite patient with you," he pressed "but now I need your full cooperation."

165

She walked directly to the window in the corner of his office and was vacantly admiring the parking lot. It seemed she had not heard him but was in a deep conversation with herself. She muttered something under her breath, her brow was furrowed and her arms were defensively folded over her chest.

"Dr. Hunter" he pressed with great agitation "are you harboring some guilt over your actions with Mr. Scott? What was the true nature of your relationship with him? What is it about your past you have failed to disclose?" He provoked.

"When did your son die?" Jeanine asked still facing the window. Snyder and Donovan were taken aback.

"What?" he asked quickly.

"It was last year wasn't it? He was killed in association with a drug dealer named Carlos Colorado."

"This is insufferable!" he exclaimed.

"How have you dealt with his loss? Has your guilt prompted you to act inappropriately?"

"Dr. Hunter!" he roared, as he shot up from his desk.

"No!" she quieted him as she turned from the window to face him. Her voice overpowered him, sedated him.

"No! You will not lecture me on the appropriate conduct of a physician. Not anymore you supercilious tyrant," her expression was resolute and her eyes were on fire.

"For the last six months, you have been conferring about my life with Monica, my friend, behind my back. You made erroneous conclusions that have affected my life. You want to know who I am? I am a daughter, a sister, a child of God, and a doctor. What else do you need to know? Everything about me is obvious. You don't need to delve into the corners of soul to know who I am. I wear my heart on my sleeve. So these sessions are over for me. But as for you, you need to deal with your own guilt. You think you are doing the world a favor as some great benefactor to the art of medicine. I advise you to examine yourself, sir!"

Donovan silently watched the exchange. He was getting more information about Snyder now than his agents had produced in the last four weeks.

"My guilt? I am appalled that you would address me in this way. You of all people have no right to..." he was shaking with anger. She was calm and completely in control.

"I, above all people, have every right!" she interrupted emphatically "I am the only one who has ever had the gall to confront your self-righteous arrogance. I am not your pupil I am your equal! You should feel guilty for every doctor you have psychoanalyzed and manipulated into feeling insecure and unworthy. I am not here at this University, at this time, by accident. I am here because I am supposed to be here and I will remain until my training is complete.

Furthermore, you are a pipe smoking, asthmatic with untreated arthritis in your left hip. You should be evaluated for post-polio syndrome and the lesion on you right cheek that you have convinced yourself is benign is not a mole it's skin cancer. And before you ask, I didn't read those things in a file. I see them as clearly as I see you because contrary to your opinion I *am* a doctor!" With that, she turned on her heel and walked out.

Snyder was so full of rage he was literally foaming at the mouth. She had dealt his ego an enormous blow. Jeanine may have come in wounded like the rocks on the pier but she had clawed and fought her way out. The waves had not overtaken her. Donovan gave Snyder a sardonic smile and coolly strolled out.

CHAPTER 20
ICU

Jeanine absently looked over some charts in the ICU. She was still tingling from her experience with Dr. Snyder. Donovan was standing at the opposite side of the rectangular open-spaced nurse's station facing her. Serena, an ICU nurse, addressed Jeanine.

"Hey doc," Serena said in her smoky, sultry, Southern accent, "how did you get so lucky?"

Jeanine did a double take to make sure she was addressing her. "Me? Lucky? What are you talking about?"

"How did you get so lucky to have that hunk of a medical student to fall for you?" Serena asked as her accent slurred the 'u' in hunk so that it became a polysyllabic word.

"What are you talking about? Did he say something to you?" Jeanine continued.

"No, not to me but he gave Carlton a what for. I've never seen Carlton flinch the entire three years he's been here but your boy made him blush like a schoolgirl who just had a boy reach up her skirt for the first time! Carlton was speechless."

"Really?" Jeanine asked amazed. "When did this happen?"

"Right after Carlton said all those mean things to you. Don't worry girl, we got your back. Me, and some of the other girls that are on call this weekend have his number. We will page his sorry ass every thirty minutes all day and all night long. He won't sleep for shit! Anyway, back to your boy, you must have cast some spell over him for him to take up for you like that. I've never seen anybody around here do that for someone else. Anyway, I've seen the way he looks at you. I'd cut off my right arm to have somebody look at me that way, even my husband!"

"I never noticed," she said distantly as she considered what Serena was saying.

"By the way, I like what you've been doing with your scrubs. That crease in the pants and the sleeves really looks nice."

"What?" Jeanine asked dumbfounded.

"The crease, in your pants, it looks nice. Geez, doc, you need to get some sleep. You're a little slow today." Jeanine looked at her scrubs and noticed the fine crease. Donovan must have been ironing them. He did love a good crease.

"Well, I better get back to work. You're on service call tonight right?" Serena asked.

"Yeah, everybody seems to be stable." Serena shot her a look of horror.

"Doc!" she exclaimed "there's a full moon tonight! Knock on some wood now! Hurry!" It was a superstition to never mention how peaceful or quiet a day was. It was a sure invitation for disaster. But it was too late for wood or anything else to prevent what was about to happen. Just then all hell broke loose.

Mr. Richard's heart monitor started going off signaling he was in cardiac arrest. Jeanine was the first to respond and called "CODE BLUE!"

She ran into the room and started doing chest compressions. Because of his large size and the height of the bed off of the floor, she had to stand on a step stool just to reach his chest. Donovan was pushed into a corner by the flurry of medical personnel rushing in trying to save Mr. Richard's life. Although it looked like chaos, it ran like a well-oiled machine.

Jeanine was calling out orders as a nurse relieved her from chest compressions. "He's in V-Fib! We need some paddles now!" she demanded as she jumped off the ladder. As the order was called out, a nurse simultaneously retrieved the machine to shock Mr. Richard's heart out of its erratic pattern. To Donovan, the heart tracing on the monitor looked like someone was being horribly dishonest on a polygraph machine.

"We're charged and ready to shock, doc," Serena called.

"Clear!" Jeanine shouted as they delivered a shock to Mr. Richard's chest to regulate his rhythm. They continued advanced life support under Jeanine's direction until the rest of the code team arrived, which included her friend Dr. Tony Liberty. After thirty minutes of CPR and advanced cardiac life support it was over. They had lost him.

Jeanine called the time of death. "Time of death 17:20," she said sadly as she watched the ICU recording nurse, who sat quietly in the corner of the room, jot down the time in the official record. There was always one person responsible for writing down all that occurred for record keeping purposes.

Jeanine wiped perspiration from her forehead and watched as Serena opened the window to Mr. Richard's room. This particular crew of ICU nurses was quirky, bright, enthusiastic, and actually loved their jobs. They had a superstition that the spirit of the dead had to be released so they opened the window of the patient's room. There were many deaths here; that was just the nature of things in intensive care. Even though Jeanine did not take stock in superstitions she always felt comforted when they did it.

"Hey kid, you okay?" Liberty asked looking at the disappointment in her face.

"Yeah I'm okay. I just have to talk to his family. Not my favorite thing", Jeanine answered. She searched the ICU waiting room for Mr. Richard's family. As it turned out, his only living family member was his elderly, eighty-year old, nursing home confined mother. Jeanine had to deliver the news via phone.

"Mrs. Richard, I have to talk to you about your son," she said to the elderly lady.

"What's wrong with him?" She asked. "Is he alright?"

"No ma'am, Mr. Richard is not alright."

"What? What did you say?" she asked. It was obvious severe presbyacusis had afflicted her hearing.

"I have some bad news about Mr. Richard."

"What about the Jews?" she asked so loudly over the phone that everyone in the ICU could hear her. Jeanine had never been through this before. She was trained to break back news carefully and soberly.

"Mr. Richard has passed on," Jeanine pronounced loudly.

"What?" she shouted back.

"Mr. Richard has passed away," Jeanine rephrased.

"What? He's passed out?" she yelled.

Jeanine looked at the Serena for suggestions to which she could only shrug an "I don't know" in response.

Calmly, she blew the air from her chest and simply said, "He's dead."

"What?"

"He's dead!" Jeanine shouted.

"What, honey?"

"He's dead!" she shouted again.

"I can't hear you honey. What's that?"

"He's dead! Dead!!" Jeanine yelled emphatically.

The entire ICU, including the staff, patients and visitors, were in hysterics. Jeanine felt embarrassed and strangely relieved with this unexpected catharsis.

"Oh, he's dead," Mrs. Richard finally understood.

"Well, it's for the best, he was always sick and big…big, big, man, always did need to lose some weight. Thank ya for tellin' me honey," she stated matter-of-factly and promptly hung up.

Jeanine was exhausted. Her palms were sweating. "Geez, doc, you handled that one well! Dr. Sensitivity!" Serena said jokingly. "Well, that was a first," Jeanine sighed.

Tony Liberty flashed a big approving smile. "Kid, it's never the same day twice!" he said brightly, slapping her on the back approvingly. "You see Donovan, Dr. Hunter can teach you a lot of things." Liberty continued.

"Yes," Donovan agreed as he approached the counter with a gait and expression that caused Liberty to take notice. "She's great," Donovan observed as he locked eyes on Jeanine.

Jeanine's pager went off again. It was the obstetrical floor. "Hey, this is Hunter, did some one page me?" she asked while finishing the paper work on Mr. Richard.

"Doctor Hunter, we have one of your continuity of care obstetrical patients down here and she's having problems. Can you get down here, fast?"

"I'm on my way!" She informed the nurse.

"Sorry Liberty, I gotta run," she said apologetically wishing for more time to visit.

"Don't worry, I'll catch you later…." He said to her back as she and Donovan flew out of the unit and down the stairs to the second floor.

From death to life, that was the way of the family physician. One moment your patient is dying and the next moment one is delivering a baby. Jeanine arrived on the OB floor excited that one of her patients was going to deliver.

"Hey, Ms. Johnson, are we ready to have this baby?" Jeanine enthusiastically.

Katy Johnson, a 15-year old patient who had received very little prenatal care, just started seeing Jeanine 2 months ago after finally admitting to her parents that she was pregnant. At which time she was already seven months along. When Jeanine saw the results of the fetal monitoring strip, her heart sank. Donovan could see from the look on her face that things were not well.

"Rachel, are you seeing this?" Jeanine whispered dejected.

"Yep," the seasoned obstetrical nurse answered flatly.

"Has she ruptured yet?" Jeanine asked.

"She doesn't know. I've positioned those leads all over her belly and I can't get heart sounds. And there's the smell..." Jeanine knew that smell. She had experienced it once before when a patient had delivered a twenty-two week stillborn two weeks after it had died.

"I'm going to check to see if your water has broken," Jeanine told the patient.

"What are you gonna stick up in me?" Katy yelled as she shot up the back of the bed as far as her wires and IV fluid lines would carry her.

Young girls, even though they were having sex, were not accustomed to having pelvic exams. Katy was alone, scared, and uneducated. Jeanine and Rachel, the OB nurse, would have to be her family as well as her caretakers.

"Katy," Rachel advised, "Doctor Hunter is a physician. We don't 'stick' anything up anywhere. She is going to *examine* you to make sure you and your baby are okay. Now just relax and take some deep breaths, we'll get through this together. Your baby is having some problems and the doctor has to figure out why. And by the way, some boy got you pregnant so obviously someone has been in there before so..."

"Thank you, Rachel," Jeanine interrupted quickly before Rachel finished her vivid explanation. Rachel's heart was in the right place, but at times, she could be very blunt.

Jeanine donned sterile surgical gloves and examined Katy to see if her water had broken. She felt for the usual landmarks in the pelvis. They had guessed she was thirty-two to thirty-six weeks pregnant because Katy couldn't give more definite details about her last menstrual period and had failed to keep her appointments for an ultrasound. Jeanine hoped to feel a closed cervix; instead she felt the unmistakable hard skull of the baby. There was no protective placental membrane.

Jeanine had learned that patients could easily read her face. So she would never look them in the face while doing a pelvic exam. That way if she observed something abnormal she would not betray her feelings before she could collect her thoughts into a clear and cogent thought.

Consequently, she was looking right at Donovan who was standing by the windows to the patient's right. As Jeanine felt the skull, Donovan watched as she closed her eyes, knitted her eyebrows together and silently and slowly mouthed the word 'shit'. He kept his face steady so as not to betray what he knew, even as his stomach turned with the knowledge of the inevitable.

Jeanine shot up quickly and started giving calm and firm orders to Rachel. She did not want to alarm Katy.

"Rachel, page the on call OB faculty and tell him to get here STAT. While we are waiting for him please have radiology perform an ultrasound."

Jeanine felt all the color leave her face. She knew the baby was dead. It was just a matter of time before Katy knew. "What's wrong?" Katy asked nervously.

"Katy," Jeanine said calmly as she sat next to her on the bed, "when was the last time your baby moved?"

"I don't know, a few days ago, I guess. I don't really keep track of that stuff. Babies are born every day and they don't need no one counting' kicks and stuff. Why?"

Jeanine analyzed Katy to determine the best way to tell her this. There was no good way. Katy was not the hand holding type. She responded to authority not kindness. She was emotional, even on a good day, and very suspicious of doctors.

"Katy, I need to do an ultrasound of your baby. I think your baby is very sick."

"Ooh, on that ultrasound will I find out if it's a boy or a girl?"

"We might be able to tell. But I need you to hear me right now, Katy, your baby is sick. I don't think the baby's heart is beating."

Just then, Dr. Gregory arrived, the OB faculty. "Hey, what we got?" He asked matter-of-factly.

Jeanine showed her senior physician the chart and her findings. Dr. Gregory donned some sterile gloves and repeated Jeanine's exam to a much more sedate Katy who seemed intimidated by a male physician.

"Hunter, call the OR," he instructed as he completed his exam. He took Katy's chart and looked at the fetal monitoring strip. "All right Katy, Dr. Hunter has something to tell you about your baby," and he walked out without ever looking her in the eye. The doctors went outside.

"We got dead baby, Licious" Dr. Gregory announced as they left the room.

"Yes, sir," she said quietly.

"No fetal heart tones, she's been ruptured for at least a week by that smell, but since she's not contracting we gotta get the baby out before she gets septic, right?" he asked flatly. Dr. Gregory taught by doing. He was not big into didactic speeches.

"Yes, sir," she answered.

"Hey, perk up, this is an easy one. Not much to mess up," he said dryly.

"Meet me in the OR after you give her the news," as he slapped her on the back collegially.

Donovan studied Jeanine's face. He admired her for the work she did. His attraction to her was becoming stronger even though he denied it to himself. This was different than anything he had ever experienced with a woman. She was physically attractive but not the most beautiful woman he'd ever met. Yet none had ever tempted him in this way. There was something more: poise, grace, and dignity that overcame him.

Jeanine sighed and said a silent prayer before she went back in to give Katy the news. "Katy," she started slowly, "where is your family?"

"They ain't here. They say they ain't comin'," she replied. Jeanine sat on the bed next to her and repeated a silent mantra in her head: keep it simple, keep it simple, keep it simple. "Katy," Jeanine finally said, "your baby is dead."

"What? Why?" she asked in shock and fear.

"Katy, look at me. Since I have been your doctor, have I ever lied to you?" Jeanine asked.

"No," the child said shaking her head as tears fell down her cheeks.

"I don't know about your family. But whenever you needed me I have been there for you haven't I?"

"Uh-huh, yeah, I guess so," she answered nervously.

"Then listen to me now. Your baby is dead. No one knows why and we will probably never know. But your life is important. We have to get the baby out or you could get sick and die. Do you understand?"

"Mmmm hmmm," she muttered as her cheeks blushed crimson against her pale complexion.

Jeanine nodded silently, rose, and left the room to prep for the surgery. Katy was given an epidural injection for anesthesia and went through the delivery very calmly. It was a life changing moment for her. In one moment, she went from being a child to a woman, and she had to go through it alone. Only time would tell if this moment would mature her or devastate her. Jeanine hoped for the former.

After Katy's surgery, Dr. Gregory and Jeanine went to the postoperative unit to do paper work.

"Licious, I didn't know you were on OB call today," Gregory said as he wrote something illegible on the required hospital forms.

"I wasn't sir. They paged me because I was her primary care doctor and I happened to be in the building."

"Oh," he said, "well, it went as well as could be expected. It's good you were here though. She probably wouldn't have taken the news as well from a stranger. You did well in surgery; you should really think about OB/GYN instead of Family Medicine but we've already had that discussion. Anyway, good work, Licious." He announced in his flat tone as he did his characteristic slap on the back of the shoulder.

"Thank you, sir," she sighed as she finished her paperwork.

"Which resident is on call tonight, Rachel?" Dr. Gregory asked the nurse standing at the nurses' station, even though it wasn't Rachel. He only knew one nurse's name and that was Rachel's. He knew Rachel, he liked Rachel, and that's all he needed to know.

"It's Johnson. He's having some problems with another patient. She's going slowly," the nurse responded.

"Alright. Well, have him call me if he needs me. I'm going home," Gregory announced.

Jeanine peered at her pager. It was quiet. She hoped this meant her work for the night was done. It was about 22:00 now. Usually, service call can be handled from home via phone. Donovan addressed her.

"That was really..." he searched for the words

"Crazy?" she finished for him.

"How do you do this...?" he asked bewildered.

"And not go nuts?" she completed the question.

"Yeah,"

"Faith," she said simply.

"Faith?" he asked.

"Faith is a personal thing. It may appear as lunacy to you but to me it's perfectly clear. I have faith that I live for something bigger than all of this. Faith that I live for a purpose," she answered followed by a grimace forcing her to find the roll of Tums in her pocket.

"What's up with the Tums?" he asked with concern.

"Best case scenario? It's just indigestion or stress induced gastritis. Worst case scenario is an ulcer."

"And which do you have?"

"I've decided to call it stress induced gastritis"

"You've decided? Have you seen a doctor yourself?" he pressed. She smiled at him mischievously. "Are you kidding? They are all quacks!" she laughed.

"Doctors are the worst patients you know," he chided.

"You should take care of yourself," he said advisedly.

"Careful Donovan, it looks like you are worried about me."

"I am"

"And what does your rule book say about that? Aren't you crossing that line in the road again?"

"Haven't you noticed? I'm off the book Jeanine," he said definitively.

The tone in his voice caught her off guard. Something felt different. She could feel his attraction to her and for a moment she liked it. They slowly meandered back to the ICU. "Jeanine, what if your job, your faith, is causing your ulcer. Is it worth it? I mean, you seem pretty miserable doing this," he observed.

"Faith is not a feeling, Donovan, it's an decision. As a doctor, I see people act on their feelings all the time and it leads them into trouble. But God did not create us to be dominated by our emotions. I know this is a hard life I have chosen but I couldn't do anything else, even though *many* times I wish I could. It's who I am. Sometimes I hate parts of it but this is earth and not heaven. Nothing on this side of eternity is perfect."

He listened carefully and considered her reply. Then, he asked a more specific question. "Jeanine, what was that, with Dr. Snyder?" She swallowed. "You said you needed information from him," she answered.

"Yes, but there were many conversations going on in there. I feel like there's something between you two I'm unaware of."

"I dated his nephew for a while last year," she informed, "I don't think he approved."

"Jourdan?" Donovan asked.

She shot him a look, surprised that he was aware of Jourdan. Then she remembered he was privy to one of their conversations. "Yes, Jourdan. But we were more friends than anything romantic, actually." She said feeling a little embarrassed.

Donovan could see there was more to this than she was admitting.

"Was it helpful to know about his son?" she asked.

"Yes, I knew his son had been killed. I did not know it was in relationship to Colorado," Donovan admitted.

"When you mentioned Colorado's name yesterday it reminded me of it," she replied.

"Why do I get the sense you know something I do not?" he asked.

"Technically, I know a lot of things you do not," she said in a sultry tone. He grinned widely. She'd won that round.

Just then, Serena approached, "It's Mrs. Thibodeaux. She's awake and she wants to be extubated," Serena said somberly.

Donovan regarded Jeanine's face. She stood transfixed for a moment as though she had not heard what Serena had said. She did not even blink.

"Doc?" Serena asked bringing her back to reality.

"Yeah, ok," she finally said "I'll be there in second."

Donovan could see she was steadying herself. Then, as her mind acquiesced the reality of Mrs. Thibodeaux's wishes, she relaxed. She knew what she had to do. Jeanine soberly entered ICU room eleven and pulled back the curtain. In the room sat Mr. Thibodeaux and his two children.

"Hey doc," they said quietly. Mrs. Thibodeaux was awake and looking at her from her bed. Now that she was conscious, it was difficult to see her tortured by being attached to these machines. Donovan cringed at the image but he pushed through it.

Jeanine slowly walked to the bed and took Mrs. Thibodeaux's hand, "Are you sure this is what you want?" she asked already knowing the answer. Jeanine was really asking it for herself; she didn't want to lose her.

"We've already signed the papers, doc," her son announced. "We are ready for whatever happens."

Jeanine just kept looking at Mrs. Thibodeaux and thinking about his words 'whatever happens'. Jeanine had been with a lot of patients before they died. Some she had known only a little while and some she had known quite well; each experience with death was different. This one would be heartbreaking.

The respiratory therapists came in and helped Jeanine extubate Mrs. Thibodeaux. It was an ugly process. It involved the patient breathing out as hard as they could while the therapist pulled the tube from their throat. Everyone in the room held their breath hoping and praying she would breathe on her own after being removed from the ventilator.

A collective sigh of relief was released when she finally took a breath. That said, her breathing was agonal and harsh. It was obvious she did not have long to live. Jeanine left the room as the nurses gave Mrs. Thibodeaux a sponge bath and her family brushed her hair.

As Jeanine placed her hands on the ICU nurses' station counter, she felt physically ill. Of all the things going wrong around her, she still held the hope that Mrs. Thibodeaux would recover.

Mr. Thibodeaux came out of the room and spoke to her. "Doc, we want to thank you for all you have done," he said. He was a tall man, about 6'5" with a belly that hung ever so slightly over his pants. He was wearing a white shirt with pin stripes, neatly pressed charcoal colored pants, and burgundy suspenders with wide straps. There was a characteristic sweet and pungent aroma to his clothes like the smell of an old but well kept home. For many decades, he and his wife shared one of Galveston's characteristically brightly painted 19th century colonial homes.

"Yes, sir," she answered respectfully.

"We want her to be comfortable now," he said firmly. He was a quiet man but his manner was straight and good.

"I will move her to one of the hospice rooms on the eighth floor. No one will disturb her and she can rest. It also has room for your family and you can be with her more comfortably."

"That would be nice," he said thankfully. Jeanine went back into Mrs. Thibodeaux's room. She mustered what happiness she could and put on a brave face.

"Hey sweetheart," Jeanine smiled. "We're going to move you to the penthouse," she finished, but not before tears welled up in her eyes.

"No baby," Mrs. Thibodeaux instructed, "don't you cry for me. I'm ready to die." Mrs. Thibodeaux's throat was sore from the tube being in her throat and it was hard for her to speak.

"I have lived my life and I'm going home to the Lord!" she exclaimed as she panted a little.

Her children tried to quiet her. "It's okay momma. Save your strength, don't get upset," they instructed.

Mrs. Thibodeaux raised her thin, feeble little hand and quieted them. "I'm alright...I'm not upset. I'm happy!" she said slowly as her elderly voice cracked. "We have been fightin' for a long time to be seen as equals in this country! I have seen my dreams come true in my children and in this girl, this woman, this doctor! The Lord has granted me the time to see it all happen and babies this is a time to rejoice!" she said looking at her family.

Her daughter approached her and held her hand. Mrs. Thibodeaux returned her attention to Jeanine; storing up some breaths before speaking again. "My time is short, baby. But I gotta tell you this, don't let them assholes take your joy from you!" she said with a smile.

Jeanine smiled back at her. "No ma'am. I won't let them," she said assuredly.

"You did not lose me honey," Mrs. Thibodeaux continued, "don't let anybody tell you different, not even yourself. You can't lose what was never, ever yours! This is my life. God gave it and God can have it back."

+++++

Jeanine arranged Mrs. Thibodeaux's transfer to the hospice wing. There were cherry wood stained cabinets, hardwood floors, large comfortable beds, and extra large sofas that held pullout beds so that her loved ones could be with her. These were private rooms built for one thing and one thing only: to allow people to die with dignity.

Jeanine especially admired the large vases of lilies that decorated the hallway. The space felt more like a bed and breakfast than a hospital room. Jeanine knew her patient's time would be short, but she wanted Mrs. Thibodeaux to die with dignity and peace. It was easy to see that her family appreciated the change, as they seemed more at ease. Jeanine remained in the hallway until Mrs. Thibodeaux was settled in.

Donovan observed Jeanine admiring the flowers in the vases along the hallway especially the gardenias. "It's my favorite flower," she said noticing him in her peripheral vision. "They are small and unassuming but their scent is so powerful." He only nodded in response.

"Doctor?" a nurse called to Jeanine, "You should come now."

She and Donovan returned to Mrs. Thibodeaux's room. Her breaths had become agonal and shallow. The sound of each inspiration was anxiety provoking to her family because the time between breaths was getting longer and longer. As the carbon dioxide levels in her blood rose, she lost consciousness.

It was the body's way of calming the mind and stilling the body. The room, otherwise, was quite peaceful. Mr. Thibodeaux held his wife's hand and said to her, "Thank you baby. Thank you for being my wife. It's all right now. You can go home, baby."

With that, as if waiting for her husband's release, she slipped away. There were tears but no hysterics, shouting, or anger. Mrs. Thibodeaux's life ended in the same dignified way she had lived. Jeanine rose silently and opened the window to Mrs. Thibodeaux's room. The chancellor was summoned to be with the family and pray with them. Jeanine slipped out to let them grieve alone. She went to a window down the hall as tears flowed freely down her face. Her heart ached.

"Come with me," Donovan instructed as he took her hand in his. She yielded to his direction, as he took her to the top floor of the Shriner's Hospital for burned children.

It was a separate facility, connected to the main hospital by a causeway suspended above Market Street. It was one of the tallest buildings on the Island and the top floor had 360 degree panoramic views of the entire Island via floor to ceiling windows. A large harvest moon loomed on the horizon above the ocean. It was the largest and brightest moon she had ever seen; it hung in the crystal-clear sky, bright and so close one could almost touch it.

"This is my favorite place," she whispered.

"Yes, I know," Donovan said, "a little bird told me you spent a lot of time here." She nodded in agreement perceiving Serena had been his informant. At this time of night, they were the only two people present.   Silver moonlight filled the room with radiance almost as bright as the sun and silhouetted them against the window.

Silent tears ran down her cheek as she thought of Mrs. Thibodeaux. It saddened her that she was gone. The world was less special now because her kind soul was not in it. Jeanine felt the need to fall into someone, to give her heart to someone, to let someone take care of her. She was not sure if this need was driven by the wild emotions of the night, loneliness, or fatigue but she knew it was right.   She felt contaminated with the dirt of humanity; a million showers could not cleanse her. She walked to the glass and pressed her hand against it, feeling the coldness against her palm.

Donovan, sensing her needs, came to her. She could feel the closeness of his chest to her back. For both of them, the voice of caution was over ruled by the manifold attraction they shared for each other. Donovan pulled her to him and held her in his arms as she sobbed silently into his chest. It was, perhaps to most, a small thing. But to each of them, it was more profound and intimate than anything they'd ever experienced. He held her silently as they were bathed in silver moonlight reflecting off of the night's sea.

CHAPTER 21
THE SHAKE UP

The following day Donovan and Jeanine rounded with her team. She informed them of the night's events. The team started the month with 18 patients. Between discharges and deaths, only Mr. Graham and Mr. Morrow remained. Given this fact and after her experience on call, Dr. Rucker had pity and gave Jeanine the rest of the day off.

Before leaving, Jeanine went to Mrs. Thibodeaux's room in bed 11. They had moved Mr. Graham into it after she had moved upstairs to the hospice floor. As she looked over Mr. Graham's chart, Donovan took the opportunity to call his agents at the warehouse to check in on some things. Jeanine was paged overhead. Donovan was a good ten feet from her and had a clear view of her face as she spoke on the phone.

"Dr. Hunter?" a male voice asked Jeanine.

"Yes, this is Dr. Hunter," she replied distractedly while hurriedly signing orders from the night before. She wanted to get out of the hospital as soon as possible.

"Do you realize where you are standing?" the voice asked.

"What? Who is this?" she asked feeling irritated.

"That question is irrelevant. Do you realize where you are standing?" She looked around her curiously, wondering who was playing a joke on her.

"Do you realize where you are standing?" the male voice asked again.

"I know where I am, who is this?" she answered getting frustrated.

"That is still the wrong question. Tell me, is that FBI agent still facing you?" Her eyes grew wide and her countenance changed.

"Is he watching the expression on your face change from frustration to absolute horror?" the voice asked. In that second she met Donovan's gaze and he knew she needed him. He flew across the room. "What's wrong?" Donovan demanded. He pulled the receiver down so that he could hear the conversation. Jeanine's heart was racing at the thought that someone was watching her.

"Good morning Agent Donovan. We just wanted the doctor to know that she is standing in the room where we killed her patient."

Jeanine felt her knees grow weak. This had been David Scott's room-ICU bed 11.

"What do you want?" she asked.

"That is the right question. We want to know everything you have told the FBI and everything they have told you. We want you to know that we can reach you any time and any place. We can get to you and to your father, your mother, and your sisters. We will be in touch and we expect your full cooperation."

If the acid in her stomach had not been churning before it was definitely burning now. She was trembling, her hands were sweating and she felt flushed. Donovan sat her down in a chair in the corner of the room. Fortunately, Mr. Graham was unconscious and no one else was close by enough to have heard their conversation. Donovan's movements were precise as he took charge of the situation. He took the receiver from her and dialed the operator.

"Who paged Dr. Hunter to this number?" He was informed it was an outside line and was untraceable. He then called his team into action. "O'Donnell, get a trace on this phone. Find out who just called. Someone has made contact with Hunter. Also, trace any and all calls to and from Dr. Snyder. I don't want him to piss unless I know about it first."

He looked at Jeanine. She was still unsettled but more in control. "Jeanine, I need to get you out of here. We're going back to the nest." She nodded silently in agreement. After their arrival, Jeanine recounted the details of the call to the agents. They went over the details a few times with her before excusing her to Donovan's office to rest on a cot in the corner of his office.

"You can get some rest here. Try to sleep," O'Donnell instructed. "I'll try," she said feebly. He patted her arm reassuringly. "Don't worry. We'll find out who is doing this. We are one step closer to catching Colorado and ending this. You're doing great," he encouraged. He gave her a blanket and joined his team.

Donovan addressed the team. "Analysis," he demanded.

"Someone has been watching us watch her. And we must have rattled someone's cage because they think she knows something and they are willing to blow their secrecy to find out." O'Donnell said.

"Affirmative," Donovan responded, "Lorna, what do get out of this?"

"Sir?" she answered meekly.

"What is your psychological analysis of what just happened?" Woo looked around in confusion. Glenn looked at her and in his eyes said, 'Come on Woo! Think!' But her time to shine passed.

"Glenn?" Donovan pressed, displeased with Woo's hesitation. "I think it's the shrink, sir. The guy was messing with her head. It was obvious he wanted to rattle her. Plus, she really pissed him off yesterday. I don't think it's a coincidence that she got this call today" Glenn stated with military sharpness.

"Very good, Jake. I concur" Donovan added.

"Do we have a lock on Snyder yet?" Donovan asked.

"His office says he is out of town on vacation. I don't have a position on him" Glenn replied.

"Well get one!" Donovan instructed sharply, "he's our best lead so far."

He noted Swenson was detached and silent. He had done this job long enough to know she was more than dissatisfied. She had a reputation of being power hungry. She was looking for a case to make her mark. Donovan pressed her in order to expose her motives.

"Swenson" Donovan patronized, "are you planning to participate in this investigation?"

"I think your obvious feelings for the suspect have clouded your judgment. My duty calls me to question your decisions and to report your inadequacies to the appropriate committee."

By this statement, it was obvious that she had already surreptitiously reported her findings to someone; the question was to whom and when and if their response was worth consideration.

He spoke with a disarmingly calm eloquence. "And what do you plan to report to the Special Agent in Charge, Mellicent? That I am working a mark? That I am using appropriate and acceptable methods to accomplish a task? And, by using such tactics I have accomplished more on this case than any one else could have done? I don't think the SAC at the Houston field office would appreciate your interruption into his already busy schedule."

He was as smooth as silk making Swenson's protestations appear illegitimate and saccharin. She was unsettled by his calmness. She had expected a violent and physical protest from Donovan. He held a commanding presence punctuated with clairvoyance and finesse. But she would not easily succumb.

"What?' she asked, as she walked toward him provocatively, "no quaint well rehearsed chide? No oversimplified catch phrase like, 'come at me with all you've got or tangle with me and you will always lose' or some such? Donovan, I'm disappointed," she taunted.

"Furthermore, if you think the local SAC is as high as my reach goes you are mistaken!" she continued.

Glenn and Woo were highly uncomfortable. Woo backed away from the table; she expected Donovan to launch at Mellicent and snap her head off of her shoulders. Glenn walked toward the table hypnotized like someone drawn to the sight of a train wreck; wanting to look away but unable to pull his attention away from the horror.

But Donovan was in command of himself. There were no fireworks, no hot words, and no emphatic speech. Furthermore, Donovan knew most of the SAC's and had a good relationship with them. He also knew many of the deputy directors in Washington. She had already betrayed that she had not contacted the Special Agent in Charge. She was easily manipulated. Her arrogance was her weakness.

"Mellicent, you must do what you think is appropriate. That is all I have ever hoped to teach any of the agents under my charge. If you believe I have acted in a way that is dishonorable to this position, it is your right and your duty to report me. Now, if you will excuse me…"

"Wait!" she yelled angrily. "I'm not finished with you!" she yelled blithely. She had rehearsed all that she would say and she had not gotten to the end of it yet.

"You are a poor excuse for an agent and you don't deserve to be in command. I will prove, once and for all, this bitch you have obviously lost sight of is a murdering tramp and I'll send her to prison where she belongs!"

O'Donnell was very impressed with Donovan at this point. He could see what Mellicent was trying to do and she was failing. The thing about Donovan is that he could get inside of your head with a look, an expression, or a simple phrase that would annoy the hell out of you. And he could do it without raising his voice; he could just use his presence. That is what he had done with all of the agents. With his peaceful reply, he had diffused a situation that had all the potential of becoming violent and, if it had been up to Mellicent, it would have been.

She wanted him to become violent to prove to Glenn and Woo that he was irrational and dangerous. But, he proved the contrary. He was very much in control and she looked hysterical and power hungry. In a last effort, she suddenly came at him but he seamlessly caught her by the throat and pressed his thumb to her carotid artery.

"I could break your neck right now and I'd have every right to. The next time you come at me, you'd better know what you are doing," Donovan informed. He released her and Mellicent stormed out of the warehouse coughing and rubbing her neck.

Donovan addressed Woo, Glenn, and O'Donnell. He sighed slowly and thought about the mistakes he had made in handling this case.

"I want you all to listen to what I have to say. I am not a man that apologizes often. But when I make a mistake, I admit it and I correct it. I have not handled this case to the best of my ability. Looking back, I see things now that I did not see before. That is a fact that comes with all cases and you have to learn to adapt. But what I see now is that I should have made all of you more involved in this case. I tackled it as though it was my own and that you were along for the ride.   I have not communicated well and that has left room for derision."

Donovan leaned casually against one of the large metal desks, folded his arms across his chest, and stroked the goatee ruefully. He spoke slowly and to each of them.

"In the next few days, you are going to see a lot happen. Many things will be asked of you, chiefly your loyalty to me, to the Bureau, to this case, and to yourselves. What I said to Swenson is what I meant. At the end of the day, you have to answer to yourself and to God. Your choice to follow me or not to follow me should not be made flippantly.

You have to be able to answer whether or not I have acted according to the principles and responsibilities given to me as your commander. You may not agree with all or any of my decisions but you should be able to respect them. If you cannot, then we have a problem; we are not a team. From this moment, I need you to act like a team to find out who is trying to abduct Dr. Hunter and who absconded with David Scott's organs. That's it. It's that simple. Everything else is politics."

They each nodded their heads affirmatively. Donovan gave them specific tasks. Jake Glenn was sent to find out how and why encrypted phone calls were leaving the hospital and who was making them. He was also assigned to interrogate Monica, who had been in the FBI safe house on the Island, and to delineate what Monica had told Snyder about Jeanine.

Lorna Woo was assigned to profile all of the doctors working with Jeanine including Dr. Snyder. And Ben O'Donnell was sent to do some undercover work regarding Colorado's organization. Donovan needed him to engage the criminal underworld and determine who was selling organs on the black market; he also needed him to work their South American contacts for more intel on the ever-elusive Carlos Colorado. Donovan set out to communicate with the FBI SAC in Houston for more support. He knew he would need more agents than those assigned to him. It was very clear that Swenson had leaked information to Dr. Snyder about the case. This is how he knew about Monica being in their custody. Now the question was why.

"Sir, might I make a suggestion?" Woo asked uncertainly. She looked like a doe standing up for the first time on unsteady legs. "I believe Dr. Hunter is at a breaking point and that will not help us very much if she succumbs."

The room waited with held breath as Donovan thought quietly. "Alright," Donovan replied, "what do you suggest?"

"She needs some time to recover. Maybe some time with her family? Or some time away from the hospital?" Donovan thought for a while.

"Good idea, Woo. I will have a list of things I will need. I will discuss them with you later. Thank you." He stated.

She sighed in relief as Donovan passed by. She had gotten something right. The feeling was intoxicating.

Donovan had to swallow a lot of pride to admit all of this. But he had to be honest with himself before he could be honest with them otherwise he would lose them. He was frustrated with himself, more than his team would ever know. He had already lost this team. To have an agent in your charge question your authority openly is one thing, but to have the agent already going above your head without any sense of fear but with pure disdain was a failure in itself.

Mellicent was not the kind of agent to announce she was staging a coup. She had already contacted whatever powers she had in the Bureau and it was just a matter of time before he would be out of a job and she would have his position. He figured he only had a week before the shake-up would happen. He was frustrated that he could not have prevented this from happening. But he knew what wheels to put into motion to defend himself. He had worked long enough in the FBI to have many friends.

Maybe if he had not been distracted with his feelings for Jeanine he could have seen this coming earlier. He was sacrificing a lot for her. Was she worth it? He still believed there were things she was hiding from him that she was not admitting.

If Renee was there she would have said, "I told you so! I told you this case would envelop you. I told you that you would lose yourself in this one" followed swiftly by a "Pull your head out of your ass and start thinking like an agent, dip shit!" And of course she would be right. As he dealt with these internal demons he caught Ben looking at him from the corner of his eye.

"I am curious. It's no secret that you have never been my biggest fan. What side of the line are you leaning toward?" Donovan asked.

189

O'Donnell looked Donovan up and down before he spoke. He answered, but in no particular hurry. He had learned from Donovan that speech was a form of control and speaking slowly held a power all its' own.

"I need to hear it from the horse's mouth. I need to know how good of an actor you are. Do you only see Jeanine as a mark, bait, or?" He did not finish the question. He did not have to. Among men of honor, some things need not be said or even asked.

Donovan was wise enough to see the origin of this question. As an undercover agent, you can lose yourself in a part or you can become so antisocial that you don't care who you are lying to or what you are lying about. Jake wanted to know if Donovan was a good agent or a good man. The two issues were often mutually exclusive.

O'Donnell continued, "If you tell me you have been using her to advance your career, I can accept that, but you are an asshole. If you tell me you have fallen for her and you have no idea of what you are doing, I can accept that, but you are an idiot. So I just gotta know, are you an asshole or an idiot? Either way, I would not follow Swenson, she's fuckin' crazy. But I would like to know the truth."

On the surface, he seemed to be nonchalant and indifferent. But in reality, Ben O'Donnell was invested in Jeanine and wanted the best for her. Donovan looked O'Donnell squarely in the face.

"What do you think?" Donovan asked.

Ben, unabashed said, "I think you had every intention of fucking her. Whether that was literally or figuratively, I don't think it mattered much to you in the beginning. Now things are different. She's part of this somehow, but not the way the Bureau thought. Now you're into her, she's into you, and Swenson has you by the balls. So what do I think? I think I'd like to know what you're gonna do chief?"

Donovan looked at O'Donnell approvingly. Donovan could see some of the useless arrogance in O'Donnell he used to admire in himself years ago. Donovan only smiled with equal arrogance and said nothing further. The smile conferred all he was going to say, which was he was in control. It was one of those moments that words would only pollute rather than clarify. Ben was satisfied.

CHAPTER 22
BURIAL

The next few hours passed slowly, day became night and then day again. Donovan had been up most of the night doing research and speaking with his sub-commander. He rose early the next morning and gently woke Jeanine. She was sleeping soundly but not peacefully. Before rousing her, he thought of their last night together. He knew he was in love with her. His mind tried to deny it; but his heart would not let him. But he wondered if she knew it. And if so, would she honor or betray his emotions? Would she return them?

Jeanine's pager rang out and she woke to Donovan's gaze as he stood over her. Her body ached as she awoke on Donovan's uncomfortable cot. Donovan handed her the phone and immediately began the recording device attached to it as she returned the page.

"Do you recognize the number?" he inquired as the phone rang.

"Yes, it's from President Sardo's office."

"Don't mention anything about yesterday," he instructed.

She nodded and waited for Sardo to answer. O'Donnell, Glenn, and Woo joined them donning headphones to listen to the conversation.

"Good morning, Jeanine. I have some news for you," President Sardo chirped brightly.

"Yes, sir" she replied surprised at his joviality.

"I don't know if you have been keeping up with Mr. Scott's family, but they have decided to proceed with his funeral and I would like you to attend."

"What?" she said barely above a whisper as her heart sank into her chest.

"Yes, the family has let out a press release. They initially wanted to wait until the FBI closed the case but due to various events, they have changed their minds. I think it would be a good gesture if you attended the service."

She gripped the phone firmly and tightly shut her eyes. Waves of anguish were flooding over her. As much as she loved David, she could not go to his funeral.

"Sir, I really don't want to go," she insisted, "besides the FBI might have an objection to my attendance." She eyed Donovan to see if this was the case. His silence on the subject did not support her hopes.

"I'm sure I can persuade them. It's just a funeral, after all. The hospital has already sent flowers and cards in anticipation of your arrival. Your attendance will hopefully sooth any hostility the family may have."

"Sir, I can't..."

He interrupted. "Thank you Dr. Hunter. Your cooperation in this matter is greatly appreciated. I have already spoken to Dr. Rucker and he is aware of your absence for the next several days." He hung up.

It was not a request that she attend the service. It was an order. She held the phone a long time after he had hung up. She slowly replaced the receiver on the phone. Donovan carefully regarded her as she listened to the soft click the phone made as she returned it to its base and studied the phone as it rested in its cradle.

When she finally returned his gaze, he felt captured by her large brown eyes. They were like endless pools of innocence and he felt deeply compelled, from somewhere deep within, to protect her. She seemed almost transparent, ghost-like with the knowledge of what she had to do. She was overwhelmed but in control of herself.

For Donovan's part, he knew this was an opportunity to flush out any potential assailants. From his experience as an Agent, he knew the noose was tightening around Jeanine. There were too many loose ends; too many ways she could be hurt and too many factors that were beyond his control or knowledge. While he was confident he could protect her he was unconvinced that she was prepared to be bait.

Meanwhile, several agents from the Houston FBI field office had arrived downstairs. He assigned two of them to escort Jeanine back home. Donovan had done his homework on the Island. He prepped the twenty agents that had been assigned to him from the

Houston SAC for the op. He wanted tight surveillance and wanted it to be obvious she was being protected by anyone who would be looking for it. This would be followed by an opportunity that would appear less guarded and the perfect chance for potential assailants to make a mistake.

He engaged the agents in a large room with slides and maps showing the entire Island and their points of interest.

"David Scott was Catholic and the funeral will be a traditional mass at Sacred Heart Church located at 1302 Broadway. The church is well over one hundred years old; originally established in 1884. It had been destroyed in the Great Storm of 1900. The current structure was erected in 1903. It's a sound structure and there is a lot of street access. I want every entrance to be covered. I also want agents across the street at the Bishop's Palace and across Broadway," he announced as he pointed at the illustrations.

"Do you suspect sniper activity will be an issue?" O'Donnell asked.

"I suspect everything," Donovan answered sharply. His response awakened the sleepy audience with a snap-to like quality.

He continued, "every detail from the ceremony to the internment needs to be prepped. O'Donnell, I want you on point for the op. I want your eyes open for anyone or anything out of the ordinary."

"Do you think the guys that killed Scott are going to be at his funeral?" Glenn asked slightly perplexed.

"That is affirmative. This is an unusual case so anything can happen. For lack of a better word, she has become the bait and we need to see how others react to her."

"Then, I'd like to volunteer to guard the suspect," Glenn continued nervously with as his cheeks blushed.

"Suspect? No, Agent Glenn, I think our perspective has changed. Dr. Hunter is no longer a suspect. If anything, she is a witness and needs protection. In that regard, I will continue my role of direct surveillance and protection. Whoever is behind the phone call she received yesterday and, I suspect, this sudden development regarding Mr. Scott's funeral will be looking for a change in our normal operating procedures. I need all of you to keep our top priority in mind which is to end Carlos Colorado," his words hung in the air as the realization of what was happening finally donned on the twenty or so agents in the briefing room.

"This is not just a routine action. This may be a moment that defines your careers as agents. Colorado is not just another perp to be marked off a list. This one is personal. He has killed many of my friends and your predecessors and if left up to him he will kill you. Unless we stop him first. Prepare well."

They only had twenty-four hours to prepare. Donovan was thankful for the structure of the Catholic Church. It lent very little in the way of flexibility. Everything would be well organized and coordinated, as it had been done for centuries. To keep as much control as possible, he made sure the media was banned from the ceremony. One of the first things Renee had taught him was to control the media as they could make or break a case.

According to plan, he and Jeanine arrived at the church very early before any one else. Upon entering the church, instantly, they were transported back in time. Sacred Heart church was living, breathing history. It was an architecturally beautiful structure and different than any other edifice on the Island.

Jeanine revered the statues and seamless lines of the building, running her hand along one of the columns outside that lined the entrance outside front door. She thought about all of the changes this church had seen; all of lives that had come through these doors, all of the joy and pain, the rise and fall of the Island, and the many, many storms.

As she entered the great hall, the only sound she heard was the echo of her high-heeled shoes on the glistening, rich, hardwood floors. Wooden pews created a long aisle leading to the altar. Above the altar was a statue of Jesus and his Sacred Heart. There were pristine white arches supported by grand alabaster columns aligned in perfect symmetry. She admired the elegant stained-glass windows. Jeanine deeply breathed the air and even it seemed from an older time. She felt the presence of all those who had gone before and all those that had lived and breathed and scratched out an existence for themselves on this Island; this Island that was so well defined by its dichotomy. It was full of dreams and nightmares, life and death, renewal and extinction. It held the blessings and curses of the Sea.

Sacred Heart Church was able to accommodate the well over three hundred guests in attendance. Jeanine sat in the back of the church hoping not to be noticed. She was still concerned about the call she'd received a few days ago. Donovan had not spoken to her about it. But she could hear parts of conversations and could read the agents well enough to know that her being out in the open was as much of a concern as it was an opportunity. There were agents in plain clothes as well as suited ones with concealed weapons. Fortunately, the guests in attendance thought it had everything to do with David and no idea it was all about Jeanine.

If the threat of death was not enough to make her uncomfortable, she had to contend with David's family. Over the last year, she had come to know David's parents very well and was fond of them. However, since David's death, his mother Florence had grown to despise Jeanine. Florence blamed her for calling them too late to say goodbye to David and in her grief, she had convinced herself that Jeanine was at fault for David's death. Despite President Sardo's directive to actively engage the family, Jeanine planned to do everything in her power to avoid them.

She tried to remain inconspicuous by sitting as far back as possible and wearing a classic black sleeveless cocktail dress. It was the first time Donovan had seen her wearing anything besides scrubs. He had noticed her beauty before but today, despite her sadness, she was stunning. The length of the skirt was just above the knees and the heels she was wearing accentuated her shapely calves. She was modestly dressed but an elegant woman in modest attire is more attractive than an indiscreet woman dressed seductively. It was just enough to make him want to see more.

The funeral mass started promptly at 10 A.M. Quiet sobs could be heard throughout the sanctuary. Although the family had requested the mass to be delivered in Latin, the funeral coordinator had made an error and asked it to be delivered in Spanish. The crowd murmured for a while, but since all masses follow the same routine, no one objected and the mass proceeded.

Interestingly, Donovan noticed that Jeanine followed the ceremony quite easily even though she was neither Catholic nor spoke Spanish. At least, that had been his assumption. Silent tears fell down her face as the mass proceeded. She thought of David's life and the tragic way it was taken.

As much as she tried to conceal her grief, she ached with sadness. She didn't know how much longer she could silently sit in this pew. Just when she thought she would go running from the church, she felt Donovan's hand on top of hers. He peered into her eyes and felt her misery. He was perhaps the only person in that room who knew the extent of her heartache. He wrapped his arm around her shoulders as she laid her head on his chest. He was her tether to stability and she needed him.

The service ended as the priest blessed the casket with holy water. Jeanine had never been to a Catholic funeral mass. She was glad that the body had been viewed the previous night at the wake. She knew she couldn't handle viewing the body. Though she had experienced death and loss several times and in several ways, this was exquisitely painful.

When the ceremony ended, it was almost noon and the full, unrelenting heat of the sun was upon the parishioners. This time of year, due to Galveston's tropical climate, it was not uncommon for the heat of the day to evaporate enough moisture to produce an afternoon storm. The burial was to take place at Calvary Catholic Cemetery on 65th Street. She really didn't want to go, but Donovan persuaded her to attend.

It was the right thing to do. It was a chapter that needed to be closed. As though perceiving the sadness of the event, thick black cumulonimbus clouds emerged from the Gulf as the funeral procession made its slow, trek down Broadway Avenue. Gradually, a heavy rain erupted as the solemn procession of slowly moving headlights led by a pair of motorcycle police officers inched its way through the Galveston streets. In respect of the ceremony, opposing traffic pulled over as the mourners proceeded to the cemetery. This was a southern tradition Donovan considered polite and honorable.

David was interred in the family mausoleum, and just as promptly the rainstorm had emerged, it ceased. In its wake was the choking mosquito-laced, thick, hot humid air. While hundreds of guests attended the mass, less than fifty attended the interment. Therefore, Jeanine's hope for discretion was lost. She made eye contact with David's mother and the resultant confrontation was inevitable. Knowing this was a possibility Jeanine had prepared a few words of consolation.

"It was a very nice service," Jeanine stated as the words choked from her throat.

"What are you doing here? My son would still be alive today if it weren't for you!" Florence vehemently exclaimed as she tried to approach Jeanine.

But her high-heeled shoes kept getting stuck in the mud and thick grass of the cemetery so that every step looked like she was walking through wet cement. Her arms were flailing in all directions as she tried to keep her balance and with each step an increasing amount of mud was thickly encased on her shoes. In any other context, the scene would have been comical but currently it was horrific. Jeanine was taken aback by her outburst but remained flinty.

"I'm sure he is at peace. I wish there was something I could do to ease your pain."

"At peace? Ease my pain? He's in pieces thanks to you! You want to do something for me? Give my son back. Give back those moments you stole!" she shouted vehemently.

Jeanine absorbed the verbal blow gracefully. Carl, Florence's husband, placed a hand on her shoulder signaling her to stop. His somber eyes made contact with Jeanine's. It was enough.

Jeanine backed away and left them in peace. Donovan walked with her, his hand calmly placed in the center of her back. He made a signal with his hand as they approached his car and about ten well-hidden agents emerged almost magically ready to depart. They were hidden behind trees, garbage cans, and even headstones. She sat in Donovan's car staring blankly at the dashboard as he discussed his plan of action with his field crew. Most of the detail returned to the nest. Jeanine was unsure of where the rest went; she assumed they were released to some other errand. She felt empty, detached, and vacant. Donovan started the car and proceeded to the Seawall.

"What are we doing here?" she asked after they'd been parked there for several minutes. It took a while before she even realized the car had stopped.

"Let's go for a walk," he instructed as he opened her car door.

"Is that safe?" she asked tentatively looking around skeptically.

"I am an FBI agent you know," he winked, "come on."

He was a difficult man to refuse.

After a few yards of walking on the hot sidewalk of the Seawall, Donovan decided it was much too hot for dress clothing. They stripped off their shoes, quickly ran across the scorching hot sand, and made their way to the wet sand nearest the water. Here, close to the water, the breeze was the strongest and the welcome shade of the partially clouded sky made the heat bearable.

Jeanine enjoyed the feel of the waves and the foam that came up and tickled her toes. Donovan had chosen a relatively secluded part of beach near the west end of the Island. Since it was near the end of summer, there were fewer tourists and the beaches were less touristy. They must have walked for over a mile before speaking.

"Thank you," she finally said "for everything."

He didn't answer. The roar of the ocean filled her ears. The kiss of the wind was against her face. For a moment, Donovan considered what it would have been like to meet her as a regular person and not as a suspect. He shook it off when he realized she had noticed him watching her.

"We should get back," he advised.

Looking down at her watch she answered, "Oh, has my tenure as bait ended?"

He smiled and chuckled a little. "What made you think you were bait, Jeanine?" he asked slyly interested to hear her answer.

"While you have advised me that I can't get you to divulge anything you would prefer not to, I am quite sure that this escapade was an attempt to… let's say create an opportunity?" she asked.

He stopped and turned to face her. "Alright, you're right. I didn't want you to worry but that's exactly what you were today. Now, if it's all the same to you, since no one has capitalized on this investment I'd like to get you back to the nest. I need to plan our next move."

"Really? So you have suspects to interrogate or something?" she chided suspecting he didn't.

"Alright smart ass," he smiled back furtively, "let's get ice cream."

"You eat ice cream?" she asked skeptically.

"As long as it's not mint chocolate chip," he answered lightly.

This made her recall a moment earlier in their relationship when he mentioned how he hated mint with chocolate. She realized she hadn't eaten all day, so by the time they got to the ice cream parlor on Galveston's historic Strand she was starving.

"Do you like your work?" she asked as they made their way to the counter.

"It's work," he replied.

"That's not a yes," she noted.

"It's not a no, either"

"You have the tendency of speaking but saying nothing."

"It's a gift" he smiled back.

"And so modest! I'm speechless," she retorted feigning shock.

La Kings was a short walk down the Galveston Strand. It was a throwback to the early 20th century style soda shops. They made ice cream on site, had an authentic 1920's soda machine for sodas and malts and even made their own salt-water taffy. Everything was authentic to the creaks in the hard wood floors to the soda jerks. They each got ice cream cones and sat at one of the quaint tables in front of the shop.

"Thanks for ice cream," she said gratefully. "You didn't have to do this"

"Please stop thanking me. You make me feel like I'm a decent human being."

"Aren't you?" she asked curiously.

"Sometimes," he replied knowing this would peak her interest and perhaps get her to open up.

She eyed him curiously.

"Do you ever answer a question honestly?" she asked.

"I never speak in absolute terms but I get as close as I can."

"As close as I can?" she repeated.

She wrinkled her forehead sensing an issue behind his response.

"That sounds like avoidance," she informed analytically making him feel uncomfortable.

"No, not really" he said somewhat nonchalantly, trying not to feel drawn in by her.

"Is that a fear of commitment?" she asked surprised at her own curiosity.

He smiled, despite himself and said, "I never trust people who think in absolutes."

"Never?" she asked as she mocked him for using the word 'never'.

"Usually," he replied.

"Why not?"

"People who think in absolute terms do so because they are either unwilling or unable to accept reality. The truth is that life is gray and not black and white. There are only a few true absolutes in this world: God, death, and taxes. Besides, it only takes once to eternally transform what was never into sometimes, twice to turn sometimes into often, and three times to change often into always."

"So, when does always become never again?" she mused happily enjoying the conversation.

"Usually never," he replied in like fashion with a bright smile.

"Never?" she asked with a raised eyebrow.

"Well, sometimes" he replied.

They equally enjoyed the flirtation in their tennis-match-like banter. He loved watching her facial expressions and especially her eyes. Those gorgeous eyes could say a thousand things all at once while she never uttered a word. It was not so much the dark almond color that captured him but it was what they represented.

Of all the souls he had met, she had a pure heart. She felt deeply and she gave to others with the same passion. Her ability to weather the verbal assault by Florence Scott earlier today was compelling. He knew the depth of Jeanine's sorrow; he had felt the poignancy of it himself. Yet, she rallied from that place of misery to a state of peace. Where bitterness could, and in others, would have crept in she had kept it at bay. And now, here she was in plain sight willing to be a target to help him solve a crime. She fascinated him.

After finishing their much-needed frosted treat, they walked along the Strand admiring the different shops. A light and calming rain began to fall; it fell hard enough to wet but not soak them.

"Did you order this too?" she asked referring to the rain. "Is this cleansing enough for you?"

"Almost, it needs to come down a little bit harder for my taste," he replied admiring the gentle fall of the mist. She regarded him thinking how perfectly and irresistibly arrogant he was. She was feeling increasingly more comfortable with him. She let herself imagine what it would be like to be a part of his life. Forgetting, momentarily, the current context of the situation and allowed herself to   wonder.

CHAPTER 23
THE TROUBLE WITH BAIT

They walked on for a few more moments before returning to Donovan's car. Upon their approach two men flanked them. With great celerity, one of them pulled Jeanine by the arm while the other attacked Donovan with a knife. Donovan subdued his foe with his own weapon, killing him quickly with a slice to the neck; preventing him from crying out and calling attention. Instantly, the crew that had been following Donovan and Jeanine sprang into action.

Meanwhile, the other assailant had forced Jeanine down an ally. A third man joined them as they nudged her forward while holding a knife to her side. A shot rang out and the man holding her slumped, dropping his weapon. He'd been shot in the head. The Agents quickly surrounded them and handcuffed the third assailant to take him back to headquarters.

Donovan recovered Jeanine, "are you alright?" He asked quickly as he took her by the shoulder and looked her over. "I'm...I'm ok," she stammered.

"But you're bleeding!" she exclaimed seeing the blood on his hands. She took off the scarf she had been wearing and dabbed the blood away from his hands looking for a contusion.

"It's not mine," he said as he stilled her hands that were busily searching for his wound. Something about his tone made her shudder. She knew he had just killed someone. She looked into his eyes and blinked back in silence. All the breath left her chest.

"Jake, let's get to the nest," Donovan commanded as his crew cleaned up any evidence of their presence and rounded up any other possible suspects or conspirators. Everything happened so quickly, Jeanine wasn't even sure anyone else had seen what had happened. Her head was spinning.

They returned to their headquarters. Donovan decided to keep the twenty agents from Houston under his command. The situation on the Island was intensifying and he needed more manpower. The only surviving member of the trio that attempted to capture Jeanine was being placed in one of the one-way mirrored interrogation rooms. Jeanine caught a glimpse of his face. She froze in shock when she realized it was Miguel her long time patient. Before entering, he stared at her with nonchalance and submissively went into the room to be questioned.

Jake informed Donovan, who had noted the interchange, of their relationship and of what he had observed between them in the clinic. As the Agents waited to see who would get the prize of interrogating the witness, they were all surprised with Donovan instructed them to have Jeanine question him.

"Jeanine I want you to ask him what he was doing there and what his intentions were. He'll probably talk to you before he'll talk to any of us. I need to know what he knows. This was not coincidental," he said.

Jeanine eyed Donovan. She was not naïve. This was not just a fact-finding mission. He wanted to see her interaction with Miguel as well as hear what he had to say. Donovan and crew would be poised on the other side of the mirrored glass while she questioned Miguel. She complied with his request but she felt manipulated by Donovan. The look in her eyes stabbed at him and he felt it immediately.

Jeanine sat down across from Miguel. He was facing the mirror while she had her back to it. She eyed the steel bracelets on his wrists.

"Miguel, what are you doing here?"

"*Yo podría preguntar el mismo!*" he snapped at her.

"What?" she asked.

"*Tu me entiendes. Por que estas aquí? Por que trabajas con la migra?*"

"Does she speak Spanish, sir? Should we get an interpreter?" Glenn asked.

Donovan, in his typical ramrod straight posture, was watching the interlude between them. "No," he commanded quietly, "we don't need an interpreter."

Woo went to turn down the thermostat in the room to make it colder but Donovan asked her to turn the heat up. "Sir?" she asked confused. "I want it hot," he finally said. The glare in his eyes was enough to burn a hole into her soul.

Her hand melted away from the thermostat and she scurried back to her position at the one-way mirror as quickly and quietly as possible.

"Esta la hija del Rey, pero vives con cucarachas," he spat angrily.

"Basta!" Jeanine ordered standing up and slamming her hand down on the table.

"I know who I am! But do you know you who are? Let me put this in perspective for you. Whoever sent you to kill me knows you are here. When you are released they will think you were turned and for that they will kill you. And if by chance, they think you did the honorable thing and kept quiet, they will still kill you because they cannot take the chance of you leaking information to the police. Because, as you know, there is no honor among thieves."

This quieted him. He quickly recognized his position. If he walked out of this office a free man or even if he went to jail, he was going to die. She sat back down and placed her hands on top of his. She admired the scar she had just sutured earlier this week. It was healing under the glint of his handcuffs. Oh how she had hoped he would change his life.

"I have always been honest with you Miguel. Here me now," she pleaded. The agents watched the transformation of Miguel Sanchez from an angry, provocative street-wise kid to a lamb in the palm of her hand. His rage subsided in the wake of her grace.

"Miguel, it's easy to confuse loyalty with honor. Families do it all the time. Blood is thicker than water is what we say. About a hundred years ago, there were two brothers that were weather specialists here on Galveston Island. The older brother, Isaac, was the chief meteorologist for the Island. He was sure he had built a house that was indestructible.

During the Great Storm, a hundred people took refuge in his house because he was sure it would be safe. His younger brother waded across waist high flooded streets to warn his brother and everyone inside to get out. To tell them that his brother was wrong

204

and they were in grave danger. But no one would listen to him. Unable to persuade them to leave he stayed with them.

Night came and the storm grew stronger and stronger. A huge wave overtook a nearby railroad trellis and blew it over like tumbleweed. The massive twisted steel rolled end over end toward Isaac's house. I can only imagine the horror they must have felt watching that trellis tumble toward them in the helpless knowledge that it would kill them all. Right before the trellis hit, the younger brother grabbed his nephews and threw himself and the children out of the window into the water. He saved their lives.

You have an opportunity Miguel. You have remained loyal to a proposition you know is fated to kill you. And now you are here, watching that trellis tumble toward you. You have the option to stay where you are and let it over take you or make a decision to move out into safer waters. The choice is yours."

Donovan entered the interrogation room and excused Jeanine. She and Miguel gazed at each other once more before she left unsure if it was for the last time. She gave him a reassuring smile and exited.

As she passed the observation room, she could overhear Jake O'Donnell remark, "Damn, look at that guy. He's putty in her hands. She should work for us."

Miguel detailed his involvement in a local gang and how that gang was loyal to Carlos Colorado. They were told to capture her and bring her to a deserted pier on the East end of the Island. He had no formal contacts within the Colorado regime that he could disclose. Donovan left the interrogation room and committed Miguel to the responsibility of his Houston sub-commander. He would be held in custody in Federal jurisdiction until the case was over.

"He can't give us Colorado. Miguel is just a pawn. Probably sent here to distract us or test our defenses," Donovan concluded.

"What was he saying to Dr. Hunter earlier in Spanish? Was that significant? She's indirectly denied speaking any other languages with Dr. Snyder," Glenn asked standing next to him by the glass.

"What do you think, Agent Woo?" Donovan inquired.

"Given her ability to discern your accents it would seem likely she speaks at least one other language. Given the region in which she lives, Spanish seems the most useful. I have to say, she has some trepidation in confessing it," Woo replied.

Glenn, Donovan, and O'Donnell turned toward her in surprise. She had finally made an Agent-worthy observation stated in a clear cogent argument.

"Good Woo. Very good," Donovan said approvingly. Woo beamed with pride with the recognition.

"Sir, why transfer him to Houston?" Glenn asked.

"Until I know where Swenson is and what she is doing I will use the utmost caution. I know he'll be safe in Houston and won't be exploited for any political or personal gain. Speaking of Swenson, where is she?"

No one knew.

Donovan continued, "I have some questions that need answers. Woo take care of the task I gave you earlier. I think now is the time." Woo left to complete her errand.

Meanwhile, Donovan looked around and noticed something was terribly   wrong.

CHAPTER 24
SLOW, HONEY KISSES

"Where is she?! What happened?" Donovan roared.

Agents O'Donnell, Glenn, Woo and the new entourage from Houston were working rapidly to determine where Jeanine had gone.

"We planted a tracking device in the necklace she usually wears but we are having some difficulty tracking it," Glenn informed.

"Resolve it now!" Donovan demanded. "I want to know where she is!"

Jeanine had snuck out of the warehouse undetected. She slipped into the quiet night and arrived at Dr. Savage's house around 10 PM. He greeted her warmly. "Jeanine, what are you doing here? Did you lose your key to the carriage house?"

He stopped abruptly as he observed her countenance. She appeared weary and completely not herself. It was like the Jeanine he knew was hidden underneath a mask of the person standing before him. "Tell me everything," he said with grave sincerity.

A faint light from the bulb over the sink was all that illuminated the room. Savage drummed his fingers quietly on the red and white-checkered tablecloth as she told him the long sad tale of events from the details with David to the events in the ICU and her recent escape from FBI headquarters. Dr. Savage sat for a while thinking about all she had said.

"It's all right, Jeanine. I'll do everything I can to help you. Though, I must say that running is not a good option for you. And from what you've told me of Agent Donovan's tenacity, he is not going to stop until he finds you. That's probably a good thing; a good thing that he is relentless that is. I get the sense that this situation will denigrate in ways you cannot imagine. You will need someone you can trust."

"Trust?" she asked recoiling abruptly. "I don't know that I can trust him especially after tonight." Her face twisted in pain as she felt a sickening pang in the center of her stomach. She hunched over in her chair at the kitchen table hugging her arms. Dr. Savage came over and patted her hand comfortingly.

"Jeanine, he was assigned to protect you and find out what happened to your patient but it seems to me he has taken a very personal stake in all of this. He has put himself on the line when he could have assigned this to anyone of his subordinates. He's even taking call with you, which is just mad! But the point is this; he cannot protect you if he does not know what you know.

There is more to this than you or I can see. Let Agent Donovan do his job. Trust has to start somewhere. And when he comes to get you, and yes it will most likely be him, you will know what is on his mind by the first question he asks you. If he is angry with you then you may assume he is more concerned about his own career. But if he genuinely shows concern for you first before getting angry with you then his concern is you vs. himself. But realize; I am just making a guess. I don't know the man and you have to remember that sometimes when you care about someone your first reaction is the craziest, not necessarily the best."

His words comforted her. Dr. Savage's best guess was usually more accurate than most people's well-informed decisions. He noticed Jeanine rubbing her stomach again and brought her a glass of milk and a roll of Tums. "By the way, when are you going to take care of that?" he asked, referring to her gastritis. She only smiled as she sipped the milk to ease her pain.

Savage began to stroke his bearded chin in quiet reflection. He sat forward placing his elbows on the quaintly decorated kitchen table. "Jeanine," he said ruefully, "I have been considering what you have said about Dr. Snyder. I have known him for several years. Snyder is not one to outwardly show his anger. He thinks it demonstrates a lack of refinement. But to display level of rage, especially in front of Donovan, was extraordinary," Dr. Savage continued.

"Why do you think he did that?" Donovan asked. They both turned around startled since they were unaware of his presence. He was standing silhouetted in the doorway like an apparition.

"Donovan!?" Jeanine gasped. The mood in the room was taught with anticipation. She was unsure what to say but could determine from his countenance he was both anxious and angry. His clenched jaw was evident even in the softly lit kitchen. "Please continue Doctor Savage, I'd like to hear what you have to say," Donovan requested coldly. It was obvious he was perturbed with Jeanine.

Dr. Savage, a patient, unhurried man, stood up quietly and said, "Why don't I let the two of you catch up for a moment. I'll be back shortly." He stood up to leave but paused for a moment, admiring their regard for each other quizzically, before exiting with a subtle, almost undetectable smile.

Donovan unleashed a symphony of emotions. He was angry, hurt, disappointed and pissed off simultaneously. Much like the way a parent feels towards a child that has run out into the street and narrowly misses being hit by a car. The impulse is to ascertain safety while the second is anger regarding such a foolish decision that provoked the danger in the first place. He was battling between two urges: to hold her passionately or to violently shake some since into her.

"Are you alright?" he asked hotly. Interesting, she thought to herself, his first question was just as Dr. Savage had predicted. Jeanine could see the waves of feelings spreading over him. "I'm fine," she finally answered tentatively.

"Then why the hell did you run?" He roared back angrily.

"I was angry!" She replied with equal rancor. "People are trying to kill you, Jeanine! How could you do something so dangerous?"

"I'm sorry that my absence inconvenienced you. But as it is my life that is at risk, I hardly see how it is a problem for you. Unless, of course, there is someone else you wanted to manipulate."

"What are you talking about?" he asked feeling a little hurt. She backed away from him a few steps before turning her back to him.

"I'm no simpleton, Luke Donovan. I am fully aware that I am bait for you. I figured you would use me to bring out the organ smugglers. That's what police do. I resolved at the beginning of all of this that if that is what had to happen to bring justice to those who killed David, I could handle it. But today was...more than I expected. What I did not expect was what happened this afternoon and what you did to Miguel tonight."

"What I did to Miguel?" he seethed.

"Yes, what you did to Miguel. You could have had any of your agents question him. But you knew of his relationship with me and you used it. I'm not the first and I won't be the last person you use in this way," she turned back to face him.

"It's my fault really. I made the mistake of trusting you. I thought you were..." she paused looking for the right words. "Sincere...I thought you were sincere. I believed you in that elevator at Old Red. But you are here to do a job. I lost sight of that."

"Is this what you think of me?" he asked. His throat was dry. She had hurt him more than she could have ever realized. He walked towards her and stopped less than a foot from her. Both of them were emotional.

"Let me clarify some things for you, Dr. Hunter," he said sharply. She bristled at his use of her formal title and arched her neck.

"I asked you to talk to Miguel first because I knew it would soften him. If I questioned him initially, I would have gotten the truth from him but I would have broken him in the process. He knows you, trusts you, and in case it missed your notice he deeply admires you. I gave him a chance I've never given any other suspect. I let him have a friend talk some sense into him. I was trying to protect him. And I can tell you it's not a career making move but a career-breaking move to have a witness question another suspect. I did it for...."

He paused and backed away from her. He had not even realized he was only inches from her face. He walked over to the sink and placed his hands on the counter taking some time to cool off.

"You did it for?" she asked quietly.

He was struggling with what he wanted to say. She could see it in the muscles of his back as he tensed his shoulders. Then slowly, he relaxed again, as though regaining control of himself.

"People are trying to kill you Jeanine," he said softly.

"I'm not afraid to die, Agent Donovan," she said with quiet defiance.

"What?" he asked incredulously.

"Don't mistake my meaning. I'm not actively planning it. But I'm not afraid of it."

"What are you afraid of?" She looked at him for a long time before she answered. Studying him to see if he was right to hear her answer.

"I'm afraid to live a life of no meaning. To always feel like I've missed the purpose of my life. I don't want to look back and realize I had lived it for all the wrong reasons. I'm afraid to fail mostly," she finally said.

He stood close to her. "That will not be your fate, Jeanine," he said assuredly. Her eyes were deep, dark pools. When she looked at him, he felt something special. It made him confident to ask another question. "Why did you really run tonight?"

She pulled away from him and sat down at the table. "I thought that would be obvious," Dr. Savage answered as he entered with his characteristic dry humor. Jeanine and Donovan exchanged glances. It occurred to Donovan that Jeanine had informed him of their relationship. She nodded affirmatively confirming his suspicions.

"You said you had a theory about Dr. Snyder," Donovan asked still peering at Jeanine.

"Yes, I have a theory. I think Snyder is involved in the trafficking of the stolen organs," Dr. Savage stated bluntly.

"What?!" Jeanine exclaimed, "That's unbelievable! He would never do something like that. He's always talking about the honor, brotherhood and nobility of medicine. He'd be the last person involved in something so...so hideous."

"No Jeanine, he would be the perfect person," Dr. Savage said gently correcting her. He was saddened to have come to a conclusion this grave about someone he had once called a friend. But he continued his line of reasoning.

"Remember your courses in anthropology and psychiatry. He's an elitist, narcissist, with a Napoleon complex. Consider all that is involved with this process of organ harvesting. Snyder would be in a prime position to interview every medical student and resident that entered the institution.

He'd be the perfect person to analyze who would and who would not be willing to assist him in this pursuit. He knows every doctor on the campus; he knows all the policies involved with surgical schedules, organ donation, and can even manipulate the schedules of the residents to place specific allies where he wants them in order to accomplish his objective.

Snyder is meticulous. He would know which residents to place on ICU and ER duty and at what time. Those are the best places to get organs as people in these scenarios are at the highest risk of dying. And it is also the best place to draw the least suspicion. And consider whose organs would be the most desirable. Vagrants, transients, runaways, e.g. people no one would miss."

"But Dr. Snyder is wealthy and established. What does he have to gain by doing this?" Jeanine questioned.

"Not all status is about money; it's not about the money, Jeanine." Savage replied thoughtfully as his gaze became distant.

"It's a disguise for another purpose," he continued as he turned his attention to Agent Donovan.

"Agent, how long have these organs been leaving the Island?"

"Almost a year now," Donovan answered. Jeanine wrinkled her forehead.

"And where have the organs been going?" Savage continued.

"All of them have gone to South America. We believe a narcotics dealer called Carlos Colorado is the recipient; not only for trafficking purposes but also for his son who apparently had kidney failure."

Jeanine thought for a moment. A flood of thoughts swept over her face.

"Oh my God," she finally said as she closed her eyes in an attempt to thwart the facts being revealed to her.

"There's more Jeanine," Savage said as he cleaned the lenses of his glasses with a small silk cloth, "when I was at the University, there was a rumor of a group of doctors who believed medicine was a tool for social reformation. They believed they had the obligation to correct society's errors through the power of medicine. Until now, I did not believe this existed. But now I must believe it exists and that Snyder is involved."

"Even if all of that is true, why would he bring Jeanine into this?" Donovan asked.

"I don't know. It seems very personal as far as Jeanine is concerned. But Snyder is smart enough to know that all roads lead somewhere. He knows someone has to go to jail and he needs someone in place to take the fall, perhaps someone who had no friends in the administration, someone expendable. But, what I don't know is how Snyder is involved with the FBI?" Snyder finished.

Donovan answered, "The link is still the organs. Let's say your supposition is correct and Snyder is the leader of this organization to sell organs to the black market to correct social evils. He would still need a portal by which to accomplish this. And for the process to have gone on for at least a year indicates someone well connected with the government here in the States as well as the cartels of South America.

It would have to be someone willing to take a big risk. Dealing with some of these characters is very tricky. They are lethal, quick to question and kill and not necessarily in that order. They would have to have one hell of an ego and really hate people."

They were all quiet for a moment as they reflected on what had just been resolved. Jeanine's forehead twisted into an almost audible groan. She was looking down at the tablecloth studying the patterns in it when something occurred to her.

"Monica," she said simply.

"What?" Donovan asked.

"Monica is the link between me and Snyder and the FBI. She was my friend, she had an association with Dr. Snyder, and she turned me in to you."

Donovan pondered for a moment. It was Donovan's turn to groan as a grave look came over his face.

"What is it?" Jeanine asked concerned.

"Agent Swenson has pulled some strings to get herself promoted. She's going to try to take over this op. But I realize now that it's more than just about her career ambitions." He paused looking concerned and disappointed. "She would have the temerity to get involved in organ smuggling. She would be in position to transfer information," he continued quietly as if working it through in his mind. He seemed to pity Swenson.

"If she has control of this case," Jeanine started. A myriad of thoughts flooded her mind; most of them involved her going to jail or dying and neither was palatable.

"Swenson is not the main problem," Donovan said as he massaged his bearded chin. She's a puppet being used by someone else only she's too blind to see it. Her pride makes her believe she is in control. She is a self-indulgent, self seeking, sociopathic sycophant."

"Well, that puppet and all of those s-words you just used wants Jeanine dead." Dr. Savage said as he regarded Jeanine.

"I'm not so sure about that. I think your hypothesis is correct. Jeanine is a convenient scapegoat not only for Snyder but also for Swenson. They need the flow of cash to keep going," Donovan said.

"I have to determine who's pulling the strings. Otherwise..."

"Otherwise, I'm on borrowed time," Jeanine finished.

Donovan focused on her eyes. The connection between them was palpable and emotions were still running very high.

"We've covered a lot of issues tonight. I suggest we call it a night," Dr. Savage sagely advised as he rose to retire. They noticed it had begun to rain, as the sound of crackling thunder ripped through the sky. Pouring rain came down in sheets so thickly that the view of the cottage house was obscured. They resolved to wait until the storm lessened before walking to the carriage house. As they waited, Donovan addressed her again.

"Jeanine, I need to ask you some direct questions. I need direct answers," he stated simply.

She sighed quietly in patient anticipation of his questions.

"Do you know Carlos Colorado?"

"No"

"You have never met or seen him?" he pressed.

"No" she insisted.

"Does your father know him?"

"You would have to ask him"

"What happened eight years ago?"

"What do you mean?"

"Jeanine, I told you once that you could not make me reveal anything to you against my will. Similarly, I'm a trained investigator. It's my life and my passion. There is nothing you can conceal I cannot discover."

"Always the detective I see," she responded sharply feeling probed.

"I'm not trying to hurt you. I'm trying to help you. If you don't answer these questions for me, you'll have to answer them for someone else in the Bureau and they won't be as interested in your well being." He was exasperated.

"And you are interested in my well being?"

"Of course I am," he said hurtfully.

"What do you want from me?"

"I want the truth."

"I've told you the truth!"

"What about your father?"

"My father?" she recoiled. "I cannot answer for my father," she said emphatically. Her devotion to her father was resolute and unshakeable.

Donovan was frustrated. He knew there was information she was not giving him. Then it clicked. He reviewed her words in his mind, 'I cannot answer for my father.'

"That's it isn't it. You can't violate the oath you've taken to your father?"

She fidgeted restlessly but remained quiet. Her eyes were fixed on his face silently confirming his suspicions.

"Let me help you," he pleaded, "What can I do?"

"You can't do anything for me," she said barely above a whisper. Her face was twisted with pain. She wanted to tell him what she knew but she couldn't. He nodded in acquiescence.

After the storm passed, Donovan escorted her to the carriage house. As Jeanine entered, she was surprised to see it was full of flowers: roses, tulips, and her favorite, gardenias. The entire cottage was illuminated with candles. In the bathroom, the claw foot tub was drawn and full of mountainous suds. She turned to Donovan in surprise.

"I had Lorna make the preparations right before you disappeared. I thought you could use this after all you've been through. Don't worry, no one will get to you and I won't disturb you. This Island is full of agents and at least 20 of them are undercover on the perimeter of this location. Every door and window is covered so don't strip in front of the windows. I'll be back in a few hours," he said appearing fatigued.

"Donovan," she started wanting to apologize. She felt badly about how she had treated him. It hurt him that she did not trust him. She never realized a man could be affected in this way.

"Don't say anything, Jeanine. I don't understand your reluctance to trust me. But I am trying. You are not business as usual. Not to me," he said softly. He turned and left quietly closing and locking the door behind him.

Jeanine needed this time alone. She submerged in the warm water of the bathtub surrounded by thick, foamy suds. The small bathroom was thick with steam. *The Flower Duet* played in the background. The celestial voices rose and fell in perfect harmony as hundreds of candles flickered softly yielding a rich ambience.

After a while, Donovan returned to find Jeanine still in the bathroom and, content their location was secure, he rested on the chaise in the den listening to the gentle fall of the rain before succumbing to sleep.

Jeanine emerged from the bathroom wearing a large white terry cloth robe followed by puffs of billowing steam. She quietly walked to the chaise and sat next to him regarding him as he slept. The hardwood floors creaked under her bare feet as she tiptoed across them. She studied him in the flickering candlelight for what seemed an eternity: his long eyelashes, full eyebrows, and chiseled jaw line. She found herself yearning for him. Not just the superficiality of physical pleasure; she desired his happiness.

Even though he was obviously tired he still lay straight as an arrow. That was the one thing that was constant about him. Even in a cesspool, he was regal and right. She felt badly for accusing him unjustly regarding Miguel. Ashamed of her feelings, conscious of her body under her robe, and distracted by thoughts she slowly rose from the chaise. As she did so, Donovan caught her by the hand, halting her ascension. The action did not startle her, although she would have expected it to do so.

"Don't go," he requested softly. His voice was quiet and tired; appealing to her sense of need. She gracefully descended to the seat beside him. His eyes were still closed but his hand was gently but firmly grasping hers. Slowly, his eyes opened and trained on her face.

"You could see me with your eyes closed?" she asked.

"I could see you anywhere," he responded decisively.

She raised a curious eyebrow and avoided his gaze. His statement pleased her. He admired her face.

"Indeed," she answered feeling her heart skip a beat by his answer.

"I did not mean to disturb you. Sleep well?" she continued.

"Not enough," he answered warily releasing his grip of her hand.

"You seem…" he searched for the words, "peaceful. Did this help you?"

Her dark eyes were engaging and he found solace in them.

"Yes, I feel well. It's amazing what you did here," she said as she admired the flowers and candles. She arched her back and stretched her neck. Donovan tried to keep the mental image of what was under her robe out of his mind.

"It's beautiful," she finished as she returned her gaze to his.

His eyes had never left her. "Yes, beautiful," he responded.

She blushed at his advances. "What are you doing Agent Donovan?" she asked already knowing the answer to the question.

"Were you watching me sleep?" he asked shifting a bit higher on the chaise and avoiding her question.

"Yes, I couldn't help it. You look terrible!" she remarked smartly.

"Ouch! You know how to hurt a guy! Please excuse my appearance. I had to forgo a shower when I had to track you down. I am trying to save your ass, you know," he shot back jokingly still half asleep.

"I see," she said, "and how are you doing that, exactly? With bad coffee, lack of sleep, an absence of hygiene and…." she sniffed, "cigarettes?" she asked with an arched accusatorial brow.

"I should have the forensics unit test your senses to see if we can put it to use on some of our unsolved cases" he lobbed back. He propped himself on his elbow to be closer to her face.

"Oh, is that the keen intellect that's going to save me? I think I'm in trouble. I have a half comatose, lung damaged, smoker protecting me," she shot back.

Donovan liked Jeanine this way. It was flirtatious and sexy. Renee was right about Jeanine being his bullshit detector. There was not much he could put past her. No one else in the department would have ever guessed Donovan used to smoke.

Her thoughts were getting muddied as she thought about the things she could not tell him. "You should shower. I think you would feel better," she advised warmly as she patted his hand reassuringly.

He toyed with her hand. "I don't want to leave you alone," he replied seriously looking into her face.

"I'm not going anywhere," she reassured him.

"But, you should get some rest. You are exhausted and in this condition you cannot help either of us. And, you stink like cigarettes!" she said as she hit him in the ribs with her elbow.

He huffed.

"On every possible level of insult that hurt! Besides, the cigarettes are your fault! I stopped smoking five years ago and haven't been tempted until I took up your case!"

"Really?" she asked.

"I would have never pictured you as a smoker. You seem to have that 'my body is a temple' thing about you," she said teasingly.

"Well, you're right. That's why I quit," he admitted.

"So why did you start again?" she asked intrigued.

"I don't know, stress I suppose," he said thoughtfully as he massaged her hand.

"You know what a psychiatrist would say?" she asked, "that you are sublimating your need for something else with smoking."

"Oh really? What do you think I need?" he fired back flirtatiously through a smoky-eyed stare.

"I don't know, Agent Donovan," she answered quietly, feeling the heat of his gaze. She averted her eyes from his in embarrassment. Passions were running within her that she had never experienced, not even for Jourdan. He knew what she was feeling: nervous, excited, and longing. Her skin was on fire; every nerve

218

ending was tingling with anticipation. Their fingers were intertwined playing a game of chase that was almost wholly independent and ignorant of their owners. The feel of his skin against hers was electrifying.

"Agent Donovan," she started. She was overcome with emotion, wanting to run, wanting to stay, and mostly wanting him.

"Luke," he corrected her as he brushed a hair away from her cheek.

He waited patiently for those elegant eyes to come back to his own. He would wait. Steadfastly regarding each slow breath as a masterwork, he would wait. Then, as slow as honey on a cold day in January, she looked up from the floor and brought her eyes up to meet his... Magic!

Donovan gently placed his hand behind her neck bringing her face to his and instantly they were locked in a passionate kiss. Her hands gently caressed his face, then, softly caressed his neck and toyed, ever so sweetly, with his hair. This was the best kiss of Donovan's life. As they parted, he gazed into her face with wonder. A passionate fire bright and burning inside of her rivaled and challenged his own. It both attracted and frightened him.

Jeanine's heart pounded in her chest. The kiss left her feeling like the Earth had tilted on its axis. She quickly collected herself and silently left him to return to her bedroom.

Donovan made several calls that night. He had to start setting things in motion. He needed to know whom he could trust. Still, it donned on him how little he knew Jeanine and that she was more complicated than she seemed. Donovan could not have been more correct.

CHAPTER 25
THE CALM BEFORE THE STORM

The following day, Jeanine woke with an unsteady sensation. This was partly due to her emerging feelings for Agent Donovan. But today, she felt anxious. She likened the sensation to the feeling one gets when they fall backward from climbing a high fence. The feeling of being suspended precariously somewhere between heaven and earth and that soon she would hit the ground, hard.

With nervous anticipation she rose from bed with a definite sense of dread. She had had these sensations before and usually they were spot on. She was off for the weekend and glad of it. She debated for a moment and considered whether she should call her father. She wanted to make sure her family was all right. Knowing that her phone was probably tapped, she would have to exercise caution in what she said.

"Dad?" she called.

"Hey honey how are you?"

"Worried about you. I woke up with a sense that something bad was going to happen."

"We are all fine. I'm more worried about you. There is a large tropical storm near Cuba. They expect it will hit Galveston in a few days. It could be the weather you are premonicing about."

"I'm not sure 'premonicing' is a word, but regardless, maybe you're right. It has been raining a lot here lately," her voice trailed off. She knew weather was not her concern, at least not today.

"What else is on your mind?" he inquired sensing her preoccupation.

"Dad, when did," she paused carefully, "you call your brother?"

"Actually, he called me about 9 months ago."

She cringed. "Do you know why he made contact after all this time?" she probed.

"I had hoped he decided to repair the rift in the family."

It occurred to Jeanine that more sinister things were in the mind of her uncle.

"Dad, do me a favor, don't talk to him again. Not until I call you back. Something isn't right" she discouraged.

"Jeanine, what are you thinking? What's really going on with you?"

She hesitated. "Dad, I need you to trust me. I'm not crazy. Just," she paused, "go on vacation. I think it would do you good."

The other end of the phone was gravely silent. Finally, "Alright honey, maybe the Caribbean this year." Thomas offered.

"No, dad, how about the Rocky Mountains? You've always liked the Rockies." While the FBI agents listening in couldn't have been less interested in this conversation and their supposition that it was useless chatter couldn't have been further from reality. Jeanine was giving her father a warning and with perfect clarity he had understood her. He knew in an instant she was telling him to get the family to safety.

The pieces were coming together. Jeanine thought through the timing of it all. Nine months ago her uncle reinitiated contact with his family after a thirty-year absence. At the same time, organs were being illegally transferred off of the Island. This had to be more than simple chance. What frightened her more than anything was the purpose behind why her uncle had reinitiated contact with the family.

Was it to get organs for his dying son? Was he planning to kill her father? Kill her? She shuddered at the thought. Then her father had mentioned something else. Something so concerning that he wanted to discuss it with Jeanine in person. Ever since Donovan mentioned Colorado's name in the elevator in Old Red where they had been stranded, the thought of Colorado had toiled in her mind.

The only person, outside of her immediate family, who knew about the Colorado relationship was Monica Rubio. Jeanine had confided in her, now she realized it was an ignorant mistake. She guessed, probably accurately, that Monica had told Dr. Snyder about their kinship and this is probably why he was so critical with her. He basically confirmed as much when she confronted him in his office at their last meeting. She also wondered about Miguel. How long had he known of her identity? How long had Colorado been watching her through him or countless others?

At some point, she would have to tell Agent Donovan the ugly truth. That would be the end of any relationship they had, at least any romantic one. There can be no fellowship without intimacy and no intimacy without honesty; she had learned that from Jourdan.

But for now anonymity was her cloak and she would wear it until she had no other choice. Besides, telling him now would only confuse things. If she was wrong about her supposition, then she had time to tell him the truth. If she was right…she was probably going to die. Someone already wanted her dead, probably Dr. Snyder's group of doctors, and Colorado probably wanted her kidneys.

She lingered in her room for most of the morning. She knew Agent Donovan would likely not disturb her there. Besides, she was unsure of how to handle her feelings for him. They were growing stronger and equally strong was her fear she would yield to temptation. She could not afford to be foolish and fall under the spell of physical lust. As long as she avoided him, she was safe.

Yet, there was that unrelenting sense of dread nagging at the corner of her consciousness like a splinter in her mind. Perhaps Donovan would be the recipient of her premonitory suspicions. In the end, her concern for his welfare was greater than her fear of herself and she had resolved fear would not rule her life.

She exited her room carefully and was greeted by the smell of something warm and sweet: aromatic coffee and hot buttery biscuits. The heavenly aroma filled her lungs and lulled her into sense of calm. It reminded her of Christmas, giving her a feeling of home, of safety and love. She could almost taste the butter-laced air and feel the light and fluffy tickle of biscuits and sweet honey on her tongue before even entering the kitchen.

And that's when it occurred to her. Donovan was not just protecting her. He loved her. Truly. Deeply. Loved her. That realization stopped her in her tracks. This was followed by another thought really, another question. Does his love obligate me to love him? Can I love him? She wondered. She didn't know how much time had passed before she was able to move or think of anything else. She proceeded from her room with mixed emotions.

On the small kitchen table there was a platter with warm biscuits a carafe of hot coffee and a note that read: *"Jeanine, I'll be back before these are cold. Love, Luke."*

'Love' she read over and over again. Her fingers traced words on the page. She started thinking about the implications of his note. Does he really mean that or is that a polite salutation? He is a man who says what he means so if he wrote 'love' then he must mean it. Why am I so simple? He's a mature man of the world. It was just a closing for goodness sake. She silently chided herself. She continued this internal debate for a while without reaching a conclusion. While she pondered, Donovan returned and startled her.

"I see you found breakfast," he began, pretending not to notice her reaction.

"Yes," she replied distractedly, while dealing with her milieu of feelings.

"Are you alright?" he asked perceiving her internal anguish.

"Uh, yes," she answered unconvincingly.

"Come on, let's eat," he instructed as he pulled out a chair for her. He liked that he could have an effect on her. He hoped it meant she was developing feelings for him.

"It's unhealthy to skip breakfast," he advised.

"I never eat breakfast," she said toy-fully referring to their previous conversation about absolutes.

"Never?" he bantered back.

"Well, sometimes when I'm eating mint and chocolate, putting bumper stickers about honor students on my car and listening to Prince albums" she joked.

Donovan smiled and shook his head at her. "You know I'm right about all of that," he replied "most of my convicts were prissy prep school honor graduates."

She buttered one of the biscuits quietly while she appreciated the scent of a small gardenia on the table.

"Seriously, how did you know all of that about me?" she asked pensively.

"Know what?" as he poured coffee into her cup.

"That I hate mint chocolate, admire Prince and U2 etc. You mentioned it in a session with Dr. Snyder."

"Jeanine," he said slowly, "those are my feelings. I never knew any of those things about you. I guess we just share good taste."

She was taken aback but tried to conceal her feelings. "So did Lorna arrange this also?" she asked referring to breakfast. She needed to quickly change the subject.

Donovan recalled the conversation he had with Lorna.

"Lorna, do you know how to cook?" Donovan asked.

"What sir?" she asked incredulously.

"Do you know how to cook biscuits?" he asked again with irritation.

"Uh, well, yes sir there is a difference between cooking and baking. To the professional, cooking and baking are quite different. I am proud to say that I was the Rhode Island scone bake off champion back in high school and I have a mean rhubarb pie recipe that..."

He interrupted her, "Lorna!"

She could feel him rolling his eyes.

"Too much info sir?" She asked.

"Way too much. Look, just find a way to get some hot, fresh breakfast here by 8 AM," he commanded.

"Yes, sir," she replied and he could imagine her with a miniature spiral note pad and pencil writing down his orders as if they were complicated.

He wondered how she ever made it through training or if nepotism alone had prevailed.

"Lost in thought, Agent?" Jeanine asked interrupting his thoughts. "I hope you didn't stay up making these yourself?" she asked referring to the biscuits again.

"No," he replied with a furtive smile "I have connections."

"Lorna, right?" she asked.

"How did you know?" he asked.

"She seems the type. I don't know how I knew. It just made sense," she finished. "By the way, was everything alright?" she queried.

"What do you mean?"

"At the nest this morning"

"Oh, yes, just routine. We're still trying to find out who phoned you in the ICU. Don't worry about Miguel. He's fine. I've transferred him to Houston. He will be safer there."

"I see," she said concerned.

"Don't worry," he said warmly. It made her smile but still she was concerned. "What is it?" he asked sensing she was disturbed.

"This may sound weird but I had a feeling this morning that something bad was going to happen today."

He took pause and eyed her seriously. "Do you have these feelings often?" He inquired earnestly studying her.

"No"

"When you have them are they usually correct?"

"Always," she replied gravely.

He looked on her for a long while stroking his beard and contemplating what she had said. She did not stir or fidget. Her resolve was straight and sure.

"Then I will take it seriously," he countered.

"I have to say, I'm a little surprised. I thought you would consider my feelings ridiculous," she stated feeling relieved.

"You've taught me that faith is a very powerful thing. God speaks to each of us in His own way. If He is speaking to you then I will listen."

They talked on a few moments. Donovan could not help but notice she seemed preoccupied and it was not just about her premonition. He wondered if it was about the kiss they shared the night before. He wondered, really hoped, her feelings for him were genuine. She was still very guarded. Still, Renee's thin yellow line analogy was haunting him. He was crossing the line regarding a suspect and that never turned out well, even if the suspect was innocent. He was losing his objectivity and that was dangerous for both of them. Soon he would have to make a choice between her and his job. The writing was on the wall.

Honey gently fell onto her delicate fingers. She brought her index finger to her lips and licked her fingers. He was in raptures. He subtly shifted in his seat; a habit she would learn meant he was deeply uncomfortable.

"Jeanine," he started tentatively unable to help himself, "can I ask you something?"

"I hardly think I can stop you," she replied casually. Her eyes flashed large and mischievously.

"What happened with you and Jourdan? I mean, why didn't it work out?"

She averted her eyes from his gaze and fought hard not to drop the cup of coffee creamer. He had a way of staring at her that was powerfully unsettling. She studied the patterns in the hardwood floor as she answered. She groaned at the mention of Jourdan's name. Donovan was encouraged that all interest between them was dissolved.

"It was my fault really. Being in medical school, it was my first experience with people in physically and emotionally tense situations. I mistook our ease of conversation, our sharing of thoughts and feelings, the intimacy of trials we endured as something more than it was. We could talk for hours about nothing and it was so seamless, so easy; I thought it meant something. I forget that it's an American way of life to say many words that have no meaning."

"You say 'American' as though you are not one yourself," he observed.

"Always the investigator, Agent Donovan?" she challenged with a sultry cut of her eyes. She was not simple enough to fall into that trap. "You have all of my records. You know that I was born and raised in the U.S.," she defended.

"Yes, and to borrow a medical term, I'd have to say your childhood was a little schizophrenic. You moved more places than a military brat. Why was that exactly?"

"Lots of reasons I suppose. My parents wanted us to have a broad knowledge of the country. It's probably why my view of people in the States is different than most. Anyway, to answer your question about Jourdan, I think I was in love with the thought of him. But we both wanted different things. He made me feel special because he noticed me. I thought that if someone as special as Jourdan noticed me that it had to mean something. It didn't."

The sway of trees and the howling winds outside the window caught her attention. She turned back to Donovan's intimidating stare. He locked eyes with her and said the most striking thing she had ever heard.

"Someone as special as you are," he paused, "you don't have the right to sell yourself short. You injure everything you are and everything you stand for when you do it. Your life doesn't just belong to you and you don't have the right to pollute it with people like him."

She blinked back in silence and swallowed down her biscuits in one gulp. His words hit her hard. She searched his eyes and in them there was no deception. She believed he meant what he said. Feeling overwhelmed she averted her eyes and nervously rubbed the honey from her fingers with a napkin. "I...I don't know why you say these things to me" she stammered back hardly able to breathe.

"Yes, you do," he simply replied causing her to blush violently. He leaned forward, unrelenting. "Yes, you do."

She had to suppress the urge to run from him. His knowledge of her was unsettling. "Who are you?" she finally asked her voice barely audible, her brow confused.

"You know who I am. Men are not hard to understand. We go where our passions lead us. Our hearts are not divided."

The words reverberated in her mind, 'we go where our passions lead us. Our hearts are not divided'. For a moment, she saw his mind.

"Agent Donovan," she said finally able to collect her thoughts, "contrary to popular belief, I..." she paused searching for the right words. "I like to know that things are well defined. I like to know that everything has order. And the same is true of relationships in my life. I need to know how to categorize them. I made the mistake of giving my heart to Jourdan when all he wanted was a punching bag. I can't make that mistake again." She swallowed hard before continuing.

"You are an FBI agent investigating me for murder. I am a doctor on the brink of being expelled, imprisoned or...killed. In any possible situation, anything between us is doomed to fail. Do you really think...what do you want from me?" she finally finished clumsily.

He was quiet for a long time only shifting in his seat ever so slightly until he finally said, "Jeanine, you know what I want from you. The question is what do you want for yourself? You've seen the impossible happen. I know you have. You have to tell me what you want."

Fortunately, her pager sounded and they were pulled back to the moment. "I didn't know you were on call this weekend," Donovan stated surprised to hear her pager sound. "I'm not on call," she said as she looked at the number on the pager's screen curiously. "Do you recognize the number?" he asked with growing concern. "It's a hospital number. Usually, I can recognize which floor by the suffix but I am not familiar with this one. I don't know why they would be paging me. Maybe there was a mix up. I should call them back."

"Don't worry, this phone is tapped, if anyone is trying to get to you, we'll be able to track them."

She dialed the number and tentatively waited for it to answer. She anxiously played with the cord. Kent Carlton answered.

"Hunter?" he inquired.

"This is Dr. Hunter"

"Look, Dr. Rucker wants you to scrub into Mr. Morrow's surgery today. Since you admitted him, he thinks it would show good form for you to be present in his surgery."

"Why?"

"It's a Rucker thing, does it ever make sense?"

Donovan signaled her to make him elaborate.

"No, I suppose he doesn't. I'm off this weekend," she continued.

"He wants continuity of care on this case so he wants you to attend anyway."

"Who's doing the case?"

"I don't have the details, I think it's Cahill. You can find that out when you get here."

"Actually, I'm right in the middle of something. I wasn't expecting to be on call. I don't know that I'll get there before the case starts."

"Blah, blah, blah Hunter, the case starts in an hour."

"What?"

228

Click. The line was dead. She called back several times but there was no answer. "Maybe this is what I was dreading" she mused aloud.

"Hmmm," Donovan pondered. "It may be. Or it could be another opportunity for them to contact you. Does the surgery make sense to you or does it appear false?"

"I believe it's justifiable. Remember, he's the man whose heart catheterization you attended with Liberty and me. His heart attack damaged so much of his heart that a bypass is necessary; it's not uncommon. What do you want me to do?"

"I'm still suspicious. Let's get to the nest and brief my team."

CHAPTER 26
CABBAGE…NOT THE VEGETABLE

Woo had retrieved a lay out of the hospital's surgical floor. She was reviewing it with Donovan while Glenn fitted Jeanine with a tracking device that she would wear under her scrubs.

"Mr. Morrow is having a…cabbage", Woo informed Donovan and O'Donnell.

"A what?" Donovan asked confused.

"It's a kind of surgical procedure. I don't know why doctors call it a vegetable, sir" Woo replied with a condescending tone toward the medical profession.

"That's what my intel says sir and I am confident it is correct."

Jeanine could hear them over her shoulder and corrected her information.

"It is pronounced similarly but it is not a vegetable it's an acronym. CABG stands for Coronary Artery Bypass Graft" she informed and she redressed and joined them.

"As Yoda said, try or try not," Woo smiled back sarcastically. Woo did not like being corrected, it hurt her pride. She enjoyed her position of being uselessly available with trivial information. She had found her niche: to fly beneath Donovan's radar, always have the right answer when asked, and to get back to Washington with hopes of working in the Justice Department.

"The line is 'do or do not, there is no try'. If you're going to quote from the classics, get it right," Jeanine corrected jovially with a wink.

Woo continued ignoring the correction of her *Star Wars* reference.

"Mr. Morrow is in operating room twenty three and Dr. Hunter is scheduled to assist Dr. Adak…sorry, Dr. Cahill. A switch of the surgeon was made at the last minute.

"Why was the switch of surgeons made?" O'Donnell asked.

"I am still trying to find out," she answered.

"Woo, show me diagrams of the operating rooms. What are their strengths and weaknesses? Is there any way for someone to get to Jeanine?" Donovan queried.

"Well, it's a little complicated sir," she answered but looking at his expression she quickly added, "but I've narrowed it down from the *Reader's Digest* version to the *TV Guide* version, sir, as you have so repeatedly asked me to do in the past." She cleared her throat and pointed to the diagrams mounted on an easel she had found. She pulled out a laser pointer and began her presentation.

"The surgery center can best be described as a central core, a big circle, surrounded by two larger concentric circles. The core is called sterile well. The only way to get into sterile well is through the operating rooms that make up its outer wall. Each operating room has two doors. One door that enters sterile well and the other door enters from the surgical hallway. The only way into the surgical hallway is through the pre and post operating rooms located here and here or via the male and female dressing rooms."

"Excuse me, Agent Woo, but that's not exactly correct," Jeanine interrupted. "There's another way into sterile well, there is a long corridor that runs down the middle of sterile well and has an entrance at either end. Those entrances are not located in operating rooms." Woo looked at her incredulously.

"What is sterile well anyway?" O'Donnell asked.

"It's basically a sterile storage center. That way if an instrument was not functioning properly, there is an immediate replacement and you don't have to wait several hours for a new one to be sterilized. Consequently, anyone going in or out would have to be masked and sterile in order not to contaminate the instruments. Also, it's a way to pass from one OR to another without having to use the hallway," Jeanine informed.

"I was just getting to that sir," Woo stated feeling upstaged by Jeanine's knowledge. Sensing that Donovan was getting impatient, Woo summed up.

"Sir, you enter the male dressing room from the main hallway and change into scrubs. You leave the dressing room through a second set of doors that actually enters the surgical hallway. You will need to scrub and then enter the operating room. A surgical tech will be there to help you into your gown. Make sure you keep your hands elevated with your palms facing you. They should be no higher than your shoulder blades and no lower than your waist."

"Finally, the surgical nurse, will ask you what size glove you wear. I have taken the liberty of determining that you are a size seven and a half. Drive your hand downward into the glove."

"Like a boxing glove?" he interjected.

"Uh…" she stammered confused unfamiliar with the reference.

"Never mind, I'll figure it out," he concluded realizing she had no practical experience.

"From what I'm told, once this occurs you are considered completely sterile" she finished stiffly.

"Sterile," O'Donnell and Glenn chuckled to themselves quietly at the word. Jeanine shook her head at them. After thousands of dollars, an immeasurable amount of time training, and a significant investment by the FBI, boys are still boys, she thought to herself.

Donovan looked at Jeanine to confirm Woo's information.

"Keep your hands at chest level. And yes, drive your hand in like it's a boxing glove. Everything else she said was correct," Jeanine answered. Woo beamed happily.

"How many operating rooms are there?" Donovan asked her.

"Thirty, sir"

"Woo, you've been studying these plans for two weeks. What's our liability?"

"The room will have only two doors. The one that you enter from the hallway after scrubbing and one on the exact opposite side that will lead to sterile well, the central core I referred to earlier. We're pretty much vulnerable everywhere, sir. This is a closed system. There's no easy way in or out for our agents. Although the loss of life would fall into an acceptable level of loss according to current guidelines."

He eyed Woo harshly, "Who's loss of life are you referring to, Dr. Hunter's? I think she would consider your analysis particularly insensitive, Agent Woo." Woo took a step back. She had only considered the numbers. As she brought her eyes up to Jeanine's she simply blinked back in solemn silence and shame. O'Donnell, who had been listening stepped forward to diffuse the situation.

232

"Donovan, I think Woo is trying to say we have definite limitations. We cannot use our recording devices here because it would interfere with the surgical monitors. The only way I see it is to have our guys camouflaged as OR personnel and hanging out in the hallways ready in case something goes wrong. I think putting any more than you and the doctor in the OR would be too obvious. We don't have the same freedom we had at the funeral. There's no other way to say this but this is probably going to draw out Colorado's people and even Dr. Snyder's accomplices."

They continued to talk for a while as Jeanine studied the diagrams Woo had provided. "How old are these diagrams?" Jeanine asked over her shoulder as she studied sterile well schematics.

"They are current," Woo replied sounding wounded at being questioned.

"Something's not right here," Jeanine observed.

"What is it?" Donovan asked quickly.

"Well, these two rooms in the corner of sterile well are marked as storage but they are actually OR's"

"What do you mean?"

"I've been in that corner several times and nothing is stored in those rooms," she said pointing at the rooms marked storage on Woo's figures.

Donovan mused for a moment. "That's how they did it," he concluded. "That's how they were able to remove David Scott's organs without any record or trace of it. They used those rooms in sterile well for the procedure. The organs never left the Island. It wouldn't raise any suspicion and they could come and go without anyone ever noticing."

"Is that possible?" O'Donnell asked turning toward Jeanine.

"Yes, they'd just flow into a sea of blue surgical gowns into the recovery room and no one would think anything was unusual."

"So is Colorado here or did they transport the organs to South America and do the transplant there?" O'Donnell questioned.

"Either is possible," Jeanine answered. "Under ideal conditions, the transfer is made as quickly as possible to prevent as much cell death to the donor organ. The transplant was probably done here."

She took pause when she said the 'donor organ'. The words stuck in her throat. It made her think about David and both saddened and angered her. Donovan noticed her reaction but pressed forward. Now was not the time for emotion.

"Alright, I want agents placed in these areas," he commanded as he circled the specific post-operative suites, recovery rooms and dressing rooms of interest.

"Since you won't be able to hear me I'll have to signal you if you are needed," he concluded.

Swenson entered the conference. She had been missing for most of the morning.

"Where were you, Agent Swenson?" Agent Donovan asked.

"I was with Monica Rubio," Swenson informed, "I felt it important someone should be guarding our most important witness." Donovan scrutinized her countenance.

"Good, I have some questions for Dr. Rubio. Bring her from the safe house for interrogation. Dr. Rubio looked over these same diagrams and had nothing to offer on these two rooms in sterile well. I'd like to know why her memory is not as good as Dr. Hunter's. I think she's been lying to us. Also, go over the sketches and wiring for the Old Red building. I bet there are some passageways that were also ill marked. O'Donnell brief Swenson on our meeting. You two should coordinate tech ops since that is your specialty."

He gave a nod to O'Donnell whom he'd earlier discussed the issues regarding Agent Swenson. A small detail of agents had been set aside to discretely follow Swenson's actions and investigate her background and her bank accounts. They had discovered some interesting details.

The agents dispersed to start their tasks. Jeanine went with Donovan to his office. He removed his leather holster from his chest and strapped an ankle holster to his leg.

"What should I do?" Jeanine asked him quietly as she watched him arm himself.

"Act as though nothing is out of the ordinary. Whatever happens, know that you are not alone. Wherever you are, look for me," Donovan informed her. She swallowed hard. Thinking about David allowed sadness to creep back into her eyes.

"Take heart Jeanine," Donovan encouraged, "we are one step closer to finishing this." He gently wiped the tears from her cheek. She smiled meekly; he could feel that her heart was heavy.

Jeanine and Donovan made it to the second floor surgery center, scrubbed, gowned and made it to the case just in time. Everything in surgery is about precise movement and efficient use motion and space. There were already two students, a resident, two surgical techs, and a surgical nurse assisting the surgeon. Jeanine was positioned behind the surgeon, who was the size of the average NFL defensive lineman. He towered several feet above her and she couldn't see anything around him.

From a staffing standpoint, her presence during the surgery was purely political. Her task was to stand in the OR and be ready for any questions about the patient hurled her way by the surgeon. This was useful during complicated cases so that the surgeon wouldn't have to page the primary care doctor for answers. As for Donovan, he was positioned across the room from her near the back wall of the surgical suite. She could see him watching her across the room and would hold his gaze for as long comfortably possible before looking away to follow the progress of the surgery.

Jeanine found it difficult to concentrate on the case. During the surgery, her mind kept coming back to her circumstances. She thought about David, her parents, Dr. Snyder, Mrs. Thibodeaux and surprisingly she found more than anything she thought of Donovan. She thought about how their relationship was changing. Thinking of him made her feel warm in a sea of otherwise cold experiences. She wondered if this is what love felt like.

For Donovan's part, he was doing a mental analysis of the room: looking for weaknesses and strengths, analyzing the best points for escape, and considered ways he could get into sterile well if the need should arise. After a thorough analysis of the room, he went down a checklist of the things he needed to do including analyze a few phone calls the team had monitored and review Swenson's connections in the Bureau. He had put some things in motion that would snare Swenson in her own trap. He just had to make sure the timing was right.

Before their arrival, Glenn handed Donovan some intel he had received from Washington regarding Jeanine's father. Apparently, her father was the critical witness in Donovan's case against Colorado case eight years ago. Mr. Hunter was lined up to testify against Carlos Colorado but when the team assigned to protect him was killed, he changed his mind. He did not believe the agency could protect him.

Since Thomas Hunter's testimony was the proverbial nail in the coffin, the case fell apart. Interestingly, back then Thomas Hunter was using a different name, Thomas Cazador, and never mentioned he had a family. He had been kept in the witness protection program until he decided not to testify. Then, he disappeared off the grid, even from the FBI's view, soon after.

His file was sealed under his previous alias of Cazador. That was why he couldn't make the connection to Jeanine's father earlier. Glenn had to do more digging to find the name. With more information came more questions. Donovan didn't recall sealing Thomas Cazador's records. If he didn't, then who did? And now Donovan was more curious to know what Jeanine knew about her father. Maybe there were things her father had not even disclosed to her about his relationship with the FBI.

He looked up to see Jeanine watching him. Even with most of her face masked, he could understand the meaning behind her glances. They were not the kind of business type glances he had become accustomed to but the furtive romantic ones of late. He assumed, most correctly, that her thoughts were bent towards him. The clang of metal hitting a concrete floor pulled him from his reverie, one of the medical students dropped one of the sterile surgical devices.

"Who is back there that has a free hand? Hunter? Hunter, please go to sterile well and get a new clamp please." Dr. Cahill asked. She silently obeyed and went into sterile well. While looking for the probe, the lights flickered in the room for just a second.

When they came back on, Jeanine was surrounded by four masked figures all in surgical garb. She could only see their eyes. They all stood closely around her and very still. She was petrified. When she tried to get away, one of them grabbed her from behind while another stepped in quickly and put a scalpel before her eyes making sure she saw it, and then to her throat. Their movements were precisely choreographed as though designed for this very moment. None of them spoke save the one who was holding her.

"You know what this is," he hissed referring to the scalpel at her neck.

"You know how sharp it is and how quickly you can die by a cut from its' blade. All we want you to do right now is listen. We know the FBI is watching you. We will create another opportunity to separate you from them. The lights will flicker again and we will be gone. We know where your family is and we will not hesitate to use all powers at our disposal to affect them. Your cooperation is expected."

Just as the voice said, the lights flickered off and then on again and they were all gone. Jeanine was shaken. She was afraid and was unsure what to do. She collected herself as much as she could. The instrument she was holding was clenched tightly between her gloved hands.

She pulled herself together and tried without success to stop trembling. She went back to the surgical suite, carefully opened the sterile package to expose the clamp, and gave it to the surgical nurse.

"Find everything you needed?" the nurse asked with a suspicious tone. It was as though the nurse knew what happened.

"Yeah, Hunter, did you get a manicure while you were in there?" Dr. Cahill asked. 'Were they both involved? Was she being paranoid? How long had she really been gone? Were these questions justified?' Jeanine's mind was all abuzz. She didn't know if she was being logical or not. She felt woozy and her stomach burned.

Donovan discerned she was shaken. She would not make eye contact with him although he was desperately trying to see her eyes. Those eyes that told him everything were obviously and conspicuously hidden. Those beautiful, smoked chocolate globes flowered by those long black eyelashes told him everything he needed to know. But something happened while she was in sterile well and she would not look at him, she would not tell him what had happened to her. Whatever it was had taken her away from him.

The surgery labored on tenuously for another two hours. Donovan's body ached and he kept shifting his weight to stay awake and diffuse pressure points on his feet. It was agonizing not knowing what had happened to her.

As soon as Mr. Morrow's surgery was finished, there was still a lot of busy work to be done before the patient was wheeled out. Everyone had a part, especially the medical students, including Donovan. As they went up the ramp into the recovery area and around the corner, Donovan's job was to help pull the gurney and hold the Foley bag to make sure it was not accidentally ripped out of the patient's urethra. The other part of the team pushed the gurney as he pulled. He kept his eyes trained on Jeanine.

As they made it into the recovery room, they were immersed into a sea of blue-green scrub wearing bodies suited with blue hairnets and blue footies. As Donovan turned to find Jeanine he was shocked to see that she was gone!

CHAPTER 27
THE GET AWAY

After leaving the OR, two gowned figures approached Jeanine each taking one of her arms and forcing her down another hallway. They came upon her so quickly she had no time to react. She had never seen this hallway before. It led to a second corridor that emptied into a service entrance. A third figure, also gowned and masked, joined them and she was silently delivered to this third person's charge as the other two fell into synchronous and calculated step flanking them.

The figure looked Jeanine in the eye and jammed what Jeanine could only assume was the barrel of a gun into her side. They said nothing but walked her briskly down the dark hallway. She could only hope that Donovan had seen what had happened. Her heart was pounding and her mind was racing. She was trying to think of something to do, someway of alerting Donovan or getting help. This was even more terrifying than her last abduction.

"That's far enough. Let her go!" A voice commanded behind them. It was Donovan.

The three figures flanking her broke their formation. The third that had joined them lastly kept walking with Jeanine, grasping her arm even more tightly and urging her forward with greater speed. The other two suddenly spread out, obviously to look for Donovan. The hallway was lined with gurneys, enormous 10 by 10 by 10-foot towel bins, and other miscellaneous equipment.

Jeanine could hear low guttural animal sounds of what she could only imagine sounded like someone being subdued. She could not discern if Donovan was succeeding or if he himself was injured. She assumed he was still alive when she heard another fall. She perceived the high-pitched whizzing sounds of bullets flying from silenced barrels flying around her. She assumed this was the case as there wasn't the loud boom of a gun.

"Let her go," he commanded forcefully "I won't ask again." He was much closer now, maybe 10 feet behind them. Her abductor whipped her around so that they were facing Donovan but they kept moving backwards. His firearm was drawn; it was the Walther PPK he had packed into his ankle holster earlier. He was partially hidden behind a column of medical supplies. Jeanine's eyes were trained on his.

Suddenly, she saw movement out of the corner of her right eye. There was a fourth assailant. The one who held her was slowly backing away with the intention of drawing Donovan into a crossfire. Jeanine kept her gaze down and to the right fixed on the man. Donovan kept moving forward focused on the one holding her.

At the moment Donovan was about to cross paths with the assailant on the floor, she suddenly brought her eyes up to Donovan's. Instantly, Donovan rolled forward onto his right shoulder and coming up he shot the man who was on the floor. He quickly whirled around to shoot the man holding Jeanine with a single shot to the head. Jeanine fell to the floor with the weight of her assailant pulling her down. Donovan raced to her.

"Are you alright?" he said collecting her.

"Yes, yes I'm alright," she said breathlessly coming to her feet. She was covered with bloody spackle.

"I'm sorry, I didn't know what to do," she panted removing her surgical gown and gloves.

"You did fine. You did more than fine," he replied hugging her tightly.

"Stay down, I need to see who they are and if there are more of them," he instructed.

He had assumed her abductors were Colorado's men or those working with Snyder. He was wrong. He asked Jeanine if she recognized any of them. The three in the long hallway were unknown to her. To his dismay, they were not doctors, they were FBI agents. All of them had recently been assigned to Donovan from the Houston Bureau. The fourth man was Jake Glenn. He could not believe his eyes. Donovan covered his face before Jeanine could see him. He did not want her to know the horrible truth. They had been set up.

"We have to get out of here" he quickly advised, "Where are we?"

"We're in the belly of the main hospital. UTMB has large bowels and dark places. I never knew you could get into surgery from here."

"Let's make it back to the surgery suite," he instructed. His right arm was burning. He was fairly sure he'd been shot. For one of the few times in his life, Luke Oren Donovan was afraid. They were being hunted.

"We have to be invisible, Jeanine. Do what I do and stay right behind me." The look in his eyes told her everything. She nodded silently and became his shadow. Donovan knew how to avoid being seen; his Israeli military training had taught him hand to hand tactics and his stint in Bureau had taught him civilian stealth. He disarmed or evaded any security cameras they encountered. They blended in wherever possible and avoided any areas where she would be recognized.

They were able to make it out of the hospital and to the main parking lot without being noticed. They went to the fourth level of the parking garage where Donovan had a car. His company car was at the nest. He always kept a private car whenever he was on a case. A trick he had learned from Renee. Always have a way out she had told him years ago. This trick had kept him alive on numerous occasions. He whipped out his keys and opened the door. Until now, he'd been able to hide his injury but in the car Jeanine could see he was bleeding.

"You're bleeding!" she exclaimed.

"Not now!" he snapped. She recoiled and strapped herself into the leather seat of the black four-door older model BMW sedan feeling small and scared. It was 3 AM at this point. They reached the gate of the garage. It would not open without a code or the swipe of a security badge.

"These are new," she observed quietly not wanting to provoke his anger again.

He chuckled at the irony. "I know. I advised the University to install them to increase security. Now they'll use them against us. What's your badge ID?" She gave him the number and he punched it in. The gate rose. Donovan knew this would signal their location and would likely get them a make and model on their car through the garage cameras. At least they had the night to hide them, if just for a little while.

The car flew out of the garage with so much speed sparks flew from the undercarriage of the BMW as it scraped its muffler on the concrete. They flew down Market Street on rain slick streets that were as black as the night. Fortunately, most of the streets were bare due to the oncoming hurricane.

Soon, two dark sedans were following them. Donovan spotted them and evaded them for as long as possible as he flew down Seawall Boulevard at 90 MPH. Suddenly, a hail of bullets flew and the back window shattered. Donovan swerved and told Jeanine to get down.

He slammed on the breaks while turning the wheel in order to spin the car around so that he was facing the cars chasing him. The tires screeched on the wet streets of Galveston's Seawall. He whipped out his gun and shot the front tires of both cars so that they flipped over. One flew over the 17 foot Seawall and landed upside down on the beach crushing the people inside. The other ran into a Wendy's restaurant, exited the other side, and wrapped itself around a steel pole.

Donovan panted. His arm and his shoulder were injured and both were really starting to bleed now. Jeanine came up from the floorboard. Her eyes were wide with fear. She was panting and dizzy from the spin of the car. She saw Donovan's arm and looked for something to apply to stop the bleeding. She could find nothing save the scrub top she was wearing. She took it off and pressed it against Donovan's arm. He winced but said nothing. He looked at the necklace she was wearing and realized Glenn had placed a homing device in it. He pulled it from her neck and threw it out the window.

"They are tracking us," he informed. They drove on silently enveloped by the night to the west end of the Island far past the protective edge of the Seawall. They were alone on a two-lane highway. Just them and that thin yellow line down the center of the road. What fragments of the radio that remained eked out a song by

U2. As the wind whipped into the car through the broken glass windows, Jeanine began to tremble. Donovan reached over and took her hand. After half an hour, they had arrived.

"Where are we?" she ventured to ask as they parked by a remote beach house.

"This is a safe house. I always secure an extra in case of emergencies like this. No one knows about this one except for me. We'll be safe here."

Since they were now in the city of Jamaica Beach, and outside the protection of the flood zone, the house was characteristically built on stilts, as were all of the homes in this area. If a hurricane or tropical storm caused a flood, the top floor that contained the living quarters, would be protected.

They walked up the stairs to the freshly painted beach house. The front door led to an open floor plan that encompassed the living room, kitchen, and had access to the two bedrooms and bathroom. The living area was surrounded by windows and had a set of French doors that led to a wrap around deck.

For being built in the 1960's, it was well kept without the musty stale smell of similar period homes. It had access to a private beach and was separated from view of neighbors by sand dunes. The normally suffocating heat was quelled by the power of the constant ocean wind. The wind gales were becoming harsh as the storm that was approaching from the southeast was gaining strength. In about 3 days, it would be on top of them.

Donovan checked the house thoroughly to make sure they were secure. He assured Jeanine he was well enough to do a few things before she looked at his arm. In truth, he knew his injuries were worse than he let on. He'd lost a fair amount of blood but nothing he hadn't survived before.

"The house is well stocked. We have food and provisions for at least 2 months. I'm going to make sure no one can see the bullet holes in the car. We don't need any curious eyes." Donovan announced.

Jeanine looked through the cabinets in the kitchen. He wasn't kidding about provisions. There was enough food for several months. To her surprise, there was also medical equipment: gauze, penicillin, sterile instruments, IV tubing, lactated ringers solution, and a hyfercator for cautery. She knew Donovan to be a thorough man and this confirmed it. She also found a great deal of money.

She found some clothes in the bedroom and put on a tee shirt since she had used her own to help stop Donovan's bleeding. He returned from downstairs and was looking worse. His shoulder ached. Donovan went to the bar in the kitchen and opened a large silver briefcase. Inside was an odd looking telephone with what looked like a rotating satellite dish.

"It's a satellite phone; they're untraceable. Before you operate, I need to make a call."

CHAPTER 28
FAVORS FROM FRIENDS

A telephone rings in an oak paneled room at 5 AM. An aged hand holding a freshly lit cigarette reaches over a black, plastic ashtray overflowing with cigarette butts to answer the phone. Thin nuanced wisps of tobacco smoke dance through the air.

"What the hell took you so long to call?"

"I don't know. I was waiting for the proper alignment of the stars and planets. How did you know it was me, anyway?" he asked.

"I knew you before your own mother did, hot shot. Don't trifle with an old dinosaur, sonny, you just get stepped on. Enough with the pleasantries, something foul is smellin' up Galveston besides the fish. Is she worth it?"

"I wouldn't be calling you if she wasn't." A tense silence was followed by a sigh.

"Where do we stand?"

"Deep."

"Do you have enough chips to cover you?"

"Renee, I wouldn't be calling you if I didn't."

"Alright, enough with the bullshit; roll it out for me."

"You're right. The stench is foul and goes all the way up to 'quarters in D.C. I don't know who I can trust on my team, if anyone."

"Who carried the tools, who built the house, upon the hill that Jack built....yada, yada, yada. You've flushed out moles on your team before. Why do you need my help? Please tell me the only difference on this one is not because it's personal?" she asked annoyed.

"The difference, Renee, is I've got two bullets in my arm and one of them is from my own Rookie, I have a mole that is being funded by someone I cannot reach within the Bureau and at least half of my team has tried to kill me. I need your help. How high you can reach?" he asked.

"High."

"How high?" He demanded.

"God!" she exclaimed.

The line was silent for a while on both ends of the phone. "This one is going to cost you. I told you before that on this case there is no going back. Are you prepared to do that?" she asked

"Affirmative," he answered with certainty.

"Alright, you have to pinch the pimp or you're taking the fall for this case going bad. Not only that, that little filly of yours is going to jail or worse."

"Well, I've never really been into long distance relationships, conjugal visits, or necrophilia so I'd like to come up with a plan that doesn't end with either of those scenarios." Renee smiled widely on the other end of the phone. She loved talking with Luke Donovan.

"My price has gone up, sport. I hope you can afford me."

"I wouldn't be calling you if I couldn't," he fired back in like style.

"There's something else," he said quietly, "I don't have a motive for this. What's the profit to the pimp?"

"Damn, sport, I taught you better than that! The motive is always the same. Follow the money. At the heart of corruption, there is always greed. Whoever wants Dr. Hunter out of the way on the State side is doing it because of money. Ever since those organs from this case went down South, the rate of drugs coming into the country has dribbled to nothing from South America. You find the one who has the most to gain by keeping the drug trade in action then you'll find the one that wants Jeanine out of the way.

My take is that Colorado is getting old. He's coming face to face with the fact he's old as shit. Whenever that happens, the old codgers start thinking about family as a way to preserve themselves. He wanted to save his son; he couldn't and now he wants revenge for what he has lost and he's called off business as usual with the drug trade until that happens."

Donovan was quiet for a while. He looked over at Jeanine who was staring at him curiously as he sat at the kitchen table. A single light over the kitchen sink barely illuminated her face. She was anxious but calm.

"I need bait," he paused. "Renee, I need you to plant an idea, a notion, a thought that will haunt our pimp and force him into the light. I need you to flush out the pimp but have him, not Swenson, take over the Op."

"Hmm," she mused (as close to gleefully as Renee could ever get). "That will be an interesting challenge. An ego this size will undoubtedly want to be known for their accomplishment. But their professionalism will make them cautious. It can be done, but will take some time. That is a luxury you do not have. By the way, sport, how's that line?" she asked.

"What line?"

"That thin yellow line I told you about" she sneered with wicked delight.

"Damn thing is driving me crazy! I can't drive without thinking about it. That's all there is out here in the middle-of-nowhere-Texas: black pavement and bright yellow lines drawn smack in the middle of them," he laughed but stopped short from the pain in his shoulder and arm

"How's the other line, sport?" she asked sincerely. He paused for a long time. She was asking about Jeanine. She was asking how far he would go to protect her.

"There is no line, Renee. Not when it comes to her." He looked up at Jeanine again who stared at him bewildered. Jeanine knew something of this conversation concerned her but it was cryptic and full of strange metaphors. He could hear Renee smiling on the other end of the phone with an unsaid, *"you got it sport!"*

"Sport, did I mention you owe me?"

"Yes, Renee, I'm in your pocket," Donovan replied humbly.

"Damn straight! I own your ass!"

"Care to double your wager?" he asked provocatively. She could not resist the temptation, "Of course, I wouldn't mind owning you for a couple of years. I, too, need favors from time to time."

"I'll double what I owe if you can tell me honestly that you are not talking to me on an avocado-green colored phone from the 1970's" he smiled widely. He could hear her tighten her grip on the receiver.

"Asshole," was the last the he heard as she hung up her avocado-green colored phone.

CHAPTER 29
THE BEACH HOUSE

"I feel that I owe you an explanation," Donovan admitted. Jeanine was preparing a surgical tray with instruments to remove the bullets from Donovan's shoulder. She had been uncomfortably quiet, tacit in fact. It made him a little nervous. They had placed a kitchen chair up on some crates they had found so that Donovan's sitting height was at her eye level. He caught her arm and pulled her close to him. She could feel his breath on her cheek as he looked into her eyes; her hands were trembling.

"It's always more difficult to do something like this on someone you care about," Donovan observed. "I know this from experience. I've allowed myself to become personally involved with you. That has affected my judgment. I'm sorry." He finished.

Her mind was all over the place. She had to focus. She pulled her hands away from his and held pressure against the wound in Donovan's shoulder to control the bleeding. He'd been shot twice. One bullet grazed his right arm and the other had passed through his shoulder missing any vital structures. He had been fortunate. The bullet that passed through his shoulder had lacerated a small artery that was bleeding quite steadily.

Jeanine needed to cauterize it but she knew it would cause him great pain. Her hands were shaking for many reasons. In less than a week, she'd been threatened, abducted twice, shot at, and almost killed. And now here was Donovan. The way he was looking at her right now was strangely more troubling to her than almost all of her other experiences.

Though she had participated in this procedure on many patients she was afraid to proceed. Donovan's observation hit the nail on the head. Her feelings for him were affecting her judgment. This is why doctors shouldn't practice on their loved ones. All doctors do it because most of the time it's fine: a cut here, a scratch there, and high blood pressure medication or two for a cousin out of town on vacation. But with every experience there's the fear that nags at them. "Did I make the right decision?" It is much more profound when it's someone you care about. When it's someone you love. Feeling her reluctance, he looked deeply into her eyes.

"I trust you, Jeanine. Trust yourself."

She swallowed and nodded slightly. She turned her attention toward the Mayo stand beside her that held her surgical instruments. She took a moment to focus and pray and then, the doctor went to work. Her movements were subtle and precise, comforting and calm. She was graceful and meticulous just as he had observed her so many times before.

Jeanine decided to talk her way through the procedure. It was a way to reassure herself. "I'm going to talk through this, so…"

"I know," Donovan answered confidently as he let out a sigh. He was mentally preparing himself. He had endured great pain before; this was neither his first nor his worst injury.

"I've cleansed this first wound. It's the worst one, I think," her throat was dry and her voice was cracking. She was tired and her eyes were drying from the bright halogen lights they'd arranged for her to see. She blinked constantly to moisten them. Where fatigue would have been a factor; adrenaline had taken over.

"I've started some IV fluids to support your blood pressure it was a little low with all the blood you've lost. Do you take any medications or have any medical problems? Do you have any allergies to medications or latex?" she asked instinctively.

He shook his head negatively; his eyes trained on her face. "I couldn't find any narcotics or pain relievers," she apologized.

"I wouldn't want them anyway," he answered reassuringly. She found his fortitude compelling and somewhat liberating. Since he was not worried about the pain, she was less preoccupied by it.

"Okay, I'm going to start some antibiotics now. They'll drip in with your IV fluids. Ideally, I would have an hour before doing the surgery but these conditions aren't exactly," her voice trailed off. She closed her eyes and focused on what was important. The entire time she prayed she was making the right choices.

"Ok," she shook her head and thought to herself stop saying 'ok' just do what you need to do.

"I need to cauterize the bleeder here in your shoulder. This is going to hurt," she advised honestly. He remained speechless and rested his head against the tall back of the kitchen chair and closed his eyes.

"So, why did you kill Agent Glenn?" she asked.

"What?" he asked surprised.

As he started to answer she inserted the tip of the cautery tool into his shoulder. A course of electricity pulsed through the tip instantly burning the skin and adjacent tissue. The distinctly pungent smell of burnt skin was instantly released into the air. Donovan grimaced and grunted a little but otherwise maintained his typically refined posture. She looked at the artery to see if it was still bleeding.

"I was trying to distract you," she countered smiling meekly, "sorry."

"Oh, I see. No more of that counting down backwards?" he panted softly.

"I use whatever method suits the patient," she replied.

"You, for example, I would not use a count down."

"Why?" he asked curiously.

"It's beneath you. You would think through the countdown and it would prove useless. Five would be too early, four is too obvious but by the time I got down to two..."

She cauterized again. This time she hit three areas and the burn was longer and more intense. He grimaced, clenched his fists and breathed rapidly through his nose. His chest heaved but he bore his pain well.

"That's it. I'm sorry," she said sincerely. "The first burn wasn't enough to stop the bleeding and..."

"And you needed to distract me"

"Yes," she sighed. Beads of sweat were forming on her brow. She wiped them against the back of her arm, keeping her hands sterile.

"Ok, I'm going to stitch up your shoulder and your arm now. I looked in the supplies and there wasn't any lidocaine so, you're going to feel some of this but it won't be as bad as the cautery."

"I've sewn myself up before. I can handle stitches."

"Really?" she asked bewildered. He showed her a scar on his left pectoral muscle. She peered at the scar seriously.

"Hmmm," she said concerned, "at least I won't have a hard act to follow." She glanced at him furtively.

"Cute" he mocked and arched his eyebrows feigning a sinister look, "I still have a gun!"

She was able to laugh now since most of the serious work was done. She still wished they had some morphine in their supplies.

"The bedside manner is definitely hard to beat. I've never had a doctor as beautiful as you."

She blushed. "You really have to stop that."

"Why?" he probed.

"It wrecks my concentration."

"Is that all? It's only fair, that's how your perfume affects me," he said coolly.

"Donovan," her voice pleaded.

"Would you please call me Luke?"

"I need to see your backside," she said matter-of-factly.

"We haven't even been properly introduced," he countered making her blush.

"I mean that I need to examine your back to make sure you don't have any other wounds. I've finished sewing your chest, Agent Smart Ass," she teased.

He leaned forward compliantly and she examined his back. He braced his hands on his knees as she glided her hands over his back and his neck looking for exit wounds and lacerations. His muscles were well defined, not monstrous or bulky, but contoured and masculine. She helped him to lean back into the seat. Though gloved, he liked the feel of her hands gliding over his back.

"Find anything?" he prodded. She blushed enough for him to notice even under her cinnamon skin.

"No, nothing interesting."

"You've never been a good liar, sweetheart."

"I meant, no other wounds. How are you feeling?" she asked somberly. She was dreading her next series of questions. She looked apprehensive.

"What?" he read through her.

"Nothing."

"Jeanine?" he urged.

"You know what," she replied. They were growing to a point in their relationship when full sentences were unnecessary. He knew what she wanted to know. And of course, there were those eyes again pleading with him to know the truth. With her assistance, he got down from the make shift operating table and sat with her on the couch. She supported him under his good arm.

"Let's hear it from the horse's mouth shall we?" he leaned forward and hit a few keys on his satellite phone. "It's going to be on speaker. I don't want you to say anything. Just listen."

Agent Swenson answered the call. "Swenson here," she answered quickly as if she was anticipating a call.

"Not for long," Donovan challenged. His eyes were trained on Jeanine's face.

"Your days in the Bureau are over," he stated.

She laughed. "You are a resilient bastard. I'll give you that. Where are you, Donny, on a satellite phone somewhere? Let me guess, you are still on the Island formalizing a plan and thinking you are going to get control of this case and save the damsel in distress? Come on Donovan. Is that they only way she'll give you a piece?"

"You tried to kill me you insolent bitch. Others, more skilled than you, would have never tried. Your arrogance is disgusting."

"Is this speech over?" she asked with a faux yawn.

"I don't roll over for anyone," he said.

"I hear you've been rolling over and under that little whore you've been protecting for months now. Where is she? Underneath you now?"

Donovan tensed. This was part of the game. He would push her for information and she would push back.

"She's in hiding. In the last place you'd ever guess. I can't say the same for Glenn or the other snot-noses you sent. The next time you send someone to kill me choose someone that is competent. It's a waste of my time otherwise. This failure confirmed your lack of leadership ability and general ineptitude," Donovan taunted.

She was quiet for a moment but quickly rebounded. Obviously, she did not know that Glenn was dead.

"Don't flatter yourself, Donovan. I care little about your existence and neither does the Bureau. You and your little doctor are an obstruction, like a clot, a cancer, or a baby. A process has been set into motion that will go forward despite you.

I have two masters: the United States Government and Senior Carlos Colorado. And in my service to both of them, I have been assured of two very important things. First, that the apprehension of Carlos Colorado is more important to the Justice Department than you or even this mirage of a case we were sent here to work on. And second, that Senior Colorado has promised me direct control over his U.S. narcotics trade routes in return for your delivery. Usually, the goals of my two masters are in direct conflict. But this time, they are in perfect sync. Your intolerable presence will be removed and I will be the youngest agent to ever be a district SAC."

She took a drag of her cigarette. Jeanine imagined that angry little banshee-like wisps of smoke circled around Swenson's head.

"Colorado is very insistent; he never takes 'no' for an answer. In that sense, we are very much alike. He sees something he wants and he takes it. That is why I am his only FBI contact and why we forged this relationship," she continued

"You don't have your prize yet, Swenson. If you don't deliver what you promised, Colorado will kill you."

This angered her. "I would worry more about yourself! Getting rid of you will help us put things back on track. You should thank the doctor for one piece of the puzzle I was unaware of. I did not know that my superior, Agent Crookshank, had also been your superior once. You remember Crookshank don't you? You know the same man that fucked your wife all of those years ago! He is going to promote me as lead over this case. That's just an added bonus to my pleasure. Come on, tell me the truth, despite all of your poise, isn't the back of Crookshank's head plastered over your ex-wife's face all you see when you think of him?"

Donovan tightened momentarily. Jeanine could see his struggle and admired his sense of control.

"Goodbye Swenson" was all he said as he hung up the receiver. It was more than a salutation. It was a proclamation. Somehow Swenson was going to die. Jeanine sat quietly contemplating all that had been said. She was sitting on the edge of the cushion as if about to spring up into action. Donovan was also quiet for a moment, thinking. The winds outside were gusting and howling.

"I can't believe this," she finally said "all this time, Glenn was working with Swenson? How do you know who to trust?"

"We have allies, believe it or not."

"What do we do now?"

"Let's watch some television," he answered. Jeanine studied him dubiously but followed his commands. She did not like all of this mystery. As the television came on, she turned the channel to a news   station.

CHAPTER 30
THIN YELLOW LINE

"Is this good for us or bad for us?" Jeanine asked as she watched in horror at the news broadcast. There, in full color for the world to see, was a picture of Jeanine's face on the national news. The news anchor in Washington was discussing Jeanine's case with his partner in the field who was outside Donovan's FBI headquarters in Galveston. Gusts of wind were blowing the newscaster mercilessly whipping him in his bright purple parka. The media had the fortune of covering two stories once: the storm at sea and the storm in Jeanine's life.

"Yes Barry, we have confirmed reports from an undisclosed source in the FBI that the South American drug lord, Carlos Colorado, has been coordinating with sources at the University of Texas Medical School in Galveston to sell organs on the black market. Apparently, Dr.'s Monica Rubio and Dr. Snyder have been implicated in the sale of these organs as well as a dozen others that have been named. Furthermore, one of the resident physicians has been threatened by these groups and has been secretly under the guard of the FBI, Dr. Jeanine Hunter. From confirmed sources, the FBI has been keeping her under tight security with the hopes of finding out who else has been involved in these horrific deeds."

"Jeff, how long has this been going on and why has the source chosen to speak out at this time?" the first anchor asked intensely.

"Barry, the source would not disclose much more than that in order to protect the interests of the case. We do know Dr. Hunter is currently missing and one of the reasons officials have released this information is to help secure her return. So if anyone has seen Dr. Hunter or knows of her whereabouts, the FBI needs your help to find her and protect her from these miscreants. We can only assume she has some information on the parties involved and may even be a key witness for the FBI's case. The officials believed she was abducted because the FBI was closing in on the suspects."

They plastered a photo of Jeanine's onto the screen.

"This is a photo of this very brave student. We can only hope she is in safe hands. If anyone has seen this woman, please contact the FBI at the number on your screen," Barry advised.

Suddenly, the camera whirled off of Jeff and onto Mellicent Swenson who had emerged from the warehouse. She had been caught completely by surprise and was notably stunned and angry. There was Mellicent, live on television, with hundreds of cameras and reporters surrounding her.

"This just in, Barry, we have an interview with the coordinator of this FBI operation here on the Island, Special Agent Mellicent Swenson" Jeff reported anxiously with a lust similar to one would expect from a hungry dog. He and hundreds of other reports swarmed around her with microphones extended and thrust into her face.

"Agent Swenson, can you tell us how long Dr. Snyder has been involved in this? How many organs have been stolen from patients? Are patients safe in this hospital? What about Dr. Hunter? How did the FBI lose her? What are you doing about Carlos Colorado?"

Agent Swenson's pale face, even more translucent than normal, loomed large on the television screen. She was angry and was pushing through the crowd of cameras to enter their FBI headquarters. She avoided making any comments accept a few obscenities. She pushed her way through the sea of reporters and closed the door angrily behind her.

"Was this your idea?" Jeanine asked with full hopes that it wasn't.

"Renee," he muttered under his breath as he rubbed his forehead so hard she was sure he was going to rub off some skin.

"What?" she asked confused.

"My mentor: I asked for her guidance to flush out the FBI agents helping Swenson."

"And this was her idea of helping?" she asked skeptically.

"Renee has the uncanny ability of knowing the exact means of teasing out a situation. She knows when to be discreet, when necessary, or when to use a more blunt instrument for attack. That said she has obviously opted to dismiss the notion that discretion is the better part of valor."

"I think she just used an atomic bomb to kill a cockroach," Jeanine stated frankly.

"Affirmative," Donovan agreed. Donovan thought for a moment as he surmised Renee's reasoning for giving this story to the press. "Knowing Renee as I do, I believe her philosophy was to turn the lights on and flush out the roaches, if I can borrow your analogy" he said with a wink. "When you turn on the lights in a dark room, roaches tend to scurry for the dark corners. Any roach that comes out into the light or refuses to run away is the one you want to watch out for," Donovan said insightfully.

"So what happens now?" Jeanine asked wistfully. She was deeply troubled at the thought of her face being plastered on the evening news. It was a photo from her first year as a student. She had just left the cadaver lab when that photo was taken; thus it was not her best image.

"It's going to stir things up around Snyder. Even though we don't know all the people involved with him, this is likely to flush a great deal of them out. Snyder is not going down alone. There is no honor in going to prison and if he's going he's going to take as many with him as he can or at least bargain with the pawns to get a lighter sentence. He'll try to make it look like he wasn't involved.

Finally, it's going to either lure Swenson's supporters to Galveston so they can clean up her mess or drive them away leaving her vulnerable. With this in the national media now, the Bureau has a black eye. The Bureau has one prevailing philosophy…no black eyes. They will send a crew to clean up it up and do it quickly. We have to make sure that the split ends are tied up in your favor."

When she looked at Donovan's face, however, she was not comforted. A foreboding storm was brewing on his brow and he shifted in his seat. "What aren't you telling me?" she asked recognizing his discomfort.

He sat down close to her so they were face to face. He gripped her hands so tightly it hurt. His usual perfect frame was bent and tortured but it wasn't his physical wounds that were affecting him. She cast a long glance at him, as flashes of lightening lit up her face in the darkness. He studied her eyes, watching them through her long pensive lashes. He was quiet for a long while. All she could hear was the sound of the ocean waves churning and crashing in the distance. Then he answered slowly at first then increasing in speed. It was like waiting for rain to come. Slow, fat, heavy drops of rain that dropped randomly and then increased in frequency and intensity into a furious storm.

"For a long time, I thought I was afraid of nothing. I have been in the Israeli army, I have killed and nearly been killed, but through all of that I have never known fear until now. I am afraid I will lose you."

"Why are you telling me this?" she whispered. She knew he had done something, something that would tear them apart.

"I needed bait to flush out the moles in my organization and to bring Colorado to justice."

"Bait," she repeated, feeling hurt. She recalled their previous conversation on this subject.

"No, not you this time" he said looking at her intently, "me."

"What?" she blinked back, "What did you do?"

"I knew I had to bring down Colorado and the agents working with him. To do that, I had to dangle a big prize. The first was the press conference that Renee organized. That was just the beginning. I've been in contact with my agents here and in South America for weeks. I've informed Colorado that he has been betrayed by the agents he has been working with here in the U.S. and that if he wants justice for the ones who killed his son with infected organs, he would have to come to the U.S. and talk to me."

"Why would you do that?" she asked exasperated.

"Do you know...do you have any idea of what they could do to you?" She asked as she shot up in protest.

"I know what he will try to do. My goal is to flush out Colorado as well as Swenson and whomever she is working with. If I can convince Colorado he has been betrayed, then he will be more willing to do the same to her."

"But what if that doesn't work? What if he blames you for his son's death? What if he does not believe you and decides to kill you?"

"Either way, you will be safe. That is what matters most to me."

"Either way?" That is not good enough!" she stammered emotionally.

"Do not fear for me, Jeanine. A faithful man craves the things God puts in his heart. God has made me for this purpose. To me, you are everything. And when you live for what matters most, there is no sacrifice," he said calmly.

She was crying and running her fingers through her hair. "When is all of this supposed to happen?" she asked refusing to hear him.

"Probably tomorrow when they come for us."

"They are coming for us?" she paced.

"Yes, as I said, I have been in contact with my agents. I told them to slip information to Swenson about our whereabouts tomorrow morning."

She huffed rubbing the tense muscles in the back of her neck as she started pacing still trying to digest everything he had said.

"What if this doesn't work?" she asked looking at the floor and knowing the answer.

"Worst case?" he asked. "Worst case, Colorado kills me, goes back to South America. Swenson and her colleague keep doing their jobs in the FBI and nobody knows any difference."

"Best case?" she asked.

He walked up behind her and placed his hand on her shoulder turning her around to face him. "This is no fairy tale sweetheart. Best case, Swenson, Colorado and their accomplice go to jail."

"And you," she asked with a penetrating stare. Her eyes welled with tears. She knew what he was going to say. "I'm ready for whatever happens," he said.

"Come on!" she shouted as she pushed him away. "Don't you have anyone you can call? I mean this is the FBI! The US government! This is the most powerful country in the world. Why do you have to…to possibly die to…?" she could barely consider the thought of him dying. The all too familiar and unpleasant sensation of stomach acid started churning in her stomach again.

"Because right now all I have his supposition. I have to tease out all of those involved. Remember, Swenson is now in command.

If I go to my superiors with what I have, it just looks like I'm trying to get my job back. It looks personal. I have no tangible evidence. And in the Bureau's eyes you are still the prime suspect regarding David."

With a loud sigh she exclaimed, "How can this be so easy for you? How can you be so...so damned calm?"

He placed his hands on her shoulders to steady her. "Jeanine, this is not easy! I had to make a decision between bad and worse."

"What if this is what Swenson wants you to do? What if this whole mess is just a way to get rid of you, get you out of the way? You would be one neat and tidy end to all of her problems. What are you going to do if they give you to Colorado?" she asked.

"A trap is exactly what this is. She wants to get rid of me. The last thing she's expecting is for me to help her do it. I know how to be a hostage. I'll find a common ground; find a means to negotiate from a position of power by ascertaining the ultimate goal of my captor. Determine a way to keep that goal out of my captive's reach thereby prolonging my life by securing my own value.

In the meantime, I will lull him into a false sense of security by using disarming honesty to every question he asks while waiting for the opportune moment to use his trust to my advantage. And when that moment arises, I will break free from him with or without the aid of the FBI and secure my own release."

She blinked back at him and twisted her face with disbelief. "And that works? That's the best all of that FBI, Israeli army, covert ops training could give you?" she asked almost screeching.

He raised one of his eyebrows and tilted his head in thought. "I've never tried it but it sounded good when I read it in the manual," he said laughing. It was enough to break the tension between them and they laughed despite their agony. They embraced passionately laughing and crying simultaneously.

Donovan pulled her away but held her by the shoulders and placed a kiss on her forehead. He smelled her hair as though it was for the last time. As he spoke to her, he could not bring himself to look into her eyes. It was a pleasant torment for him to feel the skin of her brow against his mouth. He held her still as he rallied the last of his bravado. It was a strange moment of peace, agony, weakness and strength. A thin line separated them all.

"Renee gave me some advice before I started this case. She told me to think about the thin yellow lines that separate cars on the road from having head on collisions. That the only thing that separates life and death sometimes is the power of suggestion. That line has no power. It only separates north and southbound lanes because we say it does.

I never meant to cross the line with you. I thought I could handle your case and never get involved with you. You were supposed to be another case, another deadline. But somehow, I fell in love with you," he paused momentarily shaking with the emotions that were tearing him apart. He knew they couldn't run. He couldn't hang on to her even though he desperately wanted to do so. He had to sever the tie between them.

"Jeanine you have to let me go," he said slowly. "I can't do this if…. I have to play this like I have nothing to lose. I have to know you are safe. Too many people have died. This is the only way to stop them. Please, Jeanine," his voice broke as he choked back tears. She could feel his body shaking. His arms were trembling as he held her but he would not let go and would not look at her. He drew his strength from knowing he was sacrificing himself for her and that his sacrifice was not in vain.

It was then that she understood what he needed of her. She could feel her heart breaking. She felt the weight of the entire ocean crushing her chest. She could not cry or else this would weaken him. She could not argue because she knew what affect it would have on him. She slowly placed her hands on the center of his chest feeling his heartbeat.

"Alright," she acquiesced, "alright."

He planted a small kiss above her left eyebrow turned and went to his bedroom. Jeanine rubbed her heart with her hand as if to rub away the ache of heartbreak. The air felt heavy in her chest.

CHAPTER 31
CALM BEFORE THE STORM

Jeanine did not sleep that night. The howling of the wind, the sharp and steady assault of the shudders by the rain, the sound of waves crashing against the shore were nothing compared to the storm in her head as she postulated her life. She lay on her side in complete darkness.

Frightful, spastic shadows cast by the movement of wind-whipped palm trees outside her beach house bedroom window danced violently across her view. The approaching storm, though terrifying, was still less frightening to her than the thoughts that were assaulting her mind.

She tried vainly to reason against that part of herself that she knew was trustworthy and right and at moments made suggestions, no, demands of her, that she felt impossible to perform but knew just as rightly would have to be done.

All night long she wrestled with her convictions and they whipped her as adamantly as the wind whipped the beach house. As night gave way to morning, she rose from her slumberless bed and went into the shower. The hot water fell and steamed the small bathroom to the point of blindness. She sank down to the corner of the tiny shower stall, no small feat given its narrow walls.

Yet, slowly she rose from her desolation, as resolve against the truth was attenuated by conviction to do and be all that God had purposed in her life to be. As she accepted her God given mission she rose to stand and literally and figuratively felt the cleansing of the water over her and the liberation that comes when one stops fighting against the will of their Creator. She knew this was right with every fiber of her being even though she was still afraid and unsure of what her exact steps would be.

As impassioned as Donovan was to save her, it was nothing compared to the dictum in her heart. She had to save Luke

Donovan; it was not an option, a whim, or passing fancy but an absolute necessity.

Where once there had been weakness and fear, now she felt the surge of strength with honor and purpose. She did not know how she would accomplish her task, but as her mind came to rest, so came the answers.

The most important thing was that she had to get back to FBI headquarters. Donovan had mentioned something the night before but made it sound like Jeanine would be staying in the house and he would be going alone. That could not be. She would have to go with him. She exited the bathroom surprised to see Donovan. He was standing in the living room waiting for her. She knew he could read her face better than anyone, so she tried earnestly to hide the truth of her decision from her expression. He would not understand or allow her to pursue her plans.

"How did you sleep?" he asked bare chested and wearing white linen pajamas. He had become uncomfortable wearing the shirt during the night.

"I didn't," she replied honestly.

"The storm?" he inquired.

"Something like that," she replied calmly. She was peaceful and he was glad for that. For her part, he seemed particularly bright that morning as though he was unburdened for the first time in a while. The storm had quieted and barely a wind could be heard outside.

Instinctively she examined the bandages to make sure he had not bled through them. "How are you?" she countered. The wounds were intact and had not bled much. Touching him made beads of sweat form on her forehead. But now, her attraction to him transcended simple physical allure; it was physical, emotional, and spiritual. Here before her stood a man who was willing to die for her.

Donovan observed her countenance. It was different than he had ever seen before. She seemed distracted in thought as her hands rested on his heart.

"I'm surprised the weather is so calm this morning," he remarked, "it should facilitate their arrival."

"The weather is calm?" she asked rhetorically. "That's terrible!" She gasped.

"What? Why?" he watched confused as she ran to the window facing the Gulf. The waves were almost non-existent; almost a dead calm.

"Oh no," she whispered to herself.

"What is it?" he asked again.

"The storm is back building. You've heard the term calm before the storm?"

He nodded.

"That's what's happening now. The storm is gathering strength, pulling forces towards itself. I read about it in an article written on the Great Storm of 1900. I don't remember the timing but we may have less than a day before it hits and it will hit hard, very hard."

Her eyes were serious.

"We should check the weather," he advised, taking note of what she said.

As she switched on the TV, they were surprised to see that only one channel was still accessible, Univision, the Spanish language channel.

"Well, this won't do us much good will it?" Donovan said shaking his head at the television. It was obvious they were discussing the weather in Galveston by the maps that flashed across the screen. As Donovan was about to switch off the TV, Jeanine asked him to wait.

"Please, leave it on."

Donovan agreed silently but eyed her for a moment. "Can you understand this?" he asked.

"From what I can gather, yesterday the storm had been downgraded to a tropical storm, but as it reached the hotter waters of the Gulf of Mexico, it picked up momentum and is now a category 3 hurricane; it's projected to be a 4 by landfall."

"You got all of that?" he asked suspiciously.

She ignored his question. "I know the Island. If it maintains its current heading toward Galveston, no one on this end of the Island will be safe. There is no Seawall to protect us from the storm surge."

That would be her out, her reason for getting back to the heart of the Island. Still, she needed a reason to go to HQ with him; a reason he would be willing to believe and support. He was reluctant to agree but knew she was right.

The next image that flashed across the screen caught them both by surprise. A camera crew was standing outside of Donovan's headquarters and Mellicent Swenson was talking to reporters. Standing beside her was none other than Jeanine's father. Jeanine literally fell to her knees in front of the television.

"What's wrong, Jeanine?" he asked greatly concerned.

"That's my father!" she said breathlessly.

The reporter translated the interview from Swenson but the delay in the audio feed was just enough that they could hear Swenson's words before translation came through.

"I am here with Dr. Jeanine Hunter's father, Thomas Hunter. Dr. Hunter has played a vital role in our case. She and I have developed a very special bond and I will do anything to secure her safe recovery. Her father arrived this morning to stand with me to plead for her life. I beseech her captors to set her free and strongly warn them that we will use any means to find them. We have received permission from the highest authority for maximal engagement. We will find you," she finished emphatically as she looked directly into the camera.

The interview ended and the news moved on to another segment. Jeanine rose to her feet. This was her way in.

"You realize this is a trap? They have involved your father to get to you," Donovan advised reading her mind. He knew she'd want to go to her father.

"Yes, I realize that," she said calmly. The pieces kept coming together, seamlessly, gradually, falling into place. He nodded in agreement. Then, reached for her and embraced her tightly.

"There are no guarantees now, baby" he panted softly in her ear trying to summon words of encouragement but nothing else would come. This was not a card he expected Swenson to play. He needed time to think and strategize but time was a commodity in short supply.

"I trust you," she said boldly looking into his eyes, "I'm not afraid." He was humbled and moved by her confidence in him. He simply nodded and went to his room to dress.

As they prepared to go, Jeanine felt a sudden violent pang in her stomach more severe and vexing than she had ever experienced. She made it to the restroom just in time to vomit into the toilet. She was hoping this was just a case of nerves but as she was mortified to see coffee ground emesis. A sign all doctors know to mean blood; old blood. She'd been bleeding for a while. Obviously, the gastritis she'd been nursing was an ulcer and it was bleeding. She crept out of the bathroom hoping Donovan had not heard her. He would want her to go to the hospital, which was probably already being evacuated.

Donovan was in his room getting dressed and had not heard her. She covered her illness from him and they began the journey back to the nest.

"Sorry about the wind," he apologized referring to the blown out windows from the gunfight from the previous night.

"Well, it's no Oldsmobile," she joked with a half smile.

CHAPTER 32
SWENSON'S TRAP

The drive to headquarters was tumultuous. The hurricane was predicted to slam directly into the Texas coast; it would make landfall slightly west of Galveston by midnight. The storm was fast upon the Island and its dark clouds obscured the light of day and hid the fact that the sun had begun to set. Day and evening were similar shades of black. Perhaps appropriately, the closer they got to the warehouse, the worse the storm became.

The rain was coming down in sheets and in horizontal angles to the windshield. They could barely see the road. Lightening flashed around them touching the ground in the not too far distance. Suddenly, a bolt of thunder roared so loudly it seemed to split open the sky. Donovan drove hard so they could make it to the warehouse before the storm hit. Reports were coming in that the west end of the Island, where the beach house was, had begun to flood. Getting off the Island would almost be impossible. They would have to take shelter wherever they could find it.

"Well, here's your cleansing rain," she replied shifting in her seat to find a comfortable position that did not exist. He could hear the strain in her voice.

"No," he replied trying to ease her fears and his own, "this is not what I had in mind. In Ireland, in the village where I grew up, when the rain falls it sounds like music." He accentuated his Irish accent for her notice. She returned his smile and relaxed for a moment; the thought of a happier place was comforting.

Donovan parked in front of the door of the warehouse. No one was outside or near the windows. It didn't feel right. While they were still sitting in the car, Jeanine once again checked his dressings to make sure they were all right. She knew the wounds were fine but she wanted to check it anyway. During their approach to headquarters, Donovan began to change becoming more observant, rigid, and less talkative. He was studying the outside of the building, noting changes, and making mental calculations. It was a few moments before he noticed Jeanine fidgeting about his dressings like a moth around a flame.

He focused his attention on the task at hand. As much as he loved her he had to press forward. "Jeanine," he caught her hand "it's alright. We need to go in now."

"Before we leave," she started, "there's something I need to tell you."

"Jeanine, please" he was irritated with her hesitation believing it to be a stalling tactic.

"No, really, there's something I need to say; something about me you need to know"

"Honey, I know what you are going to say"

"Do you?" she asked surprised.

"Yes, you're going to tell me you love me."

"No, that's not it" she shot back quickly as she shook her head negatively.

"What?" he asked shocked.

"I mean, yes I do but that's not what I need to tell you"

"So you do love me?" he asked furtively with a wink.

"Yes, I do" she answered warmly as her heart pounded in her chest to admit this openly, "but there's more you need to know. It won't be easy for you to hear this but I…"

"No, Jeanine" he instructed holding her hand. She studied his face sensing he couldn't or wouldn't handle what she had to say. She wanted him to know the truth but she couldn't force it. She nodded silently in understanding. Maybe it was better this way. All she had to do now was get to her father and stop Donovan from making contact with Colorado, although she had no idea of how to do this.

She was thankful, actually, for the bad weather. It would make it difficult for Colorado to reach the Island and would buy her some time. In the same vain, she wondered how her father was able to get here so quickly. With the Island being evacuated, all roads were converted to outbound lanes so the only way in would have been to land at Galveston airport, which in Jeanine's mind, surely would have been closed.

They entered the warehouse and were immediately surrounded by Agents. Swenson ordered Donovan to be handcuffed and took Jeanine away to Donovan's office. There was no sign of O'Donnell or Woo. There were two agents with Swenson that Jeanine had never seen before. She caught the sensation Donovan knew them well and vice versa.

After about an hour, Swenson had Donovan brought up to meet them. Jeanine was there, sitting in a chair next to her father. Instantly, Donovan was struck by the coldness in the room. It was not just from Mellicent. He sensed the interaction between Jeanine and her father was particularly grim. He observed a tangible friction between them. It was similar to the reaction she had to President Sardo. Though she was seated next to him she couldn't have been further away.

There were three pine chairs in front of the metal desk. Jeanine was sitting on the far side of him closest to the windows, her father in the middle, and Donovan was closest to the door. Swenson was facing them seated behind the desk grinning with supreme satisfaction like a Cheshire cat.

"I couldn't have asked for more," she exclaimed pleased with herself as she sat rigidly in her chair. Her incredibly pale skin was glowing under the incandescent light produced by the single bulb hanging from an ancient wire chandelier.

"Christmas has come early to this wretchedly humid, mosquito infested, hell hole. I have victory over the mighty Luke Oren Donovan. And all of the loose ends," she looked over at Jeanine, "will be neatly tied."

"I'm not a loose end," Jeanine fumed.

"Talk again and I will shoot you," Swenson countered sharply as she put her hand on her side arm. "Amateur night is over and it is time for you to leave the stage," she hissed. Jeanine retuned the glare undaunted.

"Will you kill your prize before delivering it to Colorado?" Donovan interrupted quickly.

"Colorado will believe whatever I tell him to believe. I will suggest that it was your fault that Dr. Hunter was killed. He will, of course, demand your murder and I will happily oblige. I will do

270

anything to get Colorado's narcotics industry up and running again. My funds are getting low. Colorado has been consumed with finding Dr. Hunter so much so that he has misplaced his priorities. I'm just helping him realize his goals."

"And yours, of course" Donovan reminded.

"Of course, I am first and foremost, a businesswoman."

Donovan provoked her. "You still have an opportunity to do what is right. Turn yourself in, and I'll make it easier for you. You were a good agent once. I can negotiate a lesser sentence."

She huffed and continued in a malevolent tone. "You arrogant ass! You have nothing to offer me! I'm in control. There is no part of this that I haven't already conceived. Colorado has been so consumed with his son that he has taken his focus away from business as usual. Now, he has finally put his attention back on narcotics. It's all politics and money at this point. I needed a contact in South America for narcotics and Colorado needed a kidney. Monica and Dr. Snyder helped us organize the organ transfer. We needed a scapegoat and Dr. Hunter was conveniently in the right place at the right time."

She reminisced with sadistic satisfaction. "It was Snyder's idea to send the infected organs to Colorado's son. He thought it was justice since I told him Colorado was responsible for killing his son. Of course, Snyder never knew that I actually killed his son. He was expendable and I needed him to die in order for Snyder and his quaint little crew to get on board with our plans. Since you involved the press, I need her to disappear permanently. I will blame that on Colorado."

"Furthermore, Snyder and Monica will serve a new purpose as the orchestrators of this malicious organ transfer scheme. They will conveniently be killed, of course, in an escape attempt. That will leave you and the good doctor as the last two pieces of the puzzle. Colorado will kill you, Donovan. And I'm sure Colorado will make Dr. Hunter spend the rest of her short insignificant life in a South American brothel praying for death," she said savoring the imagery.

"Of course, Donovan, don't discount your role in the good doctor's demise. It wasn't until after your press conference that Colorado's interest in her surged. Before your pathetic little stunt, he just wanted her dead. Now, he wants her very much alive, although in what state he didn't say." Swenson cut her eyes sharply at Jeanine as she recalled her earlier threat. The savage tone was not subtle.

Jeanine took an opportunity, "how are you going to explain to Mr. Colorado that you killed his son when you had the chance to save him?"

As Jeanine spoke, Swenson jumped up from the desk, ran around it and back handed Jeanine across the cheek with enough force to throw her to the floor. Donovan tensed but remained still otherwise. He noticed Mr. Hunter was perfectly motionless and calm, much too calm for a father who just witnessed his child being attacked in this way.

"What did you say?" Swenson seethed as she pulled Jeanine upright to a sitting position. Shaking off the pain, Jeanine answered, "You have the opportunity to save Colorado's son. Are you going to let him die?"

"He's already dead!" she fired back emphatically.

"No, he isn't" Jeanine replied quietly. The winds howled ominously outside and debris could be seen flying through the air.

"How do you know that? What are you talking about?" she inquired irately; oblivious to the storm's aggressive assault.

"You don't think the FBI is my only source of information do you? I have contacts in the hospital. There's a VIP patient in the Shriner's Hospital for Burned Children. Very little is known about him and only special hospital staff are even allowed to care for him. The funny thing is that he's an adult in a children's hospital and he was not admitted for burns. I have a source that says he's on daily dialysis and he's from a small city near Cancun. Señor Colorado is not the kind of man to take chances on something as frivolous as revenge. His son is still alive and here on the Island."

"That's ridiculous," she snarled dismissing her and returning to her seat.

"Is it? Don't sit yet, Agent. I am not done with you," Jeanine demanded. Swenson shot up in anger.

"You indignant little…" Swenson seethed.

"In all of your plotting and scheming, when was it that my death became a priority for you? Was it for your mission or for Colorado's? Dr. Snyder used you! You heartless whore! You manipulated Dr. Snyder's anger with Colorado regarding his son's murder. Manipulation and hate have strange ways of backfiring on their users. Snyder knew the organs going to Colorado would fail but he knew something else that he never told you. Something I shared with Monica Rubio."

Swenson became irritated and went back to sit down behind her desk.

"Humph, you would do anything to save your neck right now. Even make up some sad story about a man you know nothing about. Donovan's gamble with putting your face on the national news intensified his desire to find you. When he gets here, I hope he kills you slowly and that I get to watch. He's known for that, you know; just keeping you alive enough to make you suffer longer until you beg for death. I hope you've accomplished all of your meager dreams."

"I have. I have lived my life for a purpose. Soon I will die and you with me. But I will die knowing my life was not in vain." This statement drew the gaze of both men in the room but Swenson continued completely and utterly unaffected.

"And for what purpose do you think you have lived?" Swenson mocked.

"To give my life for someone else's" she replied soberly.

"Who's life you saving?" Swenson asked patronizingly.

Jeanine fell quiet. While they were talking, Donovan had quietly slipped out of his handcuffs. The sound of the wind, rain, and thunder was a useful cover for his movements. He'd hid a transmitter in the heel of his shoe that he used to signal O'Donnell to engage their plan.

The other two agents that had met him and Jeanine at the door were secretly working for him. They hid inside the warehouse waiting for the signal. Donovan kept his arms clasp behind his back to continue the illusion that he was incarcerated. He was grasping a small single shot pistol in his right hand and was waiting for the moment to use it. In this position his shoulder throbbed but he pushed through the pain to wait for the opportune moment.

Just then two very muscular Hispanic men burst into the room. The first man, named Raul, had a 45-caliber handgun and was pointing it at Swenson. Instinctively she reached for her 40 mm Glock but was too late to use it. He fired and grazed her arm, an intentional flesh wound, then pinned her against the wall pressing his forearm into her throat. The other gunman, Daniel, caught hold of Jeanine by the nape of the neck and put a knife to her throat.

"Don't move!" he commanded Donovan. As if to insure Donovan understood his intent he pierced Jeanine's neck with his blade. She winced in pain as blood began to slowly dribble down her neck. Donovan sat back in his chair thankful he had not pulled out his insignificant weapon at this juncture.

"*Es tiempo, Señor Colorado?*" Raul asked nervously glancing at the storm outside.

Donovan and Swenson were equally confused. These men were addressing Jeanine's father as Colorado. The man they addressed sat quietly for what seemed an eternity. He took a long look outside as debris flew past the windows. When he finally spoke, it was slowly and deliberately and with a rich Latin accent.

"*No, Raul. No es tiempo,*" he said wistfully. It seemed their interruption was planned but prematurely executed. The man stood up and walked to the window. Lightening flashed in brilliant displays across the sky. He folded his hand across his chest and chuckled to himself. "I have a dilemma" he began slowly. He spoke with an unsettling and chilling nonchalance as though he had all the time in the world, as if the danger surrounding him was inconsequential.

"Dr. Hunter made an arrangement with me. She told me she could convince Agent Swenson to voluntarily confess she tried to kill my son. And if she succeeded I promised I would not kill Agent Donovan." He stepped away from the window and turned to Donovan.

"You would be happy to know I have been completely aware of your every move. Agent Swenson has provided all of the recordings between you and this woman, at least up until you were wise enough to stop recording yourselves. And while I know this room is likely equipped with audio surveillance equipment, I still find the need of…clearing my mind. And since this storm is upon us I am obliged to take my time," he announced as he carefully stroked his sideburns.

"Thus, my dilemma," he continued, with the exaggeration of his vowels sounds consistent with Spanish influence. "In front of me, I have Agent Swenson whom I always knew would betray me. Betrayal is the nature of my business. For this reason, I have never allowed her to meet me in person. Yet, I had not considered she would be the author of my son's decline.

To my right, I have a man who has hunted me and thwarted me for the last eight years. And on my left, is a woman who does not even know who she is but is willing to give her life to save my enemy and my son. Life is full of contradictions wouldn't you say Donovan? So, while I should kill you for your defiance and interference in my affairs, I have given my word that I would not and I am a man of my word."

Swenson gasped. "Señor Colorado I am so glad you are here!" Swenson blurted out with as much deference as she could muster through her shock. Her obsequious mannerisms were nauseating. "We have so much to discuss. I'm glad we can talk face to face and as you can see I have ascertained Agent Donovan for you as you requested!" she panted hoping to reach his approval. Her blatant denial of her egregious acts was so insulting it infuriated Colorado who shot her a malevolent glare so horrifying she immediately quieted.

"Not to worry, Agent Swenson. You will get all you deserve," he answered with throaty cynicism and brewing wickedness. She swallowed hard and held pressure against her bleeding gunshot wound praying for a way out of her situation.

Colorado peered at Donovan who was perplexed and was searching Jeanine for answers. She did not look well. Her color was poor and she looked a little peaked.

"I see, she has not told you Agent Donovan? How wonderful," Colorado observed with twisted satisfaction. He simply looked at Jeanine and nodded giving her permission to state what was so horribly wrong. *"Dile tu héroe"* he commanded, *"en español, por favor."*

With large tears welling in her eyes, she looked directly into Donovan's face and admitted most painfully, *"Soy la hija de Tomas Cazador Colorado; la sobrina de Don Colorado. Su sangre es mi sangre. Por su rescate yo le doy mi riñón."* Donovan did not need the translation that she proceeded to give. He could see the answer in her face, in the faces of the men in the room, and the man he assumed to have been her father but who was obviously her uncle, Carlos Colorado.

"I am the daughter of Thomas Cazador Colorado; the niece of Don Carlos Colorado. My blood is his blood. And for your life and for his son's, I am giving him my kidney."

Earlier, while Swenson and Donovan were outside of the office, Jeanine and Colorado had been left alone. It was then that she realized the man with her was not her father at all but his brother, her uncle Carlos Colorado. Her father had never mentioned they were twins. She took the opportunity to negotiate with him for Donovan's life. The man who had been holding her released her instantly as if he was caught touching the daughter of a king.

Swenson whispered to her captor, Raul, "His name is Don?"

"¡*Silencio idiota! Se llama Carlos Colorado pero Don es su título*. Silence idiot! Carlos is his name and Don is his title."

Donovan was astonished. The Agency had informed him Colorado was tan skinned. This was the typical view that all South Americans were tan whereas in truth, they are just as racially diverse as North Americans. Donovan could hardly believe it. All this time Jeanine had been lying to him, deceiving him. How could she have done this? How could he have been so blind? He had to focus. Think. He had to find someway out of this mess. Did O'Donnell get his signal?

While Donovan was postulating his conundrum, Colorado had his own. Colorado was now leaning against the wall, regarding Jeanine very strangely. Donovan noticed his regard and was unnerved by it. The best description was…almost lustful towards her.

"I thought I could wait to reveal this to you but the more I see you the more I am inclined to yield to my desires," Colorado finally said to her. Jeanine felt uncomfortable. She didn't know what he was talking about and she didn't want to know. She pleaded to him.

"Señor, please, I am willing to save the life of my cousin with my own. But please, may I ask, you spare the life of this man who has protected me from Agent Swenson. If it had not been for him, she would have killed me, and your son would surely die. I beg for mercy on his behalf." Colorado approached her stealthily adding to her discomfort.

"I like to know the heart of my enemies. What is Agent Donovan thinking?" he asked her surreptitiously. She blinked back at him blankly. "I don't know what he is thinking Señor," she answered.

"*Mira su cara*," he commanded in Spanish, "look at him!"

She peered at Donovan instinctively. The look he gave her was worse than any torment she had ever received. Even the pain in her belly was nothing compared to this. The venom of knowledge slowly broke into his body poisoning him against her; betrayal and pain were in his eyes. Tears welled in her eyes as slowly and painfully Donovan was forced by disgust to look away from her. To make matters worse, the knowledge that Colorado was pleased by Donovan's feelings made it worse.

The conviction of it stabbed him in the chest. He would have preferred death. He could not hide feelings from Jeanine; as much as he tried, he could not suppress his disappointment, disapproval and distrust. Betrayal was, above all things, the hardest thing for him to forgive. He could neither forgive Sherry, his former wife, nor Jeanine. She was stained, tainted, with the sins of Colorado. And Donovan, for as much as he loved her, could not love past it. Colorado smiled sardonically. She had wounded Donovan and this brought Colorado great sadistic pleasure.

"I don't think he knows you as well as he thought, my niece. You are a Colorado, a descendent of kings. We are people of character and culture from the royalty of Spain."

She swallowed hard still reeling from Donovan's silent rejection. Colorado looked at her approvingly and smirked at Donovan.

"You see, how easily love dies," Colorado said savoring the moment with as much ease as though swirling brandy in a large sifter. "He has abandoned you. A Colorado would never stand for that. Do you think his life is still worth saving?" She kept her eyes trained on Donovan's face. With elegance and grace she arched her back and righted her posture pushing through emotional and physical pain.

"When you live for what matters most, there is no sacrifice," she announced with clarity. Colorado was deeply disappointed in her answer. She had not freed him from his commitment to keep Donovan alive. He had hoped to poison her against Donovan. It would sweeten the moment of Donovan's death especially if he could convince her to kill him. It would not be the first time he had used such a method. Her guilt over killing him would, of course, consume her and Colorado could use that guilt to control and manipulate her even against her father who was his next matter of business.

Colorado turned away from her and peered out the window. From the second story window he could barely see the harbor. The rain was falling in torrents and the winds were very high. They could all see debris being picked up and carried by the wind. Soon, this second floor office, with a solid wall of windows, would be too dangerous to occupy.

"While we wait out the storm, tell me. How do you know you can trust me?"

"I don't," she responded flatly. She was still standing but was starting to swoon a little. She kept her movements as small as possible. She still had one card left in this hand to play. No one, including Donovan knew of her illness. It might be enough of a distraction to save their lives.

Colorado needed her alive. Once her illness was made manifest, he would be forced to move quickly to get her to the hospital and remove her kidney. If she died in the warehouse, he would lose. If he was desperate enough, he might even try to leave their shelter

278

during the hurricane. It would be suicide for him to do so but if her sacrifice saved Donovan and rid the Earth of Carlos Colorado she would be happy.

"Hmm," he mused.

"And how do I know I can trust you? Even though you are my niece, you are not loyal to me. How do I know this isn't some scheme?" Her answer sent a chill through both Donovan and Colorado, although neither would outwardly show any effect.

"The FBI has been training me for this moment," she replied with unassuming frankness.

"And what did they tell you to do?" he asked curiously.

"To do whatever you asked me to do and to be completely honest."

"Why?"

"So that you would trust me implicitly"

"To what end?"

"My eventual escape"

"So you will answer any of my questions truthfully?"

"Yes."

"Where is your father?" he asked directly. Jeanine felt a hammer hit her chest. She had not expected him to ask this.

"He is in hiding."

"Your answer does not placate me. I assume this FBI tactic is meant to work with answers you are willing and unwilling to give. With answers such as these you will be in my possession for quite some time," he replied with dissatisfaction.

She sighed and plunged ahead. "I am sure Agent Swenson's recordings can confirm our conversation. I spoke with my father yesterday. He has been afraid of you for years. But after you contacted him earlier this year he decided it was time to mend his relationship with you. At least, that was until I told him to run. We have a code word in the family for trouble, for you specifically. I told him the family needed to take a vacation in the Rockies, referring to the mountain range in Colorado. He knew it meant you had found us. He took the family and left for Los Osos, California. He will contact me when he thinks it is safe." "Los Osos?" Colorado smiled to himself. "Much better," he said.

"I wish I had known the FBI was using such tactics. It would have saved me a lot time and trouble with my interrogations of Agents I have questioned in the past. Yet, I would have missed the thrill of torturing them for information" he announced as he eyed Donovan savagely.

"Does Agent Donovan have any injuries?" he salivated. She hesitated. Donovan sat perfectly still. His posture betrayed nothing. This annoyed Colorado and he nodded to the man who had held Jeanine. Immediately he walked over to Donovan and clicked open a switchblade.

"Yes, he does!" Jeanine blurted out. Colorado held up his hand signaling his accomplice, Ernesto, to halt momentarily. "Where? How?" Colorado commanded.

"His right shoulder and arm," she answered quickly. She was learning that hesitation was displeasing to Colorado. "It happened last night when you tried to kill us. Your men shot at us as we drove down the Seawall"

"Is he right handed?"

"Yes" she answered. She felt her heart sink. If she didn't answer, Colorado would attack him and if she did answer she put Luke more at risk. She didn't know who came up with this scheme in the FBI but she was forced to agree with Colorado, it was not a very good one. She noticed he didn't respond to her accusation that he had attacked them last night. Perhaps it was his men and not Swenson's that were involved.

"*Ernesto, enseña me*" Colorado instructed.   Ernesto, disappointed he couldn't stab Donovan, closed his blade and hastily ripped open his shirt. Seeing the bandages, he whipped out the blade again and cut through them. Making sure to scratch his skin with the tip of the blade to make up for the previous loss. Donovan locked eyes on him and didn't show any sign of pain. Compared to being shot, this scratch was really not that painful. But the lack of fear in Donovan incensed Ernesto to the point he wanted to strike him; but he checked his anger noticing Colorado had not given him permission to act on it, at least not yet. "*Pendejo*," he muttered under his breath and walked away.

"I like this game," Colorado announced smiling and clasping his hands together "but I don't think it will have the effect you desire." Jeanine was silent. "But something confuses me. You still want to protect the Agent even though he has abandoned you?"

"Yes"

"You will soon learn that love is weakness."

"Love is power, Señor," she replied candidly. He cut his eyes harshly at her. "Will you still love your father even though he has betrayed you?" he asked hotly. Colorado was baiting her. Any answer she would give would play into his hands. "I will always love my father," she answered resolutely. He donned a sinister smile.

"Really?" he scorned, "Your entire life is a lie! Your father never told you how close we were. He has painted me as the dissident of the family. But in fact, he taught me everything I ever knew about the business. He was a much better Don than I ever was. I admired him. But for a woman he gave up everything! He probably told you he moved from place to place to evade me? *Pobrecita*, he was not evading me; he could not give up on his own blood. Even when he went to the *federales* 8 years ago to testify against me he could not do it. He realized family is more important." He paused for a moment considering her face.

"Tomas never told you about his involvement did he?" he asked.

"No," she replied solemnly. There was some truth in what he said but how much she was unsure. She could tell he was trying to manipulate her but she would not let him. "Families have many secrets, *querida*. Your father has many secrets from you. He was very influential in my arrival here today. But we will discuss that later. For now, tell me how you knew my son was alive?" Colorado continued.

"I wasn't lying when I told Swenson I had contacts in the hospital. I started thinking about it a few weeks ago when my father told me you had contacted him. I figured you weren't just involved in smuggling organs for profit. You were looking for a match; it did not seem consistent with your character to make a gamble of being caught for such as simple issue of revenge or money. I asked a friend to do some checking, discretely. I had her match my blood with the mystery patient; we are an exact match."

"What do you expect to happen next?" Colorado asked.

"The transplant can't be done at the Shrine. They'll have to take him back to the main hospital through the underground tunnel that connects the two hospitals."

He smiled for a moment.

"Now doctor, you aren't giving clues to your FBI friend here, are you?"

"Of course I am, señor," she replied honestly. He regarded her for a moment. His expression changed only slightly but never revealed enough to betray his thoughts. "Besides, you have already tried to kill me. I am sure your third attempt will not fail." She was baiting him hoping her gamble would further damage his relationship to Swenson who was almost painfully quiet at this point.

"That is your second referral to such an incident," he asked slowly. He was cunning in his own right. Baiting him would prove difficult. "Yes, the first was downtown and the second was last night," she answered. He shot a quick look over at Swenson. It was clear that he had not authorized these attempts. He continued, "If I had been trying to kill you, you would already be dead."

This pricked everyone's ears. His tone was more malicious. Colorado let the moment pass and pressed her with another question. Coming face to face with her he probed again. She was starting to perspire from her forehead. He took it as a sign of fear and was pleased. He used questions like surgeons used instruments to carefully dissect his specimens.

"Are you afraid to die?" he asked eyeing her harshly. She considered her words carefully. She was getting cold and was perspiring. She realized it as a sign she was going into shock. Luckily, she had not vomited again. She would have to keep her answers short and conserve her energy.

"I am not afraid," she answered simply. She held his stare unabashed. She was more like him than he realized. He smiled with a level of satisfaction that perhaps surprised even him. This time, Donovan could read his thoughts. The same fire and passion he saw in Jeanine, Colorado also appreciated.

But she would have to be careful that his amusement with her as one who was unafraid to challenge him wouldn't dissipate into something sinister. She'd have to be careful not to cross the line between an amusement to an annoyance. To men like Colorado, amusements were short lived. "You are not afraid to die?" he asked wickedly.

"I am dying," she replied seizing the opportunity. He raised an eyebrow. "I will control the time of your death should it be necessary," he replied satisfied with himself. "I am hemorrhaging from a gastric ulcer. I have already lost a significant amount of blood. I've been vomiting blood most of the morning. I doubt I will live through the surgery," she said matter-of-factly playing her last card.

Colorado eyed her sharply for a moment trying to decide whether or not to believe her. He assumed her admission of bleeding was a lie to convince him not to do the surgery. If she died and the kidney failed his son would still be in danger. He would need her alive in case the other kidney was needed as well. Colorado assumed this part of the manipulation to secure her escape. Donovan, despite his anger with her, was compelled by this admission to search her face. He could see no sign of deception. He realized that what he thought was fear was actually illness: the tremulousness, the perspiration, and the weakness.

"Ah, you are indeed your father's daughter," Colorado observed with disturbing happiness. He took an opportunity to provoke her. "We are a family of contrasts. We are ruled by our passions and those passions are wildly and often equally diametrically opposed to each other. But one constant is our blood. This business is in my blood just like it is in yours! You cannot deceive me even if you tried."

"Like AIDS, señor?" she asked bluntly as she fell back into the wall, leaning on it for support. It was not intended to be an act of deception, to convince him of her weakness, it was a necessary means of shouldering her growing frailty.

"What do you mean?" he asked sharply as he approached her. "Your son has AIDS by now. The organ they gave him was from a patient with an aggressive form of AIDS and was actively infected.

283

The kidney is one of the body's filters and has a large blood supply."
Colorado was no longer amused with her. He flushed with anger and
grabbed her by the shirt collar bringing her face close to his.

"You may not be afraid to die but by my hand you will
experience such fear and pain that you will pray for death before I
am done!" he seethed. She looked him straight in the eye and said
nothing. She controlled herself and did not let fear creep into her
eyes.   And for a moment, she saw fear in Colorado.

CHAPTER 33
COURAGE

Suddenly there was a muttered sound followed immediately by the shattering of all the glass windows of Swenson's office. The force of it threw them to the floor. Colorado yelled as he dusted off shards of glass, "It's the storm! Get them down to the first floor!"

The deafening roar of the wind and rain all but drowned out his voice. Jeanine was dazed and time passed slowly and strangely. It seemed she'd been unconscious and on the floor for hours wherein reality it was only a few seconds. To her surprise, Colorado assisted her to an upright position. His countenance suddenly changed once he observed the position where she had been laying. She had been lying in a pool of bloody emesis. It was that moment he realized she had been truthful about her illness.

Sudden sharp downdrafts of wind and rain whipped against them from the shattered windows. They made their way down to the first floor. Soaked with rain and blood from broken glass, Jeanine and Donovan were taken to the center of the first floor while Colorado and his men went to the front of the warehouse to check the roads for flooding. Donovan admired his surroundings. They were in the exact same place as his first interview with Jeanine almost a month ago. Surrounded by metal desks on the concrete floor where he had rescued her from Agent Woo's offensive line of interrogation.

They were seated on the floor facing each other. Donovan's arms were still behind his back. Jeanine panted softly and she was speckled with blood. She was decompensating.

"Why didn't you tell me?" he asked vehemently.

"We don't have much time," she quickly answered. Donovan bore down on her adamantly. She tightly closed her eyes and prayed to strain out all the pandemonium around her. Her purpose was to save Donovan and hopefully herself.

Donovan continued his questioning. "All that time I tried to earn your trust you were lying to me" he pressed.

"They'll be back soon," she reminded. "You betrayed me!" he roared back.

"I made a mistake in not telling you about my family. I admit that. But I didn't know, I swear, I didn't know until recently how much he was really involved. Then once I did I thought it wouldn't matter to you…." she paused shaking her head negatively. "No, that's not true. I hoped it wouldn't matter to you. But I knew it would. I didn't want to lose you," she finished remorsefully.

"I'm surprised. The truth?" he asked mockingly. She felt hurt by his sarcasm. The comment found its mark.

"Monica was my friend. After she betrayed me, I didn't know whom I could trust with this information. I wanted to tell you but I didn't know how or when. That was a mistake and I apologize. Please believe I didn't want to hurt you," she insisted.

"Don't worry. You didn't," he scoffed as he cut his eyes at her sharply. She swallowed hard but did not answer. She felt guilty for her role in his deception but she resolved to go forward. She had held her own against Colorado whom she despised and someone she loved would not intimidate her. But the last remark smarted.

"I could have done something if I had known!" he reprimanded angrily. She looked at him earnestly. "Donovan our time is short. Let's both of us be frank. I tried to tell you in the car but you wouldn't listen. You knew didn't you?" she asked pointedly. Her eyes were penetrating even in the poorly illuminated room. He could feel the intensity of her gaze.

"I didn't," he defended.

"Donovan," she insisted unwaveringly. He sighed and clenched his teeth angry that she could still read him. "Alright, I knew something. I started putting things together: the languages, your ability to distinguish my accents, your view points on things, it all told me you were more than you were telling me but never…" he halted momentarily distracted then finally continued.

"Then Glenn found information. Cazador. Colorado's full name is Carlos Cazador Colorado. Cazador means Hunter in Spanish. Your father changed his name after he left the witness protection program. Then I realized your father was my lead witness 8 years ago. He didn't mention he was Colorado's brother or that he had a family. Then, something spooked him into recanting his testimony. He was the link to that case! Without him it fell apart! You and your whole damn family…!" he cursed hotly.

"Don't assume we are the same," she replied patiently checking her temper, "we are not."

"What makes you think I can trust *you*?" he asked sharply. She eyed him defiantly, "Do you think this was easy for me? All I could think about last night was the sacrifice you made for me and how I couldn't let you do it. When I came here tonight, I thought it was to save my father from Swenson. I was fully aware she might kill me. My intention was to save you not destroy you."

Her pain increased again. Donovan noticed her progressive decline but he looked away trying to convince himself he didn't care about her. He wanted her to know how much she had hurt him and to feel it as acutely as he did. He was quiet for a moment. Colorado and his men had not returned.

"The storm seemed to be weakening earlier. It must really be bad to have knocked out all of those windows," she said filling in the silence.

"That wasn't the storm," he informed with a calculated tone. "That was my team. They used an explosive. By now they should all be inside the warehouse. It was part of our plan until you interfered."

She eyed him curiously.

"What?" he asked indignantly, "angry that I didn't tell you about my plans? You would have just told Colorado anyway."

"I was using your techniques," she countered, "remember? You said, 'I will lull him into a false sense of security by using disarming honesty to every question he asks, while waiting for the opportune moment to use his trust to my advantage. And when that moment arises, I will break free with or without the aid of the FBI and secure my own release.' Wasn't that what you were going to do?"

He replied with a heavy heart. "I would have died for you, Jeanine."

"But you won't live for me?" she replied tearfully.

He felt convicted. Before he could answer, Agents O'Donnell and Woo crawled toward them dressed in black urban camouflage and with faces obscured by black paint.

"Boss?" O'Donnell whispered. Donovan acknowledged him.

"Yes O'Donnell, are all of you in position?"

"Our team is in place. There are only ten of us. The rest got cut off by the storm," he informed.

"Are you armed?" O'Donnell asked. Donovan released his arms from behind his back, another secret he held from Jeanine.

"I had this," he replied showing him the single shooter he'd been concealing, "but I'm hoping you have something better for me."

O'Donnell flashed a mischievous grin and pulled out the biggest handgun Jeanine had ever seen. It was a Desert Eagle .50 handgun. Donovan inspected it, nodded approvingly, and loaded it.

"Used one of those?" Woo asked hoping he hadn't. She was looking forward to impressing Donovan with pedantic details.

"Yes, it's made in Israel. I used the prototype while I was there a few years ago," he informed as he checked the weapon.

"Oh," Woo replied disappointed at her lost opportunity to be impressive.   O'Donnell patted her on the shoulder with mock consolation. "Come on, let's get in position," he commanded. He handed Donovan a few other weapons from a large black canvas bag: a MAC 10, a 45 Magnum, and a 9 mm handgun.

Jeanine silently watched, as the arsenal of weapons was unpacked. It occurred to her that they were in for a tremendous gunfight. Woo joined the conversation.

"We recorded the conversation from Swenson's office as you instructed. We have enough evidence from her own testimony to convict her and doctors Snyder and Rubio," she informed.

"That is if we get out of here alive, Woo" Donovan interjected as he took his position behind the overturned metal desks. "We're pinned down in the center of this office and these metal desks will help but they won't give us much cover. Where are the other agents positioned?" he asked.

"Two are forward of our position, four behind us and two are flanking us," O'Donnell stated. "Dr. Hunter does not look well," Woo observed, "is she alright?"

"She can speak, why don't you ask her yourself?" Donovan replied sharply. Woo and O'Donnell exchanged glances. They had heard Jeanine's revelation and all that had been said between she and Donovan. They smartly decided to remain quiet.

Jeanine, indeed, did not feel or look well. She was starting to see double and what Donovan initially thought was rain on her forehead he was alarmed to learn was perspiration. She was going to need medical attention soon.

"How's the storm?" he asked Woo.

"It's the most amazing thing sir. Someone up there must be rooting for you. It was a category 4-hurricane set to slam into Galveston then about half an hour ago it just lost strength and was downgraded from a hurricane to a tropical storm. It sharply veered west, away from all the predicted hurricane models and is fading fast over south Texas. That said, half of the Island is at least 2 feet under water and there is no power on most of the Island. The hospital is running on its own generator" Woo informed.

Donovan instinctively looked at Jeanine when Woo referred to a higher power rooting for them. He heard Jeanine say she wanted to live for God's purpose. He considered how God's purpose was affecting all of this and how God was watching over them now. What were the odds of this massive storm dissipating and changing course precisely at the time of their most urgent need, he wondered.

Donovan redirected his attention to his agents. "Do we have a visual on Colorado?" he asked Glenn.

"Affirmative, there are three of them inside the warehouse near the entrance. Swenson is with them."

"It isn't like Colorado to travel this lightly. He must have other men with him. Be on your guard," Donovan commanded.

They nodded and quietly turned over the metal desks to give themselves cover from any fire. Donovan signaled the other agents via an earpiece to get ready. The agents on the catwalk would be his eyes. He instructed two of the agents from his rear position to move forward to his flank giving them more of a front against whatever arsenal Colorado had procured.

"I've got your six," O'Donnell replied as he took position behind Donovan. The three agents formed a tight triangle with O'Donnell covering the rear of their position.

"Doctor, tuck yourself into this crevice and keep your head down. We're going to get you out of this," O'Donnell instructed patiently. He made sure she was tucked well within a corner of the desks out of the line of fire. His hand brushed hers as she got slunk in between the desks. She was cold and clammy and this alarmed him.

Instinctively, he shot a look over to Donovan that made him shudder. He knew that expression. He'd seen it before. Jeanine didn't have a lot of time. Yet, the reality was that Donovan couldn't save Jeanine or anyone else if he was dead and Colorado would stop at nothing to kill him.

"Get ready," he commanded.

"Wait," Jeanine said feebly, "you should know Colorado's men aren't completely supporting him. Before they knew I could understand them, they were speaking to each other privately. They respect his power but not the man. If Colorado falls and they are captured they'll want a deal. If he's taken and they escape they'll take over Colorado's operation but their loyalty is not to him personally. They referred to someone else as the real strength in their camp but it was not Colorado himself."

O'Donnell nodded, "Understood. Now, get in there!" She grabbed his arm as he pushed her into her little cubby.

"O'Donnell, Donovan won't hear this but you must. Colorado wants Donovan dead but he needs me alive. Given the two options, he'll take me first before he kills you or Donovan. If this confrontation ends badly and he takes me to the hospital, follow the tunnels between Shriner's Hospital. It will lead you to the adult burn unit and then directly into the surgery suite. From there, Donovan can guide you to the hidden suite in sterile well. That's probably where they'll do the surgery."

"It will be fine, doctor. You'll see," he comforted with slight patronization.

But as he pulled away from her, he could see there was more to this. She knew they were in dire straits and all the weapons in the world might not be enough to save them. He eyed Woo, who was nervous but holding her own and Donovan who was intensely focused. This could be the last moment he was alive. The poignancy of it all hit him profoundly. He secured his position and for the first time in his life, he was afraid. It just wasn't for fun or adventure anymore. This was for real. He could handle the possibility of his death but Woo? Jeanine? Donovan? For this reality he was not prepared.

Once all positions had been confirmed, Donovan commanded them to open fire on Colorado's position. Their goal was to neutralize Colorado's men but not terminate them. Donovan would draw their fire while the other teams would surround and neutralize them. Almost as immediately as Donovan's team began to fire, Colorado's men returned fire. As Donovan had suspected, there were more of Colorado's men present in the warehouse than they had seen. Initially, with the element of surprise, the FBI had the upper hand but soon they found themselves outnumbered. Donovan's concern about being pinned in the middle of the room found fruition.

Bullets were flying everywhere and Donovan was trapped in a crossfire. Two agents were killed and four others were injured. To Jeanine, everything was happening in slow motion. The bullet casings fell down in slow motion like rain falling down all around her. She was conscious enough to know they were all going to die. She knew what she had to do but earnestly prayed she would not have to do it. She mustered the strength and intestinal fortitude to press forward. While the agents were distracted, she soldier crawled to an open space behind the desks in the darkness and found an area not under fire. She called out to Colorado.

"*Tio Colorado!*" she called, "*Tio Colorado estoy aqui!*" Colorado heard her and ordered her to come forward. "*Tio,*" she called from her hiding place, "please stop! I will go with you. But I don't have much time left. If you want to save your son, now is the time."

"Jeanine no!" Donovan yelled at her looking for her vainly in the dark.

"It's the only way Donovan!" she called back to Donovan. She stood up meekly ten feet away from Donovan. With her arms raised in surrender, she walked slowly toward Colorado. As she approached Colorado's position, both sides ceased firing; admiring her courage in eerie silence as she surrendered herself to certain death. Even the storm outside was suddenly stilled. All that could be heard was the soft sound of raindrops falling from the roof to the ground. Then, unexpectedly, a shot rang out in the darkness.

"Hold your fire!" Donovan yelled uncertain who fired the shot.

The breath halted in his chest as Jeanine slowly sank to the floor, bending at the knees. A sharp assiduous fire more piercing than anything she had ever experienced was burning in her lower abdomen. She'd been shot. Soon they realized the shot came from Colorado's area. Swenson had pulled a 25-caliber pistol out of her ankle holster and shot Jeanine in the abdomen. Colorado realized what occurred, yelled in outrage, and jabbed a knife into Swenson's neck slashing her trachea. She died slowly gasping for air in agony.

Donovan, without concern for his own welfare, leaped over the desk he'd been using as shelter and raced to Jeanine's side with Woo and O'Donnell not far behind with weapons drawn to cover him.

"Jeanine!"

She was conscious and in agony. He found her wound and placed pressure on it to control the bleeding. She wailed in pain and struggled to breathe.

"It hurts," she gasped slowly.

"I know, I know, don't talk, Jeanine. Lie still!" he instructed.

"Put something under her legs! We have to keep her from going into shock" he yelled at Woo who promptly follows his commands. He could not see the wound, but from the amount of blood she was losing, he knew it was bad.

"I'm sorry," Jeanine apologized in between gasps for air.

"Don't talk, Jeanine," he whispered softly cradling her face with his hand.

"No, I really am sorry. I thought you were a big baby last night after you got shot but this hurts," she said slowly as they both chuckled.

"Good, humor is good," he replied encouragingly. She moaned and had a hard time opening her eyes.

"Stay with me, stay with me Jeanine. Don't give up! Come on, stay with me," he pleaded shaking her until her eyes opened again. Colorado and his men came to them.

"We have to move her now," Colorado instructed. Donovan refused to let her go without him.

"Her kidneys will mean nothing to you if she bleeds to death. We can kill each other later. Your vehicles have all been compromised. My car is around back." Donovan informed.

Colorado reluctantly agreed to allow Donovan to come with them but promised to kill him as soon as feasible. One of Colorado's men would stay behind to keep O'Donnell and Woo from following.

Colorado and Ernesto removed Donovan and Jeanine from the warehouse. Donovan carried her limp body to his car. She was shivering and barely conscious. The rain had stopped and there was a disturbing stillness to the Island. Once they reached the hospital, Donovan lifted Jeanine out of the car. Blood had heavily stained the tan leather seats where she had been sitting.

Back at the warehouse, the rest of their FBI team soon joined O'Donnell and Woo. They had been kept at bay by the storm. Once securing their position, O'Donnell recalled Jeanine's advice and knew where to find them.

In the surgical suite, an anesthesiologist was gowned and standing above the bed where Jeanine was to lie. In the bed adjacent to hers presumably lay Emilio Colorado. He was awake, prepped for surgery and waiting for them.

Donovan gently laid her on the surgical table. He recognized the surgeon, Dr. Cahill, who had done Mr. Morrow's surgery and sent Jeanine to sterile well. Dr. Cahill evaluated her wound and determined the bullet had passed through her body. It was unclear if any vital structures were damaged. Colorado was concerned for her life as long as her kidneys were still viable. They stripped Jeanine from the waist up, bandaged the gunshot wound and hastily prepped her for surgery. They would be removing the organs from her back as the kidneys were in the retroperitoneum.

The anesthesiologist avoided Donovan's gaze and focused mainly on the many adjustments he had to make for her anesthesia. He touched and adjusted monitors and tanks hastily. Donovan could see that his presence during the surgery was most unexpected and unwelcome. The doctor knew, as well as Donovan, that they were now liabilities. There could be no witnesses. It was the way Colorado operated. He would have no more value to Colorado after the surgery.

The only reason to keep Jeanine alive would be if the organ failed so they could harvest her other kidney. Jeanine was barely conscious but fully anticipated dying. Yet her grace and courage were obviously perceived; even Colorado's callous heart was touched momentarily.

"We will have much to discuss after you are revived," Colorado informed her as he stood before her. "No, we won't, Tio," she replied barely above a whisper. He did not reply but her honest purity riled his wicked nature. From anger at Jeanine, and for the perverse thrill, he commanded Ernesto to bring Donovan next to Jeanine's bedside. He was forced at gunpoint to sit in a chair adjacent to the head of her bed so that they were face to face.

"Make him watch," Colorado instructed.

Ernesto stood above Donovan as he sat down on the steel framed, wheeled, black leather cushioned doctor's stool. Jeanine was placed in the prone position with her head facing Donovan. He looked into her face. Time stood still; he could almost hear the slow steady pace of her heart beat. She was at peace. There was still love in her eyes for him. Love he felt he did not deserve. She was dying to save him. In that moment, he understood, his love for her was more powerful than his hate for her uncle.

He parted his lips to say something to her but the words did not come. The anesthesiologist placed a mask carrying anesthetic gases over her mouth and nose. Her eyes became heavy with sleep until they no longer opened. It was then that Donovan realized this was Dr. Sardo, President Sardo. Sardo and Cahill must have been members of Snyder's coven of doctors. The same group that was repairing society's ills with their own brand of reform. It was clear their reform had been seduced by the power of money. This is how he would save her.

Donovan asked, "Don Colorado, did president Sardo tell you of his relationship with Dr. Snyder?" Sardo's hand trembled violently barely able to keep his hand steady on the tanks and cylinders that controlled Jeanine's breathing. When Sardo realized Donovan had discovered his identity, he knew he would be even more of a liability to Colorado and that he would not live through the night.

"Did you act against my orders, *El Presidente?*" Colorado asked angrily realizing the truth of Donovan's statement.

"The president was afraid you would eventually kill him. He made a deal with Agent Swenson and worked with her to kill Jeanine. Only Sardo would have had the information on the back ways of the hospital. He was responsible for the ambush that almost killed her the other night, Don Colorado," Donovan revealed.

"Don Colorado," Sardo started meekly, "I think we have a problem." The words got caught in his throat.

"Yes, I believe we do," Colorado continued. "But it will have to wait until after her surgery. I prefer her alive but my main concern is her kidneys. At this point, take them both out. If she survives, she can have the luxury of dialysis." Colorado instructed.

Cahill stood paralyzed and speechless while tentatively holding his scalpel in his right hand too afraid to move. He had not anticipated any of this. He was only involved for a fat check. Death was not on his agenda. Sardo mustered what was left of his cojones.

"There are new rules, Señor. I carry in my hands the life of your son and niece. One turn of my canisters and they both die. I'm going to walk out of here untouched. I will call you with instructions on how to revive them. If I die, they die."

Just then, Agent O'Donnell and a crew of armed FBI agents burst through the OR doors. The lights were immediately dimmed to fifty percent of their typical illumination. Sardo was struck in the shoulder by a bullet. Donovan quickly jumped up grabbed Ernesto's wrist, pulled him forward and hyperextended his elbow breaking it. He then pulled him across his shoulder and onto the floor.

Ernesto wailed in pain as he crawled to his feet and managed to draw another gun out of his waistband with his unbroken arm. Before he could aim his weapon, Donovan whipped out the small pistol he had concealed earlier and shot him in the head. Colorado managed to slip out in the darkness. O'Donnell secured the area and then went after Colorado to no avail.

Jeanine and Emilio Colorado lie unconscious side by side. Then Donovan put a gun to Sardo's head and commanded him to revive Jeanine, "You wake her up without any harm or I'll shove this gun so far up your ass even a skilled surgeon won't be able to extract it." If there was any doubt to his sincerity, the unmistakable sound of Donovan cocking his weapon secured Sardo's attention. Sardo reversed the anesthesia immediately but he could not revive her. She did   not   resume   breathing   on   her   own.

CHAPTER 34
TRANSFUSION

A skeleton crew of physicians and nurses stayed behind to weather the hurricane and assist people affected by the storm. Jourdan, Jeanine's former acquaintance, was among them. O'Donnell brought Jourdan to the operative suite to help Jeanine. When he saw her, he went pale. The reaction was fleeting but obvious. After being briefed by Donovan as to her condition and to his true identity, he clenched his jaw but remained gravely quiet. He quickly assessed her heart rate and respiratory status.

"She's going to need exploratory surgery to assess any internal hemorrhaging from the GSW," he informed referring to her gunshot wound. "She also needs a scope to see if her ulcer is still bleeding and if so to be cauterized. She's lost a lot of blood. Her pulse is thready and her nailbeds are pale. It's a good thing she's intubated and on a ventilator otherwise she'd already be dead. Despite that, the blood bank is running low and she needs at least two units of blood to survive surgery. I can give her volume expanders but she is going to need blood or she's going to die."

A male nurse interjected, "We have to type and cross match! Plus she is your friend. You cannot operate on her it's a breach of ethics!"

Jourdan grabbed him by the collar. "We are in MASH mode! If we don't operate and get blood into her she's going to die! How ethical would that be? Don't hit me with that pansy ass ethical shit! We're going to save her life!"

"We don't have her blood type," the RN replied hurtfully. "I looked in her records. She's B-negative one of the rarest types there is." Jourdan looked deflated upon hearing the news.

"Of course you do," Donovan injected. Jourdan studied him. "Take mine," Donovan urged as he rolled up his sleeves and lie on the gurney next to hers. "We'll need two units," Jourdan advised the nurse. He examined Donovan's arm and shoulder wound and recognized them as being very fresh.

"Make that one unit," he corrected. Donovan caught Jourdan's arm as he started to recline on the gurney.

"You need two units then take two units!" Donovan demanded.

"You've recently lost a lot of blood yourself. You don't have much to give me. I need to preserve you in case she needs more blood later. Now lie back, we're wasting time." Jourdan's logic caused Donovan to yield.

"This is highly irregular!" the nurse continued to rant, "I don't like this. What if he has hepatitis or something! I don't want to be sued by her! People are suing RN's now a days."

"Given the option of immediate death vs. the possibility of life with hepatitis I think Dr. Hunter, who has saved your sorry ass on many occasions, would choose life. Now stop bitching and get to work!" Jourdan demanded.

+++++

Jeanine lie in her bed beneath the muddy waters of unconsciousness. The soft monotone ping of the ICU cardiac monitors was soothing to her ears. Like the gentle ring of the buoys that sing out quietly on calm weather days were these familiar single-toned beeps to her subconscious. Her eyes slowly opened and she recognized Jourdan standing over her. She was still too weak to speak. He noticed her eyes were open and smiled gently as he caressed her forehead.

"Hey," he called gently, "I always wanted to see you naked in my bed, but not like this!" He said causing her to chuckle a bit. "But if I had to lose you to someone, I guess he'll do," he stated glancing approvingly over his shoulder at Donovan. Donovan was sleeping in the bed next to hers receiving intravenous fluids. She gave a small smile and fell back under the gentle pool of unconsciousness surrendering herself to the healing of a deep sleep.

CHAPTER 35
ANSWERS

Jeanine's eyes hurt. As she opened them, the brightness around her was painful. Slowly, as her eyes adjusted to the light, she discovered the pain in her throat was significantly worse than what her eyes had been. Talking seemed impossible. Her vision was blurry but she could make out the image of a person hovering over her. She was initially frightened but as her vision corrected she recognized the smiling face of Dr. Savage.

"Hey, kiddo" he said while affectionately taking her hand, "glad to see you're awake."

"Lie still, the answers are coming. Just rest," he said reassuringly.

"Where am I?" she asked.

"In John Sealy Hospital."

"How long have I been here?"

"About 2 weeks."

"Why does everything hurt?"

"Everything's been broken," he replied solemnly. This caught her attention and her eyes searched him.

"My memories are fragmented. I have images but I can't make them into anything cogent."

"It will come with time."

"Do I... do I still have my kidneys?" she asked cautiously, afraid of his answer, as her hands cautiously roamed over her body searching for scars. "What happened?" she asked as her eyes grew wide as she felt the scar from her abdominal surgery.

"That's what we want to know," said a voice coming through the door. It was an FBI agent named Arnold Crookshank who was directly followed by Luke Donovan. "I'm very pleased to meet you Dr. Hunter; your heroism precedes you. I am Arnold Crookshank the FBI deputy director. You are acquainted with our special narco-terrorism director, Agent Donovan, I presume?"

Jeanine immediately read Crookshank as someone not to be trusted. He reeked of false modesty, self-importance, and seemed altogether foul. She also had a vague recollection that Agent Swenson had mentioned him as her boss. This added to the negative opinion of him. Donovan briefly made eye contact with her. Jeanine could see that he was unsettled and this made her all the more uncomfortable.

"Doctor," Crookshank addressed Dr. Savage, "would you mind leaving us for a moment?" Jeanine and Savage exchanged quick glances. It was all she needed to say. "Yes, I would mind," Savage answered dryly. He remained planted at her bedside. "Very well, you may stay...for the time being," Crookshank answered patronizingly. "What would you like to know, Agent Crook?" Jeanine inquired as she struggled to find a comfortable position in her hospital bed.

"That's Crookshank, Miss," he corrected condescendingly.

"That's doctor, sir," she countered smartly through painful winces as she wrestled with what seemed a hundred different cords and wires all over her body. He regarded her momentarily before proceeding. She was no simpleton.

"Perhaps, Dr. Savage, you can serve a useful purpose after all. Bring us up to speed regarding the doctor's medical issues."

"Agent Donovan found you intubated and unconscious. Apparently, Agent Swenson shot you and your peptic ulcer ruptured. You had lost a significant amount of blood and your hemoglobin was life-threateningly low at 6. We had GI to do an endoscopic procedure and cauterize the bleed and Jourdan repaired the guns shot wound to your abdomen.

Even with the success of those surgeries you were in trouble hemodynamically. With so many people off of the Island and with the limited supply in the blood bank due to high demand from the hurricane and everyone injured in it, we almost lost you. Fortunately, Agent Donovan was a match. He donated quite a few units of blood and quite literally saved your life," Dr. Savage informed.

Jeanine listened intently digesting it as slowly as she could. She regarded Donovan who was looking at everything in the room but her avoiding her gaze at all cost.

"Your heroism in terms of Agent Swenson has been most useful. You discovered her illegal organ smuggling activities. But we need your further assistance. Where is your family, doctor? What can they tell us about Colorado?" Crookshank asked as he engaged her with a slithering and calculated coldness that made her recoil. She was glad Dr. Savage was with her. As she started to answer, she took notice of Donovan. He shifted his stance. It was slight but enough not to escape Jeanine's notice.

"Tell me something Agent Crookshank. Where is Carlos Colorado?" Jeanine inquired. She saw Crookshank glance at Donovan. She knew then that Colorado had escaped.

"We were hoping you could tell us," he answered slyly as he righted his posture. The longer she was with him the less she liked him. "I don't know where he is," she responded "Why would I?"

"Are you refusing to answer my questions, *doctor*?" he asked haughtily.

"I've answered the only one you've asked."

"Don't play games with me!" he said irately.

"You may ask me a question and the answer may not please you. Regardless of your disposition, it is still the truth."

"Do you want to dance with me?" he provoked. He had a higher opinion of his intimidation skills than he actually possessed. It was like being interrogated by an angry butterfly. Jeanine wanted to laugh but it hurt too much to try.

"Is that a question I'm supposed to answer?" she countered.

"Look, in this room I am God!" he roared next to her face.

Jeanine's countenance became serious. "Of few things, I am certain. And with absolute assurance I can say in no uncertain terms that no sir, you are not God," she answered firmly.

The pale imp of a man clenched his teeth. "I am going to turn your life upside down!" he yelled.

She relaxed her head back into her pillow and for a moment Crookshank thought he had dominated her.

"I've been dead, Agent Crookshank. You do not frighten me," she answered somberly pitying Crookshank as fatigue caught up with her.

Crookshank flushed finally conceding defeat. Apparently, he had told Donovan he could get the answers he wanted from her without his help. He felt she had been holding back and thought intimidation would get her to respond to him.

"Alright, did Colorado say anything? Where he was going or what he was going to do?" He asked in an apologetic tone.

"Not that I recall," she answered quietly. Crookshank noticed her answer had the polish of a well informed witness; never giving away more than desired.

"Indeed," Crookshank acknowledged her realizing this line of questioning was at an end.

"Well," he continued, "I congratulate you on your service to the Bureau. Almost as soon as you were discovered, the media got hold of your story and has painted you with such elegant brush strokes that any other portrait would be damaging to the general public and the image of the FBI." She was silent. Crookshank merely nodded and turned to leave. Donovan remained silent and left with him.

Jeanine hoped to see Donovan again soon. She wanted to talk with him about all the things that had happened. A day passed, then another, then a week with no sign of him. She felt anxious but knew there had to be a good reason why he stayed away so long. The guard planted outside her room for protection in case Colorado returned was the only tether she still had to Donovan. Finally after almost three weeks he returned. He didn't say much to her but seemed wholly distracted, almost dismissive, as he had been before.

"Donovan, what's wrong?" she asked quietly trying to reach out to him. He seemed further away from her than he had ever been. It seemed to pain him to be in her presence. With great effort he looked into her face. Seeing the pain his mood was causing her, he flashed the largest smile he could muster which was much like a forced grin.

"I just have a lot on my mind. I wanted to see you. I'll be gone for a few days then I'll be back," he said stoically. He patted her hand gently and left without another word.

At this point, she didn't know how he felt about her especially now that he knew who she really was. He had cared enough to save her life even with his own blood but from what she knew of him, he would have done that for anyone in need. Was his love strong enough to endure the fact that she was related to Carlos Colorado? Only time would tell.

After a few days, as promised, Donovan returned. She was just leaving her room to do some physical therapy by walking with her therapist around the nurses' station. The nurses' station was in the center of the room and the patient's rooms formed a perimeter around it. Donovan seemed more at ease now than he did a few days ago.

"I didn't know if you were coming back," she said quietly as he entered her room.

He admired her for a moment. She had lost a significant amount of weight and appeared frail reminding him of Mrs. Thibodeaux. Ironically, the very thing Colorado wanted, he almost caused her to lose, as she'd come very close to losing one of her kidneys due to the severe blood loss she had endured. Despite this, she was still remarkable.

"I told you I'd be back," he replied warmly. The effect immediately brightened her countenance.

"I have to do some PT now," she replied as she nervously and desperately trying to close the gaping hole in the back of her hospital gown.

"Go ahead, we'll race on your next turn," he smiled. As she carefully made her way around the perimeter with the assistance of two physical therapists, it caused Donovan to reflect on his own circumstances. What she had endured physically, he was going through emotionally: tattered and torn and far less bright than what he used to be. Only a semblance of his old self remained.

As Jeanine rounded the corner she witnessed some commotion and caught sight of Donovan's wild eye. At first, she was terrified at first glance thinking Carlos Colorado had returned. Then fear gave way to recognition. Jeanine's father had arrived and when Donovan saw him approach he mistook him for Carlos Colorado and pinned him face down on the nurse's desk in a half nelson with a gun firmly pressed behind his left ear.

"No!" she yelled. "No Donovan, stop! He's my father!"

As quickly as her frail legs, IV pole, befuddled physical therapists, and multiple lines and cables would allow her, she went to Donovan walking towards him with hurried caution as she did not want to accidentally provoke him into shooting her father. She placed her hand gently on the arm holding the gun. His bicep was fiercely tensed. At first, he kept his eyes fixed on Thomas, seething with all of the anger he had for Colorado. But under the calm call of his name, like the lure of a siren, she called to him.

"Donovan...Donovan," she gently called using her voice to pull him to her. Finally, he averted his eyes to hers; but unwilling to give up his prize he kept the man pinned to the desk. What her voice started, her eyes finished causing him to relinquish his hold.

Thomas stood up and rubbed his neck with more fervor than was really necessary. He reached for Jeanine and hugged her long and tight with his good arm while nursing his bad arm and glaring at Donovan over Jeanine's shoulder. Donovan left them to get some coffee but made sure one of his agents was still present for surveillance. He did not know if Carlos was near by but somehow he suspected he was close.

Thomas helped his daughter back onto bed. "I got here as soon as I could," he apologized. "The streets are still a mess from the storm. Damned Feds! Crooked bastards!" he said emphatically.

"Dad?" she asked concerned and confused for such an outburst.

"It's alright, baby. You couldn't have known. You probably wanted to tell me what was going on but they wouldn't let you. That's how they operate by separating families from each other."

"That's how who operates? What are you talking about?" she asked confused.

"It's okay honey," he repeated fidgeting over her. "I was angry at first but now I see what was going on. They forced you to cooperate and not say anything to me. But I'm here now. I won't let them do anything else to you. Least of all that bastard!" he exclaimed referring to Donovan as he cut his eyes at the door awaiting his return.

She started to understand his meaning. Her wish to defend Donovan and facilitate a positive relationship between them superseded, perhaps tragically, the wiser voice advising her to tread carefully. She forged ahead hoping to argue on behalf of Donovan. The effect only polarized them against each other.

"Dad, it's really not what you think. I made the decision not to tell you about what was happening not the FBI. I didn't want to put you in danger. If I told you I knew you'd come."

"You don't have to defend them!" he spat scornfully.

Jeanine was taken aback by his vehement response but it did not lessen her interest.

"He defended me, dad. If it weren't for him I would be…"

"If it weren't for him you would have never been in this mess in the first place! They are all the same, a bunch of crooked, conniving assholes. You should have come to me!" he roared bitterly. With each attempt she made to calm his anger it just exponentially increased.

"Don't be naïve Jeanine. He used you. That's why you are here in this condition. My baby! Nearly dead because of him. I'm going to file a complaint with his superior and get him fired. But you should have known better! How could you endanger the family in this way? You don't even know him."

Jeanine noticed how the tide of anger was now flowing towards her. She was hurt deeply. She could not believe her father was so hateful towards Donovan and even towards herself. Not once did he even inquire about her condition. He kept telling her what she was feeling and what she was doing. Yet he never owned up to his own involvement in the process. She needed to walk a fine line between these two men she loved. She had no idea of how to do so.

"If it weren't for him, dad, Tio Carlos would have my kidney and I would be dead," she said calmly. He huffed at her dismissing her allegation.

"Carlos wasn't going to hurt you Jeanine!" She was surprised by his defensiveness on the subject.

"How do you know that?" she probed. He refused to answer but went on about other issues.

"What happened between you and Donovan eight years ago?" she probed.

Barely able to disguise his surprise at her question, he answered her with as few details as possible. "Eight years ago, Carlos was very close to discovering us. We were in Pennsylvania at that time, so I decided to make the trip to FBI headquarters in Virginia and told them I knew Carlos Colorado and could testify against him.

I never told any of you. I worked with Agent Donovan, who promised us safety in the witness protection program. However, I reconsidered and refused to testify so that bastard, Donovan, cut me loose from any safe harbor. I was forced to work with another Agent in the Bureau who has been using me even up until this day. They told me that if I did not cooperate my family would be sent back to South America."

"You cannot trust them!" Thomas insisted adamantly. "I love you Jeannie bug and I am going to protect you. I forbid you to continue whatever agreements you have started with that man!"

Jeanine listened carefully. His story and Donovan's contradicted each other. She had the distinct impression her father was not being completely honest with her, which surprised her greatly. Moreover, she recalled from her own memory never meeting Donovan or any agents 8 years ago. She also recalled Donovan's descriptions of that time period. He specifically said the witness changed his mind and decided not to testify and the case fell apart. He never mentioned anything of the witness after that.

Her father continued, assuming her thoughtfulness was a sign that she believed his testimony. He advised her more tenderly.

"Jeanine, I am no fool. From our conversations, I know you have feelings for that..." he paused struggling with the impulse to call Donovan a bastard again. "That man," he finished with difficulty.

"He's a scoundrel. He lies for a living. You have to think about it. He works undercover. He lies every day. For all you know he could have a wife. I'm telling you this as a father who loves his daughter. You think he loves you but he doesn't. He's going to leave you. He's going to say you misunderstood his feelings for something else. That he was just doing his job to protect you."

Unknown to them, Donovan was listening outside the door. As Donovan overhead them, he realized their conversation was a key to an unfortunate task he had to complete. He flashed back to a conversation he had with Crookshank on the day before Crookshank interrogated Jeanine.

"Donnie boy," he started with an insidious smile, "I savor so many of my moments with you." He crowed coolly with a swagger he could only imitate from his impressions of greater men.

"I've taken count and so far every woman you've had has come under my power."

"A greater man would never boast of conquests of another man's leftovers," Donovan replied unaffected.

"Avoidance is your hallmark. You can keep that. What I've come for is Dr. Hunter. Rather your relationship with her. I've received orders from on high that Colorado still wants her alive. So, she's free to roam as bait. To that end, you cannot have any relationship with her." He stated nonchalantly.

"On high?" Donovan repeated, "Crooked I know you are bent but do you think you are Moses now?"

"There you go avoiding the issues again. Scoff if you will. Colorado slipping through your fingers, yet again, has not left a palatable flavor in the mouths of the Bureau chiefs. Colorado surfaced for her once he'll do it again. And this time I'll be waiting. That said you cannot associate with her. And you need to end things in such a way that she won't come after you like some lovesick puppy with its nose wide open. Make it...distasteful" he sneered.

"Speaking of distasteful, don't you have some reports to file or handcuffs to don for your involvement in all of this?" Donovan pressed.

"Poor simple Donovan; this is why you will never be more than a foot soldier, a pawn in a broader game you will never understand. Didn't you know? Your friend, your mentor Renee has absolved me of all association with Swenson's misguided assertions. You don't know how far up the chain of command I reach. Poor Swenson had a terrible misunderstanding."

Crookshank could see the effect on Donovan. His eyes were sharp and his breaths quickened. Crookshank pushed him farther.

"So, either you break it off or I'll charge her as an accessory after the fact with narco-terrorism and organ smuggling. And before you mount your self-righteous high horse, I don't care if the charges stick. You of all people know how damaging allegations can be. The press is easily manipulated as Renee has already proved. They love to form all kinds of conspiracy theories. In a second, I'll turn Jeanine from a heroine into villain. The "killer doctor" they'll say. They will convict her in the court of popular opinion and the damage to her career will be irrevocable. She'll never work as a doctor again."

He turned and called over his shoulder. "Now if you could hurry, I have to get back to your wife...oh, excuse me, my wife. You know how she hates waiting. She's a horny little minx!"

The words hit Donovan in the chest. As much as Donovan tried to deny Crookshank his satisfaction, he knew something of what the man had said was true. But he had to know for himself. He had to confront Renee. During the weeks he was absent from Jeanine, he flew to see Renee in D.C.

"What is it sport?" she asked irritated not bothering to look up from her desk.

"I have questions," he answered shortly as he forced the door closed with resonance to her Bureau office in Washington. She glanced up for a second but never skipped a beat in the memo she was writing.

"I don't have time to deliver a lecture," she replied tersely.

"I'm not asking for one. I want the truth."

She huffed. "When has truth ever been your priority? But let me come to the point. I know why you're here. You want to know if I'm the one pulling Crookshank's strings. The answer is yes I am. You want to know if I ordered him to charge the doctor unless you agreed to leave her alone. No, not really. But it was a nice touch. I can get what I need from her just like I have from her father for the last decade."

"What?" Donovan asked incredulously.

"You don't think I really benched myself do you? I've been in charge of an undercover Op for the last 10 years. When you asked how high I could reach I wasn't being facetious. I've been pulling the strings on this case even before you arrived. I was the one who chose you for this case. After Thomas Hunter refused to testify for you all those years ago, I placed him in the witness protection program and under my thumb and I used your authority to do it. I knew there was going to be a need for him so I kept him quietly in my pocket.

I had no idea he was Colorado's brother but I knew keeping you on the scent would prove useful. Crookshank was dirty but I needed you to find out how dirty. He doesn't know the Bureau is onto him. He wanted credit for Colorado's capture but I gave it to you, as you deserved it. Subsequently, Crookshank won't be charging anyone with anything, as he'll be protecting his taught white little ass from harm in a federal prison. You have a lot of clout in the Bureau now chief. That's my gift to you. But for now, he roams free until we figure out how far up the chain this thing goes."

"You lied to me! Manipulated me! I trusted you!" he demanded. She responded with blithe indifference to his feelings.

"Good God! Don't be an infant! I'm giving you a gift. Don't fuck it up! I told you that working in this industry was like that thin yellow fucking line! I don't talk just to hear myself think I had a damned point. I don't owe you a thing. Get that sonny? I didn't have to tell you jack. I don't like many people but I like you. You're sharp and smart and you and kiss my ass in such a way that pleases me. I'm gonna give you a little room on this to vent some steam but don't be a pussy. My patience is short. Now either fuck her or marry her but get the hell on with it and out of my office!"

Donovan left. He felt debased and dehumanized. He wandered aimlessly for a few hours before finding himself back on a plane to Galveston. He had to talk to Jeanine. He didn't trust anyone now- not Renee, not Jeanine, and not even himself. He had to get out of the country, clear his head, and get perspective on things.

Over the next few weeks he made his way back to her. Jeanine was discharged from the ICU to the regular floor. She had several visitors including her Doctors Ivory, Rucker, and Black. It was there that Donovan finally came to see her. Late morning sunlight was flooding in from the window. He brought a small vase of gardenias with him and set it on her table in the light. She was facing the window as eastern sunbeams decorated the room with brilliant color. She had her back to Donovan and was silhouetted against the window.

"You look stronger," he observed. She said nothing.

"I have to apologize for Crookshank," he continued.

"Am I still under investigation?" she asked directly.

"No, I think he was satisfied with your answers," he responded.

"And you? Are you satisfied?" she continued.

Donovan raised an eyebrow but said nothing. His cheeks burned red and he slowly came to stand beside her. His posture was meek and unassuming.

"Look, Jeanine. As far as the Bureau is concerned the case is closed. Colorado got away but we are tracking him. Swenson will take the blame for all appropriate crimes. Rubio, Sardo, Cahill and Snyder have been arrested for their involvement. They've given up the names of at least 10 other doctors involved in the ring."

"What about Crookshank?" she asked.

"I couldn't find enough evidence besides what Swenson told me. And, since she's dead now we don't have anyway to confirm her allegations." He hung his head down and slowly said, "Jeanine, I'll be leaving the Island in a few days. I won't be coming back."

"What about...what about us?" she asked turning to see him.

"There is no 'us', Jeanine," he said quietly. He felt sick to his stomach at saying the words.

She closed her eyes to his words absorbing them as she absorbed the sun's warmth on her skin through the window. "He said you would leave," she finally said.

"Who?"

"My father. He said you would hide behind your job and that the FBI has done nothing but tear our family apart."

"I promised to protect you and I have done that. It's just that simple. I had a job to do and I did it. It was never meant to be personal."

"Simple?" she asked exasperated turning to face him, "can it be that easy for you? Is this the same man who stood before me in that beach house staring into the face of death?"

"I'm sorry if I left you with the wrong impression. Sometimes that happens with people who work together closely on a case. It's really not your fault."

"The wrong impression? Fault? How can you even say that to me? What was I supposed to understand when you said you loved me? Is there any other way to interpret that?"

"I was working a case. I did what I had to do to accomplish it."

"I see," she paused pushing through her pain, "my father said you would say that too."

"You should listen to your family. They love you," he advised distantly.

"I have to thank you for sparing me the pain of confessing to my father that he was right about you. I have the comfort of knowing he can't chastise me over this at least."

"This isn't about you Jeanine. Please understand this is about me," Donovan insisted.

"Please don't feed me a line Donovan. At least have the courage to tell me the truth."

He sighed painfully. "Alright, you are right. There is more. I was hoping to spare you the pain of this but you asked to know. It's your family. I cannot get passed the issue of your uncle. Every time I look at you I see him. There is no difference in my mind."

This answer, although more plausible, was much less palatable. It affected her deeply but, less than she revealed. Her experience had taught her to take her feelings off of her sleeve.

"Forget about me, Jeanine. Rest, recuperate, and live your life." Donovan encouraged.

"That's impossible, Agent Donovan," she said as tears welled in her eyes, "you see my father has disowned me because I defended you. He doesn't understand why I would trust you. Ironically, because of his dismissal, he confessed he encouraged my uncle to find me.

They had decided that the family needed restoration and the way to do that was through me. My father had promised to give him my kidney. It never occurred to him that I might protest. Now, he's angry with me for being angry with him. He's lost in some delusion about a family reunion and I cannot even reach him. It does not even bother him that his brother almost killed me. So, you see, you are leaving at the right time. It's time for everyone to exit this show, you included."

Donovan gasped at this news. With each aspect of what she told him, she saw his expression change accordingly. First the look of love was in his eyes but it faded into horror and worst of all pity. He quietly turned to go.

"I would have died for you Jeanine," he said over his shoulder as he reached the door.

"What is true love if it is not tested? What use is it to die for someone if you are not willing to live for them?" she asked poignantly. He dropped his hand from the door and left without a word.

CHAPTER 36
MOVING ON

Jeanine was released from the hospital after a few weeks. Dr. Savage and his wife Mrs. Roundbottom convinced her to spend her last year in residency with them. It was a comfortable living but the carriage house reminded her daily of Donovan. After a month, she finally found the courage to go to the FBI warehouse to speak to him. She didn't know if he was still there but she gave it a try. She found Ben O'Donnell there packing up the site.

"Knock, knock" she announced upon entering.

"Hey! Come on in," he greeted warmly as he helped her step over cords and around boxes.

"You're looking good."

"Thanks," she replied taking his hand, as she was still physically fragile and very thin. He caught a glimpse of her face as she spotted the place where she had been shot. The bloodstains could still be seen. She noticed his regard and for a moment they shared the moment together in quiet empathy.

"Are you looking for Donovan?" he asked intuitively.

"Yes, is he here?" she asked peering around the room.

"No, he's gone."

"Oh, on to the next case I guess," she said coldly.

"No," he said mystified by her censure, "he's taking a leave of absence. No one knows when he'll be back."

"Really? Why?"

"You don't know what happened do you?" O'Donnell asked.

"I only know what he told me. That I was just part of the job and he had to go back to work."

Ben nodded silently. It took him less than a second to tell her the truth of what really happened. She deserved to know and since no one told him he couldn't inform her, he proceeded. He recanted to her Crookshank's ultimatum. That Donovan had to end their relationship or Crookshank would have her arrested. He also informed her of the betrayal by his friend, Renee.

As she heard the news, she turned pale and looked unsteady. He regretted the fact that he did not have her sit down before discussing these details. He helped her to a chair. She was overwhelmed with emotions. Donovan did love her. He loved her enough to let her go. But she was also angry that he didn't tell her the truth. He didn't have the courage to fight Crookshank.

"How long has he been gone?" she finally queried.

"Over a week now"

"When will he come back?"

"I don't know. Actually, he gave me his badge and gun and told me to turn them in."

"Have you?" she asked.

"No. I think he gave them to me because he knew I wouldn't. I think he doesn't know what he wants to do. But this job defines him. I think he's running right now but he'll come back, eventually. I think that's why he left them with me. Maybe I'm wrong."

"Do you know where he is?"

"I get the feeling he doesn't want to be found"

She sighed thoughtfully. "Can I ask a favor?" she asked. "Can you find his mother's address in Ireland?"

"Why?"

"He'll go there," she answered.

"How do you know?"

"I just know."

+++++

The next year was difficult for Jeanine. She had to repeat several courses before entering her third year and final year of residency. Her relationship with her father was practically nonexistent. They hardly spoke and when they did it was sparse. Her parents had even separated from each other under the strain of all that happened. Her father blamed this event on Jeanine as well.

Jeanine was paranoid that her uncle Colorado was still looking for her. She had seen and heard nothing of his arrest, which bothered her. Most of the time she tried to put it out of her mind.

Through it all, there were times, she could almost feel as though Donovan was still present, watching her from afar. But after a year of hoping, it became clear he was not coming back to her. And even if he did, she was not sure she could accept him. There was too much pain and hurt on both sides, perhaps a chasm too wide to cross.

There were unforeseen benefits to their previous relationship, however. Her brush with the press had given her some notoriety in the hospital. Dr. Rucker was too afraid to challenge her on anything for fear she was still under the protection of the FBI so he gave her a definitively wide berth. During the year, she had a brief interchange with Kent Carlton as she was instructing her own interns. As their third year resident, she was detailing her expectations of them as Kent was walking passed.

"I'd be careful not to set your expectations so high that you can't live up to them. I hear you have a problem with that," he mocked snidely.

She simply smiled, "I wouldn't put too much stock in what you hear. From that standpoint, I heard you were being audited by the IRS for tax evasion."

He looked worried for a moment before countering. "You shouldn't spread rumors. I call your bluff," he replied childishly.

"It's not mine to bluff. But to be on the safe side, I'd declare all the money you supposedly didn't earn moonlighting," she said as she made the quotation signs with her fingers around the word 'didn't'.

"It's probably nothing," she encouraged, "I mean, why would my friends in the FBI be interested enough in you to talk to the IRS?"

She turned smartly and led her interns down the hallway. Carlton felt faint.

Meanwhile, an ocean away, Donovan was healing from his own scars. He'd traveled through Israel, Western Europe and finally made his way back to Ireland where his family still resided.

"You look tired son," his mother observed brushing hair away from his eyes.

"Mother, please don't start," he protested. She arched an eyebrow in a way only a mother can do.

"Sorry mother," he apologized for his disrespectful tone.

She paused to evaluate him. "Your father will be home soon. Why don't you get ready for dinner?"

After a few days, she confronted her son again. "Who is she?" she asked.

"Who?"

"The woman you're running from?"

He couldn't deceive his mother. "I got too close to a mark. I should have known better. I got burned that's all" he stated blankly.

"You've only come home like this once before. This one cut you deeply. It was Renee wasn't it? She's finally betrayed your trust? I always knew she would."

"How did you know when I didn't?"

"There are some things you must learn for yourself. I would have told you but you would not have believed me. There are some things a woman knows. She can look through the women in the lives of the men she loves and tell who is genuine and who is not. It is a God given gift and it must be used with great discernment. I never trusted her. But," she hesitated before continuing, "there may be more to this than you think. Even Renee's actions are more profound than you know. Give it some time."

"It's complicated, mom," he finally answered rubbing his neck.

"You love her don't you? Not, Renee, the woman you are running from?"

"It's complicated, mom," he said wearily.

"Love usually is. But why should that stop you? Do you think my love affair with your father was easy? Different languages, cultures, families, etc., everything was a mess for years. With love comes pain. You are wondering if she can still love you after all you have done?"

"She reads me like you do."

"Well, that counts for a lot. She must be special for you to let her get that close to you. Do you think she still cares for you?"

"There's no way to know"

"What would it take to convince you that she did?"

"A miracle," he sighed.

"By your answer you still care for her?"

"Yes, I finally had to admit that to myself. I'm lost without her. I ache without her near me. But I cannot go back. There's too much water under the bridge for her to love or trust me. *An rud nach féider, ní féider é.* What can't be done can't be done," he said quoting an Irish proverb.

His mother fished something from her pocket and laid it on the table.

"This came for you last week," she announced as she kissed him on the forehead. It was a letter written to Donovan. He realized it was Jeanine's handwriting.

"My son, '*na biodh eagla ort*'. Don't be afraid," she quoted her husband's native Gaelic and she left him with his letter. Donovan fingered the letter carefully as though it was priceless.

Dearest Donovan,

I hardly know how to write this letter. My heart advises me to come to the point and the point is that I love you. There's nothing else that I can say that can be more relevant of my heart. I totally, completely, and essentially love you. So wherever and whenever this letter finds you I hope it finds you well. I hope it conveys that I am eternally yours.

Always,

Jeanine

P.S. I'd rather be a civilian with you than a doctor without you. I wish you would give me the chance. I am not afraid.

Donovan read it over and over again. He knew exactly what to do.

CHAPTER 37
WEDDING PLANS

Jeanine entered a large room on the east side of the beach house. It was a 6000 square foot estate used for weddings and other special events. She had arrived in a hurry; unprepared, flinging half a dozen half packed bags in various directions. Her hair was a mess. An older unattractive woman attended Jeanine as she hurriedly threw on her wedding gown, combed her hair, and put on her make up for the ceremony that would take place in a few short hours.

The wedding preparations had been hastily done. Her fiancé had pushed for a quick wedding in order to avoid the anticipated and inevitable change of mind from Jeanine.

"This isn't right," Jeanine complained to the mirror. She barely recognized herself. "I'm rushing through this. I don't even know what I am doing. I can't do this," she complained.

"Dear, I know you have only known each other a short time, but sometimes that is a good thing. Even with all of *your* history, this man has stood by you through some pretty tough times. He could have cut and run but he didn't. That proves that he loves you. He may not be your first choice, but he is a good choice. There is no guarantee that you will get the one you want but you have to take the one that wants you. You owe it to him and all of his relatives he flew here to go through with this."

She finished by aggressively tightening the corset on Jeanine's bodice, attending a few other busy details, and leaving. Jeanine felt depressed. The corset was cutting off her circulation. She sat at the vanity peering at the view through the window. She could barely see through the sheers that covered the large bay windows. They let in a slight breeze that caused the sheers rise and fall in a hypnotic and tranquilizing cadence characteristic of the lazy sigh of summer.

The room was quite lovely. It was decorated in beach house pastels from the windows to the oversized white couches to the throw rugs over the walnut stained hard wood floors. French doors were behind the vanity where she was seated. To her right was a sitting area with 2 sofas that faced each other framing a large fireplace. Behind her were 4 large windows each opened to different heights. She could hear the ceaseless, steady roar of the ocean outside.

The corset kept her frame rigid. It was a quaint ivory colored sleeveless dress. It was simple except for some intricate detailing down the back of the dress to the train. It was nice but not the dress she would have picked for her wedding day. It was consistent with the other choices she'd made. Her fiancé had admired it and, as he said, since he was paying for everything his vote should have more sway.

She didn't argue, although she could have. To her, it was just a dress and this was just a wedding and this would just be a marriage. She respected her fiancé and would honor him but she could not completely love him. Her family wasn't even in attendance. With all that had happened, she was not surprised by their absence.

She knew her choice to marry him was not the best one. She knew he would be kind to her and that was enough for her at least on some level. Her heart told her he was not the one. But, as her companion had previously said, he had done so much for her that she owed this to him. She knew this was not the purpose for her life. But she felt isolated and without sound advice from family or friends, (besides Dr. Savage who adamantly advised her to flee in the opposite direction of the buffoon she was marrying), she plodded forward against all that she knew was right.

As the guests arrived, she could hear the quartet playing soft music in the main entrance of the house. In half an hour, she would hear the wedding march. She stood up to prepare herself and immediately doubled over with grief and pain as she clutched the vanity for support. She bit her lower lip and fought against the natural urge to cry. She knew at that moment, she could not marry him. She just wished she had a way out. God was listening.

"Hello, Jeanine" a voice behind her called softly. The voice floated to her in the same tranquilizing way the window sheers did in the wind. She did not turn to see his face. She had dreamed and hoped to hear his voice many times and now here he was.

"Donovan" she whispered. She sighed, righted her posture, and turned to see him standing only ten feet behind her. He looked different. He was a little thinner, had shaved his beard save a little five o'clock shadow, and was wearing a very smart black tuxedo with the tie undone.

"Hi honey," he said tentatively.

"What are you doing here?" she asked feeling her heart quicken.

"I heard you were getting married. I needed to see you."

"Your timing is interesting," she said with a smartly raised eyebrow.

She admired his tuxedo. "You're over-dressed. It's a casual wedding," she informed flatly.

"I must have missed that on the invitation," he rallied back.

"Funny, I don't remember sending you one," she answered.

"I got your letter."

That answer caught her for a moment. It seemed a lifetime ago that she'd sent it. She inhaled deeply considering what he'd said before proceeding.

"That was over a year ago. Is the mail slow in Ireland?"

He took their ease at slipping back into this kind of jovial tennis match like banter, like a close to the net rally of barbs, as a good sign. He coolly approached her with one hand in his pant pocket. The last time they were together, his internal demons had made him restless. He was different now, more at peace. He wore it as easily and beautifully as the Armani tuxedo he sported. He still had that puma like stroll that was confident and utterly attractive. Instantly, she wished he were by her side at the altar. Her heart yearned for him.

"So what does he do?" Donovan asked referring to her fiancé.

"Is that why you are here to do a background check of the man I'm going to marry?" she asked wrinkling her forehead. He noticed the smooth contours of the nape her neck, the fine angle of her jaw, and the line down her back to her waist.

"I still care about you. I want to make sure you moved forward instead of back. What is he? An IRS agent?" he asked condescendingly as he flashed a bright smile. She knew Donovan was tenacious. He already knew the answer to every question he was asking.

"He's in the medical profession," she answered playing along.

"A chiropractor?" he teased.

"He sells medical marijuana," she fired back keenly.

"Is that lucrative?"

"Not as much as you would think. Once the government gets involved it loses the street value," she smiled.

He smiled furtively.

"Have you been saving that?" he asked referring to her marijuana joke.

"I thought you'd like that. Too punchy?" she shot back wittingly.

"No the delivery was great, nicely sharp," he answered.

A glow was returning to her that had been gone for a long time. After a long silence she asked. "It's been a year. Where have you been?"

"I benched myself."

"A desk?" she asked sorrowfully.

"Yes,"

"I'm sorry."

"Don't be"

"That's not who you are"

"It's who I wanted to be for you"

"You should have asked me first," she replied, "I didn't want you to change for me."

"I didn't know who to trust, Jeanine. I didn't know what they would do to you."

"You could have trusted me," she said simply. They were uncomfortably quiet for a moment. "Why are you here?" she asked again as her eyes shot over to the door nervously expecting it to open at any moment.

He never took his eyes from her face, not even for a moment. He was drinking in every aspect of this moment. The way the morning light bathed her skin. The soft pastels on the sofas behind her, the quiet movement of the window shears, and the white vanity behind her; they all framed this moment in his mind.

Every aspect of this moment he languished and lavished; she was radiant and with every breath he wanted her more. He hoped his gamble would work. His gaze made her uncomfortably warm. It was not hard to know what he wanted and she did not feign ignorance of it. They were interrupted by Bertha, the wedding coordinator, who had attended Jeanine earlier.

"Oh, excuse me" she apologized as she continued curiously, "Are you a guest?" She eyed him suspiciously with a guess of who he might be. "Bertha, give us a moment please," Jeanine requested. Reluctantly Bertha departed. It was clear her purpose was to obtain the groom as quickly as possible. She did not want this intruder to ruin her perfectly planned wedding, or her commission.

"She's going to get Steve. He'll be here shortly."

"You don't love him?" he asked, really more observed.

"Is that a question?" she asked evasively.

"That's not a 'yes'," he noted with hopeful observation.

"I'm going to marry him," she said certainly.

"That isn't an answer"

"Was there a question?"

He paused as emotions were tearing through both of them. The air was tense with feelings. His eyes softened and he approached her slowly so they were only a few inches apart. She felt the urge to run from him but fought it and remained steadfast. He could see her resolve and was glad she was not moving away from him. It further attracted him to her. If he wanted her, he was going to have to earn her.

"We communicate better when we're in crisis," he started.

"I could shoot you would that help?" she joked as she wiped tears from her eyes.

"I left because I couldn't face another rejection, another person lying to me," he pressed.

"Is that an apology or an accusation?" she countered defensively.

"No, Jeanine, I'm sorry. I had it in my head how I wanted this to go and it was much smoother in my head than now. Yes, I am sorry. I hurt you."

"I'm sorry too. I tried to find you," her voice trailed off, "but you were already gone." She nervously shifted her weight.

"I didn't want to be found. I discovered your letter in Ireland after I'd been traveling for a while."

"I could tell," she smiled noticing his Irish accent had thickened.

"Sorry, it's not the easiest accent to lose" he apologized.

"Don't apologize, I've always admired it," she said sadly.

"Don't tease me girl," he said with an Irish flare on the 'girl'

"Don't tease me," she demanded painfully her bright eyes were glazed with tears. She was pressing her hand against her side trying to ease the discomfort of the corset cutting into her ribs.

"I'm sorry," he said seeing her pain. "It's so easy to fall back into our rhythm."

She nodded carefully wiping the tears from her eyes.

"I've hurt you deeply, Jeanine. But please, don't do this. Don't choose someone else just because I was an ass," he urged.

"Don't you think your opinion on the subject of who I marry is slightly biased?" she asked sharply.

Suddenly, Steve burst into the room and addressed them. He was only 5'7". He was a thin Caucasian man with a narrow nose and nasal voice. He buzzed around Donovan like an angry Chihuahua.

"What? What? What is this?" he stammered. "I knew you would be coming around! She's mine now and we are going to get married. You may think you are something because you are in the FBI but don't think for a second that a podiatrist can't raise some hell buddy! You are trespassing and the laws still apply to you. Jeanine, don't you fall for anything he has to say. This wedding is already paid for including the honeymoon. All that's left is to consummate...."

Donovan and Jeanine had not moved from their previous positions. They were still admiring each other. When she'd had enough of Steve's interruption, she interjected.

"Leave us," she commanded. Since she was looking at Donovan, neither man was sure whom she was addressing. Her tone was so formidable even Donovan almost took a step back. As he went to speak again, she took her eyes from Donovan's face and peered at Steve.

"Leave us, now" she ordered. Steve eyed her blinking quickly. She was indefatigable. Steve left immediately with his tail tucked conservatively between his legs and murmuring something indiscriminant to himself.

Donovan regarded her as the creature he had come to love. A beautiful contradiction in terms: strong and soft, tempestuous and temperate.

"It's never easy with us is it?" he asked.

"All relationships are complicated. My family tried to kill you and you tried to kill them... In most families that's just a figurative statement but for us it's quite literal."

"I've decided to move past that little detail" he replied.

"That's very big of you," she answered coolly and laughed as she moved the bangs from in front of her eyes. He could drink every movement she made.

"That's good to know. I thought you might be here to arrest me. I'm glad to know those aren't handcuffs in your pocket," her eyes beamed for a moment before he could see sadness in them again.

Her emotions were raging and wearing the tight bodice wasn't helping. She couldn't breathe. Being this close to Donovan was driving her crazy. She massaged the nape of her neck.

"What happened?" she asked barely above a whisper.

He tentatively raised a hand to her check as though asking permission to touch her face. Her eyes didn't disagree with his nonverbal request. He took the chance and slowly caressed her cheek. She started to sway a little with the weight of all the pressure she was feeling. He gently placed his hand on her contoured waist to support her.

"I've been here, in Galveston, for the last month. I tried to contact you every day but I couldn't bring myself to see you. I was afraid of your answer. I'm here now because I have to know if you love him. If you do, I can live with it. But I had to know."

She shifted her weight ever so slightly and wetted her lips. Her heart was racing. Inside she was dying to say the words she so desperately wanted to say.

"Would that knowledge change anything for you?" she pressed.

"It would tell me why you are marrying him," he answered.

"I decided to marry him because he was good to me. He is decent. He's not perfect, mind you. Aside from being a self-centered egocentric idiot, he's honest and he is what he is. He rushed the wedding because he figured I'd change my mind. I don't even know where we're honeymooning."

"Belize," Donovan informed. "Belize?" she questioned frowning. "I hate Belize!" She exclaimed passionately.

"I know you hate Belize, honey." Donovan interrupted gingerly.

"They don't even speak Spanish there!" She persisted, annoyed at Steve's dismissal of her feelings. "It's the only South American country whose official language is English. What's up with that? British Honduras, hah! Why would I want go there? He knows how I feel!" She realized she was rambling and stopped herself.

"That's how I knew you didn't love him. That and I overheard you before I came in. Jeanine, please tell me. Do you love him?" He pleaded.

She looked deeply into his eyes. He seemed ten years younger somehow. Despite his physical changes, he was still the same man less whatever demons had been haunting him. She knew he wasn't asking if she loved Steve. He was asking her if she loved him. She could not avoid answering him any longer. A well of emotions erupted inside of her and for all the ways she wanted to be eloquent only the truth would come.

"How could I love him when my heart has always been yours?" She collapsed into him as he wrapped his arms around her. She turned her face away from his shirt as she wept an ocean of tears.

"I'm going to ruin your suit," she exclaimed pulling away from him. He peered down at her cradled her face in his hands, "Ruin it, baby!" They embraced tightly.

"I love you, I love you," she repeated through deep sobs.

"I so hoped you did," he said over and over again as he planted kisses all over her face. She pulled away as far from him as her arms would allow.

"I guess I should let the groom know there won't be a wedding?" she laughed through tears.

"Don't be so hasty. Maybe there can still be one." He released her for a moment and reached into his pocket.

"If you're just determined to get married," he paused as he knelt before her. She eyed him with great anticipation and curiosity as he pulled a ring from his coat pocket. He took her left hand and peered at the thin golden band and diamond solitaire Steve had given her as an engagement ring. He shook his head at it.

"Did he know you at all?" he asked.

She stared at him with wonder as he produced a ring that in all estimation was the ring of her dreams.

"How could you know what I wanted?" Jeanine gasped.

"I know you baby," he started, "and when you love someone you live for them."

As tears welled in his eyes, he slipped off Steve's ring, tossed it over his shoulders and gently slid a 3 diamond, princess cut, engagement ring over her finger as he kissed her hand. She stared at him in wonder as he knelt before her.

"I love you, Jeanine. With all of my heart I love you," he said.

"Donovan, I have to tell you, I wasn't going to marry him," she admitted.

He stared down into her beautiful diamond eyes, as he came to his full height. "Honey, you're a lady, it never even occurred to me that you would."

"I missed that cocky little arrogance of yours," she teased.

"Just a 'little cocky'? Baby, don't hurt me. Nothing about me is small," he said feigning insult.

"Hmmm, next thing you know you'll be putting bumper stickers about honor roll children on the back of your car or mixing chocolate and mint together," she replied smiling brightly.

"Come on," he advised, "we have to break up with your fiancé"

"Do you think he'll mind?" she joked.

"Nah, I saw him fondling the cocktail waitress as I was heading in."

"That bastard!" she exclaimed at Steve's unfaithfulness.

"Baby?" Donovan chided with a sly grin.

"Okay, okay. He can have his waitress. They can go to Belize! By the way, where will we honeymoon?"

"I was thinking South America. Thought it be nice to see your folks," he grinned arrogantly.

"Damn, that thin yellow line!" she smiled back, as she wrapped her arms around the love of her life.

####

ABOUT THE AUTHOR

"Melissa J. Urrea, MD is a native Texan. She received her medical degree from the University of Texas Medical Branch in Galveston. While completing residency training in medicine, Dr. Urrea was inspired to write Thin Yellow Line. Dr. Urrea currently lives in Austin, Texas with her loving family. She continues to write fiction novels and practice the art and science of medicine."

Connect with the author:

Website: www.mjurrea.com
Facebook under Thin Yellow Line;
and
Twitter @melissaurreamd

Made in the USA
Coppell, TX
24 April 2020